IDAHO CODE

BY
JOAN OPYR

Ann Arbor
2006

Bywater Books, Inc.
PO Box 3671
Ann Arbor MI 48106-3671

Printed in the United States of America on acid-free paper.

Bywater Books First Edition: March 2006

Cover designer: Bonnie Liss (Phoenix Graphics)
Cover painting by Patricia Koch

ISBN 1-932859-15-2

For Benjamin D. Huskey, 1970-1996
You probably think this book is about you.

ACKNOWLEDGMENTS

I am terribly nervous about writing this. What if I forget someone? What if forget someone really important? What if I forget someone who was vital to the writing of this book? Someone who helped me way back in the early days when this novel was just an outline and a 25-page draft? It's not just possible that I'll forget someone from that early struggle; it's probable. I began writing *Idaho Code* in 1992. It took me seven years and seven drafts to finish it, another five years to sell it, and three more edits to hammer it into the book you now hold in your hand. Throughout this process, I have been shameless about asking friends, relatives, and the occasional unwary stranger to read a draft and let me know what they thought. A surprising number did so with apparent pleasure, and I am grateful to them. I don't have the luxury of posing as an unloved, unappreciated, starving artist. I have received nothing but unstinting encouragement, flattery and praise, and many a helpless belly laugh in all the right places. What writer could ask for anything more?

Okay, I'd also like to sell Steven Spielberg the movie rights for a cool million, but I'm not greedy. Well, not excessively greedy. I'd donate at least ~~ten~~ five percent to charity.

These are the people who must be thanked. With the exception of my wife, they are not listed in order of importance but in order of memory, so, please, no fighting.

I thank my wife, Melynda Huskey, for her patience, her encouragement, her love and affection, and her cruel and ruthless editing. Melynda is herself a fine writer, and she is the smartest, bravest person I have ever known. She has read and re-read this text in search of "flagrant assholery," and she has never been afraid to tell me when a joke or a scene or a character has fallen flat. Those of you who have the misfortune of living with a writer will know the courage this requires. Melynda is the Chesty Puller of author spouses, and I adore her.

I thank my in-laws, Rose and Don Huskey, Heather and Micah Jordan, Lew and Jill Huskey, and Molly Huskey for reading draft after draft; for their support and encouragement; and for always putting up a good fight. They are a constant source of inspiration to me, though, for legal purposes, I would like to point out that they are in no way reflected in any of the characters in this book. Any resemblance to Rose, especially, is purely coincidental. (What's the difference between Rose Huskey and Emma Hardy? Emma has to do exactly what I write.)

Thank you to my wonderful, hilarious, ass-kicking agent and future sister-wife, Victoria Sanders, to her long-suffering partner, Diane Dickensheid, and to Victoria's assistants, Imani Wilson and Benee Knauer. VS: when Steven Spielberg calls, tell him the price is now two million.

Thank you to my publishers, Kelly Smith and Marianne K. Martin of Bywater Books, and to Jean Redmann, who first said the magic words, "We want your book." Thank you to Val McDermid for encouragement, advice, and a terrific blurb. (Did you know that your girlfriend really wants a border collie? You should get her one. A nice puppy sired by Scottish champions. Very cute. Very lively.)

Thank you to Marah Stets, genius editor, and to Patricia Koch, genius painter. Patricia's paintings of the Palouse are a constant source of inspiration and I am so grateful to her for allowing her work to grace the cover of this book. What an honor.

To Polly Opyr, Julia Gothe, Jennie Staples, Saundra Lund, Keely Emerine Mix, Lois Blackburn, BJ Swanson, Robin Woods, Nicole Opyr, Micheal Opyr Pender, Johnny Pender, Mable J. Watkins, Lilah Amos, Kate deGroot, Laura Kemmink, Eve Strongoni, William Doelle, Connie Gibbs, Debi

Robinson-Smith, Deborah Love, Janice Corey, Dave Tilley, Carol Lorenger, Brian Carver, Mary Lowe, Maggie Thacker, Lisa Matthews, Mel Ashby, Lesa Luders, Lee Smith, Linda T. Holley, John Kessel, Gitta Bridges, Carmen Wilbourne, Pam Southworth, Kym Dye and Linda James, Carrie Bickle and Sally Blank, Cheryle and Teresa Myers, Bill London, Benton Falkirk, the entire Moscow-based Palmer family, librarians par excellence Donna Hanson and Pauline Baughman, Betsy Dickow and Bob Greene of Book People, Courtney Lowery and Jonathan Weber of New West Magazine, Mike Schultz of Stonewall News, and the late, wonderful, and much-beloved Marla Kale and Robbie Knott—thank you all for reading my work and for encouraging (and, in some cases, paying) me to write. I owe you a debt of gratitude that can never be repaid.

Unless, of course, Steven Spielberg calls. Then, I promise each of you ~~one~~ some percent of the net film proceeds. That's if it makes a profit. A really big profit. I mean truly enormous. Like *Raiders of the Lost Ark* or *Jurassic Park.*

"Everything turns from sugar to shit."
—CHARLES RANDOLPH WATKINS

Chapter 1

What's more shocking than a phone ringing in the middle of a funeral? The corpse sitting up in the coffin and taking a look around, but not much else.

When the phone rang, the sound was so close that I nearly fell off the pew. When it rang a second time, I knew why. The sound was coming from my mother's handbag. Now, I know my mother, and I know her faults. She's a typical Idaho woman, a cross between Ma Ingalls and Norman Schwarzkopf. If she were caught in a bear trap, she'd chew her own leg off, drag the bloody stump home, and reattach it with a staple gun. In many ways, I admire that, though it doesn't make her easy to live with. For a brief moment, I dared to hope that she would reach into her purse and switch it off. Instead, she pulled it out and hesitated. With my mother, hesitation is fatal. It's always in those moments between right and wrong that Emma Hardy hears the call of the wild.

"Don't answer that," I whispered sternly.

We both knew who was on the other end of the line. The only person who ever calls my mother on her cell phone is my criminal wretch of a brother, Sam. Who but Sam would have the bad luck, bad timing, and bad karma to call in the middle of a funeral?

I hate funerals. Maybe it's because they're so heavy with arcane ritual—particularly funerals at St. George's Episcopal Church, which are all robes, candles, and incense—but once the organ starts playing, you might as well be in the sixteenth century as the twentieth.

Then again, it could just be that funerals are creepy. They creep me out, anyway, like séances. I don't want to talk to the dead, and I don't want the dead to talk to me. In this, I differ very strongly from my mother, who likes to think that once she's passed through the misty veil, she'll still be able to reach back and slap the living. We were sitting in the front third of the church, only three rows behind the mourning family. The phone rang a third time, louder now, as it was in Emma's hand. Several people looked over their shoulders at us, including Sylvie Wood, only daughter of the deceased.

I caught Sylvie's eye and tried to look like a hostage. She looked away. I cast a pleading glance at my mother, but it was too late—she'd already turned the phone on and put it to her ear. Please God, I thought, don't let her get into one of those hissed conversations about Sam's pot-smoking. Or his larceny. Or his tramp of an underaged girlfriend. From the pulpit, the minister cast a damning eye upon us but continued his sermon.

"Not a good time," Emma murmured. "I'll call you back."

"Let us pray," said the minister.

I prayed for a small black hole to open up beneath my mother.

"What?" Emma spoke sharply, her whisper rising. "What do you mean they've arrested you?"

Someone cleared her throat loudly, and I noticed that Helen Merwin was sitting on my mother's right. In fact, there was the whole Merwin family—Helen, her balding father, Fairfax, and his oversexed wife, Agnes. I was surprised they weren't sitting with Sylvie and her mother, Kate. Agnes was Kate's sister. She had a right to the family pew, and it wasn't like the Merwins to hang back when there was a chance to be in the spotlight. Helen in particular was a notorious drama queen—as my mother says, the bride at every wedding and the corpse at every funeral. The deceased was an uncle she hadn't seen for nearly two decades, and yet there she sat in a black crepe dress, just like a Mafia widow. When it became clear that my mother was going to ignore her, Helen cleared her throat again, this time adding a sanctimonious little cough. Subtlety, alas, gets you nowhere with Emma. She twisted in the pew, leaving Helen free to cough on her back but not in her ear.

The church was packed to overflowing, and at least half the congregation was now staring at us. Emma continued to mutter into the phone. I closed my eyes, practiced deep breathing, and silently chanted my mantra: I am not responsible for my mother.

"Fuck," said Emma, clearly audible.

I opened my eyes and pinched her thigh. Hard.

My mother looked up, her features glazed with fury. I cringed like a dog. Resting the phone on her heaving bosom, she leaned over so that her lips were right next to my ear and said, "Where are we?"

"The Episcopal Church. Are you having a stroke or something?"

Emma rolled her eyes and tried again, this time louder. "I mean, where are we in the service, you idiot!"

"Nearly to the benediction," I said, in as low a voice as I could muster. "For Christ's sake, would you at least try to whisper?" Sylvie was looking over her shoulder at us again. I smiled weakly and, not for the first time, considered the potential benefits of sewing a poison pill into my shirt cuff.

"I'll be there in fifteen minutes," Emma snapped into the phone. "Just keep your hair on."

The organist played the opening chords of "Blessed Be the Tie that Binds." My mother stuffed the cell phone back into her purse, seized a hymnal, and dragged me to my feet.

"I wish I were dead."

"Just sing," she replied, coming in with zest on the line, "Our hearts in Christian love."

I saw that Kate had wrapped an arm around her daughter's shoulders. They weren't singing. I wasn't surprised. Either they'd had nothing to do with the choice of hymn, or someone had a black sense of humor.

It wasn't a tie that bound Burt Wood to his family; it was a slipknot. Until he'd turned up a week ago, a prisoner in the county jail, he'd been missing since July 4th, 1978, when he'd walked out on his wife and child and, for all intents and purposes, vanished from the face of the earth. For sixteen years, Burt Wood was out of sight and out of mind, all but forgotten except as a cautionary tale, a warning to the wise against mixing with bad company and abandoning your responsibilities. Though it had been quite the scandal way back when, I was sketchy on the details. I'd been six years old at the time and more interested in singing along with the soundtrack to *Grease* than in the how, why, and where of Burt Wood's disappearance. I knew that he'd skipped town with a chronic ne'er-do-well named Frank Frost. I also knew that some money had gone missing from the Lewis County Assessor's Office where Wood and Frost worked.

So far, newspaper reports on the present-day investigation had been sparse. The body had been identified, the autopsy performed, and the funeral arranged. The town was buzzing. Who or what killed him? Who identified the body? Why did he come back? No one knew where he'd been. No one knew who he really was until he had the misfortune to drop dead in police custody. It seemed he'd given the arresting officer a false name. Nothing this exciting had happened to Cowslip, Idaho since the music minister at the Rock of Ages Fellowship had murdered his wife with a claw hammer.

I looked around me. The church was standing room only. It was also hot and stuffy. Two rows of chairs had been set up behind the last pews, and still people were leaning against the columns and walls, fanning themselves with the funeral program. The assembled congregation was a veritable who's who of Cowslip. Fred Maguire, the king of community theater, sat on the pew directly in front of me. The new mayor and her husband sat across the aisle. The Rotary Club, the Cowslip Elks, the Chamber of Commerce, and the City Council were all well represented. The Junior League had turned out in force, hats perched jauntily on their blue-gray heads. One thing was clear—we weren't all there because we were grief-stricken. No matter how many hymns we sang or pieties we murmured, any mourning was playing second fiddle to speculation and intelligence gathering. I felt sorry for Kate and Sylvie, and even a little sad for the deceased. St. George's was packed to bursting with beady-eyed, big-eared, open-mouthed ghouls.

I tugged at the collar of my shirt, feeling the heat rise to my own big ears. I wasn't exactly a ghoul, but I wasn't a mourner, either. Chalk it up to the curse of small-town coincidence, but my brother was with Burt Wood when he died. They were sharing a jail cell. Wood was picked up on a charge of vagrancy and public drunkenness. Sam was in for trying to liberate a six-pack from the Safeway. As shoplifting was one of my brother's hobbies, not one of his talents, he'd stuffed the Budweiser under his T-shirt and tried to shuffle unnoticed out the front door. My mother and I had watched the security tape of this performance in the public defender's office. There he was, tall, black, and skinny with a beer-inflated midriff—I couldn't decide if he looked more like the Hunch-Front of Notre Dame or a pregnant stork. The sheriff's deputies had him before he'd made it halfway across the parking lot.

About an hour after Sam's arrest, they put Wood, who was already complaining of stomach pain, into the cell with him. Sam didn't pay much attention—too busy reclining on his bunk, watching TV and, I suspected, coming down from a good high. It wasn't until Wood collapsed on the floor and stopped breathing that Sam sat up and took notice. He yelled for the guards, but it was too late. Wood was pronounced dead on arrival at Cowslip Memorial. Not that anyone knew he was Wood at the time—that bombshell wasn't dropped until several days later.

In the days since his release, Sam had made himself scarce, hiding from my mother and probably from justice. I'd seen him in passing once or twice, but I'd been too busy to ask him a lot of questions about his late cellmate. It was the first week of fall classes, and I was determined that this semester, unlike the previous four, I'd get off to a good start. I'd go to class every day. I'd pay attention. I'd take notes and even study. There'd be no distractions, no hangovers, and, most importantly, no romantic entanglements. I was through with all that. I was going to be serious.

Of course, I didn't tell my mother any of this. I preferred that she remain in the dark about my real reasons for transferring from the University of Washington to tiny Cowslip College. She thought I was just tired of Seattle and wanted to be closer to home, and since that was at least partially true, I didn't think it would be hard to maintain the fiction.

I've been wrong before. I stared at the back of Sylvie's head. Her hair was blond, and the ends of it just brushed the tops of her shoulders, accentuating the golden curve of her neck. A wave of guilt washed over me. If small-town nosiness accounted for the record attendance, my own reason for being at Burt Wood's funeral was even sleazier. In elementary school, I'd secretly worshipped the water Sylvie Wood walked on. She was pretty and smart, and I was tall and awkward. One day, when we were in the first grade, she reached out on the playground and ruffled my hair and lo, a baby dyke was born. It's not that I believe in the eternal love of six-year-olds, but how many of us get the chance as adults to encounter the original object of our polymorphous perversity? I'd heard through the grapevine she was back in town, and I was pathetic enough to think of her father's funeral as a chance to reintroduce myself.

When I formed this plan, it didn't seem quite so bad. Burt Wood had been a brutal and unpleasant man, nasty to his wife and mean to his daughter. I had a few hazy memories of him. He was tall and muscular with heavy eyebrows and a black mustache. He always scared me because he yelled a lot. My mother actively hated him. According to Emma, disappearing was the best thing Burt Wood ever did. She and Kate were old friends, college roommates, and though, as far as I knew, they hadn't had much to do with one another for several years, my mother always spoke fondly of her.

Sylvie turned her head, and I admired her profile. Smooth, tan skin. Regular, even features. She seemed to glow from within. Oh, hell, what was I doing? If we did speak, what would I say to her? The last time we'd met was at high school graduation, two—no, three years ago. My excuses for attending her father's funeral were visibly thin. The bizarre coincidence of Burt and Sam sharing the same cell. An old playground crush. What if she thought I was just another busy-body? What if she thought I was a stalker?

Back in the present, Emma shifted her weight from foot to foot and huffed impatiently. The minister was saying something about the Lord's countenance shining upon us. The service was nearly over. If I was going to talk to Sylvie, I needed a good opening line. I'm sorry about your dad. I'm sorry Sam didn't give him CPR. Sam doesn't know CPR. Exhaling has never been his strong suit.

I had no idea if Sylvie was a lesbian or not. Of course, there were rumors, but that meant nothing. I'd heard a rumor that my mother smoked dope and mowed the grass naked. Not unlikely, but also not true. Still, just assuming that she was gay, what then? Maybe I could invite her out for coffee and start dropping subtle hints, work the conversation around to the collected works of Gertrude Stein or hum a k.d. lang tune. I could invite her over to watch some lesbian movie like *Desert Hearts*. Yeah. And then my mother, my father, Sam, and my three older sisters could sit on the sofa with us, eating popcorn and swilling beer while Helen Shaver and Patricia Charbonneau get naked.

Jesus. What kind of soulless monster cruises a funeral? It was a no-hope situation from the get-go, even without my mother and her damned cell phone. Another case of sordid thoughts meet zero potential.

The organist began to play something uplifting, and though I failed to recognize the tune, I knew it was the recessional because no one was singing. The congregation stood up. I made a last-ditch effort to send Sylvie a psychic message. Bil Hardy is not a stalker. She's a very nice woman. Really. Unfortunately, my signal was interrupted by the maniac next to me.

"No dawdling," Emma said, gripping my elbow. "We've got to get out of here before all these old bags start clogging the exits."

"But we have to offer our condolences," I protested. Sylvie and Kate were making their way to the narthex, where the Altar Guild had set up coffee, tea, and cookies.

"We'll call," my mother replied, shoving me out of the pew and down the aisle.

"Oh for God's sake," I began before finding myself impaled on the end of a pointy umbrella. "Ouch!" I rubbed my wound and glared down at the perpetrator, a rotund midget in a large and fruity hat. "Hello, Granny. Are you trying to kill me?"

My grandmother turned around. In a voice that sounded like a cross between Katharine Hepburn and a malfunctioning jackhammer, she said, "Wilhelmina! What's the matter with you? Why are you rubbing your stomach? Where's your mother? Could you give me a ride home? I walked here. It's eight blocks, you know. My bunions are playing merry hell."

In one of those moments of perfect mother-daughter understanding, I knew that Emma, who's a foot shorter than I am, was crouching down behind me, hidden from view. There was no way my grandmother, who's even smaller, could possibly see her. I also knew that it was my filial duty to lie through my teeth, to say that I'd come to the funeral alone, and that I couldn't possibly give Granny a ride home because I'd hitchhiked, or come in on a Harley hog, or some other such mother-saving bullshit.

I smiled. "Emma's right behind me, Granny. I think she's crouching down."

In retrospect, it was well worth the kick. Granny shoved herself under my arm and seized upon my mother, who was trying simultaneously to do me an injury and blend in with the carpet.

"There you are!" Granny shrieked. "I wish I'd known you were coming. We could have sat together. Did you hear that telephone ringing and that woman talking? In the middle of a funeral! I couldn't see who it was because that enormous Millicent Rutherford was sitting right in front of me."

As that enormous Millicent Rutherford was now standing right in front of me, I whispered, "Granny, keep your voice down."

"I'm glad to see you here, Emma," she continued, unchecked. "You too, Wilhelmina. I'm sure it means a lot to the family, what's left of it anyway. It's just Kate and her daughter now. His mother died fifteen years ago, just after your daddy, Emma. She never knew what happened to her son, whether he was dead or alive. He never called her. He never wrote. And now they say he was poisoned!"

All over the church, heads snapped around to look at us. Millicent Rutherford stopped dead in her tracks and pretended to fish something out of her purse. I scarcely had time to stop myself from plowing into the broad expanse of her back.

"Mother," Emma muttered, "you are not addressing Congress."

My grandmother flowed over this as if it were a rock in the rapids.

"I made cookies," she said. "The Altar Guild provided all the refreshments. I always make cookies when anyone dies. Oatmeal lace. Your favorite, Wilhelmina. You always used to like them, anyway. Poisoned! Hannah at the Safeway told me. She heard it from Inez who cleans for the coroner's wife. I wonder who did it?"

We'd reached the narthex now. I spied Sylvie and her mother by the coffeepots, accepting cookies and condolences from a steady stream of wrinkled worthies. It was now or never. I had to ditch Granny and my mother.

"Please don't call me Wilhelmina," I said.

That got her attention. Granny raised an eyebrow. "Excuse me?"

"Don't call me Wilhelmina, Granny. Everyone except you calls me Bil. I prefer it."

"Well, I don't know why," she objected. "Wilhelmina is a lovely name, very regal. I cried when your mother told me that you were going to be my namesake. I was named after Wilhelmina, Queen of the Netherlands, and you . . ."

"I'm not exactly a queen."

Granny rolled on. "We're Dutch on my father's side. English on my mother's. Being adopted, of course, you're not Dutch or English but . . . what are you? Do you know? Have you ever thought of looking for your birth parents? Genealogy is so interesting, don't you think?"

"Go on," said my mother. "Answer her."

"I'm Samoan," I lied. "And Greek. One-quarter Egyptian and two-thirds Eskimo. By way of Louisiana."

"I forgot you were born in Baton Rouge," Granny mused. "Do you like hot food?"

Three of my parents' five children are adopted. Two, Sarah and Sam, are African-American. Though my grandmother came to grips with the reality of having an interracial family years ago, the fact that I'm white like my parents and yet also adopted seems to strike her with fresh wonder whenever she thinks of it.

"Of course. I put Tabasco on my corn flakes. Would you excuse me, Granny? Dry throat. Need some coffee. Must dash."

Granny blinked like a turn signal and immediately began addressing my mother. I grinned benignly, ignoring Emma's gorgon glare, and backed quickly away. Damned if I was going to let my mother steamroll me. Sam could just cool his heels for an extra minute or two while we behaved like decent, civilized people. I would offer Sylvie and her mother my condolences. I'd make polite conversation, talk about the weather, or the World Series. And if I happened to suggest that we meet sometime for coffee or doughnuts or *Desert Hearts*, so much the better. Nothing ventured, nothing gained.

I pushed my way through to the refreshments table. Sylvie was busy chatting with the organist. I poured a cup of coffee, examined and rejected the oatmeal lace cookies, and found a nice quiet spot next to an old upright piano where I could sit and wait.

I thought the organist would never shut up. On and on he went, like the living embodiment of perpetual motion. Eventually, I got tired of watching him. I took a pen from my pocket and played three games of tic-tac-toe on the back of the funeral program. I lost every time. In desperation, I tried to drink the coffee. It tasted like stewed cigarette butts.

"Jesus Christ," I muttered. "They filtered this through someone's gym socks."

A voice spoke, low and attractive. "Don't you know better than to drink church coffee? It's never good."

Hot liquid sloshed over the edge of the cup and onto my hand. With all the suavity and coolness I could muster, I stood up. "I'm never good," I said thickly. "I mean, I never go to church. So I don't drink the coffee. Hi, Sylvie. How are you?"

"I've been better," she replied. "Your hand . . ."

"It's fine." I wiped my hand on the leg of my trousers, remembering too late that they were dry clean only. "I'm tough. Old asbestos hands, that's what they call me."

She laughed. "How are you, Bil? I haven't seen you since . . ."

"Since high school," I finished, my heart skipping a beat.

"It was nice of you to come."

I shrugged. "It was nothing. I mean, of course it's something. I mean . . . I'm really sorry about your father, and, um, everything."

I was having difficulty concentrating, and my tongue seemed to have grown too large for my mouth. She was tall, at least as tall as I was, and she was standing less than a foot away from me. I'd forgotten how green her eyes were, like the leaves on a tropical plant. Her pupils were rimmed with gold, and there was something wolf-like about the concentrated way she was looking at me. It was disconcerting—disconcerting, but attractive.

I took a deep breath. "I'm sorry," I said. "I don't know what to say. It's been a long time and I feel sort of stupid."

To my surprise, not to mention gratitude, Sylvie laughed. "There's no need to feel stupid. What can anyone say? This isn't exactly typical, is it?"

"No," I agreed, "it isn't. Not typical at all."

A silence fell between us, and I shifted uncomfortably. To fill the gap, I said, "So, I hear you've moved back to Cowslip. Why?" I could have kicked myself. Nosy and blunt—a nice way to start.

If she was bothered by my question, it didn't show. "I wanted to be closer to my mother," she said. "I moved back about a month ago, before all of this happened." Her gesture seemed to encompass the church, the funeral, and her father's disappearance and awkward return. "I came back for graduate school. Cowslip College has a good program in botany."

"Botany?" I didn't mean to sound quite so surprised. What was I expecting her to say, modeling? Walking down the catwalk in leather and latex? Sylvie interrupted this fantasy before I actually began drooling.

She laughed. "Yes, botany—cliff botany, to be exact. That's my specialty. How about you? You were at the University of Washington, weren't you? I guess you've graduated."

"Ah, no, I haven't. I'm enrolled at Cowslip College as an undergraduate. In English." I paused, wondering how to explain my stupid and very sudden departure from the University of Washington without getting into specifics, like the fact that I left because my girlfriend of two years had jilted me. For a man. A man named, of all stupid things, Euphrates, Euphrates Jones. Fucking idiot hippie parents. I shook my head to get rid of the image of that skinny moron with his sparse goatee and his black, laced, puffy-sleeved poet's shirt. Ugh.

"I wanted to be closer to my family," I said, which was at least a little bit true. "I got homesick, and I really didn't have much to lose. In my three years at the University of Washington, I had five different majors. I still don't know what I want to be when I grow up. Maybe a cliff botanist?"

Sylvie laughed again. I liked her laugh. It was warm and smooth, and, for some reason, it made me think of toffee—good, English toffee. Before I could figure this out or say anything else, she leaned forward and put her hand on my arm.

"Bil, would you meet me somewhere this afternoon? I want to talk to you. The Cowslip Café, maybe? We could have a cup of coffee. Good coffee." She smiled, displaying a perfect row of very white teeth.

"Um, sure, but . . ."

"Three o'clock," she said. "If the rain stops, I'll be waiting at one of the outside tables. If not, I'll be inside, probably somewhere near the back. It's quieter there. More privacy."

Privacy. "Okay. Three o'clock. I'll be there."

"Good."

She left before I had the chance to say anything else, or perhaps break into a song and dance. I watched as she made her way back to the coffee table, slim hips shifting beneath the smooth fabric of her blue linen dress. I didn't have time to wonder what she wanted to talk to me about or even to say wow before, out of the corner of my eye, I saw my mother bearing down upon me at breakneck speed. She couldn't have looked more like an angry bull if she'd had horns and a ring through her nose.

"Are you quite finished socializing?" she asked, taking my arm and maneuvering me across the narthex and out the door. "Honestly, I don't know what gets into you sometimes. Your brother . . ."

"Is in jail for the nineteenth time."

"Which makes this my nineteenth nervous breakdown," she cracked. "Have pity on a poor old woman. I'm not as young as I used to be."

"Yeah, right. And speaking of poor old women, I gather we're leaving Granny to hobble home on her bunion-infested feet?"

My mother looked smug. "Nope. I've fobbed her off on that enormous Millicent Rutherford. Neither of them is happy about it, but I don't give a damn. Now stop talking and start walking. We have to go bail out your brother."

Chapter 2

"Could you drive a little faster?"

"For the millionth time, no. The speed limit is forty-five, and I can't afford a ticket."

My mother drummed her fingers on the dashboard. I knew she was dying for a cigarette, but I can't stand smoking in the car. Even when it's her car.

Though the signs weren't good, I decided to venture a question. "Did Sam say why they'd arrested him?"

"No."

"Well," I continued, "it has to be one of three things—pot, pilfering, or pussy. Since we've already had the pot and the pilfering this month, my money's on the pussy."

My mother stopped her drumming and looked at me sideways. "Nice language. I suppose you kiss your mother with that mouth?"

"Only on Mother's Day. And only because she makes me."

The Lewis County Jail was on the opposite side of town from St. George's Episcopal Church, right at the spot where Main Street turned into Highway 8. Though my mother was anxious to get there, I was in no hurry to be sucked into another of Sam's epic battles with the criminal justice system. In the short time since I'd moved back home, I'd seen enough action to have earned a bronze star.

Emma tugged absently at a loose string on the cuff of her pants.

"So," I asked reluctantly, "what's the plan?"

"The plan? We find out what they've trumped up against him this time. Then, we find out how much it will cost to bail him out. After that, we go home, you hide in your bedroom, and I break the news to your father."

"I don't think it's fair to say that I hide."

"Fine, you don't hide. You discreetly absent yourself. How's that?"

"Much better."

After my brother was diagnosed with non-Hodgkin's lymphoma, my mother gave up having friends and a social life. It was a full-time job just keeping Sam alive and out of jail. The illness struck him at a bad age. He was seventeen and already mildly delinquent. It was all petty stuff—he'd been caught shoplifting and drinking beer in the cemetery. The diagnosis changed that. Knowing there was a good chance that he might not make it to twenty pushed Sam over the edge. In the space of a few months, all the while going through radiation and chemotherapy, he managed to rack up an impressive juvenile record: breaking and entering, larceny, vandalism. Because of his illness, and because he was usually lucky enough to go before sympathetic judges, he generally got a slap on the wrist—a lecture, probation, and release on his own recognizance.

Then his cancer went into remission. Sam graduated from high school and got a job. Nothing exciting—he sold tickets and worked the concession stand downtown at the Adler Cinema. For a while it looked as if he might actually make it, that he might escape from the past and become a productive citizen. The peace lasted for three years. He went to work, he stayed relatively clean, and we came to believe that his luck would extend beyond the legal. Then, the cancer came back. Sam quit his job and picked up where he'd left off. Always stoned, always in trouble, and always somewhere he shouldn't be with people he shouldn't have known.

Sam and I never talked about his cancer. We kept our conversations superficial. He'd ask me if he could borrow some money, and I'd say yes or no. Mostly yes. I knew he was taking advantage, pressing my buttons, but lending him money went a little way towards easing my conscience. I suspected my sisters did the same. They were all professionals, a doctor, a lawyer, and a librarian. Good sources of ready cash. Between us, Sam probably raked in enough to keep half the county in beer and weed.

Although to some extent I could understand Sam's criminality, I couldn't excuse it. My mother, on the other hand, was in complete denial. She'd developed a persecution complex. The cops were out to get him. He wasn't so bad; they unfairly singled him out. Emma liked to believe that his troubles all began with the initial diagnosis, conveniently forgetting that Sam was always light-fingered. She stopped taking us to yard sales when we were kids because Sam had made a habit out of stealing old shoes. Usually just one, and usually the left. When she caught him, she'd make him take it back, but this never seemed to serve as a deterrent.

The cops were getting tired of my brother. So were the DA and the formerly sympathetic judges. Sam was nearly twenty-two now, and five years of saying, "I can't help it man, I'm dying" were beginning to wear thin. Sooner or later, he was going down for a long stretch. If he lived that long.

"You know," my mother said, getting out a cigarette and putting it in her mouth, "I wish your brother put as much fight into taking care of himself as he puts into fucking with the cops."

I tried to deflect. "You kiss your mother with that mouth?"

"Never," she replied. "But you know what I mean. If he goes into remission again, chances are good he'll get to spend several healthy years in the state penitentiary."

"Yeah. Look, you're not going to light that, are you? You promised you wouldn't smoke in the car."

"Fine," she snapped, putting the lighter back into her purse. "When did you become a Mormon? I was only going to suck on the filter."

I shuddered. "That makes me want to vomit. Why don't you get some nicotine gum or the patch or something?"

"Hmm," she said, tapping the filter against her lips. "Why don't you take up smoking?"

We turned into the jail's parking lot. I switched the car off and gritted my teeth. "You'll behave yourself, won't you? No theatrics?"

My mother smiled grimly. "Of course. What kind of woman do you think I am?"

❖❖❖

"You should be shot to the moon for this!"

Deputy Donald Smith, Jr., stood behind the counter with half a doughnut in his hand, powdered sugar sifting down the front of his khaki uniform. The other half was in his mouth. I doubted he'd be able to work up enough spit to swallow it.

"Well?" my mother continued. "What is it this time? Jaywalking? Parking tickets?"

"Mrs. Hardy, please. If you'll just calm down . . ."

"Calm down? Listen, you worthless, one-bullet Barney Fife, I want to know what trumped-up bullshit you're trying to pin on my son."

I grabbed Emma by the arm, giving her a little shake for emphasis. "You're not helping." I turned to Donny. "What my mother is trying to ask, Deputy Smith, is what is the charge against Sam?"

Donny chewed rapidly, somehow managing to choke the doughnut down. Sweat trickled from the broad expanse of his pale forehead, and he smiled faintly, a sure sign of his helplessness in the face of my mother's bull-headed fury.

"Mrs. Hardy," he said, though he looked at me for reassurance, "I'm sure we can straighten this out if you'll just calm down. All of this yelling is getting us nowhere."

Donny Smith was not a small man. He was six feet four inches of clean-living, potato-fed, caffeine-free Mormon. Next to my mother, however, he was a lightweight. I almost felt sorry for him.

Emma leaned forward and said in her brimstone baritone, "You don't know what nowhere is, Donny, my boy. I'll send you to a hot fucking nowhere if you don't have Sam out of that jail cell in the next five minutes. I'm getting pretty tired of coming down here every other day to bail out my son. My daughter's a lawyer, you know. I'll sue your fat ass!"

Ah, Naomi, that august member of the Idaho Bar. If I were a sensitive soul, my sisters might have given me an inferiority complex. They were all over-achievers. Naomi was only twenty-eight, and Ruth, the physician, was thirty. Sarah, only three years older than me, was the deputy head of the reference department at the Cowslip College Library. Each of them, by the time they were my age, had already earned their bachelor's degrees. I, on the other hand, was still technically a sophomore. Damn transfer credits, anyway. Perhaps my sisters were paying a hidden emotional toll for their collective success. They were all single, but then again, so was I.

Donny shoved his mouth into what was clearly supposed to be a patient, Latter-Day Saintly smile. He was breathing heavily, and every time he blinked, his eyes stayed shut for a fraction of a second past normal. He spoke slowly, as if he could sweeten his words by pouring them on like cold syrup.

"I'm very sorry, Mrs. Hardy, but Sam's in on a very serious charge."

My mother cocked her eyebrows in anticipation. "And that charge would be?"

Donny swallowed. Again. "I have orders not to discuss it with you until Lieutenant Young gets back. He won't be long." He looked at his watch. "Not long at all."

"I see," said my mother. "As soon as your lieutenant gets here, he'll pull the string on your back and you'll start talking. I'm a busy woman, Donny. I don't like to wait. Is there anything you can tell me in the meantime?"

"I can tell you . . . I can tell you that he resisted arrest."

"Oh really?" said my mother. "Anything else?"

"And . . . and . . . on the way to the station . . . your son urinated in the squad car."

"Goddamn it," Emma barked. "I don't care if he pissed on your doughnut. In case it's escaped your notice, Deputy Dawg, my son is sick. He has cancer. He is in the middle of a course of chemotherapy. If you keep hounding him like this, he will die. Is that what you want?"

Donny said nothing. He rocked back and forth on his heels and examined his fingernails.

"His hair," my mother went on, "is falling out. Surely you people have noticed that he wears a wig. Usually, you are thoughtless enough to confiscate it. My son doesn't sleep well. He doesn't eat. He weighs a whopping one hundred and twenty-two pounds. He's only a few inches shorter than you are, Donny, and he weighs less than your left leg. What the hell has he done to justify this police persecution? Petty shit! Nothing!" She dismissed my brother's crimes with a wave of her hand.

Donny stared at a spot some inches above our heads. "I can't do anything about it, Mrs. Hardy. Lieutenant Young is in charge, and he's gone to see Judge Andrews. Why don't you go home, and we'll call and let you know when Sam is arraigned? It won't take long."

Much to his surprise, and mine, my mother agreed.

"Okay," Emma said. Her tone was suddenly reasonable, quiet and persuasive. She smiled, a terrifying sight, and not just because she wasn't wearing her partial plate. My mother treats her teeth like a cocktail dress, wearing them only on special occasions. "Okay, I'll do that. I just want to see him first."

I felt like I was watching a cobra mesmerize a rat. Donny shook his head. "I can't, Mrs. Hardy. Visiting hours aren't until . . ."

"Visiting hours are now," she said matter-of-factly. "We're not going to make a break for it, Smith. I don't have a file or dynamite in my handbag."

"I don't know," Donny hesitated. "The lieutenant wouldn't like . . ."

Emma leaned forward and poked him on the chest with her forefinger. He winced and rubbed the spot, smearing the remains of his doughnut all over his necktie.

"Ow, Mrs. Hardy! You didn't need to do that."

"I want to see him now. You can search me if you like." She put her palms on the counter and spread her legs.

Donny shook his head desperately, and I stifled a laugh. He looked as if he'd rather chew his own hands off than pat down my mother. Fishing a key ring out of his pocket, he stepped from behind the desk. We followed him through several barred gates to the back of the jail, where he showed us into a long, narrow room.

"Wait here," he instructed, as if we had a choice. There were three stools in the room facing three windows, each of which was no larger than the glass on a ten-gallon fish tank. Next to the windows were telephone receivers on short metal cords. I cast a surprised glance at Emma.

"We're not going to get to see him in person? They've always let us meet him in the cafeteria before."

She didn't answer. There was a tap on the first window. Donny's face swam into view.

"Five minutes," he mouthed, holding up five fingers in case we couldn't read lips. He stepped out of the room, and Sam shuffled in. He was shackled and cuffed. It was with some difficulty that he sat down on the stool facing the glass.

Emma was shaking, but she picked up the receiver and held it so I could listen. Nothing happened. Sam stared down at his hands, moving them back and forth so that the cuffs caught the light.

"Pick up the telephone," Emma shouted.

Sam looked up and glared at her. Then he picked up the receiver on his side. "I'm not stupid," he said. "I've been in here before."

"Don't I know it, you rotten little shit. Do you know how sick I am of coming down here and bailing your tired ass . . ."

Sam hung up the phone and stared into space. My mother beat on the window, first with the palm of her hand and then with the earpiece of the receiver.

"Knock it off," I said, taking it out of her hand. "Do you want to get us arrested as well?"

I tapped lightly on the glass with my index finger. Sam picked up the phone.

"No," I slapped Emma's hand away. "You've had your chance. It's my turn. Okay, Sam, what's up? Why have you been arrested? Donny wouldn't tell us what the charge is."

Sam shrugged. He still had his wig. It was sitting on his head slightly askew, which for some reason made him look cock-eyed. Or something. I peered at him more closely. He wasn't cock-eyed, he was black-eyed. Two swollen half-circles, one under each eye. There was also an inch-long cut on the bridge of his nose and an egg-shaped lump on his forehead.

"Jesus, Sam, what the hell happened to you? Donny said that you resisted arrest, but he didn't say they had to use a baseball bat to get you into the squad car."

"Police brutality!" Emma squawked. "I knew it!"

Sam shook his head and smiled lazily. "Take a chill pill. The cops didn't hit me."

"A chill pill?" My gaze shifted and I looked him in the eye. The Plexiglas between us was thick, which distorted his features a bit, but I recognized those grotesquely enlarged pupils. He was stoned out of his mind. "You are in such trouble. What have you done?"

He looked away. In a voice almost too low to hear, he said, "I didn't hit her."

"Who didn't you hit?"

My mother snatched the phone back. "You hit someone?" she said. "Was it a cop? Did he hit you first?"

"Not he," I said. "Her."

"What?"

"Her. He didn't hit her. He's been fighting with a girl. I'm sure you can guess who."

Emma stared at me. "Bullshit. What are you talking about?"

"Into the phone, Emma. Ask Sam."

"Sam, what are you talking about? Who's this her you didn't hit?"

"Francie," Sam said, still not looking at us.

"Francie! You mean to tell me that you've been fighting with a fifteen-year-old girl? Of all the worthless, clapped-out, addle-brained . . ."

I took the phone. "Did Francie give you those black eyes?"

Sam shrugged, which was answer enough for me. My mother, however, had changed tack.

"He hit her?" she scoffed. "I don't believe it. That corn-fed slut makes three of him. I'll bet you dollars to doughnuts that she . . ."

"Hit him," I finished, covering the receiver with my hand. "Probably. But I'll bet *you* that he hit her back." Francie Stokes, my brother's on-again, off-again girlfriend, was a hardened juvenile delinquent—drinking, drugs, and grand theft auto. She smoked like a chimney, dressed like a hooker, and got into cat fights with other trampy girls. I spoke into the phone again. "Is that right, Sam? Did you and Francie beat the shit out of one another? I'm not judging you. I think you're pretty evenly matched. What you lack in size, you make up for in age."

In the pause that followed while he worked this one out, my mother launched a sneak attack. She shoved me off the stool. "Now you listen to me," she yelled into the phone. "Who did that to your eyes? Francie or the cops?"

"Who did what?" he asked nonchalantly, or as nonchalantly as someone can who's sitting in jail with a crooked afro and a kippered brain.

Emma inhaled deeply, her chest shaking with the effort. She held her breath for a moment, and then she let him have it. "When are you going to get wise to that fat-assed hussy? Francie Stokes doesn't give a damn about you! You're a convenient source of booty and beer. That's it. Sometimes you are as dumb as a bag of rocks. I've a good mind to leave you in here until you get some sense!"

"Call my lawyer," Sam said. "I want bail."

"Your lawyer?" Emma shrieked. "Your lawyer? I think you mean my lawyer. Or do you mean your sister? I certainly hope not. Naomi has no interest in defending you—she knows a hopeless case when she sees one. Your father's going to go through the roof this time. You know that, don't you? And for what? For a two-bit, shit-brained . . ."

I'd had enough. I grabbed Emma by the arm and gave her a look that was meant to simulate a bullet to the head. "Knock it off. Just ask him the essentials and let's get the hell out of here. In case you've forgotten, today is Friday. We can't bail him after five o'clock. Do you want to spend the entire weekend taking his collect phone calls?"

"My god," Emma said. "You're right. We've got to find your father and figure out how much this is going to cost."

She turned back to Sam, who appeared to be contemplating his navel through his orange jumpsuit. Emma tapped on the glass. "Look at me. Is there anything else I need to know before I leave? How are you feeling? Are you tired? I can't believe you've gotten yourself arrested again. You have chemotherapy tomorrow morning! What the hell were you thinking?"

Sam dangled the receiver in front of the glass, watching it like a cat watches a yo-yo. It didn't matter anyway; our five minutes were up. Donny came in through the door behind my brother and gently took the phone out of his hand. Then he waved at my mother, who was hyperventilating with rage, to indicate that the interview was terminated.

I patted Emma on the shoulder. "One of these days, you're going to give yourself a stroke. You need to be more Zen about these things. Om."

"Shut up."

"Come on. No matter what, they'll have to let him out for his ten-thirty chemo appointment. Let's go home and figure out our next move."

"My next move," she observed tersely, "is a lawsuit. Did you see what that bulbous oaf did to his eyes? And that lump on his forehead. She beat up on a cancer patient, Bil. A cancer patient! And who's in jail? Who, I ask you, have they thrown in jail?"

"We don't know what happened," I said, adding disingenuously, "Sam didn't actually say she did that to him."

"Which is proof positive, if you ask me. Why would he tell us that his fifteen-year-old girlfriend blacked his eyes? It's too humiliating!"

It certainly was. I hated to think of Sam brawling away with his jailbait girlfriend like a trashy loser on the TV show *Cops*. I hated that he *was* a trashy loser. There was no denying it. The evidence was in. Francie was a big girl and mean to boot, a bad-tempered cow with the same IQ as a bowl of cold mashed potatoes. Still, a grown man fighting with a teenage girl. It didn't bear thinking about.

I mustered my strength and gathered my aplomb. "Right, Emma. At this point it doesn't matter what happened. If we want to get Sam out of here, we have to get organized."

Under duress, my mother could swing into efficiency mode with disconcerting speed. "Yes," she said crisply. She stood up and banged on the door. "Donny! Let us out of here! We've got business to attend to. Hey! Don-boy! Jesus wept. Get your thumb out of your ass and . . ."

Donny opened the door. His face had assumed a hangdog expression. "If you'll just follow me, Mrs. Hardy, I'll . . ."

"Not so fast," Emma cut in. "The last time you had my son in here, a man in the cell with him died. Sam said he yelled for five minutes before any of you bothered to come and see what was wrong."

"It wasn't that long," Donny objected. "And we were . . . understaffed."

Emma poked him sharply in the ribs. "No excuses," she said. "This time, if my son so much as whispers, you hop to it. If he wants anything, you get it for him. Do you understand me? My eye is upon you, Donny Smith. If you put a foot wrong, I swear to God, you'll be shitting out of a brand-new asshole by quitting time."

Chapter 3

The cigarette was back in my mother's mouth, only this time, it was lit. I decided to let it go. She was sitting very still in the passenger seat, smoke puffing out of her nostrils. With her bosom heaving and her eyebrows drawn down over the bridge of her nose, she looked like Mount Vesuvius sitting on a tack.

"It's weird to watch you in action," I said.

"What are you talking about?"

"I'm talking about Donny Smith. The way you kept poking him—you're not allowed to poke the police. He could have arrested you. I don't know how you get away with it."

"It's not about me," she replied. "I've got to do whatever it takes to protect your brother. Donny's a wimp. He'll be more careful if he's afraid of the consequences." She crossed one leg over the other and tapped her foot on the armrest of her door. "You drive like an old lady, Bil."

"Would you shut up about my driving? If I were you, I wouldn't be quite so eager get home. Do you really want to tell Hugh that Sam has done it again?"

"Don't worry about that. I know how to handle your father."

Poor Hugh. My father longed for a quiet life. His hobbies were reading and falling asleep in front of the television. He did not enjoy the drama and excitement of Sam's escapades. Had it been left up to him, the Lewis County Jail would have been my brother's permanent address. But it wasn't up to him. Cancer had given Sam carte blanche with my mother. As long as he seemed to be living life to the fullest—and she took his determination to leave this world in a hail of gunfire as proof—she was always willing to fly into battle on his behalf.

I shook my head. "You know, Emma, I think Sam secretly likes it in jail. He gets to lie in bed all day, watching cartoons, smoking, and hanging out with other petty criminals. It's his idea of heaven."

I expected my mother to argue with this. Instead, she laughed. "Probably. If I keep poking Donny, maybe I'll get to give it a try."

We were silent for the rest of the drive. The family homestead was about eight miles outside of the Cowslip city limits, a small white farmhouse on a twenty-acre parcel. If you didn't count the gravel pit across the road—and we didn't—our nearest neighbor was a mile away. The house was old by Idaho standards. The oldest bits, the kitchen, the living room, and my parents' bedroom, were built in 1898. The rest had been added room by room, as the house changed hands and the families who lived in it grew. When my parents bought it, the house was generously described as a fixer-upper. The plumbing was bad, the floors were warped, and the foundation was crumbling. Twenty-some years later, the whole thing was finally weatherproof and no longer falling down around our ears, but it was still a little rough around the edges. The four shutters on the front windows were painted four different colors, and one of them was hanging by a single hinge. There was a big hole in the front porch, right in front of the door, and two dead cars sat on blocks in the yard. My mother sometimes talked about turning them into chicken coops.

As I pulled into the driveway, I saw my sister Naomi's jeep. As usual, she'd parked in the best spot, right beneath the cottonwood tree. I pulled in behind her, blocking her in. My mother raised an eyebrow.

"She's hogging the shade," I explained. "Her car has air-conditioning. Yours doesn't."

Emma nodded sagely. "Middle-child syndrome. Always has to be compensated for her contested place in the birth order. Also, it's raining."

"She's no more a middle child than I am. And I don't care if it's raining. It's a question of principle."

"You've parked in a mud puddle. Better get out my side."

I climbed over the empty cigarette packs, old coffee cups, and fast-food bags my mother had piled on the front seat. In the meantime she, unencumbered, had leapt over the hole in the front porch and was already through the door. I walked slowly up the gravel path. It wasn't actually raining anymore, just misting. There was even a hint of sun visible through a chink in the clouds. Jed, the family cat, was lying in the tulip bed, chewing something hairy and gray that made a nasty crunching sound. I decided not to investigate.

I stepped into the living room to find Emma in the middle of a high-speed monologue.

"I said, you'll let me see him, or my daughter the lawyer will . . ."

"I wouldn't have a relative for a client, Emma," Naomi interrupted. She was sitting on the sofa facing the door. She had my latest copy of *Muscle & Fitness* in her hand and was waving it around for emphasis, thoughtlessly—typically—wrinkling the cover. "Come to that," she went on, "I wouldn't have Sam, period."

My mother decided to take this as a sporting challenge. She often paid a ridiculous amount of deference to Naomi's opinions, probably because she so often needed legal advice. "Fat lot of good it would have done to tell Smith that. Where is your sense of dramatic effect?"

"In the same place as your sense of the truth," I said, rescuing *Muscle & Fitness* from Naomi's mangling grasp. "I save these, you know. Don't screw it up like that."

Naomi rolled her eyes. "Whatever. Can you tell us what's going on with Sam? Emma's making no sense. Again."

"You don't listen," Emma objected. "It's perfectly clear. Sam's in jail."

My father was sitting in the overstuffed chartreuse recliner that my mother calls Archie Bunker. Next to it was the matching but smaller chair, Edith. Many years before, the purchase of these chairs had led to a lengthy argument about sexual dimorphism in living-room furniture. I can't remember who won. It might have been a draw. Anyway, my mother always sat at the head of the table in the dining room.

Hugh yawned. There was a copy of *The One-Minute Manager* on his lap and an unlit pipe in his hand. It was clear that he'd just woken up.

He looked at Emma over the top of his black half-glasses, blinking every couple of seconds as he worked up the revs to speak.

"What's he done this time?" said Hugh.

"Fine way to talk about your son. He's done absolutely nothing."

My dad shook his head and yawned. "I'll try again. What's he charged with?"

"Taking a swing at Francie," I said. "Emma wants to bail him out, but she can't because he hasn't been arraigned yet."

"When will he be arraigned?" Naomi asked.

"Should be any time now. Donny Smith said he'd call us. He's waiting for Lieutenant Young to get back from somewhere."

"So I suppose the question," Naomi mused, "is do you really want to bail him out?"

Emma hopped from one foot to the other like a hyperactive chicken. "Of course I do!"

"I was including Hugh in that question," Naomi said. "The *you* was collective."

My mother shrugged impatiently. "Well, of course your father wants to bail him out. You do, don't you, Hugh?"

"Hmmph," said my father.

"Okay," Naomi went on. "As soon as he's arraigned, you can call Slinky Nilsson and get him to post bond. But if I were you, I'd consider leaving Sam in jail. It was only a week ago that he was released on his own recognizance. The judge isn't going to like this assault charge. It'll make him look stupid for letting Sam out on O-R."

"O-R?"

"Own recognizance," I explained. "Haven't you been listening?"

"You can get your attorney or his public defender to sort it all out on Monday," Naomi said. "A weekend in jail might teach him a lesson."

"Teach him a lesson," Emma sputtered. "You don't . . ."

"He's spent plenty of weekends in jail," I pointed out. "Hasn't taught him a thing."

"Wait," my father said. "Can he get a public defender?" So far, Emma and Hugh's lawyer had always represented Sam, with Hugh footing the bill.

Naomi laughed. "Of course he can. He's over twenty-one—you're not legally responsible for him. If he can't afford a lawyer, the court will appoint one."

"He can't afford a lawyer," Hugh said firmly.

Emma dismissed this with an airy wave. "Naomi could . . ."

My sister pursed her lips. "No, Emma, I couldn't."

They glared at one another. I wondered if Naomi knew how much she looked like my mother. Or acted like her. My oldest sister, Ruth, looked like Emma as well, though she, thank God, had my father's disposition.

"Hey," I said, interrupting the staring contest. "Why is the bail bondsman called Slinky?"

Naomi looked puzzled until she realized that I was trying to rescue her. She smiled. "It's after the toy. He's tall and skinny, and he sort of uncoils himself when he stands up."

"He's a snake," Emma remarked acidly, "but we need him. Now don't change the subject. You know that I wouldn't leave either of *you* in jail."

"I don't shoplift," I observed.

"And I don't punch up my girlfriends," my sister added.

I caught Naomi's eye for a moment. She looked away. I wasn't out to my family. Not that I was exactly closeted, but I'd never had a big sharing moment. As far as my private life was concerned, no one asked, and I didn't tell. It wasn't that I worried about their reaction—I didn't think they'd care—but I dreaded the prospect of becoming another one of my mother's great causes. It was hard enough just being her daughter without her marching in the streets and joining P-FLAG.

"Enough," Emma snapped, tapping her wristwatch. "It's five past two. We have got to get your brother out of jail. What's Slinky's phone number?"

"How should I know?" Naomi sniffed. "You'll have to look it up."

"Fine. Bil, you find the phone book. Hugh, grab your checkbook and go warm up the car."

My father remained in his seat. "The car doesn't need to be warmed up, Emma. And before I grab my checkbook, I want to know exactly what's going on here. Did Sam hit his girlfriend or not? Because if he did, I'm not bailing him out."

My mother said nothing. She looked past Hugh, fixing her gaze on a spot somewhere down the hallway.

"I'll take that for a yes," my father said. "He can rot in jail."

Here, I saw fit to intervene. "It's more complicated than that, Dad. Francie's blacked both of his eyes, so my guess is that it was a mutual altercation. As bad as Sam is," I held up a hand to forestall my mother, "I don't think he's a girlfriend beater."

"Maybe," Hugh said skeptically. "Still, bail bondsmen cost money, and that's money that you don't get back. Slinky Nilsson is a shyster."

"It's either pay Slinky or pay the full bond," Naomi said. "Take your pick."

At this point, my mother, who had been pacing up and down the room, sprang at my father with a whoop and a holler and tried to yank him out of his chair. "Hugh, listen to your daughter—get your checkbook and let's go!"

My father refused to budge. It was the immovable object meets the irresistible force. His face was beginning to harden, and soon he'd be set like a lump of cement. I racked my brains for a persuasive argument.

"Ah," I said. "Think about this, Hugh. If we don't get Sam out of jail, Emma will make our lives unbearable. Tonight, tomorrow, the next day. The entire weekend, shot to hell."

He pondered this, tapping the bowl of his pipe against the arm of the chair.

"Besides," I added, "what does he do when he's sitting in jail? He calls collect every five minutes." I pointed at my mother. "She won't refuse the charges. You know she won't. The phone bill will add up to more than his bail."

"All right," my father said at last. He turned to Emma. "I don't care if you bail him out, but I don't see why I should go with you. Use your own checkbook."

My mother hauled back and gave my father a flat-handed slap on the arm. "You're mean, Hugh. You're an old screw, a skinflint, a tightwad. You know I don't have any money in my checkbook. I live like a pauper on that measly allowance you give me."

Hugh laughed. It was always like that with them. My parents are not a lot alike, but they are compatible. Emma talks, Hugh listens;

she's into the big picture, he obsesses over the small details; she tells big fat lies, and he laughs.

Hugh is a professor of business and accounting at Cowslip College. He and my mother met there as undergraduates, and Emma dropped out after her sophomore year to marry him. They traveled around for years after that, Hugh collecting graduate degrees and Emma collecting children. When he accepted the job at Cowslip, Hugh insisted that my mother re-enroll and finish her degree in philosophy. She did. Juggling five kids and taking one class a semester, it took her ten years to finish. She'd worked off and on, only part-time since Sam's diagnosis, and always at clerical jobs she could leave with two weeks' notice. Consequently, my father was the recognized breadwinner.

"I don't give you an allowance," he was arguing, "I supplement your income."

"Whatever you call it, it's a paltry sum!"

"Then use the joint account. That's your money, too."

"Not for bailing Sam out of jail! I'd never hear the end of it." Emma turned to us. "Take a lesson from me, girls—don't ever get married. Men, even good men like your father, only want one thing."

I laughed. "From what I hear, he gets it."

Hugh stood up and put *The One-Minute Manager* on the seat of the chair. Two other books were crammed into the crack between the arm and the cushion, their spines covered in pipe ash.

"Fine," he said, "I'll come with you. I'll even pay, but you've got to call Nilsson first. I want to know exactly how much this is going to cost me."

"Done!" Emma cried. "Get your skates on, Daddy, I'll be back in a mo!"

Chapter 4

I bummed a ride into town with my parents. Slinky Nilsson's office was on Main Street, right next door to the Cowslip Café. I was eagerly anticipating my three o'clock rendezvous with Sylvie. Unfortunately, my truck, which needed transmission work, was sitting at the Toyota dealership waiting for me to come up with the cash for the repair bill.

With Hugh at the wheel, the drive back to town was slower than molasses. I drove the speed limit, but my father drove ten miles under it. Emma had her feet propped up on the dash and was performing a little toe dance on the windshield. Wisely, she said nothing. I looked out the window and tried to concentrate on the scenery.

To the north of Cowslip stood Cole's Mountain. Though it wasn't particularly tall as western mountains go, the peak was covered with snow for at least eight months out of the year. To the south was Hayman's Butte, smaller than a mountain, bigger than a hill. The top and back were covered with trees, but the front was bare. On its green expanse sat Hayman's horse farm, which overlooked our moderately picturesque town of twenty-five thousand. It was a prime piece of real estate, in the Hayman family since time immemorial, but I preferred the view on the back side of the butte. My best friend Tipper Schwartz's mother had a house on that side, and from the top of her ridge you could see for a hundred miles. Distant wheat fields, ever-green forests, and long, twisting roads that seemed to roll off into infinity. I yawned, and it suddenly dawned on me that I needed a nap. I'd been up until three o'clock in the morning watching *To Have and Have Not*, and the lack of sleep was beginning to catch up with me.

"Tired?" Emma asked.

"Yeah. I need at least twelve hours of sleep a day to feel fully human."

"You're worse than a cat."

"I didn't say I got that many hours. I just said I needed them."

Emma tapped on the window and pointed at Hayman's Butte. "How long is Tipper in town? Until this anti-gay thing is over?"

The anti-gay thing was a ballot initiative called Proposition One. I was supposed to be helping Tipper organize opposition to it, though so far, I'd been obliged to bag out. I was serious about doing better in school. Tipper, however, didn't know how to take "I'm busy" for an answer. He was a drag queen, and though he now lived in Seattle, he was a native of Cowslip. He was also really, really pushy.

"He's here until November," I said. "He'll go back to Seattle after the election."

"And what's the number of that initiative again?"

"One. It's not hard to remember, Ma."

"I'm not trying to remember. The safest thing to do is just go in and vote no on all of these citizens' initiatives. They're always written by crackpots."

"Well," my father laughed, "that's what I call informed."

"They're all anti-something," Emma insisted. "Anti-tax, anti-abortion, anti-gay. Vote no, and you don't have to waste your time reading the ballot."

"If only everyone were as lazy as you are." I yawned again and rolled down my window.

"That's it," she said, lighting a cigarette and letting the smoke blow back in my face. "Get some fresh air into your lungs."

When we finally got to town, our first stop was the bank. Hugh muttered about there being no point in having a savings account if you never saved anything, and Emma swore dramatically that she'd economize. Even better, she'd never loan Sam money again. Hugh raised his eyebrows but said nothing. I pretended I was deaf.

We exited the drive-through and headed down Main Street, past three Chinese restaurants, two bookstores, and a pizza parlor. The population of Cowslip was eclectic, part descendants of pioneers, part college transients. The division between town and gown was still evident, though it was no longer as sharp as it had once been. For reasons now obscure, a group of progressives founded the college in the early nineteen-twenties. Why anyone would want to build a small liberal arts school out in the middle of nowhere was a mystery. Before the college came to town, Cowslip was just a fork in the road with a Catholic church at one end, some grain elevators at the other, and a railroad track running between them.

It was five 'til three when my father parked the car in front of Slinky's office. I hopped out quickly, saying, "I'm going to the café. I'll get Sarah or Ruth to drive me home later."

"You don't want to come with us?" asked my mother, as if the gory details of springing Sam from the Hoosegow were of universally acknowledged interest.

"No, thanks. I've had enough excitement for one day. It's time for a triple mocha latté."

"Suit yourself," she said. "When are you getting that truck of yours fixed?"

"It is fixed. I'm just gathering up the money to pay the bill."

"You could gather a lot quicker if you didn't buy so many three-dollar coffees."

Hugh, bless him, gave her the evil eye. "In the meantime," he said, "you can use either my car or your mother's whenever you like."

Emma didn't rise to this bait, choosing instead to turn sharply and march into Nilsson's office. My father followed at a more measured pace.

Sylvie wasn't at any of the outside tables at the Cowslip Café, so I went in to look for her. She wasn't there, either. A teeming multitude was crammed around the tables next to the window, and there was a distinct smell of wet leather and wool socks. As the sky was now perfectly clear, I decided to forego the tables at the back and instead sat down outside. There were four bohemian-types near the door, but otherwise, I had the place to myself. Sylvie had said she wanted privacy; I hoped this would do.

The temperature was warming up, but the wind was brisk. I smiled at the bohemians. Although they didn't look like the Wal-Mart shoppers who comprised most of Cowslip's permanent residents, they looked just as mass-produced. All of them were wearing tie-dyed T-shirts, knitted caps, and Birkenstocks. They smiled at me and then went back to talking.

I leaned back in my chair and waited for someone to fight his or her way through the throng to take my order. I could hear the harvest trucks three blocks away, rumbling along Highway 8 to and from the grain elevators. The farmers wouldn't be happy about the morning's rain, which would delay the rest of the wheat harvest for at least three or four days. The wind stirred up stray kernels on the pavement, and I noticed a few people were out and about. An old woman and her Labrador were looking in the bike shop window, and a couple of teenage girls stood across the street with their backs to me, checking out the fine fashion on display at the Goodwill.

I drummed my fingers on the table. Eventually, a waiter came out to take my order. He was wearing a knee-length floral dress and a look of concentrated boredom. I admired his chutzpah and wondered if he knew Tipper. However, I didn't ask. Why make assumptions? Certain members of my family got pretty tired of being asked if they knew every other minority resident in town.

I ordered a mocha with whipped cream and took stock of myself. I'd only seen Tipper once in the two months since he'd helped me move back from Seattle. He'd called a couple of times and left messages with my mother, but I hadn't called him back. Schoolwork was a lame excuse. The real reason I hadn't thrown myself into political work with Stop the Prop was that their first order of business was encouraging gay volunteers to come out. I dreaded that disclosure for a number of reasons, not the least of which was my fear that it would lead to questions about my former "roommate," A. J. Josephs. We'd lived together for nearly two years until it all went to hell in a handbasket. She was why I left the University of Washington. She was why I'd come back to Cowslip with my tail between my legs. I didn't want to talk to my mother about A. J. I wanted to forget her.

The wind was becoming unpleasant. It had picked up a bit and was now stirring the dust and wheat kernels in little eddies. Still, I didn't want to go inside. The interior was far too crowded for my taste. If

I was going to be cheek to jowl with a bunch of people, I wanted to be dancing, not sipping a latté. I turned my back to the wind and shielded my cup with my hands.

A shadow fell on the table in front of me. I looked up, squinting to keep the dust out of my eyes. Sylvie was smiling down at me. Her hair was pulled back in a short ponytail, and she'd changed her clothes. She now had on a white T-shirt, a brown bomber jacket, and faded blue jeans. A black motorcycle helmet was tucked under one arm. I smiled back at her.

I wish I was the sort of woman who requires a long courtship. The kind who wakes up one day and happily discovers that she's in love with her best friend. I wish I was the sort who turns to a woman she's known and liked for several years and suddenly discovers that her feelings have grown into something substantial and mature. But I'm not. I'm like a penny on a railroad track, and beautiful women are like freight trains.

Sylvie Wood poured Novocain on the sensible parts of my brain and poked a cattle prod into the areas marked "idiot." I had no idea what I was going to say before I heard myself talking.

"Anybody got a match?"

Oh, Jesus. It was Lauren Bacall's opening line in *To Have and Have Not.* Sylvie hesitated for one interminable moment, while I sweated a case of bullets. Then she laughed.

"You know how to whistle, don't you? You just put your lips together and blow. I guess I'm not the only one who stays up late watching old movies on television."

"I'm an insomniac," I lied. "Never sleep more than an hour or two. Please, sit down."

"Thanks." She placed her helmet on the table, pulled out the chair opposite me, and sat down in a single, fluid motion. Ballet, I thought suddenly, and lots of it. Nothing else could account for the way she carried herself, erect but not stiff. Ballet and motorcycles. Interesting woman.

She sat back in her chair and smiled, or rather half-smiled. Several moments passed while she just looked at me. I waited for her to say something, my heart pounding with the effort not to babble. I stirred two spoons of sugar into my already sweet coffee, propped an elbow up on the table, and rested my chin on my hand in a vain attempt to keep my jaw from dropping into my lap.

"So," she said finally, "is this coffee better than church coffee?"

"It doesn't taste like gym socks, if that's what you mean. Oh, sorry. I'm sure you'd like one yourself. I'll flag down the waiter." I searched in vain for Mr. Laura Ashley, but he was nowhere in sight. "I could go inside and get you one, though it might be quicker if I just went to South America and picked the beans myself."

She smiled broadly this time. "The service is always glacial here."

Straight white teeth behind full pink lips. I was reminded of a line I'd read somewhere about Chiclets nestled in a red velvet case. I thought about the gap between my own front teeth and covered my mouth with my hand. Why the hell did my parents not get me braces? Selfish bastards—they'd ruined my life.

Sylvie rested an elbow on the table and leaned forward, shielding her eyes from the wind with her hand. I looked around again for the waiter and caught sight of him through one of the windows. I waved, but he either didn't see me, or he pretended not to notice.

"The service isn't just glacial," I said, "it's inept. I hope you're not dying of thirst."

"I'm not." She was looking at me curiously, as if weighing her options. "I'm sure you know why I wanted to see you."

I had no idea why she wanted to see me. I knew what I was thinking—I already had us married and living in Provincetown—but I wasn't optimistic enough to believe Sylvie was thinking the same thing. Stalling for time, I said, "I hope the funeral wasn't too upsetting."

I immediately regretted it. Of course the funeral was upsetting. Bizarre circumstances. Rumors of poisoning. Aside from that, Burt Wood was one half of Cowslip's great gay scandal; he left his family for another man. Even in 1978, a gay elopement on its own wouldn't have been that big a deal, but the Woods were an old family, and Frank Frost was the mayor's son.

Part of the surprise at Burt Wood's sudden return and subsequent death was that everyone had assumed he was dead already. The conventional wisdom was that "people like that" came to no good end. Even the gossips who weren't homophobic took note of the fact that Burt and Frank had disappeared just before the start of the AIDS epidemic. If they took off for some gay Mecca like San Francisco, what were the chances they'd escaped the plague?

The men's disappearance was also tied in with some monetary malfeasance. Money had gone missing from the Lewis County Assessor's Office—a quarter of a million in property tax revenues. The money later reappeared just as mysteriously, and the mayor claimed that there'd been an accounting error. No one believed it. He was a rich man, and people just assumed that he'd made up the difference from his own pocket.

My eyes met Sylvie's. "I'm sorry, that was a stupid thing to say. I'm sure this has been absolute hell for you."

She shrugged. "It's okay. I don't feel much like the grieving daughter. My father was gone a long time, and the truth is my mother and I were better off without him. It was almost like attending a stranger's funeral this morning."

"Still, it can't have been easy. Your mom took you out of school after he left."

"She sent me to a private school in Washington. She thought it might help."

"I missed you. Did it help?" I added quickly.

She shook her head. "Not really. It was only twenty-five miles from here, not far enough to make a difference. Eventually, I learned not to react when someone mentioned it. I grew a pretty thick skin. Thick enough to come back here for high school."

"We were moving in different crowds by then."

She smiled. "You and Tipper Schwartz, the dynamic duo."

"You and . . ." I stopped abruptly. I didn't know who her friends were in high school. I was certainly aware of her, painfully aware, but she was someone I daydreamed about in the hallway, not someone I'd have had the nerve to approach.

She said lightly, "I tended to keep to myself."

"Kids can be rotten."

"I don't hold it against them. What did they know? They were just repeating what they'd heard at home." She shut her eyes and rubbed the lids with her fingers. Then, smiling again, she leaned forward and put her hand on my arm. "Do you remember playing under the kitchen table while our mothers drank herbal tea and talked about passing the ERA? We must have been about five or six."

I laughed. "I remember sitting under the kitchen table and eavesdropping, pretending I was Harriet the Spy. Listening to adult conversations was one of my favorite pastimes. Everything they said seemed to be in some sort of code, and I kept thinking if I listened long enough, I'd be able to figure it out."

Sylvie's expression grew serious. She hesitated, and I took a long sip of my now-cold, sickeningly sweet mocha.

"Bil, the reason I wanted to talk to you is that your brother . . ."

I waited. She looked away from my face and down at the table.

"Sam was in jail with my father," she continued. "I was hoping you could tell me about that."

Though I should have been expecting this, I wasn't. I might attend funerals to pick up dates, but Sylvie had more important concerns. I said, "Of course. What do you want to know?"

She looked relieved. "I don't know. Anything. What did he say to your brother? How long were they in the cell together? How did my father act?"

"Well, I know that they weren't together for long. I think it was only fifteen or twenty minutes. Your father was clearly not well when the deputies brought him in, and he collapsed shortly thereafter. I don't know how to answer your other questions. I haven't talked to Sam about it."

"You don't know if my father said anything about where he'd been or why he came back?"

"If he did, Sam hasn't mentioned it. My brother had no idea the man was your father—none of us did until that report came out in the newspaper. My mother was shocked to death." Sylvie flinched. "Sorry," I said quickly. "Unfortunate turn of phrase."

She waved this aside. "You don't need to be delicate with me. I'm asking you all of this because . . ."

I guessed what she was trying to say. "Because the autopsy suggested something wasn't quite kosher? Let me guess, the sheriff's department has launched an investigation, but they aren't telling you or your mother anything. They're just running around, asking questions and acting mysterious."

"How did you know?"

"Because getting information out of them is like squeezing blood from a turnip. Whenever Sam's arrested . . ."

"He's in jail today, isn't he?"

It was my turn to flinch. "Damn my mother and her cell phone. I tried to stop her, Sylvie. Honestly, I think she's possessed by Satan."

She laughed. "Don't worry about it. My mother thought it was funny. She said if your mother's phone hadn't rung, the service might have gone on forever. The minister . . ."

"The minister wanted to shoot my mother. He gave her a look that could have curdled milk." She laughed again and I said, "Look, why don't I ask Sam some questions? I could find out the details for you, and then maybe we could meet again somewhere. I mean, if that's okay with you."

"That would be great. I'd appreciate it."

Her gaze became warm, and a thousand butterflies flapped their wings in my stomach. She opened her mouth to say something else, but our fool of a waiter chose that very moment to turn up, bill pad in hand, and ask if Sylvie was ready to order. In deference to the cold, he'd put a fishing vest on over his dress. I glared at him, but he gave me the same look of studied ennui that he'd been practicing earlier. Then he looked at Sylvie, and it all fell apart.

Oh great, I thought, it's a straight guy in a dress. The Cowslip College School of Design was nationally famous, and as a consequence, it drew scores of the ultra-hip from their more natural urban habitats. Our waiter was clearly a design-school denizen. The goatee alone should have clued me in.

"What can I get for you?" he drawled.

Sylvie, thank God, seemed oblivious to his fawning. "I'll have a double latté and a chocolate biscotti."

Though he had pen and pad in hand, he wrote none of this down. He just stood there, staring.

"Thank you," Sylvie said. "James, isn't it?"

He grinned like he'd won the lotto. "It's Jamie, actually. And your name is Sylvie, right?"

"Yes."

"You're in my theater design class."

"Yeah. Nice to see you. I'll have a double latté and a chocolate biscotti. Did you want to write that down?"

"I can remember it."

"Good. Thanks."

It was a clear dismissal, but he continued to stand there.

"Excuse me," I said, waving to get his attention.

"What?" he asked, giving me the briefest of glances before returning his gaze to Sylvie.

"Would you please get this woman a coffee and biscotti before she dies of hunger and thirst?"

Sylvie studiously avoided making eye contact. Sensing defeat, Jamie sighed heavily and moped off.

"And another double mocha for me, please!" I called after him. I glanced at my watch. It was nearly three forty-five. Emma and Hugh were taking their own sweet time in Nilsson's office. That was fine by me. I hoped they didn't come out until tomorrow morning. I looked at Sylvie and smiled happily. "What a ma-roon! Prepare yourself. When Jamie gets back, he's going to pull up a chair and set a spell."

"Let's hope not."

"What's the matter, you don't go for men in dresses?"

"I don't go for men," she said.

"Oh." The butterflies came back with a vengeance. "Does that mean what I think it means?"

"Of course. I understood that you were . . . similarly inclined?"

"Oh yeah. And you can just say lesbian. No need for euphemism, I'm right out there." It was a wonder lightning didn't strike me dead. "Do you mind if I ask who told you? Not that I care or anything. It isn't a big secret."

"Tipper Schwartz. I ran into him last night at a Stop the Prop meeting."

A meeting I should have attended. That would teach me to return Tipper's phone calls.

"So," I said, "how long have you been out?"

She gazed at me intently for a moment before replying, "I'm not out completely. I haven't told my mother yet."

"Oh," I said. "I have a confession to make. I haven't told my mother, either."

She seemed surprised. "Why not, if you don't mind my asking? Your mother's . . ."

"Notoriously liberal? Loudly leftie? A radical freak?" I shrugged. "It's not that I'm afraid I'll be disinherited or anything. I guess I'm afraid I'll be conscripted. My family already looks like the raw material for a sitcom. Black kids, white kids, adopted kids, gay kids. We should all learn to play musical instruments and travel around the country in a motley-colored school bus."

She leaned back in her chair, laughing. She had a big laugh, loud and infectious.

The hopeful Jamie reappeared with her latté. My second mocha was nowhere in sight. He paused, waiting for some encouragement from Sylvie. When she didn't give him any, he sighed heavily and scuttled off.

"Bil," she said, dipping the biscotti into her coffee, "when do you think you'll get a chance to talk to Sam?"

"This evening, I suppose. My parents are at Slinky Nilsson's arranging his bail. They've been in there for nearly an hour. I'm not sure what's taking so long."

"Do you think we could meet again this weekend?"

"Sure," I said, trying not to sound too eager. "Tomorrow if you like."

She thought for a moment. "Let's make it tomorrow night. I've got some things to do in the morning and afternoon, but I'll be free in time for dinner. Would you like to go out? My treat."

Underneath the table, my feet did a secret tap dance. "Absolutely. Anywhere, you name it."

"Let me think about that. It'll have to be someplace quiet. Why don't I call you tomorrow night around seven o'clock?"

"555-699-6548. I could write it on a napkin for you."

"No need. I'll remember it. I've got a head for numbers."

Sylvie Wood was a lesbian, and she'd asked me out to dinner. I felt a stupid grin spreading across my face and forced myself to think about something else. It probably meant nothing. She just wanted to know what Sam had to say. I'd wear my best shirt anyway, the dark blue one with the mother-of-pearl buttons. Too bad I'd wiped coffee on the leg of my good pants. I looked up from my reverie to find her staring at me.

"Do you think my father was murdered?" she asked abruptly.

I was taken aback. "I don't know," I answered slowly. "It seems more likely to me that he had some sort of accident. Who would want to murder him?"

"You think he was poisoned by accident?" she said, ignoring my question.

"I have no idea. Has the sheriff's department confirmed that he was poisoned? The newspaper said that the coroner was waiting for autopsy results from Spokane."

"They are. There's some sort of delay, a backlog or something." She shook her head as if to clear it. "I asked you that, Bil, because there's a rumor going around town that he was poisoned. Helen told me this morning."

"Helen who?"

"Helen Merwin."

"At the funeral? What an asshole!" Too late I remembered that Helen was Sylvie's cousin. "I'm sorry," I said quickly. "I'm sure Helen didn't mean to . . ."

Sylvie brushed this aside. "Of course she did. Helen is like that—she can't resist poking at people until she gets a reaction." She took a sip of her coffee and then continued in a softer voice, "Bil, please talk to Sam. See if he can remember exactly what my father said and did in that cell. Any small detail would help. I want to know if he was really poisoned, or if this is just more pointless gossip and rumor. Will you ask him?"

I opened my mouth to say yes, but before I could reply, cold hands reached from behind me and covered my eyes. A familiar voice whispered in my ear, "Guess who?" I nearly jumped out of my skin. Then I recognized that voice. Its owner was drawn to political drama like a moth to a flame. I should have known she'd come to Idaho for Proposition One. I sighed heavily and hopelessly.

"I don't want to guess who because I'm praying I'm wrong." I pulled the hands away and turned around to find A. J. Josephs smiling down at me. She laughed, flashing her very white and very expensively bleached teeth.

"As melodramatic as ever, Bil. Can't you just say hello?"

"What do you want, A. J.?"

"You might ask me to sit down. I've been trying to reach you ever since I got here last weekend, but you're never home. To think I came all the way from Seattle just to see you. Aren't you going to introduce me to your friend?"

I noticed then that Sylvie had pushed her chair back and picked up her helmet.

"Don't go," I said quickly. "A. J. is just passing through."

"Well," she hesitated. "I thought maybe . . ."

"Please stay." I trained a baleful eye on my grinning ex-girlfriend. "I'm sure you have other fish to fry, don't you, A. J.?"

"Nope, not a one." She plopped herself down on the chair next to me. "I thought you might buy me a cup of coffee, and we could talk about old times." She turned to Sylvie and held out her hand. "Hi," she said. "I'm A. J. Bil and I are . . ."

"Not on speaking terms," I finished.

A. J. continued to hold out her hand. Sylvie shook it politely.

I sighed. "Sylvie, this is Abigail Juliet. A. J., meet Sylvie Wood. Now, if you'll just leave me alone . . ."

"It's like that, is it?" A. J. asked spitefully. "You certainly work faster than you used to. How long has it been, four months? Five? I'm not even cold in my grave and . . ."

"I know you," Sylvie spoke suddenly. "You're with the Lesbian Avengers. You were at the Unitarian Church last night for the Stop the Prop meeting."

"That's right." A. J. shut her eyes momentarily for dramatic effect. "I've come here to do some political organizing. I got my undergraduate degree here at Cowslip College—that's how I met Bil. I was about to graduate, and Bil was taking a year off after high school. She was working on the campus grounds crew, planting trees and pulling weeds. I saw her outside one day and that was it, wasn't it?" She laughed. "We were both going on to the University of Washington in the fall, she for her bachelor's and me for my master's, so naturally . . ."

"Have you finished your master's yet?" I asked with deliberate malice. When I'd left Seattle, A. J. was on the verge of flunking out. Too many extracurricular activities.

"I'm taking a semester off," she replied coolly. "I'm here to bring professional order to the local yokels."

"You!" I sputtered. "Professional order?"

"Well, someone has to whip these people into shape." A. J. leaned forward, laying a proprietary hand on my arm. "You haven't exactly stepped up to the plate, Bil. I ran into Tipper last night, and he said he hadn't seen you for months. He said he wasn't even sure you were still in town."

Nice try, Tipper. I wondered how I could ever have found that hideous, toothy grin attractive. Her teeth were not like Chiclets in a velvet case. They were like sharks' teeth in a shoe box.

She reached out and took the mocha from my hand. "You don't mind, do you Bil? I'm parched." She took a small sip. "Yuck! That's cold. Why didn't you warn me?"

I thought about slapping her teeth down her throat, but before I could put my plan into action, she suddenly leaned across the table and spoke to Sylvie. "Wait a minute. Bil said your name was Sylvie Wood. I read about your family in the newspaper. It was your father who . . ."

"A. J.," I spoke sharply, hoping to cut her off.

"Oh shut up, Bil. Her father is some sort of gay martyr. The Avengers thought we might make political use of him. Idaho man, driven from his home by a bigoted society. Returns years later only to die tragically in the county jail, another casualty of homophobia."

"A. J.," I said again, this time so loudly that the bohemians at the next table started from their seats. "Shut up. Once again, you've gone too far. You don't know what you're talking about, and I for one . . ."

I never got to finish my sentence. As is always the case with my life, everything went to hell all at once. Over Sylvie's shoulder, I saw my mother coming out of Slinky's office. She was clearly madder than hops. Hugh was hot on her heels, sucking on his unlit pipe.

"Christ in a pushcart!" Emma bellowed. "Have they lost their minds?"

"Don't start," Hugh said. "I don't want to know what you think. I want to hear what the county prosecutor thinks. If Sam had anything to do with that man's death . . ."

I didn't hear the rest and neither did my mother. She stopped dead in the middle of the sidewalk, like a deer caught in the headlights. Well, more like a grizzly bear. Her eyes were fixed on a point directly in front of her. I followed her gaze across the road. The two girls who had been looking in the Goodwill window when I'd sat down at the Cowslip Café were now coming out of the Main Street Market. They'd stopped so one of them could light the other's cigarette. I didn't know the redhead, but I knew the brunette. She caught sight of my mother, and her sullen face registered first surprise and then fear.

Emma didn't hesitate. She set off across the road at what, for a middle-aged fat woman, can only be described as a breakneck pace. As she ran, she howled, "Francie Stokes! I want a word with you!"

Francie didn't waste any time, either. She was off like a shot, down the street and round the corner, dragging the redhead behind her. My mother, narrowly missed by a pickup truck heading north and a motorcycle heading south, took a flying leap at the curb and wound up doing a belly flop onto the sidewalk.

I pushed my chair back from the table, spilling cold mocha onto A. J.'s lap.

"Goddamn it, Bil!"

"Sorry," I said, not pausing to savor the moment. "Gotta go!"

I reached Emma a few seconds later.

"Oh Bil," she cried, bursting into tears. "They think your brother has killed someone!"

Chapter 5

That someone was Burt Wood. In the next two hours, I learned plenty of information to pass on to Sylvie. Somehow, though, I didn't think it would win me any Brownie points with her. I learned that the alias Wood gave to the arresting officer was Charlie Gibb. As the officer had recently played that role in Cowslip Community Theatre's revival of *Our Town*, he didn't believe him. Wood was thrown into Sam's cell to sober up and remember his real name. Less than an hour later, he was dead. They found out Wood's real name via an anonymous tip.

Contrary to my mother's scaremongering, no one had formally accused my brother of murder; they had decided to hold him for questioning. It took a Herculean effort to squeeze this information out of Donny Smith, who was still claiming that he couldn't talk to us because he was under orders from Lieutenant Young. When we asked to speak to Young, Donny said that he wasn't available. My mother continued to ask questions, reading meaning into each of Donny's furtive looks and poking him in the ribs every chance she got.

Eventually, the county prosecutor, Alice Campbell, showed up and explained that Wood had apparently died of an overdose. The theory seemed to be that Sam had smuggled something into jail—something meaning drugs—and given it to Wood. When Emma pointed out that Sam had only been in jail with Wood for fifteen or twenty minutes, and that he was already complaining of stomach pain when they brought him in, Campbell said that it was closer to an hour, plenty of time for Sam to have given him some illicit substance. She also said that Sam was the only witness as to when exactly Wood began complaining.

They were waiting for the complete autopsy results, including some blood tests and an analysis of Wood's stomach contents.

My mother smiled sourly. Without those results, she argued, they couldn't hold Sam. Alice Campbell smiled back at her. They were holding him on the assault charge. It was a grim face-off. We knew Campbell fairly well; she was one of Naomi's law-school cronies, a grasping yuppie with political ambitions. In the end, Sam was arraigned, and his bail was set high. My parents had to cough up a thousand dollars. Nilsson posted Sam's bond on Saturday morning, and my mother picked him up at the county jail at ten o'clock, just in time to take him to his ten-thirty chemotherapy appointment.

I offered to go with my mother, both to the jail and to chemo, but she refused, saying that she preferred to speak to him alone first. Emma seemed certain that the autopsy results would clear him. I wasn't so sure. The experts in Spokane would be able to pinpoint the exact substance that had killed Burt Wood, and if it was anything Sam was known to use or suspected to sell, he was headed to the pen.

Emma dropped me off at the Toyota dealership on the way. Hugh decided that as long as he was splashing out the cash, he might as well loan me the money for my truck repairs. I accepted, graciously. Ain't too proud to beg is my motto. When I got back home, Ruth and Sarah were perched on the living-room sofa, and my father was asleep in Archie Bunker.

"Just the woman we wanted to see," said Sarah. She gestured at the recumbent Hugh. "Sleeping Beauty has not been forthcoming. What's this about Sam taking an ax to someone?"

"An ax?"

"Emma left cryptic messages on our answering machines last night," Ruth explained. "Mine said that Sam was being treated like an ax murderer. Can you tell us what's going on?"

"I can try." I sat down in Edith and extended the footrest. "First, he didn't use an ax, and it probably wasn't murder. The cops think Sam had a stash hidden on him when he was arrested at Safeway last week. They think he passed it on to Burt Wood, who took it and died. If they can prove it, we're probably looking at involuntary manslaughter."

"What was supposed to be in this stash?" Sarah asked.

"Campbell didn't say. Pot, heroin, Drano—who knows? We're waiting for autopsy results."

Ruth nodded as if this made sense. "The lab in Spokane is backlogged right now. I sent some blood complements up there on Monday, and they haven't come back yet. It usually only takes two or three days."

"Anyhow," Sarah said, "why do they think Sam *gave* Wood anything? Since when has he shared dope out of the goodness of his heart?"

"Gave, sold. The DA thinks Sam is a big dealer," I replied. "He's supposed to be Cowslip's answer to the Medellin."

"Oh really?" she laughed. "Then why is he always borrowing money from me?"

"You, too?" said Ruth.

"And me three," I added. "It doesn't make a lot of sense. I think they're just looking for a way to get him off the streets. He's been arrested four times since June, and now twice in seven days. You can't blame them for trying."

"No, I don't suppose you can." Ruth stood up and stretched. "I've got to get going. I'm on call in the ER this weekend. Tell Emma I stopped by, and ask her to keep me posted."

When Sarah stood up as well, I said, "Leaving so soon? You don't fool me, either of you. You only stopped by this morning because you knew Sam had chemo and that Emma would be out. She's convinced you were secretly at home last night, screening your calls."

"I had a date," Sarah protested.

"And I was working," Ruth said. "Naomi may have been screening calls, but then she has even more reason to be wary of Sam's dramas than the rest of us. She said Emma was trying to get her to take him on as a client yesterday."

"True. She stuck to her guns, though. As things now stand, he's getting a public defender."

"You be careful, Bil," Sarah advised. "I know you live here now, but you've got to quit getting sucked in. How's school going?"

"Just fine. I don't need a babysitter. Besides, if I don't take an interest in Sam's affairs, where will my sisters get their information? You'll have to go right to the source." I pushed Edith into the full reclining position, closed my eyes, and yawned.

"Don't you start," Sarah laughed. "You're just like old man narcolepsy over there."

"I heard that," Hugh said.

Half an hour after they left, the crunch of tires on gravel jarred me out of a fitful sleep. I glanced over at the chair next to me. A fly was buzzing around my father's head. He kept on snoring.

Sam was first through the front door. He said, "I didn't give that guy shit" and, "Fucking stupid prosecutor" to no one in particular, then locked himself in his bedroom. Emma stopped at his closed door. Ordinarily, she would have beaten it down.

She knocked gently. "Sam?" Silence. "Let me know if you need anything."

Though she looked tired, and I felt sorry for her, I didn't say anything. My mother despises pity. I picked up my mangled *Muscle & Fitness* and pretended to read it.

Emma spent the next hour whipping through the house like a tornado—she mopped, waxed, and dusted. Our place was usually a midden, and the cleanest of us could generously be described as a slattern. My mother wasn't working off her stress, she was telegraphing a message. At some point, I got swept up in the excitement and found myself washing four days' worth of dirty dishes. Hugh opened one eye when Emma began vacuuming around him. Otherwise, he didn't stir. When the place was sparkling like the Crystal Palace, Emma sat down at the kitchen table and asked me to hand her the phone book. It was the first time she'd spoken to me since she'd gotten home.

She called Bucky's Salvage and arranged to have the junked cars towed out of our yard.

"Here," she said, handing me the receiver, "would you please hang this up?"

"I think you forgot something."

"What's that?"

"Aren't you going to call a locksmith to get Sam out of his bedroom?"

"He'll come out when he's ready."

"You could kick the door down," my father said, passing behind Emma on his way to the coffee pot.

"So, the somnambulist rises," Emma observed. "Did you have a nice nap?"

Hugh sat down heavily, splashing coffee on the newly waxed table. "A bit noisy. Especially the vacuuming."

Emma nodded. "I'll speak to the maid about that."

"So," said my father, slurping loudly, "when are we going to be treated to the tale of the jailhouse corpse? Is Ted Bundy still in his bedroom?"

I decided to shelve curiosity and make myself scarce. "Excuse me," I said. "I have to see a man about a horse."

Emma waved a hand at me, irritated. "There's no need to go haring off. Your father and I are not going to argue. He's going to drop the subject."

Hugh drained his cup. "Horseshit, Emma. You can't have it all your own way."

My parents rarely argue, much less fight, but when they do, it drags on for days and there's no living with them. Hugh retreats into stone-faced silence as Emma gets more outrageous.

The Holy Spirit descended in the form of a ringing doorbell.

"It's the Jehovah's Witnesses," I said happily. "I'll get it."

So much for divine intervention. It was not the Jehovah's Witnesses, Mormon missionaries, or even the Girl Scouts. Instead, Granny and Helen Merwin stood on the front porch, staring like a couple of extras from *Village of the Damned.* Granny smiled. Helen's expression didn't change. She always looked at me as if I were something stuck to the bottom of her shoe.

"Come in," I said. "Watch out for the hole."

Granny expertly negotiated the empty space, but Helen tripped, catching the toe of her shoe on the edge of the doorframe. It dropped down into the abyss below. "Oh sh—" she began. Then she looked at my grandmother and amended it to "darn."

"I'll get it," I said, dropping to my knees and reaching into the gap.

I tried not to think of the garter snakes I'd seen slithering around the steps all summer long. I closed my eyes and groped around. Luck was on my side. I found the shoe without touching anything slithery.

Helen stood there, lopsided, her arms folded across her chest. She held out her hand, and I gave her the shoe.

"I'll need to rinse this off," she sniffed.

"Won't that ruin the leather?" I asked, knowing full well that she was wearing cheap vinyl church pumps. Helen squinted at me. There are many, many advantages to having drag queens as friends, particularly if your own family can't tell the difference between a tennis shoe and a Gucci loafer.

"The bathroom is this way," I said. "Emma, Hugh, we've got company!"

At the sound of the doorbell, my father had vanished out the back door. He was on the patio now, doing a very convincing imitation of someone repairing a barbecue grill. He waved cheerfully through the window at my grandmother. Behind Granny's back, Emma gave him the finger. Granny settled herself down at the table.

"So," my mother said, "can I get you a cup of coffee?"

"I'd prefer tea. Iced if you have it."

"I don't have it. How about coffee?"

"Actually, we do have tea," I volunteered. "It's just not made. I'll put the kettle on."

Emma glared at me. Once my mother is mad, she finds it nearly impossible to behave gracefully. Everyone within reach gets it.

Helen came out of the bathroom, her hooves successfully re-shod. I smiled at her sweetly. She made a lemon-sucking face. She'd abandoned the Mafia widow look today for nun-in-training. Her hair was scraped back into a tight French braid, and she had on a conservative blue dress with a round white collar. Having so recently stared with lascivious intent at her good-looking cousin, I found it disconcerting to look at Helen. She was almost pretty. If she'd smiled more, or at least refrained from pulling sour faces, she might have been as attractive as Sylvie. She had a nice body, or so I suspected, anyway. I stole a look at her legs as she sat down—smooth and muscular with well-turned ankles. Nice ankles, nice body, but odder than a football bat. Helen was one of the strangest people in Cowslip, and that was going some.

She was twenty-nine or thirty and, for time immemorial, had worked part-time in the Cowslip College Library. She was one of Sarah's paraprofessional subordinates. Occasionally, my sister felt sorry for her and took her out to lunch. Afterward, she was always sorry she'd bothered. With a host of annoying habits to choose from, Helen had one that rose above all the others—she hummed incessantly. It was always just under her breath, and Sarah took it to be indicative of her mood. In staff meetings, she might hum "We Shall Overcome." In crowded elevators, she hummed show tunes. Emma once asked her how her parents were doing, and Helen hummed three bars of "Send in the Clowns."

Now she was humming "Rock of Ages."

"Tea, Helen?" Granny asked.

"Tea, yes. That would be fine." Helen looked around our clean but less-than-well-appointed kitchen and wrinkled her nose suspiciously.

"Do you smell something?" I asked. A snotty smile pulled at the corners of her mouth. I was about to let her have it with both barrels when Emma suddenly spoke up.

"Is that a new hair-do, Mother?"

Granny nodded happily. "It is. What do you think?"

Emma took a long, appraising look. "I think," she said slowly, "that it looks like a bullet from a Remington thirty-ought-six."

I tried unsuccessfully to smother a laugh.

"Don't be silly," my grandmother replied. "I just got it done this morning. Helen took me."

"Suit yourself," Emma shrugged. "It's fat in the front and pointed at the back."

"What brings you out here today, Granny?" I asked quickly.

Granny drew herself up. "We've been canvassing." She delivered this sentence as if she were announcing that the Japanese had bombed Pearl Harbor, Hawaii by air.

My mother sighed. "Another Nazi for county commissioner, I suppose."

"I am canvassing," Granny continued in a throaty rumble, "to garner support for a law that will protect the children of Idaho."

Emma rolled her eyes. "And what sort of law will do that? Don't tell me you're pushing prayer in school again because you know how I feel about that. Since when do Episcopalians evangelize, anyway?"

"I'm not evangelizing," Granny said huffily.

"You're not here to save my soul, are you? I warn you, Mother, I'm an atheist. I don't want Jesus for my personal savior, and he doesn't want me for a sunbeam. Let's leave it at that."

Helen drew in a breath and changed her tune from "Rock of Ages" to "The Old Rugged Cross." Granny looked more confused than offended.

"Emma, really. Helen and I are here to solicit your vote. Yours too, Bil," she nodded at me. "We're gathering support for Proposition One, the traditional-values initiative. I've got a copy of the text of it here." She rooted around in her purse, stirring up tissues and half-sticks of gum, and finally pulled out a pamphlet.

"We're not interested," I said, the blood pounding in my ears.

"Bil's right," Emma agreed. "I don't give a tinker's cuss about your initiative. It's sheer crackpottery."

"Surely you don't support special rights for pedophiles," Helen said.

"Of course she doesn't," I snapped. "What's that got to do with Proposition One? Look, Granny, put that pamphlet away. I'll get you some literature from the other side explaining what this thing is really all about. You've been bamboozled. My friend Tipper . . ."

"Tipper Schwartz?" Helen asked, sneering.

I glared at her. "Yes, Tipper Schwartz."

Somewhere along the line, Granny had lost the thread of the argument. "Tipper Schwartz. Isn't she married to the Vice-President?"

"That's Tipper Gore," Helen corrected.

"Then who's Tipper Schwartz? Do I know her?"

"I doubt it," I observed tartly. "He's not a member of the Junior League"

"Mother," Emma sighed wearily, "it might not look like it, but I'm actually very busy, so if you're finished . . ."

"Of course," Granny agreed without apparent rancor. She was clearly puzzling over Tipper Schwartz and that had driven everything else from cognitive. "I'll leave this pamphlet with you. Read it when you have a chance." She nodded significantly at me to indicate that I was included in this command.

"No thanks, Mother. We've already made up our minds."

Granny stood up then and smiled at us. It was an automatic gesture—she always smiled when she entered a room, and she smiled when she left it, just like Miss America. "I'll leave it here on the table. You might be thinking more clearly later on. I know you're under some stress, Emma."

"What sort of stress?" my mother asked suspiciously. "What have you heard?"

"I hope you didn't imagine you could hide this sort of thing," Granny replied.

My mother and I both held our breath. If word had reached Granny that Sam was a suspect in Burt Wood's death, then it was all over town.

Granny pushed her chair back and gathered up her pocketbook. "Emma, I know that you have a special relationship with Sam, but this really is beyond the pale. I am your mother. And I'm Sam's grandmother," she added, clearly as an afterthought. "Naomi told me that he was arrested for hitting a woman. A woman. The shame of it."

"The shame," Helen parroted.

Emma laughed. "Mother," she said, "you don't know the half of it."

Granny shook her head sadly. "You are obviously not feeling yourself today, Emma."

"I'm not feeling anyone else," Emma replied.

Helen snickered before she remembered herself and slapped a hand over her mouth.

"We're leaving, Helen," Granny announced. "Thank you for the tea, Wilhelmina."

"You're welcome, Granny." As I didn't want to delay her departure, I didn't remind her that I'd never actually gotten around to giving her any tea. "Please, do call me Bil."

Helen resumed her humming. I hoped she would trip over the hole in the porch again—this time, she could dig around for her own shoe while I just stood there and laughed at her. Granny hobbled along in pained silence, a martyr to her bunions. The performance was wasted on my mother, who remained seated at the table and simply called "bye-bye" after us.

"Let me help you over the gap," I said, taking Granny's hand. I needn't have bothered—she sprang through the doorway like a circus dog. I turned to Helen and smiled politely.

"Bye, Mildew."

She stopped humming and glared at me. "Don't call me Mildew. No one calls me that."

"You must have misheard me. Watch the hole. We don't want to trip, do we?"

She stepped through the door. Then she stopped and turned her head so quickly that her lips nearly brushed against my ear. In a low voice she said, "Get your rotten porch fixed, dyke."

I stood for a moment, dumbfounded. By the time I mustered up a response, Helen was down the front steps and out in the yard.

"Fuck you, Mildew!" I had meant to speak quietly, but it turned into a shout. Granny stopped dead in her tracks and swayed unsteadily.

"What was that?" she asked.

Helen stepped forward and took Granny's arm. "That was Wilhelmina," I heard her say. "I think she said 'bless you.' "

I walked back to the kitchen and sat down, propping my feet up on the chair next to me. Emma was smoking a cigarette, using a saucer as an ashtray.

"Was that you I heard swearing at Mildew Merwin?" she asked.

"Yes." Some explanation seemed to be expected. "She said something that made me mad."

My mother chose to accept this at face value. "Nothing like her cousin, is she? Despite the family resemblance."

"No, she isn't." How would it feel to be your beautiful cousin's freaky doppelganger? I could almost have felt sorry for Helen, but then Sylvie wasn't just any beautiful cousin; she was a beautiful lesbian cousin. Helen's vicious "dyke" was still ringing in my ears.

"Pretty is as pretty does," I said.

"What?"

"Sorry, I was just thinking out loud."

Chapter 6

Sam ended his exile half an hour after Granny and Helen left.

"Where's Hugh?" he asked.

Emma looked out the window. "I don't know. He seems to have given up on the barbecue."

"There was nothing wrong with the barbecue," I said. "He snuck around the front of the house and went back to bed. He's never awake on a Saturday."

Sam sat down at the table and picked up my mother's saucer, now full of cigarette butts. "What's up with this? You starting a cancer factory?"

"Don't blame her," I said. "I've taken up smoking. Those are all mine."

"Trying to lose weight?"

"Bite my ass, baby brother. I am the picture of physical fitness. Can't you tell the difference between muscle and fat?"

"Sounds like I struck a nerve."

"Fuck off."

"So sorry," he laughed. "I didn't know you were beefing up."

"Beefing . . . I'm not . . ."

"Stop sputtering, Bil," Emma interrupted. "You are beefing up, or buffing up, or whatever you weightlifters call it. You spend more time in the gym than Arnold Stallone."

"I'm not at the gym today," I said, casting an eye on Sam, "and it's Sylvester Stallone. Arnold is a Schwarzenegger."

"Who cares?" my mother said. "What do you want for lunch?"

"Are you cooking?"

"I am. How about fried chicken and biscuits?"

Sam's favorite. Emma opened the freezer door and rummaged around. "There's a package of chicken breasts in here. If you'll keep me company, I'll thaw them out."

My mother put the chicken into the microwave. I looked over at Sam, who was studying the tabletop. The circles under his eyes had darkened even more, and they were now topped by greenish-yellow crescents. His nose was swollen, and he had a scab on one nostril.

"You look like living hell. Once and for all, was it Francie?"

"Yeah."

Confirmation at last. Emma stood at the counter with her back to us. She said nothing, though I knew she was listening intently. She dumped two cups of flour into a ceramic mixing bowl, spraying white dust all over herself and the floor.

"Strong girl," I observed.

Sam looked up at me, and I wondered what he was going to do. It's often hard to read his mood. I can sometimes tell what he's thinking, but never what he's feeling. I waited. A slow, lazy smile lifted the corners of his mouth. He tilted his head to one side and regarded me.

"She's built like a fucking linebacker."

"No Girl Scouts for you, Sam," I said lightly. "You seem to prefer those sumo wrestlers. So, why did she black your eyes?"

He shrugged. "I said something that pissed her off."

If I'd pursued this line of questioning, we might have been in the kitchen for hours listening to he-said, she-said. Instead, I decided to be blunt. "Well, we know she hit you. Did you hit her back?"

He shook his head. "No. She hit me, and I shoved her." I must have winced because he explained, "No, I mean shoved her off me. There wasn't any other way—she was all over me, hitting me in my face and on my arms."

"And?" Emma tossed an ungodly amount of shortening into a cast-iron frying pan. She sat it on the front burner, turned on the heat, and took a step toward us. I gave her a warning look. If she interrupted Sam now, he'd never finish.

"It was after I'd shoved her off that she gave me these," he said, pointing at his eyes. "Then her mother called the cops."

Emma's jaw dropped. "Her mother was there while you two were tearing the place up?"

"What do you mean there? Her mother started it." Sam snorted. "She called me . . ." He hesitated. "It doesn't matter. She was drunk."

"Drunk my fanny," Emma gestured impatiently. "What did she call you?"

Sam closed his eyes and sighed heavily. "She called me a nigger."

"White trash," my mother observed.

"So," Sam continued, "I called her a fucking c—"

"Don't say it," I said quickly. My father hates swearing. Fuck is pretty bad in his book, but cunt he cannot abide. To my knowledge, no one had ever uttered that word in our house, not even Emma. It didn't matter that he was all the way down the hall and asleep in his bedroom with the door shut, there was still a chance that he might hear it and fly into a million pieces.

"I called her something," Sam went on. "Then Francie got pissed off at me. I don't know what her problem is—she calls her mother all sorts of shit. To her face, too." He shot me a look out of the corner of his eye. I guessed there was more to the story than he cared to tell. Crystal Stokes was as bad as her daughter. Possibly worse.

"Well, it's certainly a fine mess now," Emma said, returning to her biscuit dough and rolling it out with unnecessary violence. "Do you really have to troll among Cowslip's trailer trash to find yourself a date?"

Sam's face lost its laconic look. "Shut up, Emma," he said.

As my mother stepped away from the stove to embark on a full-scale battle, I noticed twelve-inch flames leaping up behind her.

"Hey!"

"What?" Emma and Sam spoke in unison.

"The frying pan's on fire."

Black smoke rose and spread out on the ceiling while my mother stood frozen, staring at it. I jumped up, pushed her out of the way, and smothered the flames with a pan lid.

"Way to go, Julia Child. What is the matter with you?"

"I was distracted."

"No kidding." I sat back down at the table. Sam was laughing now. I shook my head at him for a moment, and then I joined in.

"Another great day at the fucking Waltons," Emma said. Sam and I laughed harder. My mother leaned against the counter, one foot crossed over the other. Only her fingers tapping on the Formica gave her away. "Can we please get back to the business at hand? Where were we before I set fire to the kitchen?"

"You were making unfortunate remarks about people who live in mobile homes."

"Mind your own business, Bil."

"I wish you'd mind yours, Emma," Sam said. Now that we'd abandoned the subject of Francie, his tone was easy again.

"I don't know what you're talking about, jailbird," my mother said. Her tone, however, was light. "If I didn't mind your business, who would? Next time, maybe I'll just let you sit in the pokey. Bil here thinks you like being incarcerated."

Sam didn't take the bait. He looked at me and rolled his eyes until only the whites were showing. He was clearly in an expansive mood. If I could just keep Emma reined in, I could ask Sylvie's questions. She might not want to see me once she learned that my brother was a suspect, but I could always hope.

Trying to make my voice sound as disinterested as possible, I said, "So, what's it like in jail? Is there really a toilet just sitting out there in the open?"

"Yeah. You have to go with everybody watching."

"Gross."

"No kidding. It's worse when someone else has to go. Then you're the watcher."

"You could look away."

"Not if they're making all kinds of noise. That guy who died spent ages barfing."

My mother joined us at the table. "Did he? Tell us exactly what happened."

"You know what happened. He died."

"I don't know what happened," she insisted. "I wasn't there. How long was he in with you? Fifteen minutes? Twenty? An hour?"

He shrugged. "I didn't look at the clock."

"When did he start throwing up?" I asked. "Had he already been in the cell for a while, or was it right away?"

"No," Sam said thoughtfully, "it wasn't right away. At first, he was just lying on the bed, holding his stomach. I thought he was drunk or something. I wasn't really paying attention."

"Why not?" my mother asked angrily. "The man died."

"Because I was watching television. And I didn't know he was going to die."

My mother opened her mouth to speak again, but I interrupted. "Did you recognize him, Sam? I don't mean did you know he was Burt Wood. I mean was he someone you'd seen before, walking around town or something?"

Emma gave me an inscrutable look. My brother sighed heavily.

"What difference does it make?"

I shrugged. "It might make a lot. If he was sick when he got there, we can prove you didn't do it. If you'd never seen him before, why would you give him your stash?"

"He didn't have a stash," Emma snapped. "Where would he have gotten one, out of thin air?"

"Out of my ass, actually," Sam said. "That's what the cops think, anyway. I don't know if the guy was sick before they arrested him or not. I guess he must have been."

"Ha!" Emma cried. "Then how could you have given him something?"

Sam didn't answer. "It's his word against theirs," I said. "We're in the same boat they are. We're all waiting for the autopsy results. In the meantime," I turned back to Sam, "what was this guy wearing?"

He stared at me blankly.

"I'm serious," I continued. "Was he wearing something distinctive? Glow in the dark socks, a fish-shaped necktie? Maybe he was seen somewhere before his arrest, accepting a Ziploc baggie full of drugs from someone. Preferably someone other than you."

Sam thought for a moment. "Jeans," he said. "Brown boots. Black turtleneck."

"Jacket?"

"They don't let you wear coats in the cell. No coats, belts, neckties, or shirts with buttons. You might use those things to hang yourself."

I tried to picture someone hanging himself with a jacket. He'd need long sleeves and a lot of determination. "Okay," I said. "Let's go with Lieutenant Young and DA Campbell's theory. You were arrested at Safeway. You had a six-pack under your shirt and a stash up your ass. As we saw on the security tape, this impeded your walking. You got to jail, dropped your trousers, pulled out the stash, and gave it to Wood. Skipping the question of why for the moment, it seems to me that we have a problem of logistics. The toilet's in the middle of the floor. Were there other people around?"

"No witnesses, if that's what you mean. It was just him and me. When he fell over, I had to yell for five minutes to get a jailer to come check on him."

"Sam," I said, an ugly suspicion taking shape in my mind, "do the cops have any physical evidence for this theory? I mean, did they do a body search on you or anything like that?"

He shook his head. "They just searched my clothes. Lieutenant Young thinks the drugs were in a condom. I got them out, gave them to the guy, and then flushed the rubber down the toilet."

The light dawned. I looked at Emma. "You know what this is about, don't you? They're trying to cover up criminal negligence. The sheriff's department has shit in its white hat, Ma. Remember what Donny said yesterday about being understaffed? There weren't enough guys on duty to man the jail. They're trying to deflect attention onto Sam. He's going to be their fall guy, the big, bad drug dealer."

"You mean the big, bad, brown drug dealer," she said. "This town is whiter than Barbara Bush's ass. If the cops want to know who's passing out dope, they should arrest some of those rich, white farmer boys who're always hanging around Lilac Trailer Court."

My brother flinched at the mention of Francie's home turf, an action that was not lost on my mother. Before she could launch into another anti-bimbo diatribe, I said, "What we need to know now is just how Wood died. What did the vomit look like?"

"It looked like a Jackson Pollock painting," Emma observed sarcastically, cutting off whatever Sam had been about to say. "What is the matter with you?"

"This is not a stupid question," I insisted. "I was wondering if he threw up food or blood or what. It doesn't have to be drugs that killed him. Maybe he ate something that made him sick—raw meat, or shellfish." I turned to my brother. "Was he spitting up pieces of shrimp?"

"No," Sam said irritably. "Do you think I got down on my hands and knees and poked at it with a stick? Most of it hit the toilet. What landed on the floor looked like that stuff Jed yaks up in the flower bed."

My mother was nodding slowly now, a thoughtful look on her face. "You think it might have been food poisoning, Bil?"

"Exactly."

"Hmm. That's usually accompanied by other symptoms, like cramps and swelling. Did his stomach look swollen to you, Sam?"

My brother covered his face with his hands. "I didn't look at his stomach. I didn't take a magnifying glass to his vomit. When he started throwing up, I spent all my time trying to get the guards to come and do something about it. Okay?"

"Okay," I said. "Calm down. What do suppose Young and Campbell think you gave him? No one dies from eating pot."

Sam thought for a minute. "Acid," he said. "Maybe mushrooms. The guy was tripping." He ran his hands up and down his arms and shivered. Then he stopped. He crossed his arms, grabbing a biceps in each hand. "Spiders, he said something about spiders. He kept trying to brush them off, but there was nothing there. It freaked me out."

"Do food-poisoning victims hallucinate?" I asked my mother.

"I don't know," she said, "I don't think so." She gave my brother a piercing look. "What do you know about acid and mushrooms? What's floating around Lilac Trailer Court these days?"

Sam didn't answer her, choosing instead to scratch at the flaking varnish on the table with his fingernail. We were clearly heading for another standoff.

"This autopsy is taking too long," I said. "I don't care if the lab is backlogged; they ought to know what killed him by now. How many tests can they run?"

My mother, who was staring intently at my brother, made no sign that she'd heard me. Sam looked at her and then stood up.

"I'm going to my room to lie down," he said. "Could you bring me a couple of biscuits?"

Emma leaned back in her chair and lit a cigarette. "Sure."

As soon as he was out of earshot, I said, "What was that all about?"

She shrugged. "He's tired. You know how he is after chemo."

"That's not what I mean. Something happened just then, something weird." I took the cigarette out of her mouth and held it hostage. "Tell me."

Emma blew the hair out of her eyes. "When they arrested your brother yesterday," she said, "they asked him to take a urine test."

"Oh my god." I gave her back her cigarette. "Did he do it?"

She nodded. "He told me this morning that he's been drinking some kind of clean tea. It's supposed to cover up any traces of THC."

"He doesn't really believe that."

"He does." She smiled sadly. "Between the assault charge and the shoplifting, I'm sure they could have made him take the test. He thought he was being really clever by agreeing to it voluntarily. Even if he is telling the truth, Bil, it might not matter. If anything in his urine matches something in Wood's blood or his stomach contents, your brother is in big trouble."

Chapter 7

At three-thirty, Tipper called, waking me out of a sound sleep.

"What are you doing in bed?" he demanded. "The sun doesn't set for another six hours. You've got no excuse for lying in bed in the middle of the afternoon like an old lady. Unless, of course, you've got a fancy woman under your quilt. As I doubt that you do, up, up, up!"

"Christ on a cracker, Tip. Have you no mercy?"

He laughed. "Not for the lazy, sweetheart. Siesta time is over. I'm calling to invite you to a little pick-up game of softball. We're playing the Folksong Army, and you're pitching."

"I can't," I protested. "I'm expecting a phone call between seven and eight."

"Seven? It's not even four o'clock yet. You've got plenty of time. Don't argue with me, Bil—you've been blowing me off for weeks. Get your ass over here, and I'll make sure you're home by seven. Who's supposed to call you, anyway? Is it," he gasped, "a girl?"

I ignored the question. "I'll be there in half an hour. We're going to lose, you know. The Folksong Army is invincible."

"Oh ye of little faith. Don't forget your spikes."

I hung up the phone and gave myself a couple of sharp whacks on the forehead with the palm of my hand. It didn't help. I took two aspirin. Fifteen minutes later, I'd located my shoes and glove, put on my Mariners cap, and was headed out the door. No one was in the living room, and no one seemed to be stirring anywhere else in the house. Emma had probably joined Hugh in his nap. As I headed down the driveway, I saw the curtains twitch in Sam's bedroom. I walked as quickly as I could without breaking into an all-out run. The last thing I wanted to do was give him a ride into town.

The pattern with my brother was always the same. Whenever he was released, it was always on the condition that he stay away from his underage loser friends. In custody it was all "Of course, I'll stay home. I'll stay out of trouble. I'll stay away from Francie." Once he was out, that quickly changed to "Drive me to town or I'll fucking hitchhike." I wasn't taking him to town, not this time, and I didn't feel like fighting with him about it.

Once I was safely in the truck and on my way, I began to relax. A game might be just what I needed. Softball was the state-sanctioned religion at Fort Sister, a.k.a. Tipper's house. Captain Schwartz, Tipper's mother, ran her home as a kind of artists' colony-cum-lesbian boot camp. Fort Sister wasn't its real name—it was actually called Blood Moon Women's Haven. That was the official title in the brochures, anyway.

Idaho has always been a magnet for people like Captain Schwartz and my mother, a haven for the individualist, the true libertarian, and the crackpot. My mother was an Idaho native, born and bred, but even if she hadn't been, she was a pioneer hippie who had back-to-the-land fantasies about peace and justice and living *au naturel.* Tipper's mother was another kind of Idaho oddity, a lesbian survivalist. She'd spent ten years in the Army before being swept up by the women's movement. Captain Schwartz liked women and she liked guns, and after her experience as a lesbian in the military, she didn't trust the government. Fort Sister had plenty of artists in residence. It also had an arsenal, a bomb shelter, and a library of books with titles like *The Anarchist's Cook Book* and *How to Survive A Nuclear Winter*.

Crackpot or not, I often wished I could be more like Captain Schwartz. Sometimes I wished I were more like my mother. They both knew what they wanted, and they acted without hesitation. What did I want? True love and a quiet life? A little safe excitement? Out at Fort Sister, the women paired up, broke up, changed partners, and everyone stayed friends. I wondered how the hell they did it. A. J. and I had been together for two years. Then she discovered the joys of adultery. I didn't want to be her friend. I wanted her to drop dead.

When I arrived at the entrance to Fort Sister, Tipper was straddling the front gate, swinging it back and forth across the long driveway. The house was a mile in from the road, far from casual view. He waved a beer bottle at me and hopped down, bowing low before opening the gate so I could drive through. I stopped just inside. He closed the gate behind me and padlocked it before hopping into the passenger seat.

"Long time, no see," he said, his voice heavy with sarcasm.

"Don't start now. I've had a long two days." I glanced over his outfit, giving it a thorough appraisal. "Tipper, old bean, you look fetching in that black mini-skirt, but you can't really play softball in it. How would you slide into home?"

"Very carefully." He smoothed his skirt down over the top of his legs, which—like the rest of him—were long, tanned, and muscular. "I ordered it from the Victoria's Secret catalog. Do you like it?"

The Captain had given birth to Tipper at Fort Bragg, North Carolina. They moved to Idaho when he was ten. That was thirteen years ago, but he still had a pronounced drawl. He was good-looking, quite masculine when he wasn't dressed like Cher. He'd also been out forever, at least since junior high school. The one thing he seemed to have inherited from his mother, aside from her height, was an iron will. He'd be himself come hell or high water.

I reached over and flipped up the edge of his skirt. "Pink bloomers, that's a nice touch. You know, Tipper, I think you've got the longest legs in town."

"And the hairiest. Go ahead and say it."

"My mother raised me better than that. I never insult a lady. Besides, if you want to look like one of the Captain's hirsute paying guests, that's your business. I can't believe she lets you get sexist exploitation like the Victoria's Secret catalog out here."

"Well, she does. And Frederick's of Hollywood, too. Mama doesn't cramp my style."

"How sexist and hypocritical. Just because you're a boy, you get to wear lingerie."

"Ha! You don't know subversion of the patriarchy when it walks up and bites you."

I laughed. "So, what's up with the padlock? You don't usually lock the gate during the day."

"I know. And fat lot of good it does anyway since anyone could just walk around it and up through the woods on either side. It's Mother—she's insisting that we take every precaution. Some tramp wandered onto the property Thursday before last and scared the hell out of Cedar Tree. She didn't like his looks. Imagine wearing a black turtleneck in August. She said he was sweating like a pig."

I stopped the truck.

"Honey, what's wrong? Did you run over a rabbit?"

"A black turtleneck?"

Tipper nodded.

"Well, maybe it's a coincidence, but . . ." I described the man in Sam's cell and gave Tipper a blow-by-blow account of our dealings with the DA and the sheriff's department.

"Sounds like our tramp," he agreed. "If you'll pardon my saying so, I think someone's put a root on your family. Sam's had nothing but bad luck these last few months."

"It's okay. I don't believe he gave the guy anything."

"Hmm," he replied noncommittally. "Other than that, how have you been?"

"Okay. I saw A. J. yesterday."

"Did you tell her to hop on her broomstick and fly back to Seattle?"

"I didn't get the chance. Emma put on one of her more stellar performances, chasing Francie Stokes halfway up Main Street. It was humiliating."

"You poor thing," he clucked sympathetically.

"It's all right. Who cares about A. J., anyway? So, what did your vagrant want?"

"I can't help you with that," he said. "You'll have to ask Cedar Tree."

"Cedar Tree? I'm assuming that's not the name she was born with."

"No. She was née Beatrice Ann Jackson, at least according to her driver's license. She's our newest resident painter. She paints giant, psychedelic vulvas. Her latest is bright purple with big grapevines growing out of it. She calls it *Pain's Vineyard*."

"Does she ever sell any of them?"

He cringed. "Oh god, I hope not. It was twenty-three years ago, so

I wouldn't swear to it, but I think I passed through the model for *Pain's Vineyard* on my way into this world."

"No way! Your mother . . ."

"Posed."

We pulled up in front of the house. Fort Sister was actually an old hunting lodge, built in the nineteen-thirties by a railroad magnate. A good trout stream ran through the property, and there were still plenty of deer, elk, and bear around and about. A hotel chain bought the place in the fifties, hoping to turn it into a resort. They built four log-cabin guesthouses and then promptly went bankrupt. The buildings were falling apart when Captain Schwartz came along, and they continued to fall apart for some time after. She didn't complete restoration of the main house until a couple of years ago. Most of the women had bedrooms on the first floor though a few of the real die-hards preferred to stay in the log cabins—cabins being a generous term for what were in fact dirt-floor hovels.

Although he'd been living in Seattle since we graduated from high school, Tipper still claimed the entire second floor for himself. All three bedrooms, the sitting room, and a bathroom. "I cannot," he said, "be expected to share intimate accommodations with women who name themselves after garden plants and pagan deities."

Most of the women at Fort Sister were semi-permanent residents. Some had been there for as long as I could remember. Still, every couple of years, someone left and a new woman took her place, usually someone fleeing a Midwestern metropolis like Detroit or Columbus.

Tipper held the front door open for me. I curtsied and, not looking where I was going, ran smack into Captain Schwartz. It was like hitting a brick wall. Tipper's mother was one hundred and seventy-five pounds of number-ten butch, six feet tall with a tight gray flat-top. I loved her. When I was a teenager, she'd taught me how to shoot, how to box, and how to play softball. She was my role model.

"Oh," I said, jumping back. "I'm sorry."

I found myself swept up in a big bear hug.

"Bil!" she cried. "How are you? I hear you're playing for the Radical Faeries today. How's that pitching arm?" She gave it a good squeeze, and I did my best not to cry ouch.

"It's fine, Captain, and I'm fine as well. Who've you got pitching for the Folksong Army?"

"We've got a new one," she smiled. "Jane. She used to pitch for the University of Michigan. Arm like a Howitzer."

"Well, that'll be fun," I lied. Michigan my eye. I'd give Howitzer Jane a taste of Idaho she wouldn't soon forget.

Tipper grabbed my hand. "Excuse us, Mommie dearest. We've got to get our spikes on and discuss strategy. Meet you on the battlefield in ten." When we were halfway up the stairs, he whispered, "The Radical Faeries are hiding out in my bedroom. Cedar Tree was chanting her menstrual mantra when I came out to meet you, and they fled in terror."

"Wimps or just jealous?" I paused on the landing outside of Tipper's door. "Wait a second. If they're all Radical Faeries, wouldn't that give them quite a lot in common with this Cedar Tree woman? The Faeries are pagans, right?"

"No, or rather yes and no. Cedar Tree isn't the same kind of pagan as the Radical Faeries. She's what's called a solitary practitioner."

"What does that mean?

"It means that she should get out more. She's a witch without a coven. As for the rest of your question, they're not actually Radical Faeries. Well, one of them is, Suzy. Although maybe he's Episcopalian. Anyway, the rest are just odds and ends here to help fight Proposition One. Mama has been calling them 'the Faeries' as a kind of shorthand. She was calling them 'the boys,' but Anne—you remember her, the Ph.D. in women's studies? Well, Anne noticed all of a sudden that Alan and Brian are black. She also noticed that my mother has a thick Southern accent."

"So I guess 'boys' was out."

"Was it ever. The Folksong Army got together in a huge processing circle and interrogated their own racism."

"Must have been fun."

"You don't know the half of it."

"I've been meaning to ask you something," I said. "Is it or is it not bad manners to call a drag queen he? You just called Suzy he, and I always call you he, even when you're dressed as a she."

Tipper pursed his lips, thinking. "As a general rule, I suppose it is bad manners, but Suzy isn't your typical drag queen. He's like me, only more so. I do the sweet transvestite thing. Suzy wants everyone to know he's a man, particularly when he's in lipstick and high heels. He's a kind of gender-fuck kamikaze. The Folksong Army don't know what to make of him. Several are convinced that drag is inherently misogynist, but drag that isn't trying to fool anyone, what's that? There have been processing circles about Suzy, I can tell you."

I laughed. "You know, I'd never have made it as a lesbian in the seventies. They'd have booted me out of the collective."

"Bullshit," he replied, his hand now on the doorknob to his bedroom. "I can just see you all earnest and bespectacled, covered in flannel. The wo-myn would have wet themselves. Now, close your eyes in case someone's lounging around in the altogether."

Considering his taste in clothing, Tipper's room was surprisingly conservative. The walls were the pale green of Granny Smith apples, with white trim and white wainscoting. Several watercolors, most painted by Tipper himself, were hung asymmetrically around the room. The only clue that the room belonged to a gay man and not Martha Stewart was the autographed eight-by-ten glossy of Harvey Fierstein on the bedside table.

The Faeries were lounging around, all right, but all were fully clothed. I was introduced to Tom and Brian, who were on the bed reading magazines, to Jeff and Alan, who were playing chess on the floor, and, finally, to Suzy, who sat perched on top of a stereo speaker, his knees hugged close to his chest. Judy Garland was playing at maximum volume.

"Must you be so obvious?" Tipper asked, striding across the floor and hitting the stop button on the CD player. "You'd think Betty Buckley had never been born."

Tom sighed and heaved himself off the bed. "We needed a little fix. The big one from Detroit has been playing women's music festival crap all day. Filling up and spilling over. I was afraid Suzy would have a stroke." He turned to me and grinned. "Hi, Bil, I'm glad you could make it. Tipper has us terrified about this softball game."

"And rightly so," Tipper snapped. "I don't like to lose." He pointed an accusing finger at Suzy. "You are inappropriately attired. Where are your spikes?"

Suzy uncrossed his legs and waved a bare foot at us. "My spikes, Tipper, are in Seattle where I left them. I didn't know they'd be required."

Tipper sighed. "I told you before we came here that softball equals free room and board. You were obviously not listening. Lucky for you, I've got a spare pair in the closet." He eyed Suzy's feet suspiciously. "Can you squeeze those boats into a size ten?"

"A tight fit," Suzy replied, "but I don't expect we'll need to call the foot-binder."

I modestly averted my gaze while Tipper dropped his mini-skirt and pulled on a pair of blue jeans. Then we all waited impatiently for Suzy to finish lacing up.

We trooped down the stairs and out through the kitchen. Fifty yards from the back door stood the Fort Sister softball diamond, complete with dugouts and floodlights. Before the house was even fully livable, the Captain and Tipper built the diamond. It was regulation size and immaculately groomed.

The Folksong Army was first up to bat.

"Age before beauty," Tipper observed.

"Pearls before swine," his mother replied.

Brian took first base, Suzy second, and Tipper third. Tom covered right field, and Jeff took left and center. Alan, who at six foot five was the largest of the Faeries, was catcher. We hoped that his size might deter the more aggressive Army players in their rush to home plate.

The infamous Cedar Tree stepped up to bat. She was a short but substantial woman in a tie-dyed sweatsuit. She was also left-handed, which threw me a bit as I wasn't warmed up. She scored a base hit off my second pitch.

"Shake it off, honey!" Tipper called.

Jane, the Michigan Howitzer, was next. She was a tall, good-looking woman of about thirty, well built and confident. She took a wide stance at the plate, feet exactly parallel with her broad shoulders. I fingered the brim of my cap and blew softly on my fingertips. Then, heaven smiled upon me. I delivered three perfect pitches, and the Howitzer swung at—and missed—all of them.

The Captain gave a loud whistle from the dugout.

"Yer out!" Alan yelled.

"Whoo, girls, catch that breeze," Suzy called. He stood on second base and swished his hips from side to side.

The bases were loaded when the Captain stepped up to the plate. I motioned for the outfield to move way back. It didn't matter. She connected with my first pitch and knocked it over the fence.

By the bottom of the fifth inning, we were down two runs. I stood at the plate, waiting for Howitzer Jane to do her stuff. A telephone rang. The sound was muffled, and at first I thought it was coming from the house. Jane paused on the mound.

"Is someone going to answer that phone?"

"Just pitch," I said. "I'm ready." I was very ready. The bases were loaded, and Jane was beginning to tire. Alan had scored a triple off her in the fourth inning.

"I can't concentrate with that damn ringing," Jane objected.

"For Christ's sake, Tipper," Suzy said, "answer the phone. Your tit's calling."

Tipper sighed heavily, reached into his brassiere, and pulled out a cell phone.

"You're worse than my mother," I yelled.

He blew me a kiss. "Schwartz residence, Tipper speaking. Oh, yes ma'am. She's here."

He walked over to the plate and handed me the phone. Jane gave me a disgusted look and sat down on the pitcher's mound.

"Who is it?" I hissed.

"Your mother," he whispered.

"Gatorade, anyone?" the Captain called. The bases cleared.

"This had better be good, Emma."

"Can you come home?"

"No. We're at the bottom of the fifth, and I'm up to bat. How did you find me?"

"I called every number on that damned bulletin board of yours. You might have left me a note."

"Sorry," I said. "I'll remember to do that next time. I've got to go."

"Are you coming home?"

"No. I'm playing a game of softball. What do you want?"

"Sam . . ."

"Wait," I interrupted, "let me guess. He asked you to drive him to town. You refused. He hitchhiked. At first you were mad, but now you're worried. The reason I have to go find him is that he's more likely to get in the car with me than he is with you. If I say I don't want to do it, you'll say what if he's at Francie's house? What if he's sick or dead in a ditch? But I'm telling you right now, Emma, I don't care. I don't care if he's sick or dead in a ditch. I don't care if he's gone to Francie's. I don't care if he's gone to the Shrine Circus. I'm busy."

There was a long pause. "Fine."

"You know I'm right."

"You're right," she agreed.

"Well?"

"Well what?"

"I'm waiting for you to tell me off. To tell me I'm a shitty daughter and a selfish sister. Tell me why I should drop everything, once again, and go find Sam, who's probably whooping it up over at the Main Street Market with a lot of underage bimbos."

"I'm sorry," she said. "You're right, this isn't your problem. Go finish your game."

I sighed. "I'm leaving now."

Chapter 8

As expected, I found Sam at the Main Street Market. He refused to get into the truck, and I wasted nearly half an hour arguing with him. Francie was there, sitting in the back of someone's car. She had a cigarette in one hand and a bottle of beer in the other, both, no doubt, purchased by my brother. Clearly, all was forgiven. One thing I've learned about petty criminals—they're a bunch of cock-eyed optimists. The cops were bound to catch Francie drinking, she was bound to point the finger at Sam, and he was bound to go back to jail. Somehow, the inevitability of this chain of events utterly escaped him. He thought every day was his lucky day.

Back home, I found Emma pacing the floor. I shook my head to indicate that I'd failed in my mission. She gave me the bad news that I'd missed Sylvie's phone call.

"What did you tell her? Did she leave a number?"

"I said you were out looking for Sam. She said you didn't need to call her back. I didn't know that you two were friends. Does she know that the cops suspect your brother?"

I sat down heavily in Archie Bunker, my evening now thoroughly ruined. If Sylvie didn't want me to call her back, then she didn't want to talk to me. That probably meant that she knew about Sam. I ignored my mother's questions. "Sam was at the Main Street Market with Francie. They were in the parking lot, drinking beer."

Emma collapsed into a heap on the sofa. "Why does he do this?"

"I couldn't begin to answer that. Where's Hugh?"

"Gone bowling. He said he needed to get out of the house before he poisoned someone himself. He's afraid your brother is going to skip bail and we'll have to pay the whole bond."

"Sam is a skinny black kid in the middle of Idaho. Where's he going to go, Disneyland?"

"His disability check came today. He's got four hundred bucks in his wallet, and he's feeling high, wide, and handsome. And speaking of high," my mother reached into her pocket and pulled out a plastic bag containing three or four dried brown nuggets. "Do you know what these are?"

I took the bag and examined it closely. "Looks like dried mushrooms to me."

"Magic mushrooms," she corrected. "I found them in the pocket of your brother's jeans." At my raised eyebrows, she added defensively, "I was doing a load of laundry."

"Are you sure those are magic? They look like shiitakes."

"Why the hell would your brother be carrying a bag of dried shiitakes?"

I shrugged. "I don't know. Should I phone the Cordon Bleu or the Betty Ford Clinic?"

"Don't be sarcastic. You know what this means, don't you?"

"It means he's been tripping on mushrooms."

Emma stared at me. "Wood was hallucinating. The cops are going to find traces of this stuff in your brother's urine. Sam is going to go to prison."

I shook my head. "Ma," I said calmly, "listen to me. People don't die from eating psychedelic mushrooms. They trip out and see things, but they don't keel over."

"People die from eating poisonous mushrooms all the time!"

"That's not a bag of deadly toadstools you've got there. The only way one of those is going to kill you is if you choke to death on it."

She looked at me doubtfully. "How do you know so much about it?"

"Not from personal experience, if that's what you're thinking. However, I have, in my travels, met the occasional user of *Amanita muscara*. Beer is my drug of choice, and on my present budget, I drink precious little of that. Would you like a signed affidavit?"

"No," she said, shaking her head, "I believe you. I just don't know what to do about your brother. Pot is one thing, but mushrooms . . ." She gestured at the weekend edition of the *Cowslip Herald-Examiner* sitting on the coffee table by her feet. "Take a look at the paper. Lower right-hand column."

I picked it up. The article was headed "Sheriff's Department Still Looking For Leads."

> The Lewis County Sheriff's Department is still seeking information regarding a vagrant who died on the afternoon of August 25 in custody at the Lewis County Jail. The deceased, later identified as Burton R. Wood, was arrested late Friday afternoon. He was carrying no identification and refused to give police his name and address.
>
> Wood spent an unspecified time in jail before he collapsed, complaining of stomach cramps. He was pronounced dead on arrival at Cowslip Memorial Hospital. Autopsy results have not yet been made public.
>
> Wood is described as a white male in his late forties, six feet tall, weighing about one hundred and ninety pounds, with short brown hair and a bushy mustache. At the time of his arrest, he was wearing blue jeans, a black turtleneck, a brown jacket, and brown boots. Wood was arrested in the vicinity of the Lilac Court Trailer Court, after wandering into oncoming traffic at the corner of Main Street and Broad.
>
> Anyone who might have information regarding Wood or his movements prior to five o'clock on Friday, August 25, should contact Lieutenant Vernon Young at (555) 624-2695.

When I was finished, I tossed the paper back onto the coffee table.

"Still feeling sanguine about those mushrooms?" Emma asked.

I wasn't feeling sanguine about anything. Still, I thought I ought to offer at least a token objection. "Lilac Court is notorious, Ma. If Wood went there looking for a fix, it doesn't necessarily follow that he got it from Sam. The place is packed with dealers. Besides, it just says that he was arrested in the vicinity. It doesn't say he was seen going into trailer number eight, the home of juvenile delinquent Francie Stokes."

"It's only a matter of time," said my mother. "What this means is that your brother didn't have to smuggle anything into jail. He could have given Wood something before they were arrested. People come and go at the Stokes' trailer all day long. It's like Grand Central Station. You can't tell me they're just stopping by to say hello."

"I doubt they're stopping by to get drugs from Sam. He doesn't live there."

"He might as well. It doesn't matter who does most of the dealing, Bil, your brother was at Lilac Trailer Court on the twenty-fifth of August. And so was the late Burt Wood."

"But that would mean that Sam was lying to us this morning," I argued.

My mother gave me a grim smile. "Oh, Pollyanna. You don't think your brother lies?"

Sam didn't come home that night. When Emma went looking for him at all his usual haunts early Sunday morning, he was nowhere to be found. Fortunately, however, the good Christians of the Cowslip Sheriff's Department were under the impression that all crime stopped on the Sabbath, so Sunday patrols were always light. If he failed to turn up by Monday, then I'd worry.

I spent the afternoon working on homework for abnormal psychology, anthropology, and French. As the last two assignments weren't due until Tuesday, I felt quite virtuous. I also felt justified in accepting Tipper's invitation to meet him and the Radical Faeries for dinner at Fiesta Jack's. I waved good-bye to the disapproving Emma, who thought I should be helping her look for Sam, and headed into town.

I found Tipper and company sitting at a large booth, working on three pitchers of sangria. They offered me a glass, which I gratefully accepted.

Tipper leaned over until his face was only about two inches away from mine. "I have some news for you. Burt Wood was arrested not once but twice."

I nearly choked on a mouthful of sangria. "Where did you hear that?"

"In a minute," he replied, mopping at my chin with a napkin. "You've dribbled red wine all over your shirt."

"Stop it," I said. "People will think you're my nanny."

"Near enough." He poured me a fresh glass of sangria and continued. "The sheriff's deputies picked him up just before noon on Friday, not far from Lilac Trailer Court. He refused to give a name, so they reckoned he was a vagrant."

"What did they do?"

"What they always do with vagrants. They drove him to the county line and dropped him out with instructions to make his way to Spokane."

"That's disgusting."

"It's Cowslip's answer to the homeless. Anyhow, when he turned up again later that afternoon—this time drunk off his ass and wandering into traffic—they were pissed. So, they hauled him off to jail, tossed him in with your brother, and . . ."

"Ignored him when he complained of stomach pain," I finished. "The whole thing stinks. Unfortunately, the fact that they were negligent doesn't absolve Sam."

"Look," Tipper said, leaning even closer, "did Sam give that guy anything? You can tell me."

"That's the problem—I don't know. Six months ago, I would have denied it with absolute confidence, but now . . . I wouldn't put anything past him."

"Francie's baleful influence?"

I stared down at my drink. "It's not that simple. It could be Francie, or it could be that he's like every other addict. It could even be the cancer." I was surprised to hear that word come out of my mouth. "Sorry, now I sound like my mother."

Tipper took a long pull at his sangria. "Well, you can't blame him for being angry about this relapse. How's Emma coping with it?"

"Oh, about like you'd expect."

He nodded and smiled ruefully. "She's running around like her hair's on fire."

"Exactly."

"Well, don't you go putting that fire out with an ax, however tempting it might be." He gave me a reassuring pat on the arm. "Have the doctors actually said that he's going to . . ."

"Die?" I finished for him. "No, they always talk in statistics. The five-year survival rate for people like Sam is about seventy-five percent."

"That doesn't sound like a death sentence, Bil."

"It's one in four. Flip a coin." I swirled an orange slice around in my glass, trying to bring it as close as possible to the rim without letting it slosh over. Then I drained my glass in a single gulp, blocking the orange slice with my front teeth. "How about a refill?"

Tipper poured dutifully, but he said, "Why don't you and I switch to beer next round?"

"Good idea," I agreed. "Those orange slices are a choking hazard."

"They are the way you're drinking," he observed tartly.

I ignored this remark and took another long, deep drink. The Faeries were clearly having a high old time of it. Suzy and Jeff had tied their dinner napkins over their noses and were shooting at passing patrons with finger guns. The other three were playing quarters.

"Now," I said, dropping my voice so that only Tipper could hear me, "tell me where you heard about the cops arresting Wood twice."

He tapped a finger against his nose and pointed at Suzy, who was sitting close enough to Tom to get us all arrested. Suzy looked up and tipped his glass of sangria in mock salute before going back to his inchworm efforts to creep onto Tom's lap.

"That one," Tipper said, "gets around. Only been here three weeks and already sleeping with a closet-case in the sheriff's department."

"Fuck a duck. Who?"

"He won't tell me. I have managed to get him to admit that his nightstick isn't the sheriff himself; it's one of the jailers. Mystery cop is high enough in rank to know a thing or two, though. Suzy's mole says that they gave your brother a urine test on Friday. They're hoping to match any illicit substance to whatever they find in Wood's autopsy."

"I know," I began, "and Emma found these mushrooms . . ." Just then, a thought swam up through the sangria fog and floated on the surface of my brain. "Wait a second, Tipper. Sam took that urine test on Friday—this past Friday, not the Friday Wood died."

"So?"

"So any match would be purely circumstantial. It wouldn't mean a thing." Between the sangria and this flight of logic, I suddenly felt ridiculously happy. "Fuck Suzy's mole!"

Suzy looked up and pointed his finger gun at me. "Apologize," he said. "My mole is very sensitive. It's a Marilyn Monroe stick-on beauty mark, and it cost me five dollars." He dropped his bandit's mask and showed me.

"Sorry," I said.

"Don't apologize," Tipper cut in. "That may be Marilyn's mole, but it's Cindy Crawford's location. What kind of drag queen are you? That's cross-dressing 101."

"I'm not a drag queen," Suzy replied haughtily, "I'm a drag terrorist. In a mini-skirt and in your face, that's my motto."

"Off with the mini-skirt and in your face is more like it," Tipper said.

Tom laughed and gave Suzy a not-too-subtle shove, pushing him off his lap. "Move your mark, honey. These Idaho spuds might mistake you for straight."

Suzy peeled the mole off and stuck it on the end of his nose. "How's that? Now I'm Bella Abzug."

"Can I take you home to meet my mother?" I asked. "She'd be so excited if I came out of the closet and married you."

Everyone laughed, and I poured myself another drink. Several sangrias later, I was singing along to a Carpenters' song with Suzy and Tom. "We've only just begun . . ."

"Speaking of only just beginning," Tipper interrupted, "who was that blond I saw you with on Friday at the Cowslip Café? I was driving past, so I didn't see her face." When I'd told him, he said, "Sylvie Wood! How long has this been going on?"

The Faeries looked up sharply. Even Suzy stopped her renewed assault on Tom's lap long enough to glance over at us. I grabbed Tipper by the arm and gave him a little shake.

"Would you like to repeat that? I think someone in the next county might not have heard you. I met her at the funeral, and she asked me to meet her at the café. She wanted to know if her father had said anything to Sam while they were in jail together."

"Of course," he said. "She'd be curious, wouldn't she? I mean, he went off without a trace and no one knew where he was. Probably living under an alias somewhere."

"He gave an alias when he was arrested on Friday, Charlie Gibb."

"That's a terrible alias. Every high school in America does *Our Town*."

"It's better than Twatsa Moré," I replied, referring to one of Tipper's drag names. "But it does make me think that it was spur of the moment. Why would Burt Wood need an alias anyway? He didn't do the actual embezzling—the other one did, Frank Frost."

"Wood was an accessory. Besides, what if his wife wanted to track him down for child support? What if she wanted to punish him for all the humiliation and gossip? What if Sylvie wanted to find him and ask why he didn't want to be her father anymore?"

"I hadn't thought of that."

"That's what you have me for. It's all moot, anyway. There's no way of finding out now."

"There might be a way," I said slowly. "We could look him up. Wherever he went, he'd have to have a social security number. He'd have to work, wouldn't he? Maybe he and Frost lived off the embezzlement money, but sooner or later, that would run out. What's a quarter of a million to two gay men in someplace like San Francisco?"

"Down payment on a one-room studio with a massage parlor next door and a methadone clinic downstairs," Tipper observed. "But who knows—in the seventies, maybe it was a fortune. How do you propose to look them up? It's not like there's a directory of runaway gay boys."

"I'll remind you that Sarah is an information specialist."

"She's a librarian, Bil. I don't see how a librarian's going to help you."

"You obviously don't know anything about librarians," I replied. "You know the Myers-Briggs personality test? According to Sarah, the most common personality type among librarians is also the most common among CIA agents. She'll know how to find out information about Burt Wood. Newspaper indexes, social security files, who knows?" I flicked the top of my glass with my middle finger, making it ring. "Ta-da!"

"Congratulations," Tipper said. "Let me know what you find out."

Eventually, we ordered dinner. We also ordered more drinks, and somehow, I found myself sipping a margarita. I knew better—I hadn't been this stupid since my freshman year—but I had begun to forget my worries and feel truly happy. The Faeries were in fine fettle, and they seemed to think everything I said was extremely funny. By eight o'clock, we were all as tight as ticks. Suzy had broken into a chorus of "I'm just a girl who can't say no" when I noticed Sylvie Wood, sitting by herself at a table about twenty feet away.

She tipped her glass to me—it appeared to be filled with iced tea—and smiled. I smiled back. She was wearing a blue silk shirt and matching pants. Her hair was loose, just brushing the tops of her shoulders, and her earrings were long, silver blades. She was dressed up, especially by Cowslip standards. Alcohol made me brave, and I met her gaze longer than was strictly polite. She looked away first. I continued to stare, and soon, she looked back and smiled again.

Even through my drunken haze, I recognized that feeling deep down in the pit of my stomach. It was pure lust. I closed my eyes and took a deep breath, hoping to steady my nerves. Instead, I just felt dizzy. I drained my glass, whispered, "Excuse me" to Tipper, and walked over to her table. Once again, faced with the prospect of talking to a beautiful woman, I opened my mouth to speak before having any idea what I was going to say.

I was relieved to hear myself say, "Hi."

"Hi," she replied.

I put my hand on the back of the chair across from her to steady myself and said, "Mind if I sit down?" Before I fall down.

"Be my guest."

"Thank you." I wasn't certain how to begin. I felt like Don Juan, a feeling I never have when sober. I'm sure I looked like Don Knotts.

"So, what are you doing here?"

With just the barest hint of a smile, she said, "I'm waiting for someone. And you?"

"Drinks," I said, "I'm having drinks. With my friends. Those are my friends over there." I waved to the Faeries. The Faeries waved back. Suzy winked lasciviously and flashed me the okay sign. Tipper, who was wearing a pair of combat boots, gave him a sharp and visible kick.

"Yes," she said, laughing, "I can see that."

"You told my mother I didn't need to call you back," I said slowly. The muscles in my mouth had grown reluctant to move, and I was certain that I was slurring my words.

"You mean yesterday?" When I nodded she said, "Actually, I told your mother that you didn't need to call back if you were busy. I said I'd call you back."

"Oh. Did you?"

She looked down at her hands. "No, I'm sorry. Something came up."

My brother. The blood pounded in my ears. If Tipper and Suzy knew Sam was a suspect, why wouldn't Sylvie? I suddenly felt a maudlin, drunken desire to cry. "He didn't do it," I said. "It's all a big mistake."

She looked up again, gazing at me curiously. "I don't know what you're talking about, Bil. What's a big mistake?"

This penetrated the sangria fog and brought me up short. "I'm not making much sense," I said, shaking my head in a vain attempt to clear it. "I'm afraid that I'm a little drunk."

"You're a lot drunk, but that's okay. I'm glad you came over to talk to me. I don't think you would have if you were sober."

That I didn't have a stroke right there in Fiesta Jack's is attributable only to the massive amount of alcohol in my blood. Sylvie ran the tip of her finger around the rim of her glass, a gesture that poured gasoline onto my fire. I felt suddenly bold.

"May I ask you a question?"

"Sure."

"Would you go out with me sometime?"

She smiled. "Yes."

"Not to talk about Sam or your father. I mean on a date."

"I know what you mean. The answer is yes."

Sometimes it's hard to get the answer you want, particularly if you've spent several desperate seconds preparing to be disappointed.

"Yes," I said, processing the information slowly. "Yes. That's great! When?"

"Bil!" Sylvie said suddenly. Our hands had been touching on the table, and she pulled hers back quickly. For one terrible moment, I thought she was going to slap me.

Instead, she stood up.

"Bil," she said again. "This is my mom, Kate. Mom, you remember Bil, don't you?"

"Christ on a cracker," I thought, though I managed to turn around and say, with almost perfect clarity, "How do you do?"

Kate looked like an older version of her daughter. The blond hair was going gray, but she was still very attractive. Her eyes were the same intense green as Sylvie's, and they regarded me with the same expression of mild amusement.

"Of course I remember you, Bil. In fact, I remember the last time you came out to my house. You had a shoebox full of baby frogs, and your mother was trying to convince you to turn them loose. How is your mother? I didn't get a chance to speak to either of you at the funeral."

"I still like frogs," I said nonsensically. "My mother is fine." She had to know I was stinking drunk. I turned to Sylvie, not meeting her gaze. "I'd better get back to my table. My friends are waiting."

My friends, in fact, were watching this whole scene as if it were a soap opera. All eyes were upon us.

"Bil . . ." Sylvie began.

"Lovely to see you again." I nodded quickly to them both and was immediately sorry. It took me a moment or two to regain my balance. As I wove my way back to the table, Suzy graciously resumed his singing, and the other Faeries pretended to engage in lively conversation.

Tipper leaned over and whispered, "What did she say? You two seemed to be getting along pretty well there for a minute or two."

"Tipper," I said, falling forward onto the table and resting my head on my arms, "she's beautiful, she's a lesbian, and until a minute ago, she was interested in me."

Chapter 9

Sylvie and her mother ate dinner and left. We stayed until just after eleven. By this time, Suzy had exhausted his repertoire of show tunes and was singing, "Give me a pig's foot and a bottle of beer." We were politely asked to leave. Then, not so politely.

We left by the back door. There was no designated driver, so Tipper pulled his cellular phone out of his handbag and called for Cowslip's one and only taxi. It arrived about ten minutes later. The Faeries piled gracelessly into the back seat, sitting on one another's laps.

Tipper opened the front door for me. I shook my head.

"You know you can't drive," he said sternly. "Do I need to take your keys?"

"No, you don't. I'm going to crash with Ruth and Naomi. Their apartment is only a couple of blocks from here."

"Do you think you can stagger that far?"

"I don't see why not."

"I'm not sure you can see at all. Why don't you let us give you a lift?"

I shook my head again. Suzy leaned out the window and grabbed the front door. "Are you two coming or not? The meter's ticking, Tippy!"

"Shut up, Suzy," Tipper snapped. "Get in, Bil."

"Opposite direction," I replied. "Don't worry about me. What do you think I am, a lightweight?"

"Not you, sweetie," he laughed and gave me a quick hug. "You drank me under the table. Call me tomorrow." Then he hopped into the cab, and they were off.

I leaned against the back wall of Fiesta Jack's for a few minutes, taking deep breaths of cold night air. I hoped Ruth would answer the door, but with my luck, it would be Naomi the teetotaler. I decided to take the long way round to their apartment, hoping to sober up a little.

The long way round took me right past the Underground, the closest thing to a gay bar this side of Spokane, which is to say they play alternative music. I stopped and rested against the wall next to the door. I didn't recognize the band on the marquee, but they didn't sound too bad from where I was standing. A. J. and I had often gone to a dance club in Seattle that was a lot like the Underground, only much hipper and much more expensive.

I hesitated for a moment, trying to decide whether or not to go in. I had nearly made up my mind to face the music at Ruth and Naomi's when the door opened and A. J. walked out. She was fanning herself with a cocktail napkin.

"Hello, Bil," she said, smiling as if she had expected to meet me. "It's so hot in there, and I've been dancing. Are you going in?"

"I hate dancing."

She stepped closer and put a hand on my arm. "Now why do you say that? We used to go dancing quite a lot."

I didn't move away. A. J. was nearly as tall as me. She wasn't as muscular, but she was athletic. She jogged, cycled, and swam. She looked good—in fact, she looked like Elizabeth Taylor in *Butterfield 8*. I noticed that her makeup was more dramatic than it used to be. She had on red lipstick, and it suited her. While I doubted butch-femme would ever play among the granola dykes of Cowslip, I kind of liked the contrast between us. It was one of things that had attracted me to her in the first place.

"I'm glad I ran into you," she said smoothly. "I wanted to tell you I was sorry about . . . well, you know."

"I don't know," I said stubbornly. "What are you sorry for?"

She shrugged. "For the other day. I was rude to your friend."

"Oh, that. I thought . . . never mind." I looked at her. Her eyes were half-closed, and she was standing very close now. The hand on my arm had slipped around my back.

"You thought what?"

"Nothing." She'd never be sorry for the things I thought she should be sorry for.

"Suit yourself." Her breath smelled faintly of clove cigarettes, and I remembered tasting them on her lips the first time I kissed her. The flavor was sweet and spicy, and I could still taste it hours afterward. The way she was smiling at me made me wonder if she remembered, too.

"Walk me home, Bil."

"Why?"

"Because it's a dark night," she laughed. "No one will see you."

They'd better not, I thought. We walked in silence for three or four blocks.

"Where's home?" I asked.

"I'm staying with some friends. They're out tonight. The house is dark, and I don't like to go home alone."

"Don't I know it," I observed sarcastically. I knew this was a bad idea, and yet I couldn't seem to stop myself.

A. J. tightened her arm around my waist. "Come on, Bil, can't we be friends?"

"No."

"Why not?"

"Um, let's see. Because I hate you?"

"No, you don't."

We walked several blocks more, turning this way and that, before stopping in front of a large, run-down bungalow. The neighborhood seemed vaguely familiar, but between the dark and the drink, I'd lost all sense of direction. A. J. had neglected to leave the porch light on—deliberately, I suspected. We walked up the concrete path to the door.

"Expecting to get lucky?"

She laughed. "I have, haven't I?"

She unlocked the door, and we stepped inside. We were in a long hallway with a staircase going up the right-hand side. On the left, a double-door opened into a darkened living room. A row of coat pegs was hanging on the wall in front of the staircase, and A. J. had to close the front door to hang up her jacket. She held her hand out for mine. I shook my head.

"Suit yourself," she said. "Would you like to go into the living room?"

"No."

She stepped closer, until she was only inches away. I backed up, right into the closed front door. She smiled. "Well then, how about the bedroom?"

"Why not right here in the hallway? I expect that would suit you just fine."

She just laughed and put her arms around my neck. I put my hands on either side of her rib cage, my thumbs resting just beneath her breasts. I held her for a moment and looked at her. Her eyes were closed, her mouth slightly open. She was waiting.

I shook her until her eyes opened.

"Bil . . ." she began.

"I don't believe you. I don't believe you're trying this on me. Do you think I'm stupid?"

I let her go and sat down on the stairs, leaning forward with my elbows on my knees and my head in my hands. I felt sick, miserable, and tired. A. J. stood there silently for a minute or two, and then she held her hand out to me. I looked up at her.

"It's all right," she said. "I won't try anything."

I took her hand and let her pull me up, tripping a little in the process.

"I'm sorry," I said, straightening up with the help of the banister and A. J.'s arm. "I'm a little drunk."

"More than a little," she replied. "I'd say a lot."

"Funny, you're the second woman tonight who's told me that."

She laughed. "You do get around these days. Anyway, it's me who should apologize. I wouldn't have pressed the point if I'd realized how out of it you were."

"No?"

"No, and you can stop looking at me like that. I knew you'd had a drink or two—your shirt seems to be made out of red wine and orange pulp. I didn't know you were falling-down drunk. I thought you came back home with me because you wanted to."

"Because I wanted to? Why would I want to?"

She was angry now. She jerked away from me and opened the front door. "You can leave. I don't need this from you."

I slammed the door shut again and leaned against it, crossing my arms over my chest. "You don't need it from me because you're getting it from Tigris, or Amazon, or the mighty Mississippi . . . what the fuck was his name?"

"Euphrates," she snapped. "And, just for your information, that's over."

"Yeah, of course it is. The poor bastard. Did you actually bother to break up with him, or did you just let him walk in on you and whoever—no, make that whatever." I shook my head. "Don't answer that. It doesn't matter. It'll be the same old story. You got bored, you felt tied down, you just didn't want to commit. I can't tell you how glad I am that you decided to bring your dog-and-pony show to Cowslip. It reminds me of what I'm not missing."

She shoved me aside and tried to pull the door open. I pushed against it with my foot.

"Okay," she said, "what will it take to get you to leave? Would you like a big fight, right here and now? We can do it in person this time. I don't suppose calling me up once you were safely back in Idaho and telling me it was over really satisfied you. Go ahead, yell at me. Call me a whore. Tell me how much you hate me."

I took my foot off the door and stepped aside so she could open it. She didn't move.

"Go ahead," she said. "I'm waiting."

I didn't answer. Finally, she reached out and put a hand on my arm.

"What do you want, Bil?" she asked softly. "Do you want me to take you home? I could probably borrow a car from one of the Avengers. If not, you're welcome to stay here—you can sleep on the couch."

I looked at her, and I suddenly felt very stupid. Perhaps she was right, maybe I did want a fight, a chance to tell her in person what I thought of her. I had my chance now, but all I could do was shake my head.

"I'm sorry," I said. "It's late, and I've had a long weekend. My sisters live around here somewhere. I'll just walk over to their place."

"I don't think you should walk by yourself. You don't know if you're coming or going. Come on, I'll go with you."

She brushed past me and pulled a jacket off the peg, draping it over one arm.

"Is that okay? Bil?"

I put my hands on her arms and pulled her to me, forcing her to drop the jacket. I kicked it aside with my foot.

"Are you sure about this?" she murmured.

I kissed her hard until her mouth opened. A second or two later, she was kissing me back. She unbuttoned my shirt and pushed it back off my shoulders. I let it drop onto the floor behind me. Then she pulled her own shirt off and tossed it on top of mine. She never wore a bra. Her breasts were small and round, the nipples erect. I felt her hand tugging at the buttons on my jeans.

"No," I said, taking her hands and holding them together behind her back. "Not yet." I bit her gently on the neck before making my way down. She had perfect breasts, like small, firm apples.

"Bil," she said.

Some sober spot in the back of my mind was screaming at me to stop this, but I ignored it. I could be stupid, just for one night. I could be stupid forever, what did it matter?

It was just after six a.m. when I woke up. I wondered for a moment why I didn't have a headache, and then I realized that I was still drunk. A. J. turned over as I got out of bed, but she didn't wake up.

"You always were a heavy sleeper," I said. "I suppose it's too much to hope that you'll forget all about this."

She didn't stir.

I thought about leaving her a note but decided against it. What would I say? All is forgiven? All was not forgiven. I still hate you, but I can't keep my hands off you?

I felt cheap and foolish. I also felt appeased. Sex is more compelling than the best arguments. I could get mad, or I could get laid. Why did it have to boil down to that? I knew that I'd come to regret the night I'd just passed, but as I walked down the street, I couldn't help feeling just a little smug.

I was halfway down the block before I realized where I was. The east end of town, not far from campus, an old neighborhood of run-down bungalows. Some were in the process of being gentrified, but most had been cut up into apartments for students. The bungalow where A. J. and the Avengers were staying was at the very end of Broad Street, two blocks up from the Safeway. Just behind it, separated by a chain-link fence, was the Lilac Trailer Court.

Burt Wood had walked down the street where I now stood. Then he'd wandered into traffic and been taken to jail to die. I was too tired to do more than register this fact and promptly forget about it. When I got back to Fiesta Jack's, I climbed into my truck, stretched out across the front seat, and fell asleep.

Chapter 10

I slept in the truck until about eight-thirty and spent the next hour in the Cowslip Café, drinking strong, black coffee. At nine, I ordered a fried egg on toast and smothered it with enough Tabasco to kill a more virtuous woman. It was well past ten before I felt fit enough to drive home, praying all the while that Emma would be out when I got there.

Of course, I had no such luck. When I walked in, she was sitting on the sofa eating a bowl of peach ice cream.

"Good morning," I said brightly.

"Good afternoon," she replied, peering at me over the top of her reading glasses. "Aren't you supposed to be in class?"

"I only have one class on Monday," I hedged. "Abnormal psychology."

"What time does it meet?"

I looked at my watch. "Now."

"I see. Can I offer you something? Hair of the dog that bit you, perhaps?"

I shoved her feet over and sat down on the end of the sofa. My head was throbbing.

"If you were serious, I might just take you up on that."

"I'm sure your father has a bottle of Bailey's somewhere. He bought one last Christmas."

"Don't make me sick," I said, suppressing a strong desire to throw up.

"That," she replied archly, "is one thing for which you cannot blame me."

I leaned back against the cushions and closed my eyes to keep the living-room lights from burning holes in my retinas. "How about two aspirin and some ice-water, for old times' sake?"

"What old times?"

"The old times when you had some sympathy."

She got me the aspirin and a glass of water, even going so far as to put a slice of lemon in it. Still, she couldn't resist saying, "I thought you were smarter than your brother."

"Guess you were wrong. Where is he anyway? Did he ever come home?"

"Eventually. He had another fight with the slut."

"Anyone lose an eye?"

"Not that I know of. This seems to have been a purely verbal altercation."

Emma settled back down on the sofa and continued eating her ice cream. I finished my water and fished out the ice cubes to press against my forehead. When my mother had emptied her bowl, she put it down on the coffee table and looked straight at me, her lips set in a thin, hard line.

"So," she said, "are you going to tell me where you were last night?"

I pressed the now-empty glass against the back of my neck and toyed with the idea of answering her question honestly. It was only the coolness of the glass against my skin that kept me from saying, "In bed with my ex-girlfriend."

It was quiet around our house for the next few days. Sam stayed out of jail, and, as far as we knew, there was no word about his urine test. Lieutenant Young called on Monday afternoon to say that we should stop by the jail and pick up some of Sam's things that the cops had confiscated but were now ready to release. When my mother tried to quiz him, Young refused to answer any of her questions. It was via Slinky Nilsson that we learned that Francie and her mother had dropped the assault charges.

On Tuesday, I worked up enough nerve to call Kate Wood and ask her for Sylvie's phone number. Sylvie was out, so I left a message on her answering machine. By Wednesday night, she still hadn't called me back. She was probably avoiding me—after all, why wouldn't she? My brother was possibly involved in her father's death, I'd made a complete ass of myself at Fiesta Jack's, and A. J. was certain to have blabbed to the Lesbian Avengers about my lapse on Sunday night. Whatever chance I'd had was well and truly blown.

A. J. called on Monday, Tuesday, and Wednesday. I contrived to be out or otherwise unavailable, and Emma took messages without asking any questions. I spent as much time as possible at school, the gym, and Fort Sister. I also let Tipper talk me into signing up to work the Stop the Prop booth at the Pioneer Days festival. I hated Pioneer Days, which was when all of Cowslip turned out to celebrate a whitewashed version of homesteading, but I couldn't keep saying no to Tipper.

I took two tests on Thursday, one in French and the other in calculus. Both were easy. It was raining when I took the abnormal psych test on Friday. The professor, Gary Smart, arrived ten minutes late, squeezing rainwater out of his brown ponytail. By way of apology, he told us that we could skip the last of the four essay questions. He handed the test out at ten. I handed it back at ten-twenty. Not the ace I'd been hoping for, despite his generosity.

I spent the night at Tipper's house. On Saturday morning, he woke us all up at five-thirty. He had to threaten to light a fire under Suzy, who had been out until three gallivanting with his closeted cop. When we got to the festival, we saw that the Gay Christian Association, the Lewis County Bisexual Alliance, and the Cowslip College Gay and Lesbian Association all had booths on the edge of the main drag. Stop the Prop was relegated to a patch of grass behind the food vendors, which included a group from Fiesta Jack's selling burritos, nachos, and fried ice cream. Suzy asked who he had to sleep with to get us a better spot.

"Millicent Rutherford," Tipper said. Suzy decided we were fine where we were.

Though they didn't have a booth, the Lesbian Avengers did a brisk trade nevertheless. They walked around the fair in Stop the Prop T-shirts, stopping passersby and handing out pamphlets. I looked for A. J., more in fear than in anticipation, but I didn't see her.

Tipper was not so fortunate. For a time, we didn't know where the forces of evil were, so once the festivities really got going, Tipper and Tom went on a scouting expedition. They came back to report that the pro-Proposition booth was on the opposite side of the park from us. Unfortunately, this placed them very near the front gates.

"That's too bad," I yawned. "Tipper, I don't know how long I'm going to last. I'm exhausted."

He gave me a vigorous shake. "If you'd gone to bed at a decent hour instead of staying up half the night watching old movies . . ."

"I like old movies."

"Like *Butterfield 8*?" he inquired archly.

I felt queasy. "Who've you been talking to?"

"Who do you think? I just ran into her on the other side of the park. I have one question for you—are you insane?"

I avoided looking him in the eye. "It was nothing, just a big mistake."

"No kidding. Next time, you're getting in the cab."

At five o'clock, Tipper allowed me time off to grab some dinner and stretch my legs. I was on my way back to the booth when I heard the familiar shriek of my grandmother. She was standing by the outdoor stage wearing period costume, a gingham dress and a slatted sun-bonnet. I suddenly remembered why I hated Pioneer Days.

The Cowslip Community Theatre always put on a play, penned by my grandmother, about the founding of the town. Cowslip was actually incorporated by a group of miners, loggers, and enterprising prostitutes, but Granny's version reflected none of this. *Cowslip Back Then* was a westernized version of the elementary school Thanksgiving play. Some white farmers hop off the Oregon Trail in the middle of the camas prairie and bargain with three Nez Perce Indians to trade thousands of acres for a couple of rifles and some tobacco. It was a disgrace, and the county historical society should have put an end to it years ago. However, the historical society's president, Millicent Rutherford, had played the starring role in this farce for over twenty-five years. She didn't know a damn thing about history, but she was a bigger ham than Porky Pig.

I made my way over to Granny, who was holding a plateful of food that might have given Henry the Eighth pause. Millicent stood next to her, taking delicate sips from a giant martini.

"Hi Granny," I said. "What time does the fun begin?"

She squinted at me. "You mean the play?"

"No, I mean the second coming." She didn't laugh, though Millicent looked vaguely amused.

"You're staying for the performance, aren't you?" Granny said. "Millicent made rather an interesting discovery about the town's early history, which I've incorporated into the script. One of our town fathers was—" she paused as if waiting for a drum roll "—a black man. His name was Marcus Apple. He was a tailor."

"And you've added him to your play? How multicultural of you."

"I think it will be nice," she continued. "A little something different for those who've seen the show before. Do you know if your mother will be here?" Granny looked down at her watch. "I called to remind her. The show starts in fifteen minutes. In fact," she smiled at Millicent, "it's time you were getting into your costume."

Millicent drained the last of her martini and handed me the empty glass. Of course the world was her servant. As soon as she and Granny had disappeared into the dressing room, I threw the glass in the trashcan. It shattered against the metal sides, making a louder noise than I'd intended. I turned around to find Sylvie Wood standing right behind me. She was wearing a white dress with small blue cornflowers all over it and her leather bomber jacket. My mouth was suddenly as dry as a wad of cotton.

"Hi," she said. Her smile was tentative.

"Hi."

We were silent for a long moment, and I wondered if I should bring up Fiesta Jack's.

She spoke first. "What are you doing backstage?"

I shrugged. "Just curious, I suppose. I usually avoid Pioneer Days like the plague."

"Why?"

"This damned awful play, that's why. I used to have to come as a child, year after year, and watch Granny and Millicent chew up the scenery."

Sylvie straightened her shoulders and said with mock seriousness, "Be careful—some of that scenery is mine."

"Oh my god," I cried. "Did you build the set?"

"I did," she laughed. "I'm also acting in this fine production. Didn't you know?"

"No. The cast for this thing hasn't changed in living memory. Who are you playing?"

"Mrs. Apple, wife of the town's tailor. I have exactly one line."

"Please tell me it's not 'Oh lordy, lordy.'"

She laughed again. It was a big, contagious laugh, the kind that carried through a room and made everyone else laugh as well. "No, it's 'Yes, Mrs. Janson.' Millicent's character stops in to get a pair of trousers mended. My husband, Mr. Apple, gets to say 'They'll be ready on Tuesday.' That's it for the Apples."

I shook my head in amazement. So much for multiculturalism. I stepped a little closer to her and said, "You seem to be normal enough. Why are you here?"

"I double-majored in drama as an undergraduate. I've never done an outdoor production before, and I thought this was as good a chance as any to get the experience."

"I'm a double-major. Well, sort of. I've done coursework for a BA in English and a BS in Psychology, but I'm still fighting with admissions over credits. Are you double-majoring in grad school?"

"No. I'm taking the theater design class because it interests me."

"Hmm. Cliff botany and acting."

"I know," she laughed. "If I don't make it as an actress, I suppose I can always go into pharmaceutical research."

"Drugs," I said, without thinking, "you should talk to my brother." I felt the blood drain from my face as I stood there, waiting for the gods to strike me dead.

Sylvie was looking down at her boots. Without looking up she said, "I need to talk to you about that, Bil. Could you meet me somewhere after the show?"

"Sylvie, I don't know what to say or even where to begin. I don't know if Sam . . ."

"He didn't," she said firmly. She looked up now and regarded me intently. "That's what I want to talk to you about. Whatever happened in that cell, Bil, it's not what you think."

"What do you . . ."

She reached out suddenly and put her hands on my shoulders.

"After curtain call, I'll meet you at Traveler's Rest. The play's forty-five minutes, more or less."

"It seems like more," I said. "But we can just meet backstage afterwards if you like. Now that I know you're making your Cowslip debut, I'll stay for the show."

"No, I'd rather meet away from all these people."

The rest of the cast began filing back onto the stage. Sylvie handed her jacket to me. "Would you mind keeping this with you? There's no place to hang it back here."

"No problem. Don't you need to get into costume?"

She looked down at her dress and grimaced. "What do you think this is? I wouldn't be caught dead in this get-up in true life—not unless I died and went to hell."

"Sorry, no offense intended."

"None taken," she smiled. Then she was gone. I followed the rest of the inessential crowd and descended the stairs at stage right.

Traveler's Rest, a stand of cedars at the very edge of the park, was a prime make-out spot for high school students. Ignoring the stares and mutterings of several desperately horny teenagers, I sat down beneath a tree and waited.

Chapter 11

The sun was sinking behind the trees, and I shivered for a few minutes before I remembered Sylvie's jacket. A perfect fit. It smelled like Bay Rum, and I wondered briefly if she'd loaned it to someone who wore aftershave or if she was more butch than she looked.

I zipped up the jacket and tried to make myself comfortable. It wasn't easy. Grass and bits of bark kept poking up under the patches I'd ironed over the holes in the back of my jeans, and the bushes around me were filled with the sounds of labored breathing. I sat there quietly until my legs began to get numb, and then I stood up and brushed myself off. The ground beneath me was probably crawling with ticks.

In the distance, I spied Sylvie. She was leaning against the wall at the back of the stage, talking earnestly with Helen Merwin. When I waved to her, she didn't react. Helen looked over her shoulder at me, then turned back to Sylvie and began talking again, this time with a lot of animated gesturing.

I sat back down, wondering what Helen was going on about. Someone had recently trimmed off the lower branches of my tree, probably to create a nuptial bower, and the wood's aroma drifted down pleasantly. I closed my eyes, trying to concentrate on the smell rather than what might be crawling beneath me.

When Sylvie appeared, I looked up at her and smiled. She looked away. Her hands were shoved down into the pockets of her dress, and she seemed to be thoroughly pissed off about something.

"Are you ready?" she asked. The words were clipped and terse.

"Would you like your jacket back?"

"You keep it. I'm not cold."

"Are you by any chance hot?"

We made eye contact now, and I felt the scorch of it from my nose up to the top of my forehead. Suddenly I wasn't so eager to know what Helen had said.

I took a deep breath. "Before we go any further, I want to say that I'm sorry for my behavior the other night at Fiesta Jack's. I was a complete idiot. I don't usually drink like that."

She stared at me for a long moment, not acknowledging my apology.

"This is no good," she said at last. "Let's get out of here. Is your car nearby? We could take my bike, but I only have one helmet."

"We'll take my truck." I didn't fancy tearing around without a brain bucket on an angry woman's motorcycle. "I don't have a car. I don't suppose that matters, of course. Car, truck, what's the difference? Anyhow, I got here early this morning, so I'm parked close by."

I was rattling on and on, unable to stop. We climbed into the truck, and I started the engine. Then I stopped and turned it off again. I couldn't concentrate with this ball of fury sitting next to me.

"Do you want to tell me why you're mad?"

"I'm not mad," she snapped.

I leaned back against the truck door and pretended to cringe. She laughed.

"I'm sorry," she said. "It's just that Mildew told me something I didn't want to hear."

"You call her that?"

"Only when I'm angry."

"That name has sort of stuck around my house, too," I admitted. "She spends a lot of time hanging out with my grandmother. We think it's a little perverse. A thirty-year-old who doesn't have a friend under seventy-five."

"Perverse is a good term for her. She's always going after me for one thing or another. We've never really gotten along."

I waited for her to continue, but she didn't. I started the truck and began to drive forward. Then I stopped again. "I don't know where I'm going."

"Go anywhere. It doesn't matter to me."

"Am I forgiven for Fiesta Jack's?"

There was a brief pause, and then she shrugged. "Of course. I thought you were kind of funny, actually. Let's just . . . let's find someplace private where we can sit and talk."

I racked my brain for possible destinations. My house was out of the question. Though the hayfield was a possibility, I wasn't sure my allergies could stand it, and there was no guarantee Emma wouldn't wander up to see what was going on. I hadn't spotted her in the audience at the play, so she might well be at home. I circled the park three times, thinking.

Sylvie said nothing. She didn't seem to notice where we were going, or that we were going nowhere. The sun was now hidden behind a bank of black clouds, and a thick fog was settling in. I circled the park one more time before making a decision, turning left on Hayes Street and driving up Route 2 to Fort Sister. Ten minutes later, we pulled in and stopped at the gate. I got out to open it and discovered it was still padlocked.

I tapped on Sylvie's window.

"Come on," I said. "We'll have to climb over and walk up."

"Where are we going?"

"The dugouts. We'll be able to talk there." Sylvie got out of the truck slowly, clearly puzzled. "When we get near the house," I said, "try to make a lot of noise. Well, not a lot of noise. Just talk in a normal voice, and don't try to walk softly or anything."

She stopped and stared at me. "Why?"

I shrugged. "Just a precaution. You know Captain Schwartz—she's armed to the teeth. She's got sharp ears and a paranoid disposition. If she hears us talking and walking like we're actually supposed to be out here, we'll be fine."

"And if she doesn't?"

"If she doesn't, we'll find ourselves answering rude questions at pistol-point."

I started walking again. Sylvie stood her ground. "I don't think this is a good idea."

I took her hand. "Come on, it's fine. I come out here all the time. I have an open invitation. We'll walk under Captain Schwartz's window, and I'll let her know we're here. Okay?"

She looked doubtful but allowed herself to be pulled along. The light was on in the Captain's bedroom, so I tapped on the glass. The sash was thrown up a few seconds later, and a woman stuck her head out. "What?" she asked. "We've got a front door, you know."

It was Jane, the Michigan Howitzer. I stepped back. Not only had I not been expecting to see her, but she was naked from the waist up. And it was a chilly night.

"Hey, you're Tipper's friend, aren't you?"

"I'm . . . yes, I'm Bil Hardy. We just wanted to let the Captain know we were here. I thought we'd go sit in the dugouts."

"Isn't it a little late for a game," she paused heavily, "of softball?"

Fortunately, a large arm reached out and pulled her back through the window. "Hey," Jane yelled.

"Go back to bed," the Captain laughed. "I can interrogate my own visitors. Hi, Bil."

"Hi. We just wanted to borrow one of the dugouts. A quiet talk," I added quickly. I didn't know what Sylvie was thinking. I wondered if she could possibly be as embarrassed as I was.

"Be my guest. The gate was locked, wasn't it?"

"Yes, I'm sorry. We climbed over."

"No problem," she smiled. "You're always welcome, you know that. Just tap on my window when you leave, would you? Cedar Tree is still a little nervous about trespassers, and I like to be vigilant. You never know," she added ominously.

"Sure thing," I said. She went back to Jane, and I turned around to find Sylvie, who had stepped back several paces, stifling a laugh.

"One more thing," the Captain called behind me. "Do you want the field lights on or off? The switch is in the kitchen. It's a bit of an obstacle course out there right now. We've been target shooting, getting ready for tomorrow." The second day of Pioneer Days featured a black powder rifle competition that Captain Schwartz usually won.

"Why don't we leave them off?" I avoided meeting Sylvie's eye for fear that she might misinterpret. Or worse, that she might interpret correctly. "I think we'll be okay."

"Right. Goodnight Bil. Goodnight . . . Sylvie Wood, isn't it?"

"Yes ma'am," Sylvie said.

"We're neighbors. Your mother's place touches on the north corner of my property. If you climb up to the top of the ridge, you can just make out the roof of your barn. Stay as late as you want, Bil. Now, if you . . ." She hesitated, giving me plenty of time to dread what she might say next. "One of the cabins is vacant at the moment. If you want to stay, you're welcome to stay there. Looks to me like it might rain."

Even worse than I could have imagined. "Thanks," I said quickly. When the Captain had closed the window, I turned to Sylvie and whispered, "I'm sorry about that."

"Do you come out here often?" Her face was in shadow, and I couldn't tell if she was laughing now or not.

"No . . . yes, but not like that. I play a lot of softball," I finished lamely.

We walked on a few steps, and then she stopped again.

"Why did you say you were sorry?"

I didn't look at her. "Embarrassed, I suppose."

"Captain Schwartz didn't seem to mind. Besides, it's a pretty natural conclusion. Two women, it's dark, we're on our way to a dugout . . . lesbian dream date, isn't it?" Definitely laughing.

"I don't know. I think I'd prefer something more comfortable than a wooden bench in a cold dugout. Even Traveler's Rest would be better than that."

"Infinitely," she agreed. We reached the dugouts, and I led Sylvie around to the third base side. She sat on the bench. I sat before her on the ground, leaning back against the fence that separated us from the diamond. We said nothing for what seemed like ages. I felt the word "infinitely" hanging in the air between us like a patch of fog, thicker and more impenetrable than the mist hanging over the softball pitch.

"You said earlier that Sam didn't . . ."

She shook her head. "We'll talk about Sam later, I promise. First, what do you know about my father? Forget the rumors. Try to tell me what you actually remember."

"I know that he disappeared sixteen years ago, in 1978." I tried to think back to that summer. "You and I had just finished first grade. Your father left on the Fourth of July."

"Is that what you remember, or what you've been told?"

"Does it matter?"

She sighed. "It does, I'm afraid. It's true that my father officially disappeared on the Fourth of July. I remember going to see the fireworks. Then my mother brought me home and put me to bed. The next day, she told me he was gone."

"What I remember," I said tentatively, "is walking in on a lot of conversations that suddenly stopped. My mother hadn't seemed to mind my eavesdropping before, and I was puzzled that she wouldn't let me listen now. Later . . . do you want to hear about later?"

She nodded, staring out over the field and not looking at me.

"Later, people brought it up occasionally. They wondered where your father and Frank had gone. Some people said San Francisco, others said New York. All of those places seemed plausible to me then."

"And now?"

"Now I don't think they could have gotten away with enough money for that sort of life."

"Do you remember my father at all?"

"Vaguely." I paused, trying to think of a good way to phrase my thoughts. "He scared me. He had that big, black mustache, and he seemed angry all the time. I don't think he liked kids."

"Not even his own," she agreed. "Anything else?"

"I remember that everyone talked about it, and everyone said exactly the same things—imagine leaving your wife for a man, imagine Burt Wood turning out to be gay. The only person who said anything different was Hugh. He said he thought the stress of living a lie made people do a lot of things they might come to regret, and that it was a shame your father felt he couldn't be gay and keep his relationship with you."

"That's a kind thought," she said. "I think I'd like your dad."

"Most people do. He has a kind of Will Rogers take on the world."

She looked down at me and smiled. "Why don't you sit up here on the bench? That ground looks damp."

"It is," I agreed. I sat down with one leg on either side of the bench, facing her. "Would you like your jacket back? It's getting cold, and you've just got on that thin cotton dress."

She shook her head. "I'm fine. Besides, you're just wearing a T-shirt yourself."

"Yeah, but I'm a big, tough butch."

She laughed, and we sat for a few moments in silence. Muffled sounds traveled through the fog and something, possibly a woodpecker, hammered on the electrical pole behind us. Sylvie reached up and pulled out a comb and several bobby pins, letting her hair out of the bun she'd worn in the performance. As she shook her head, her hair cascaded down to her shoulders.

"What did your mother say about the disappearance?" she asked. "Do you remember?"

"Not really. The same things everyone else said, I guess. At some point, she stopped hanging out with your mother. I don't know when that happened, whether it was before or after."

"It was after," she said matter-of-factly. "Why do think that was?"

I shrugged. "I don't know why. Maybe they had an argument. Maybe your mother didn't feel like company after your dad left. I've never really asked. I know that Emma didn't like your father. She said . . ."

"What did she say?" When I hesitated, Sylvie leaned forward and put her hands on my knees. "It's all right. You're not going to offend me. Please tell me what she said."

"She said that disappearing was the best thing your father ever did. She said he treated your mother like absolute hell."

Her face had been only a few inches from mine, but she leaned back now. As she lifted her hands, I reached out and held them.

"At one time," she said, not looking at me, "our mothers were very close."

"They were roommates before Emma dropped out and got married."

She nodded. "My mom has a lot of pictures of them together. Your mother got married at the end of their sophomore year. Then your parents moved to the East Coast somewhere."

"Virginia. Hugh did his master's at George Mason. After that it was Florida, Louisiana, California, and finally back here. Academia is wonderfully accommodating to the hippie nomad. I know that our mothers kept in touch, and when we moved back, they picked up where they'd left off. They spent a lot of time together."

"When you moved back," she said, "my parents had been married for just over seven years. I remember Emma coming to the house. Sometimes she'd have you with her, sometimes Sam or one your sisters. Sometimes she came alone." She smiled. "You don't know what it's like being an only child. When your mother arrived without one of you in tow, I was very disappointed."

"It's hard to remember that my mother used to have friends. After Sam's diagnosis, she just sort of withdrew. It was like she wanted to block out anyone who wasn't part of the immediate family. I suppose that's normal under the circumstances."

"I suppose so," she said quietly.

"I remember your mother, too," I went on. "I remember her coming over to our house and sitting in the kitchen with Emma. They drank cup after cup of coffee, surrounded by a fog of cigarette smoke. I'm sure she brought you with her." I was struggling now, and I didn't think I could summon up much more from the well of memory. Impressions, things people had said, all of these were clearer to me in some ways than my own direct experience.

"She always brought me," Sylvie said. "She never left me at home with my father, not if she could help it. I used to play with your sisters, Sarah in particular. She was one of those older girls who didn't mind being followed around by a younger one. Ruth was too old to take more than a babysitter kind of interest. Naomi . . ."

"Naomi never played with anyone. She sat in her bedroom counting her Monopoly money."

Sylvie smiled. "You didn't play much, either. You just sat under the kitchen table listening to the conversation. My mother thought you were funny. She said you'd occasionally offer some pithy observation, but mostly, you were quiet. You were her favorite of Emma's children."

"When did she tell you that?"

"The other night, actually. At Fiesta Jack's. That's when she told me about Sam."

I closed my eyes and took a deep breath, trying to steady myself against the sudden sharp sting of humiliation. When I opened them again, I saw that her eyes had grown dark and difficult to read.

"Bil, do you mind if I ask you a personal question?"

"Ask me anything." I was very conscious of Sylvie's hands in my own. The touch was light, but electric.

"When did you first know you were a lesbian?"

"Elementary school." This was dangerous ground. When had I known? That afternoon at recess when Sylvie had reached out to ruffle my hair. Not that I was a lesbian, exactly, but I certainly knew that I liked girls. Sitting so close to her now, I could remember that feeling of longing and anticipation.

"You're going to tell your mother, aren't you?"

"Sooner or later." As that didn't seem like much of an answer, I tried again. "My mother can be very invasive. I want to keep some part of my life private. A. J. told me once that I was just being wishy-washy. Maybe she's right."

Sylvie released my hands and moved back on the bench. I was sure now that word of my post-Fiesta Jack's rendezvous had reached her, but there was nothing I could do about it.

I said, "When did you know?"

"I was a late bloomer. I didn't know until high school. My mother didn't know until she was married and had a child."

"I thought you weren't out to your mother."

"I'm not. I mean my mother didn't know about herself."

"Your mother's a . . ."

"My mother's a lesbian," she said. "I don't know if she's ever been with anyone. She might have—I haven't lived at home for over three years. As far as I know, she's only ever come out to one person." She paused for a moment and took my hands again. "She doesn't know this, but I was there when she came out. I was sitting in your old hiding place, underneath the kitchen table. We had a long tablecloth, thick white damask. The edges touched the floor. I couldn't see her, and she couldn't see me. She came out to your mother, Bil."

"My mother?"

"Yes. It wasn't so much coming out as confessing, really." She spoke quietly and carefully. Though I had begun to feel apprehensive,

I was utterly unprepared for what she said next. "She told your mother that she was in love with her."

"What did Emma say?" I asked tentatively, not sure I wanted to know.

"She said she was sorry, really sorry. Then my mother cried. I sat under the table as quietly as I could, not wanting them to know I was there. It's awful when you're a child and your mother is crying. You don't know what to do."

"What happened after that?"

"I don't know."

I ran a hand through my hair and looked out over the field. The wind had picked up, dissipating the mist and blowing clouds of damp leaves around the bases. I couldn't picture Emma as the object of anyone's desire. I knew my parents had an active sex life; they were private, but not quiet. Still, I didn't think of either of them as being sexual, as having a sex life that wasn't somehow parental. They had a sex life together, not apart.

"When was this?"

"Sixteen years ago. Just before my father disappeared."

What had my mother been like back then? Thinner. Long brown hair with streaks of gray, bright blue eyes. She'd been attractive.

"Christ," I said suddenly.

"It's okay." Sylvie moved closer to me. "Until recently, I didn't think it was all that important. You love someone, and they don't love you back. It happens all the time. I'm telling you now because two weeks ago my mother identified that body in the morgue as my father, and now they think your brother killed him. Bil, look at me—I don't know what happened to that man, but he was not my father."

I shook my head, not comprehending. "Your mother identified the body . . . what do you mean your father was someone else?"

"I mean my mother was wrong. That man was not Burt Wood. I think he was Frank Frost."

"You saw him?"

"Not in the morgue. My mother went by herself to make the identification. I saw him on Thursday, the day before he died. In my mother's kitchen."

I stared at her.

"I don't know what he was doing there," she went on. "I went out there that night for dinner. They were in the kitchen, arguing. I heard him say something about making her sorry, and she said she wasn't interested in making any deals with him. He could either leave under his own steam, or she'd call the sheriff and have him forcibly removed, so he left. I don't think he saw me. I was out in the yard when I heard them, and I ducked around the corner of the house when the back door opened. When I went in, I pretended I'd only heard part of the conversation. My mother told me that he was just a pushy transient, looking for work."

"You're sure it was Frost?"

She nodded. "Very much changed, but I recognized him. I didn't say anything to my mother about it, and I don't know why she lied to me. I had to leave on Friday morning to drive a friend to Spokane, and I ended up spending the night there. I was a little worried, but then I thought, what could he do? She didn't have any trouble throwing him out. On Saturday afternoon, the sheriff's department called and asked her to come down to the morgue. She identified the body as my father. I didn't know until I got home."

"Holy shit," was my inadequate response. Even through the thickness of Sylvie's jacket, I could feel the cold rising through the damp air.

"I know," she said. "I don't know what your brother did, Bil, maybe he didn't do anything. I do know that he didn't kill my father."

"He killed Frank Frost."

"I doubt it." She still seemed to be thinking something over, trying to decide whether or not to tell me.

"Go ahead," I said slowly. "I have a bad feeling that there's more to this story."

"I'm sorry." She closed her eyes and took a deep breath. "I wouldn't get you involved, but I don't know what else to do, and in a way, you're already involved. Nearly as much as I am, in fact."

"Thanks to Sam."

"No. Look Bil, you have no idea why our mothers stopped being friends, why they stopped having anything to do with one another?"

I swallowed hard and took the plunge. "They had an affair, didn't they?"

She smiled. "I don't think so. It's hard to fall in love with someone who can't love you back, who wouldn't be with you even if she were free. That's why my mother was crying. I'm sure Emma loves your father."

I felt relieved. It was fine if my mother was bisexual, what did I care? I just couldn't stand the thought of her cheating on my father. "I can't picture my mother keeping a secret like that, not from Hugh. She tells him everything."

Her gaze was suddenly so intense that I flinched.

"My father was killed sixteen years ago, Bil. He didn't leave with Frank or anyone else. My mother shot him and then she buried the body in our backyard. We had a backhoe—my father had rented it to dig a trench out next to the barn for some water pipes or something. My mother used it to dig a deep hole. There's a giant syringa over the spot where he's buried, the first in a line of bushes stretching out from the barn. He's out there."

She spoke in a low voice, and yet it felt as if she were shouting at me. A loud buzzing started in my ears. It was the sound of blood rushing up past my eustachian tubes in a feeble attempt to block out what she had to say next.

"Emma was there, Bil. She helped my mother hide the body."

As soon as the words were out of her mouth, the floodlights came on above the dugouts and six figures approached us from the opposite side of the field. One of them shielded his eyes with his hand, trying to make us out. Then he stopped.

"Shit, Bil," Tipper said. "I'm really sorry. We had some excitement at the festival, and we need to wind down. I thought we'd play a little softball, try to relax."

I stared at him stupidly, and he smiled.

"Sylvie," he said, holding out his hand. "So nice to see you again. These are my friends. Here, let me introduce you."

Chapter 12

"This is Alan," Tipper said, "and this is Tom."

Tom held out his hand. "How do you do?"

Brian and Jeff stepped forward. Jeff winked at me, a gesture I was certain did not slip past Sylvie's notice. "Don't forget Suzy," he said.

Suzy was flopped down like a cow pie on the pitcher's mound.

"Suzy!" Tipper called. "Get up for God's sake. Have some manners."

"It's okay," Sylvie began. "I don't . . ."

Suzy heaved himself up with visible effort and reeled over. "Charmed, I'm sure." He threw an arm around her shoulders and leaned in conspiratorially. "I've had a few daiquiris, and Tipper is very annoyed with me. He's a bit of a prude, you know."

"And you're a bit of a drunk," Tipper observed.

"Well," Suzy huffed, all wrists and hips, "that's a fine how do you do. So I mentioned a few names—it's not like we were at an AA meeting. It's a very bad idea to be anonymous, you know. In fact, it's downright dangerous."

"You've lost me," I said. "What happened? You mentioned some excitement."

Tipper gazed at me sadly, his arms folded across his chest.

"It's late," he said, "and I don't know if I feel up to reciting the story. Are you and Sylvie staying out here tonight or are you on your way somewhere?" I gave him my that-was-beyond-the-pale look, and he explained quickly, "I was thinking that we could bat the ball around a bit and then retire to the house. There's an empty . . . there's plenty of space for everyone. We could make a night of it, music, old movies, and a strategy session for tomorrow's booth."

"You'd better tell her," Tom interrupted. "She'll want to know."

I sighed. "What was the excitement this afternoon? Did Suzy do a striptease at the Proposition One booth?"

"It was an outing," Tipper replied. "That daiquiri queen over there outed someone he had no right to out."

I stared at Suzy, who examined his fingernails.

"Who?"

"He outed you, Bil."

"How could he out me?" I hadn't told my family, but the gay community of Cowslip knew.

"I'm sorry," Tom cut in. "I'm afraid it was my fault. Tipper pointed your grandmother out to me. Later on, she was talking to the people at the Proposition One booth, and I pointed her out to Suzy. He'd been drinking daiquiris all day, ever since Fiesta Jack's opened their tent flaps. I just wasn't thinking."

"Granny," I said slowly, turning my wrath on the lanky figure now lying flat on his back on the third base line. "You told my insane grandmother that I was a . . . that I'm . . ."

"I told her you were a lesbian, darling," Suzy said, drawling the words out. "Out, proud, and free! You're here, you're queer, and your sweet old granny had better get used to it."

Sylvie took my hand, and I gazed at her helplessly.

"Do you want the details?" Tipper asked. "Or would you rather not know?"

I thought about it for a moment or two. There was nothing I could do about it. I'd been shoved out of the closet, and Granny would make sure that the doors slammed shut behind me.

"Give me the details," I said finally.

"Well," Tipper said, "this big old drag queen, three sheets to the wind, marched up to your grandmother and the Prop One people and told them that they should be ashamed of themselves. Your grandmother has you, and one of the men working the booth, the Reverend James Jones, has a son who flunked out of Exodus International."

"Exodus?" I asked.

Jeff spoke up. "It's a fundamentalist Christian group that claims to cure homosexuals. They teach butch lesbians how to put on makeup and effeminate men how to play football. It's crazy. Suzy and I met at an Exodus meeting. We're what they call ex-ex-gays. The reverend's son, Trevor, was in our group. He and Suzy were friends. We were all living in Renton, Washington, and Suzy was . . ."

"I was married, honey," Suzy said. "I was married and living in the suburbs. They called it a bedroom community. I saw a lot of bedrooms." He giggled.

"Anyhow," Jeff continued, "Suzy and Trevor were close. He stayed in Exodus a lot longer than he should have."

"Who did, Suzy or Trevor?"

"Either of us," Suzy replied. "Both of us. We're interchangeable Stepford fags. I was in Exodus for three years." He staggered up and threw himself forward, until we were standing nose to nose. "Don't be ashamed of who you are, Bil. I was ashamed. My father was a minister, just like Trevor's daddy. Nothing I did was good enough. You know what they say about the preacher's son, don't you? It's all true. I like drinking, dancing, and great big dicks."

I let go of Sylvie's hand so I could push Suzy out of my face. I said to Tipper, "Are you sure he's just drunk?"

Tipper shrugged. "I think so. He does like a little hashish every now and again."

"At least I'm not pretending it's peyote like your mother does," Suzy shot back. He leaned towards me again, his breath so heavy with rum that I had to dig in my heels to keep from falling over backwards. "Bil, you'll be just fine. Your grandmother didn't even look surprised."

"How did she look?"

He thought for a moment, and then smacked his lips. "Blank. But perhaps you should ask Carrie Nation," he pointed at Tipper. "She was terrifyingly sober."

"Your grandmother wasn't alone, Bil," Tipper explained. "It was after the play. We were looking for you, but you'd already left. Some of the cast were with her at the booth."

"Who?"

"Helen Merwin, Fairfax, Millicent . . ."

I turned on Suzy. "You told everyone and his dog, didn't you?"

"No, I didn't. What's that? One, two, three," he counted off on his fingers, "four people."

"The four biggest mouths in Cowslip," I replied, slipping out from under him and turning to Tipper. "You know that my mother is the first person she'll call."

"I'm sorry, Bil. If I could have, I'd have shut him up, I swear. Short of casting his head in cement, I don't think it's possible. What are you going to do now?"

"I think," I said at last, casting a pleading glance at Sylvie, "that we'll take a walk up to the top of the ridge. I'd like to clear my head."

"I can't say as I blame you. Here though," Tipper grabbed Suzy by the arm and stripped him of his jacket. He smiled and handed it to Sylvie. "It's cold up there, and you've got bare arms."

"What about me?" Suzy said. "I'll freeze."

"You'll also sober up. I don't want you yakking up all over my carpet tonight."

Sylvie and I were silent as we hiked up the hill, as if we had nothing important to talk about. The fog had begun to dissipate, and patches of clear sky and stars were shining through the clouds. The big dipper seemed to be hanging just a few feet above the tall pines. We walked on and up for half a mile, until the Faeries' shouting was a distant echo and the lights around the dugouts glowed far behind us.

There was a clearing at the top of the ridge between Fort Sister and Kate Wood's farm. It was made by the original homesteader, long before the railroad magnate bought the property. Once upon a time, there was a rumor that some of the women at Fort Sister had formed a coven and were using the clearing for their naked Sabbaths. Tipper said that was just wishful thinking. The remains of an old house lay just over the top, on the side facing Kate's farm. To protect local kids, who were looking for a house in which to get laid or stoned or both, the Captain knocked down what was left of the walls several years ago. All that remained was the foundation, a rectangle of irregular, weatherworn stones.

Sylvie and I paused near the top, stopping to listen to the wind rushing through the trees and to catch our breath. A few invisible creatures shuffled about in the underbrush, but otherwise it was quiet. We passed over the top and sat down on the edge of the ruined foundation, looking down on her mother's property. A dog barked in the distance.

Sylvie said, "That's my mother's dog, Elvis. Listen—Priscilla will start howling in a minute."

I listened. There were two or three more barks and then a long, low howling began. It was definitely dogs, rather than wolves or coyotes. I still shivered. "They're so close to being wild, aren't they? I mean, we've been breeding them for centuries, and at night, they still talk to each other in the same old way, a way that has nothing to do with us."

"It's nice, isn't it?" she said.

"I suppose so. What kind of dogs are they?"

"Elvis is a mutt, a big Lab cross. Priscilla's a Samoyed. I've had her for years."

"She doesn't live with you in town?"

"No. I've got a tiny apartment and a roommate. Even if I could find a place that would have her, I couldn't take her away from Elvis. They'd both be too lonely. Besides, can you imagine the neighbors putting up with that racket?"

The howling had begun with a high-pitched sound that gradually dropped through the register to a low moan. Priscilla did this once or twice, and, after a long pause, she was rewarded by a series of short yips.

"Listen," Sylvie said, putting her hand on my arm. "It's a pack of coyotes. They're not far from here."

The yipping intensified until the pack sounded as if they were only a few feet away. I knew it was only the echo coming up over the flat, but I sat very still, glad of Sylvie's company. Finally, the yips subsided and moved away. I was tired. I leaned forward and rested my forearms on my knees. Sylvie shifted on the rocks, and I felt her hand touch my back. It moved in slow, tentative circles for a moment or two and then stopped, moving up to rest lightly on my shoulder.

"Are you okay?"

"I'll be fine. Really, it's nothing."

"Right, nothing at all," she agreed.

I smiled grimly. "Let's see. Your mother's a lesbian. My mother might or might not have had an affair with her. You don't think so, but how can we know? It doesn't matter anyway because your mother killed your father and my mother helped bury him in the backyard. But even that's beside the point because the county prosecutor is going to charge my brother with killing him only last week."

"I'm sorry," she said.

"And, finally, a big-mouthed drag queen who looks like Carol Channing has just outed me to my grandmother and all of her friends. Conservatively, the entire town of Cowslip will know by sun-up. So many presents, I'm beginning to think it might be Christmas."

"What are you going to do about it?"

Her eyes met mine. I'm going to kiss you, I thought. Here in the ruins, with the coyotes singing in the distance, I'm going to kiss you, and we'll forget about everything and everyone else. I'm going to kiss you, and we'll stay up here on this hillside forever.

Her hand rested on my back again, and I lost my nerve.

I said, "My mother runs through my life like a bull through a china shop, and she drags Sam behind her. I haven't come out to her because there's no time for it. Where would I work it in, somewhere between my brother's arrests and his chemotherapy? Perhaps I could find time while running interference between my mother and the sheriff's department, my mother and Sam, and my mother and the rest of the normal, sane world."

"I'm sorry," she said again.

The stars were bright in the sky above us. Her eyes were dark and intense. She put her arms around me, and I rested my head on her shoulder. We sat without moving until the coyotes' calling faded into the distance.

"It's all right," I said at last, lifting my head reluctantly. "The reason I'm not out is that I feel too fucking sorry for myself. I want my mother to be interested in me, not in how I can further some agenda."

She hesitated.

"Go on," I said. "What is it?"

"Don't you think you're being a little hard on her?"

I stood up and stretched, hoping to clear my head. I looked down at Sylvie, who was still regarding me intently, and discarded the flip answer I'd been prepared to give.

"I know I'm too hard on her. This thing with Sam—the cancer, the crazy shit he pulls—it's like a vortex. Everyone else in the family has pulled out except for Emma and me. We just keep getting in deeper and deeper. Sam is now the sum total of the connection between us."

"Why don't you talk to her?"

"And say what? That I'm jealous of my terminally ill brother?"

"I think," she said, "that you're even harder on yourself than you are on her."

I sat down again on the wall and faced her. "I don't even talk to Tipper like I'm talking to you." She smiled. I took a deep breath and let it out slowly. "Okay, I'm ready to listen now. Tell me everything."

"I don't know for certain how he died. I remember my father renting the backhoe. He was doing a lot of landscaping that summer, digging out the hill behind our house, pulling up trees. My mother didn't want him to do it—she wanted him to leave everything alone. The house and farm belonged to her, not to him. It's the family homestead. The original one-room cabin her grandfather, my great-grandfather, built when he first came here was still standing then. My father knocked it down to put up a metal shed."

"Why?"

"Because he wanted to. He destroyed everything my mother cared about."

I realized then that she was crying. I put my arms around her and pulled her to me. She let me hold her for a minute or two, just as she'd held me. Then she sat up and pulled away.

"No," she said. "I'm okay. I've got to tell you this." She wiped her eyes on Suzy's jacket. "I hated my father. He yelled all the time—at me, at my mother. One of the things I remember most clearly about him is that he used to grab me by the back of the neck and pinch really tight. He picked me up like that once and dragged me down the hall to show me some mess I'd made."

I took her hand, holding it in both of mine.

"I can still feel his fingers on the back of my neck. When I knew he was gone, Bil, really gone and not coming back, I was happy. It was the thing I'd prayed for as long as I could remember."

"Did he ever . . ." I wasn't certain how to ask and was grateful that she guessed what I wanted to know.

"He beat the hell out of my mother. Usually, he did it on the weekends. Sometimes it was during the week. My mother tried not to miss any work. She couldn't always help it."

"Sylvie, I'm so sorry."

She took a deep, shuddering breath, and I put my arms around her again. This time, she didn't pull away.

"That night—I think it must have been the night he died—I heard my parents arguing in the kitchen. They were fighting about one of my mother's dogs, an old mixed-breed named Jack. My father kicked him and broke one of his ribs. It punctured his lung, and my mother had to put the dog down. She shot him in the head with a hunting rifle. My father wouldn't let her take him in to the vet."

"He was going out somewhere with Frank that night. Probably to a bar or something. Frank was over at our house all the time. Occasionally they spent the weekend together in Spokane, cruising the strip joints or something. That's probably where the gay stuff came from. Anyhow, he came in the house to get ready, and my mother was sitting at the kitchen table, crying. The rifle was in the corner, leaning up against the wall. He told her to shut up about the stupid dog. She sent me up to my room."

"I don't know what happened after that. There was a lot of yelling. I know I didn't go to my own room because I remember lying on my mother's bed with a pillow over my head. I fell asleep up there, I don't know for how long. I woke up twice that night. Once, I thought I heard his motorcycle in the driveway. The second time, I heard a loud engine. That was the backhoe. I went downstairs and stood by the screen door in the kitchen. It was a bright night, the third of July. We went out the next morning and bought fireworks."

"Sylvie," I said. "What exactly did you see?"

She closed her eyes and leaned into me. I put a finger under her chin and lifted her head up until she looked at me. "You can trust me. I have no reason to tell anyone, and even if I did, I wouldn't."

She took a deep breath. "My mother stood at the edge of a trench, the one my father had started on the hill behind our house. She had her back to me. At first, I couldn't see who was driving the backhoe. They dug a tremendous hole. Then, the engine stopped and the driver climbed out. I ducked back behind the kitchen door because I was afraid she'd see me. It was a minute or so before I looked out again. I still didn't recognize the other woman, but they were rolling something into the hole. It was a man, and he was naked. When they stood back up, the other woman, the driver, lit a cigarette. She held the flame in front of her face, and I recognized her. It was your mother, Bil. I don't know who killed him—I'm guessing it was my mother—but Emma helped to hide the evidence."

I didn't doubt that my mother was capable of doing what Sylvie had described. She was fierce about the people she loved, often irrational. She'd have dealt with the body calmly and efficiently, probably without losing a moment of sleep. I've never known anyone else with such a complete confidence in her own moral rectitude.

I said, "What did you do?"

She twisted a piece of hair between her fingers, winding it into a tight curl. "I ran back upstairs to my mother's room. Then I guess I went to sleep. I don't remember anything else. The next day was normal. We bought fireworks and set them off in the front yard. The motorcycle was gone, and my father never came back. A couple of days later, my mother called the sheriff's department and reported him missing. By then, Frank had stolen the money from the county assessor's office, and he disappeared too."

"You never told anyone what you saw? Not even your mother?"

"What would I have said?" She put her hands over her eyes, pressing her palms against her eyelids. "This can't be easy for you to believe. Sometimes, I don't believe it myself."

I shook my head. "On the contrary, I don't have any trouble believing it, at least not as far as Emma's concerned. My mother is a mass of contradictory ideas. Captain Schwartz pisses her off because she's such a gun nut, and yet on some level, my mother actually believes in frontier justice. I mean, she jokes about a bullet being the only cure for some people, but under certain circumstances, she wouldn't hesitate to pull the trigger. If she knew about your father, how he treated you and your mother, she'd have helped hide that body without any compunction."

Sylvie said nothing. She seemed content for the moment to sit quietly, her head resting against my shoulder. I had no idea what to say to her, let alone what I could do to help.

"You're wondering if I could have dreamt it, aren't you?"

I shrugged but didn't answer.

"I've wondered too. I suppose I could have. What I remember most clearly are his feet. Isn't that strange? They were whiter than the rest of his body, white and stiff. His ankles were bent so that his feet were perpendicular to his legs. I thought they could probably push him up and stand him there, just like a statue."

I was now well and truly cold, and I guessed it must be past midnight. I stood up.

"Come on. Let's go."

"Wait," she said. "You're disgusted, aren't you? You think I'm a monster because I wanted him dead."

"No, I don't." I bent over her, holding her arms tightly until she was forced to look me in the eye. "I'm not disgusted. Why wouldn't you be glad to think he was dead? You don't owe him anything just because he fathered you. There's more to being a parent than just fucking someone and getting her pregnant. He wasn't your father in any real sense of the word, he was an abusive bastard. It would be sick if you didn't hate him, and you'd have to be some kind of masochist not to be happy when you found out he wasn't coming back."

"Maybe," she said quietly. "I don't know anymore. It was such a long time ago, and every memory I have of him is a bad one." Elvis barked in the distance again. Sylvie stared off down the hill in the direction of her mother's barn. "Bil, do you ever think about your biological parents?"

I shrugged. "Sometimes."

"Have you ever thought about trying to find them?"

"Sometimes," I said again. "I wonder if I look like them, or if either of them had any other children. I don't suppose they're still together. The social worker who placed me told Emma that theirs was a temporary arrangement. That's delicate, isn't it? I might have a half-brother or sister out there, though I probably shouldn't wonder about that, should I? God knows I've got more than enough siblings now."

"Do you ever feel lonely, being adopted?"

I smiled. "No more than most people, I expect. I don't know how non-adopted people feel. How do you feel?"

"Lonely," she said. "Sometimes."

"There, I guess it's universal." She laughed, and I continued, "I really don't feel a compelling need to track down my birth parents. Whatever's missing in my life, it's not anything a couple of strangers from Louisiana could supply."

"I won't ask you what's missing in your life. I don't think either of us is up for another revelation tonight. Shall we walk back down?"

"Sure." I reached down and helped her to her feet. "One more question, and then we can both stop. Does your mother have any idea that you're a lesbian?"

She thought for a moment. "She might. She's never asked me. We don't talk about relationships. I love my mother, but I can't let her know that about me."

"Why not? Especially if she's gay herself."

"That's exactly why, that and the fact that everyone thinks my father is gay. Don't you see? She's never told me she was a lesbian, it was just something I overheard, and these rumors about my father, they wall us off from each other. Every time I come to the point, every time I think I'm going to tell her, my father pops up between us like some sort of zombie."

"I don't understand."

"Don't you?" She shook her head sadly. "You can't tell your mother because of your brother, and your grandmother, and everything you think is weighing her down. I can't tell mine because if I'm right, if I wasn't dreaming that night, then my father has been dead for over sixteen years, and my mother has let this rumor that he was gay, that he ran off with another man, hang there in the air between us. She's hidden behind it like a veil. I don't know how to tell her about me without pushing that veil aside."

I kissed her. Not passionately, but in sympathy, and that was how she responded.

We walked back down the path as silently as we'd come up it. The moon was only a thin crescent shining through the dense trees, and it was hard to see where we were going. The dugout lights had been switched off. I reached for her hand.

"Sylvie," I said, stopping abruptly. "I don't want to take you home."

"That's okay, I can walk. My mother's place is just over . . ."

"That's not what I meant. I mean, let's take the Captain up on her offer and stay in one of the cabins. You can take the bed, and I'll sleep on the floor. There's probably a sleeping bag around somewhere. It's just that . . ." I stumbled, trying to think of something that wouldn't sound sordid. "I don't want to go home, not yet. My mother might be up—she's a night owl. I just can't face her."

"Okay," she said, nodding slowly in the dim light of the moon, "but let's go back to my place instead. You can sleep on the sofa. My roommate's there, but she always sleeps like . . ."

She'd been about to say like the dead.

Chapter 13

"Look," I said, "they must know what killed him, whoever he was. It's been two weeks since he died, and backlog or not, the lab should have some results by now. The holdup must lie in the fact that they're trying to pin this thing on my brother. If they're not able to do that, then they might open a real investigation. God knows what it'll turn up."

"Do you think Frank was murdered?"

"I don't know. I suppose it's possible."

Sylvie squeezed my hand for reassurance; I had to let go to change gears. I'd spent a restless night on her sofa, and we'd both woken up a little before seven. Aside from a bag of spaghetti noodles and some stale teabags, there was nothing to eat in her apartment, so we were on our way to the House of Pancakes.

"My mother didn't know about Sam," she said. "I'm sure of it. The sheriff's department called and said they thought they'd found my father. She went down to look—what else could she do? They asked her if it was him, and she said yes." There was a long pause. "Do you think they've been in contact?"

"You mean Kate and Emma? Maybe."

"You don't believe me, do you?"

I kept my eyes on the road ahead. "It's not that I don't believe you. It's Sunday morning, it's sunny, and we're on our way to get pancakes. Last night, anything seemed possible. Today, everything seems perfectly normal again."

"But if it's true . . ."

"If it's true, then my mother is bound to have talked to yours. They'd have to compare notes and decide what to do about Sam. I'll tell you another thing," I said, looking at her for emphasis, "Emma will dump your mother right in the sheriff's lap if Sam is in any real danger, and she won't hesitate to incriminate herself."

"I hadn't thought of that," she said nervously.

"Why should you? It's counterintuitive. My mother is a loose cannon." I offered her the only comfort I could. "We've got time on our side at the moment. Two weeks have passed, and Sam still hasn't been charged. Emma won't act unless he is. She hates the cops, and she doesn't trust them, so she won't make a pre-emptive strike on this. If the urine test is clear, we're over one big hurdle. After that . . ."

"After that," she finished, "we've got a thousand other possibilities to worry about. My god, I'd like to have been a fly on the wall for the conversation between Mom and Emma."

"Oh, I expect you'd have needed a telephone tap. After all this time, it would be too suspicious if they suddenly started visiting again."

Sylvie crossed her legs, resting the edge of her foot against the dashboard. "She deliberately misidentified that body, Bil. I don't know why she did it, not after all this time."

We pulled up to an intersection as the light turned from yellow to red. Realizing too late that I didn't have time to make it through, I slammed on the brakes. The car behind me blew its horn.

Something occurred to me. "It's strange, isn't it, your father and Frank disappearing at the same time? They supposedly ran off together, but if your father was already dead, then what happened to Frank?"

"Maybe it's just a strange coincidence."

"It's not just strange, it's convenient." I shook my head. "No, there's something there; we just need to find out what it is."

"And how do we do that?"

"I'll think of something." The light turned green, and the car behind me blew its horn. I gave its driver the finger in the rearview mirror. He gave me the finger back, and blew his horn again. I slammed the truck into gear and screeched through the intersection. Then I had to put on my brakes again almost immediately—we'd reached the House of

Pancakes. Sylvie was certainly getting a fine taste of my driving. I found a space near the back and switched off the engine.

"What's the matter?" Sylvie asked.

"I need to call Sarah. She works in the college library, and she might be able to find out something about your father and Frank. I'll ask her to check some newspaper indexes, find some contemporary articles, stuff about the money missing from the assessor's office, that sort of thing. Once we've got our ducks in a row, we can tackle our mothers."

"But Bil . . ."

"You know it's the only way. My mother's going to try seven ways to Sunday to get Sam out of this, and she works on pure instinct, not logic. Properly identifying the body won't clear him at this point. No matter who that man was, he shared a cell with my brother. If the real Burt Wood is buried out next to your mother's barn, then that's where he's got to stay." I hadn't spent the past few years keeping my mother's lunacy in check for nothing, and one thing was clear to me—she couldn't help Sam by sending Kate and herself to jail.

Sylvie was stirring uncomfortably in the passenger seat. "Maybe we should hire somebody, a private investigator."

"At three hundred dollars a day, plus expenses?" I objected. "Besides, do you know one?"

"There are a couple up in Spokane."

"They'd stick out like sore thumbs the minute they came down here and started asking questions. The only way we can avoid making this worse is if we do the footwork ourselves. It's natural for you to want to know about your father and for me to try to help Sam. We'll start with Sarah, who won't ask questions because she's not nosy, and we'll go on from there."

We got out of the truck and began walking across the parking lot. Sylvie paused and turned to face me.

"I don't know if we can save them, Bil. Maybe it's too late."

"We'll find a way," I said firmly and with more confidence than I actually felt. "You'll see."

I was due at the Stop the Prop booth by noon. Sylvie and I finished breakfast at eight-thirty, and I dropped her off at the park to pick up her motorcycle. We arranged to meet backstage after the show. The second night of the Pioneer Days festival always featured a cast party and a fireworks display. While it wasn't exactly a date, it would be my first public outing after my public outing. Suzy was right—the sooner I got into being out, proud, and free, the better. A gratuitous observation on his part, since there was nothing I could do about it. Damn all of them, anyway. I'd go with Sylvie to the cast party, and I'd smile at my grandmother like I was the Cheshire cat.

But first, I needed to beard the lion in her den. Buoyed by a stack of pancakes, I plucked up my courage and drove home.

My father was sitting in Archie Bunker, watching the news. I flung myself down into Edith.

"Hi, Hugh."

He smiled. "Hi, Bil. What are you up to today?"

"Nothing. How about you?" He seemed perfectly normal, and I wondered if maybe Emma hadn't told him yet.

"Nothing at all," he said. "I should be grading some papers, but I'm watching the idiot box."

Hugh is not much of a conversationalist. Bad jokes, the weather, and observations about current events, either sporting or political, make up the bulk of his social interactions. I had no idea how or where to begin.

"So," I said tentatively, "where's Emma?"

"In town. She left about forty-five minutes ago."

"Trouble with Sam?"

"Probably."

I nodded, and he turned back to the news. Don't be such a wuss, I told myself. Do it.

"Has Granny called?"

"I don't know, I try not to answer the phone. It's never for me."

And besides, I thought, talking to you on the phone is like pulling teeth. Hell, talking to you in person is like pulling teeth. My father's attention was fixed on the television, and for a long moment, I considered just letting it all go. If Emma hadn't told him yet, why should I? Why not have a few more hours of closeted comfort?

"I believe I'll make a pot of coffee," Hugh said, sitting forward in his recliner. "Would you like a cup?"

"No, Dad. I drank half a carafe at the House of Pancakes, and I'm beginning to have heart palpitations. Look, do you have a minute? There's something I want to talk to you about."

He sat back down, and I cleared my throat. "Dad, I'm . . . a . . . I'm not quite sure how to begin."

"Why don't you begin at the beginning," he suggested.

Oh great, a mindless platitude. I'd tell him I was a lesbian, and he'd probably say a bird in the hand was worth two in the bush.

"Bil." He reached over and patted me on the arm. "I think I know what you're going to say, and you don't need to be shy. I don't mind."

"You don't mind?"

"Of course not. It's easy to get in over your head. You've always been self-reliant, and I admire that in you, but I'm your dad. I'd like to help you. In fact, it would be my pleasure. How much do you need?"

He looked so earnest it made me want to laugh. "I think we've gotten our wires crossed, Hugh. What do you think I'm talking about?"

"Your truck," he replied. "You don't need to be embarrassed. The repair bill was nearly four hundred dollars. Consider that money I lent you a gift. You don't need to pay me back."

"Thanks," I said at last. "I appreciate that. The insurance is due in two weeks, and I was wondering how to cover it." He smiled happily and moved to get up. I put a restraining hand on his arm. "But there's one more thing. I want to tell you myself before you hear it from someone else, someone like Granny." Or Emma, I added silently. "Dad, I'm gay."

He looked puzzled. "You're gay?"

"I've known for a long time—years—but Granny found out last night. Someone let it slip. He didn't mean to, it just happened. I've been meaning to tell you. This thing last night has sort of forced my hand."

"Right. I can see how that would change things." He was staring blankly at the wall behind me. "Does your mother know?"

"I don't know. I haven't told her, but if she's spoken to Granny, then she knows."

"Well, you'd think she'd have mentioned it to me," he said angrily.

I cringed and took my hand off his arm. I'd always thought of my father as open-minded. I felt profoundly disappointed, embarrassed, and beneath it all, scared. I hadn't expected this from him—his creed had always been live and let live.

"I'm sorry." I spoke quietly, carefully masking any emotion. "I know this is a shock, but like I said, I didn't have much time to prepare my speech. In time, I hope you'll see that this is just who I am. In the meantime, maybe I should move out."

He stopped frowning at the wall and gazed at me fixedly. "Now who's got her wires crossed? What on earth are you talking about?"

"Look, if you're not comfortable with me being a lesbian . . ."

He looked at me curiously. "What's the matter with you, Bil? I've known lesbians before. My Aunt Jesse was a lesbian. Of course, they didn't call it that back then. She was a bull's dagger, worked all of her life as a logger in Oregon, dressed like a man."

"Dad, that's not . . ." I began, but then I realized he was right. My infamous great-aunt was a lesbian. She spent her entire life with a big honking dyke named Irene. "Dad, it's bulldagger. There's no possessive on the bull part. The point is, do you want me to move out? I'm sure I can stay with Tipper until I find something more permanent."

"Why would I want you to do that? Surely you don't think . . . Bil, your mother and I have wondered about you for ages. We talked about it only last week, when that friend of yours, A. J., was calling all the time. She said you'd left her house early on Monday morning and that she was worried about you. Your mother wasn't sure but I told her, look, no one Bil's age has slumber parties. She was all for asking you flat out. I told her to mind her own business. I said that when you were ready for us to know, you'd tell us."

I sat back in Edith Bunker, dumbfounded. "But Dad, what was all that about thinking Mom might have mentioned it to you? I thought you were furious—furious at me."

He rolled his eyes and sighed heavily. "Your mother's a fine woman, Bil, and a wonderful parent, but sometimes she thinks she's the only one who needs to know anything. She keeps things from me, doesn't tell me things she thinks will upset me. I appreciate that she's trying to spare my feelings, but I don't need protecting, and no one needs to be protected from me. I don't have a bad temper, and I'm not a moron. Sometimes, I'd like to deal with you kids without the benefit of a mediator."

He'd given me nearly as much to chew on as I'd given him. "So, you're not mad at me?"

"For being a lesbian? Of course not. It wouldn't make sense, would it? I might as well be angry that it rains so many days, snows so many others, and that the sun shines all the rest. It's a fact of nature. What's the estimate, ten percent of the population? That seems about right to me. Your mother opened my eyes to that."

"My mother opened your eyes?" I was afraid to ask, and yet I couldn't let it go.

"Of course. Who do you think she met in all those consciousness-raising groups? Lesbians galore."

"Dad," I laughed, "you're amazing."

"Hmmph," he snorted, clearly embarrassed. "No such thing. Now, how about that coffee?"

"Why not?" After all, it was a Pacific Northwest tradition. Coffee is to us what tea is to the British, the universal panacea.

I used the phone in my bedroom to call Sarah. She wasn't at home, so I tried her at work. She answered on the seventh ring.

"Hi, Sarah," I said.

"Go away, Bil," she replied.

"Why so hostile?"

"Because I'm busier than a two-peckered owl in a hen house."

"On a Sunday?"

She sighed. "Yes, on a Sunday. I was supposed to be off this weekend, but half the reference department is out with the flu, the computer system has gone down, and we're having to check out books on little slips of paper. I've just been made the network coordinator, so it's my job to coordinate getting the system back up."

"Do you have time to do me a favor?"

"You're a pest," she laughed. "All right, what is it?" When I'd told her what I wanted, she said, "I see you've chosen to ignore my advice about not getting dragged into Sam's messes. When will you learn? There's nothing you can do, Bil. If they find a match, they find a match."

"I know, but . . ."

"But you can't help yourself. Very well. I'll take a look through the index for the *Cowslip Herald-Examiner*."

"What about the national newspapers?"

"They were small-town gossip, Bil, not nationwide news."

"Just asking. When do you think you'll have time to look?"

"Would you like a fat lip? I'll get to it. Any more questions?"

I thought for a moment. "Did you get a raise when they made you network coordinator?"

"Yeah," she laughed. "I can take two extra pencils a month from the supply cabinet."

I lounged around in the living room for another fifteen minutes, waiting for Emma to come home. The lack of sleep was catching up with me, but I had an idea. I wanted to get a closer look at Kate Wood's farm, and I wasn't due at the booth for another hour and a half. I stood up and stretched. If I were late, then Suzy could cover for me; he owed me that much.

"Dad," I said, "I've got to go. If you see Emma before I do, and she doesn't know already, go ahead and tell her."

He looked up and smiled broadly. "Really?"

"Really. Tell her we had a long talk, and that I asked you to tell her."

"Are you sure you want to do that?"

"Positive. You'd be doing me a favor, and besides . . ."

"You think it would be funny?" I nodded. He laughed. "I'll do it."

On my way out, I swiped my father's binoculars and changed from loafers to boots. I couldn't find my hiking boots, so I had to wear my new Dr. Martens. The drive to Tipper's gave me time to think. I would cross the top of the ridge, drop down on the other side, and look around without the dogs bothering me. I supposed I could just drive up to the house and say I was looking for Sylvie, but I didn't feel ready to face Kate.

Fort Sister's gate was open, and I drove straight up to the front door. Captain Schwartz was practicing with the black powder rifle. In my opinion, the highlight of Pioneer Days—if you could call it a highlight—was the black powder turkey shoot. The contestants shot at targets and won frozen turkeys, sacks of potatoes, and certificates for free tire rotations. The competition was fierce, and the Captain had never left empty-handed.

She had on her hearing protection, so I waved and pointed in the direction of the dugouts. She nodded and smiled. I could imagine what she was thinking—I'd arrived to clear up the assorted detritus of my wild night. I walked on quickly.

It was certainly easier to climb the ridge in broad daylight. The path was well worn, both by the residents of Fort Sister and by deer, moose, and, judging from the tracks, a couple of elk. I passed over the summit and sat down once again on the foundation of the ruined house. I could just make out the roof of the barn and a little of the yard beyond. I looked through the binoculars. A white dog danced in and out of view, barking occasionally. That would be Priscilla. I didn't see Elvis, nor could I see anything else.

It was no good. I had to move closer. I edged my way down the hill-side with some difficulty on the narrow and overgrown path. About halfway down, my feet began to hurt and I wished I'd stuck to my loafers. As I paused to loosen the laces, I realized that I was in some sort of microclimate. The temperature was several degrees colder on this side of the ridge. I made my way down until I could see the barn again, stopping at the edge of the trees. I was about a hundred yards away, and now I had a clear view of the house. I sat down on a stump and looked through the binoculars.

Someone was standing at the kitchen window, looking down. I could see the top of a blond head. I thought it was Kate, though I couldn't be sure.

"Come on," I said, "look up."

The barking, which had become infrequent, now resumed with fresh intensity. I put the binoculars down. Priscilla had heard, seen, or sniffed me, and she wasn't happy about it. Fortunately, she was on a cable tied somewhere around the front of the barn, and though she strained against it, she didn't get very far. I trained the binoculars on the kitchen window again.

It was definitely Kate. She'd looked up and was tapping on the window, mouthing something. Probably telling the dog to shut up. She looked up the hillside, directly at me, and I froze. I was sitting beneath a large fir tree, and though I was fairly certain she couldn't see me, any movement might give me away. My mother could look up the hillside behind our house and spot a deer in the distance, just by the flash of its tail. Eventually, Kate looked away. Then, she disappeared.

I followed the edge of the trees around to the side of the house, keeping my same distance. Now that she'd spotted me, the dog was going to bark no matter what. No wonder Sylvie couldn't have her in town. Priscilla never shut up.

I made my way over until I was facing the back door; only the screen door was closed. Fortunately, it was an old wooden one, with screens on both the top and bottom. I could see two women sitting at the kitchen table. One of them was Kate. The other woman had her back to the door. I edged closer, leaving the cover of the trees just long enough to run to a large bush at the side of the barn about ten feet away. Kate was talking, and her companion was nodding, a cloud of smoke swirling up around her head.

Hugh's binoculars were a birthday present from me, and I began to wish I'd been a little more generous. Though I couldn't get a good look at the companion, I did notice a familiar-looking purse at her feet. My mother was sitting in Kate Wood's kitchen, smoking like a chimney.

I pushed down a couple of branches and focused my binoculars. I'd just made out the back of Emma's head when my field of vision was blocked by something large and black. A massive dog stood at the screen door staring out in my direction. Elvis. When Sylvie and I had sat up at the ruined house the night before, she'd said he was a Lab cross, and I'd pictured something fat and lazy. This dog looked like a cross between a wolf and the hound of the Baskervilles. He stood very still, silently waiting. Priscilla stopped barking and wagged her tail furiously. Kate stood up, and I ducked back behind the bush, dreading what I was sure would happen next. She'd let that monster out, and he'd make straight for me.

I had two choices. One, I could sit still and hope for the best. Perhaps if I seemed submissive, he wouldn't tear my throat out. My other option was to run like hell up the hillside and take my chances that they would see me. Even if they did, I reasoned, one blurred ass in jeans looks much like another. I had just settled on option two when I heard the crunch of tires on gravel. Someone else had arrived. Kate took Elvis by the collar and led him out the back door. She freed Priscilla, who ignored Kate's calls and made her way straight up to my hiding place. Kate turned her attention back to Elvis and hooked him onto the cable. My mother got up and looked out the screen door.

Priscilla had reached me now, effectively blocking my view. She was dancing happily, her tail curling over her back. She sniffed at my face and hands, then gave me a tentative lick. Kate called her again. Her voice sounded surprisingly close. Priscilla looked down the hillside and then back at me, her head cocked to one side.

"Go away," I said in a low voice. "Go on."

She seemed to be smiling at me, if a dog can smile, but she backed up.

"Priscilla! Get down here! Heel!" I guessed Kate was halfway up the hillside. "Don't make me come after you, Prissy."

"Piss off," I said, frowning at the dog. "Grrrr."

Priscilla gave me one final sniff and bounded off. I whispered a prayer to the god of narrow escapes. It was interrupted by a cry and the sound of someone falling down the hillside. I looked out from behind the bush. Priscilla had spotted the new arrival, and in her haste to cover him with sloppy dog kisses, she'd knocked Kate over.

I froze. The new arrival was Fairfax Merwin. Emma stood in the doorway, smoking a cigarette and watching him walk up the driveway. Neither of them was paying any attention to Kate, who was rocking back and forth, holding her ankle.

I made a snap decision. I dropped the binoculars behind the bush, brushed myself off, and stepped out into the open.

"Here, Kate," I said. "Let me help you."

Chapter 14

The ankle was twisted, not broken. As soon as I'd gotten Kate down the hillside, my mother got her to move it from side to side while she felt the bones beneath the swelling. I thought she should have an X-ray, but I was overruled. When we were inside and Kate was sitting at the kitchen table, her ankle propped up on a chair and packed with ice, my mother went on the offensive.

"Let's see," she said, "I believe I last saw you on Friday afternoon. You're my daughter, Bil, aren't you? The tall black-haired one between Sarah and Sam."

"Don't start with me, Emma," I replied. "I was at Tipper's on Friday night, and I gave someone a ride home from the festival yesterday."

"A twenty-four-hour drive? She must live in Anaheim."

"How do you know it's a she? Been talking to Granny?"

Fairfax sat bolt upright in his chair. My mother looked puzzled. "I expect your grandmother's not speaking to me. I missed yesterday's performance."

"You certainly did," Fairfax observed, casting a sly glance in my direction.

Fortunately, Emma changed the subject. "Never mind that now. You swooped down that hillside like the wrath of God. What are you doing here?"

I might ask you the same thing, I thought.

"I went for a hike. Fort Sister is on the other side of the ridge, you know. There's a ruined house at the top. I sat up there for a while and then decided to walk down this way." I stopped myself from going on. Too much explanation would be worse than none at all.

"Hmm," Emma said. She sat back in her chair and toyed with a pack of cigarettes, shaking one out and then tapping it back in. When she noticed me staring at her, she offered one to Kate, and they both lit up.

Fairfax waved a hand in front of his face, feigning asphyxiation.

"I came," he said, "on my way to the festival. To see how you were doing."

Kate inhaled deeply and blew out a thick column of smoke into his face. He sputtered, and Emma smiled.

"This house," said Kate, "isn't on the way to the park."

"It's not out of the way," he replied, making an obvious effort to keep the smile plastered on his face. "I thought it would be better to visit than to call. The telephone is so impersonal."

"That still doesn't explain why you're here," Kate said.

Though I didn't particularly like Fairfax, I was surprised by the hostility in her voice. Fairfax was a show-off and a phony who thought a good deal too much of himself. He was the manager of Pioneers Bank, the first and still the largest bank in Cowslip, and he'd helped to engineer its expansion from a local operation into a regional one. It was still small potatoes, but to hear him tell it, you'd think he was Donald Trump.

He said calmly, "Agnes and I have been worried about you, Kate. I know this is a difficult time for you and . . ."

"No, it isn't. I had a difficult time before Burt left, not after. You know that."

"I knew Burt," he agreed. "I knew him quite well."

Emma leaned forward and stared at him, resting her elbows on the table. "I didn't know that. I knew you were close to Frank, but not Burt. Isn't that so, Kate?"

"Could be," she shrugged. "I wasn't privy to most of Burt's social interactions."

Kate looked tired. Her hair was pulled back into a ponytail, which accentuated the tiny wrinkles at the corners of her eyes. She turned to me and smiled. "My ankle is throbbing, Bil, would you mind getting me a couple of Tylenol out of the bathroom cabinet? Upstairs, second door on your right. They're in the medicine cabinet."

I left the room reluctantly, feeling as if I were six years old again. I considered pausing outside the door and eavesdropping, but that trick hadn't worked when I was six, and it wouldn't work now. They'd expect to hear my footsteps on the stairs.

I found the Tylenol in short order and headed back down the stairs. I handed the pills to Kate and sat back down.

Emma said, "How about a glass of water? She can't swallow them dry."

"The glasses are in the cupboard next to the sink, Bil," Kate smiled. "Thanks, by the way."

"You're welcome."

The kitchen window looked out at the barn door, which was closed, Elvis lying in front of it like a sphinx. To the left was the line of syringas Sylvie had described. If she were right, Burt's body was somewhere beneath the one nearest the barn. Suppressing a shudder, I filled the water glass and returned to the table.

Emma sat with her back to the door, just like before. I looked past her, through the screen door to the bush where I'd been sitting. I was sure now that I hadn't been visible, at least not to anyone sitting in the kitchen. As I watched, something suddenly moved. A shadow shifted to one side and then quickly moved back. Someone was up there watching us now, just as I'd done earlier.

Fairfax pushed his chair back and stood up.

"Well, I must be going," he said. "I have a lot of preparations to make before this evening's performance. Will you all be in attendance?"

"I expect so," my mother said. "How about you, Kate?"

"I'll hobble in. Sylvie has a line in it, and I'd like to see her. She begged me not to come, but perhaps I'll be able to hide somewhere on the back row."

"I'm sure you'll be there," he said.

I was concentrating on the figure on the hillside, so it was a moment or two before I realized he was talking to me.

"Sorry?"

"I'll see you tonight." He gave me a wry, knowing smile. "I don't suppose you'll want to miss the performance."

"I'll be there," I said shortly.

"Well, I'm off." He smoothed the hair over his bald spot. "If you need anything, Kate, I hope you'll call us. Agnes has been very upset by all of this."

"I'm sure she has," Kate replied calmly. "She knows my number. Tell her to call me if it gets to be too much."

Fairfax was tall, and for a moment, his figure in the doorway blotted out my view of the hillside. I stared long and hard at the spot after he left, but it was no use. The shadow was gone.

"Cheesy bastard," my mother said. "Offering his condolences. Nosing around, more like."

"Oh, I expected that. It'll all die down soon enough."

"We'll see." Emma shook out a cigarette and tapped the filter on the table. She turned to me. "So Bil, can I give you a lift to Fort Sister, or would you prefer to hike back over the hill?"

I wanted to retrieve my father's binoculars and look for signs of the spy who'd assumed my place behind the bushes. I also wanted a chance to talk to Emma alone. Sylvie could pick up the binoculars later. There was no chance that Kate would venture up the hill again in the next couple of days.

"I'll ride," I said. "I'm about hiked out."

"Fine. Can I get you anything before we leave, Kate? Maybe you'd prefer to be in the living room."

Kate shook her head. "I'll be fine. You could bring me the cordless telephone, though. I think I'll give Sylvie a call."

"Won't she be at the festival getting ready?" I asked.

"Oh, I shouldn't think so, she's only got the one line."

"If you need a ride, give me a call," Emma said. "After I drop Bil off, I'm heading straight home. Hugh will be getting restless."

"Hugh will be sound asleep."

"Mind your own business, Bil." Then to Kate, "I'll call you."

Kate was lighting up another cigarette when we left. I followed my mother around the front of the house to the car.

"So," I said, determined to beat my mother to the punch, "what are you doing here?"

"Acting as your chauffeur," she replied. She turned the key, and after a long minute of grinding, the car roared to life.

"Don't be facetious. You haven't been out here in years. What gives?"

She said nothing until we were at the end of the driveway, which was even longer than the drive at Fort Sister. The house itself was completely hidden from the road, and the end of the driveway was poorly marked by a couple of pole reflectors stuck into the ground on either side. It would be easy to miss in the dark, unless you knew what you were looking for.

"What do you think gives?" she asked, pulling out into the highway and accelerating rapidly. "Considering Sam's involvement, I thought the courteous thing to do was to pay her a visit."

"Bullshit. Why didn't you call her then?"

"Who says I didn't?"

"So you did call her. Did you tell her about Sam or did you wait until the sheriff's department did the dirty work for you?"

Emma tapped her fingers on the steering wheel, her jaw set in a stubborn line. "I'm not answering impertinent questions, not from someone who vanishes for an entire weekend and then turns up with some cockamamie story about sleeping out at Fort Sister and driving strange women home from the park."

"You really are the limit, you know that? I was at Tipper's, and I did drive a strange . . . well actually, she wasn't a strange woman at all, she was a perfectly normal woman. She was Sylvie Wood, in fact. You can't get much more normal than that, can you? After all, you've just been chewing the fat with her mother."

Emma hit the brakes hard, pulling off to the side of the road. She stared at me intently. My mother's eyes are a hard, blue-gray. Sam's the only one of us who has ever been able to resist her when she turns on that cobra-like glare.

"What are you up to?" she asked. "Or should I say what are you and Sylvie up to?"

I met her gaze squarely. "You haven't talked to Granny, have you?"

"I told you, she's not speaking to me. What's she got to do with it anyway?"

I thought about my father, sitting at home, waiting to spring the one piece of news that he'd ever heard first. I also thought about saving my own hide with a quick confession. Coming out to my mother on the way to Fort Sister while steam poured out of her ears was not in my revised master plan.

"I've been doing your dirty work," I said at last, keeping my voice carefully modulated between apology and indignation. "I ran into Sylvie at the festival last night, and we talked about her father. I told her what little Sam knew, and then asked a few questions in turn. I was doing a little private investigating." Now for the hard part. "I don't know any more now than I knew before I talked to her."

Her eyes grew smaller for a fraction of a second. Then, she relaxed. "It's a waste of time trying to help your brother," she said, pulling the car back out onto the highway. "He's certainly not interested in helping himself. He's off with that slut today, living the life of Riley."

"Emma," I said slowly, "what happened with you and Kate? I mean all those years ago. We used to go over to her house quite a lot, and then we stopped. Did you have a fight or something?"

She sighed and shook her head. "No, nothing like that. We just drifted apart. Different lives, different interests. After Burt took off, she withdrew, cloistering herself up at the farm. I've seen her here and there over the past several years, but at some point, we just stopped visiting."

"What puzzles me," I went on, "is how he could have just disappeared. He must have changed his name and started all over again somewhere else. That seems really weird to me. This story that he ran off with Frank so they could go somewhere and be gay together doesn't make any sense. It can't have been that big a deal to be gay in 1978."

"Cowslip in 1978 was no different than Cowslip in 1958. Things change slowly here."

"I'm just surprised that the cops didn't try to find them. They might not have been all that interested in Burt, but Frank stole a fat wad of money from the county."

"That money reappeared in the county coffer. Frank's father put it back."

"Do you know that for a fact?"

"It's common knowledge." She tapped her fingers on the steering wheel again. "Frank was a petty criminal, a small-time thief, and one of the local pot suppliers. I don't think he dealt in hard drugs, he wasn't the type. Still, most people were glad to see him go, particularly his father."

She pulled into the Captain's driveway and stopped at the gate, which was still open.

"You're not going to drive me up to the house?"

"I think not," she replied. "You know I don't approve of guns. Schwartz is bound to be up there, practicing her John Wayne act for the turkey shoot."

I grinned at her. "Maybe I'll enter this year. I'm a crack shot—toss a beer can in the air, and I can plug it three times before it hits the ground."

"How charming. Please let me know when you can rope and spit."

I blew her a kiss and opened the car door.

"Oh, Bil?"

"Yes?"

"Don't think you've gotten away with it. You were no more hiking in those brand-spanking new Dr. Martens of yours than I was in Kate's kitchen flying a kite. Sooner or later, you'll tell me what you were doing up there on that hillside, spying down on us."

Why do I bother to lie to my mother?

Chapter 15

Tipper was working the booth when I arrived. He said that Suzy had indeed covered for me and that no one had particularly minded.

"I wondered if you'd make it," he said, one eyebrow raised in accusation. "You and Sylvie left my place pretty late."

"How do you know, did you wait up?"

"I have a life of my own," he sniffed. "You're not the only one who can find alternative uses for the dugouts."

"I'm glad I didn't see you. I might never have gotten over the shock."

"I'm sure you'd have survived. Besides, we were just admiring the stars. I do my trysting indoors on the Sealy Posturepedic, not out in the open air."

"Uh-huh. And just who is *we*? One of the Faeries?"

He looked off in the opposite direction. "It's turning cold, isn't it? I do believe we're in for an early winter."

"Fine. Shall I guess? My own personal pick would be . . ."

"Hush," he said quickly. "That's information you'll have to earn. First, you sit down and tell me all about your *nuit d'amour* with Sylvie Wood."

He was sorry to hear that there was nothing to tell, or at least nothing I was willing to tell. After much prodding, I did confess to more than a passing interest in her.

"Well then, we really must give you a makeover," he observed, casting a disapproving eye over me.

I examined my T-shirt. It was a bit ragged, but the picture of Mr. Bubble on the front was still bright. "What are you talking about, a new wardrobe and a trip to the Clinique counter?"

"No makeup for you, sweetie. You'd look about as convincing as Suzy."

I was hurt. "That's how I'd look in makeup?"

Tipper grabbed my chin and examined me mercilessly. "Yes," he replied. "And don't fall to pieces. All I mean is that you're handsome, not pretty. What you need is sprucing up. Honey, you've got to lose Mr. Bubble and get yourself a suit and tie."

I rolled my eyes heavenward. "Good lord. I can't wear that kind of stuff in Cowslip. It's terminally casual out here. Besides, isn't that, well . . ." I struggled to find the right word.

He flapped the edge of his pleated kilt at me. "Advertising? Flaunting it? You bet. Listen to me, Bil, have I ever steered you wrong? You've got to quit schlepping around in raggedy-ass jeans and disreputable T-shirts. Tomorrow, you and I are going shopping."

"Hold on a minute, Professor Higgins. How do you know Sylvie's going to go for the suit and tie?"

"I have an unerring dyke instinct, honed through years of studying my mother and her tribe. I have a doctorate in lesbian anthropology. You could use a haircut, too," he observed. "Your short back and sides has gotten a bit shaggy."

"Do you mind?" I freed my chin from his grasp.

"So," he continued, "what was the outing fallout? You seem to have come through it unscathed."

I related the complete story of my conversation with Hugh.

"So, that's one parent down and one to go. Do you really think he'll tell your mother, or will he wait for you to do it?"

I shrugged. "At this point, I don't care. If he tells her, fine. If my grandmother tells her, that's fine, too. To tell you the truth, I was more worried about telling Hugh. My mother is melodramatic, but she's all thunder and smoke. I didn't know how my father would react. I didn't think he'd suddenly embrace the Old Testament, but I did think he might be a little shocked."

"You sound disappointed."

"What will I do for a coming-out story? Where's the drama? People say, 'I told my dad, and he threw me out of the house,' or, 'I told my mother, and she fell over dead.' Well, I told my dad, and he made me a cup of coffee."

"It'll never play in Peoria," he agreed, "but I still say lucky old you. Would that everyone's father was such a gem."

"I don't mean to complain."

He smiled. "Don't worry about it. I can't talk, can I? My mother is the Great Dyke Hope, and I never had to come out because I was never in. Suzy, on the other hand, has been reliving the torments of Exodus ever since he came here. I'm afraid the Reverend Jones strikes a little too close to home."

"You know what they say about the preacher's kid."

"Do I ever. Suzy is wild, wild, wild."

"How did you meet him?"

"At the March on Washington last year. We had a kiss-in on the Capitol steps . . ."

In some amazement, I said, "Your dugout date wasn't Suzy, was it?"

"Close your mouth," he replied, "I can see your molars." I gave him a friendly shove, knocking him off balance. "All right, all right. No, it wasn't Suzy."

"You'll have to do better than that. Was it by any chance Tom?" The tops of his ears turned crimson, so I knew I'd hit the mark. "I heartily approve. I'll never kiss anyone with a big bushy mustache, so you'll have to tell me what it's like."

"Don't be cheeky," he said, pinching my thigh. "It's bad for your health."

The booth did a steady business up until show time. We sold three hundred dollars' worth of bumper stickers and T-shirts, and only a few people looked at us askance. The Reverend Jones walked by once, and Tipper and I smiled at him sweetly. He didn't stop. The Captain arrived at five o'clock sharp, toting a twenty-five-pound turkey she'd won at the black powder competition.

"First prize?" Tipper asked.

"Grand prize," she replied. "Cedar Tree is loading the potatoes into the truck."

"How many this year?"

"Four boxes, a hundred pounds."

"Christ, we'll be eating spuds thrice daily till Christmas."

"And counting yourself lucky," the Captain said. "First prize was five bushels of wheat and a certificate to get your tires rotated. I'll just stick this bird in the ice-chest here, and you and Bil can head off to the show. You don't want to miss it."

The town had turned out in force for the final night of *Cowslip Back Then*. Tipper and I could scarcely find space on a hay bale. I spied my mother and Kate sitting together down front.

"Emma's trying to make up for last night," I whispered to Tipper. "Granny's not speaking to her because she skipped Saturday's performance. Mark my words, my mother will be clapping and whistling like she's never seen the damn thing before."

"The things we do to keep on Mama's good side," he said.

Emma and I were the only representatives of the Hardy family in attendance. My mother could never coax, bully, or cajole Hugh to get up out of Archie Bunker and attend, and my sisters and Sam always contrived to have some pressing engagement—reference hours, a client, emergency surgery, or an imminent arrest. When Granny died, I'd better inherit everything.

Kate looked a bit pale, but otherwise, she seemed to have recovered from her fall. She and my mother were chatting amiably, and I wished I could read lips. Sitting side by side, the contrast between them was striking. Emma was a little over five feet tall, sturdy and compact. In fact, she was built exactly like my father, only with breasts. Kate was tall, like her daughter, with well-developed arms and legs. I suspected she ran or worked out. She seemed to be in good shape, even if she did smoke like a diesel truck.

The play began, and Sylvie delivered her line beautifully. After she left the stage, I closed my eyes and leaned against Tipper. My two hikes up over the ridge were beginning to catch up with me. When I opened my eyes again, the curtain had dropped and the audience was clapping wildly. My mother was in the lead, hooting and whistling like a sailor.

Family members and local dignitaries were invited to the cast party, so after the third curtain call, we got up and headed backstage with the other royalty.

Part of the stage was set up to look like a frontier store. I found

Sylvie in front of the counter, sitting on a pickle barrel. I walked over and took her hand, shaking it vigorously.

"You were terrific! Top notch. Broke a leg."

She laughed. "Call the Academy and tell them to hold the Oscar. I'll pick it up after the party."

The room behind the stage was hot, crowded, and noisy. Someone had brought a tape player, which was blaring selections from Gilbert and Sullivan through its tinny speakers. Along one wall was a buffet. Trays of hors d'oeuvres filled one end of the table, and bottles of gin, vodka, Scotch, and mixers sat at the other. Fred Maguire was acting as bartender, dipping ice out of a cooler with his bare hands. Behind him, in a far corner, Emma was deep in conversation with Helen Merwin. Granny had her back to both of them, and she was talking to Millicent and a couple of their blue-rinse buddies.

I asked Sylvie and Tipper what they wanted to drink.

"Gin and tonic," Tipper replied. "A slice of lime if they have it, lemon if they don't."

"I expect you'll get neither. How about you, Sylvie?"

"I'll have the same," she said, "and would you bring me an egg salad sandwich and one of those little quiches? Oh, and some chips and salsa. I'm starving!"

I smiled and bowed. Then I made my way to Fred, who beamed at me happily, his makeup rolling off in large beads of sweat down his forehead. "Ms. Bil Hardy, what can I get for you?"

"Two gin and tonics and a plain orange juice," I said. As he got the drinks, I thought I ought to add something about his performance, which was over-the-top, as usual. "You were very convincing."

He smiled and poured an extra jigger of gin into each of the glasses. "Thank you, thank you very much. Your grandmother is a pleasure to work with."

"I'm sure," I replied laconically.

"Tisk, tisk," he said. "You don't give her enough credit." He leaned in close and whispered in a husky voice, "Have you spoken to her yet? I mean, I'm sure you heard about last night."

I pulled back defensively. He reached out a pudgy hand and pulled me back. "Don't worry, you're among family."

Oh great, Uncle Fred. He went on quickly, "Your grandmother is all talk with this Proposition One thing. There's nothing she loves better than old theater queens—I'm living proof. If you hadn't come out, I might have had to."

"You?" Though it was common knowledge that Fred Maguire was gay as a goose, I could scarcely believe my ears.

He must have been reading my mind because he said, "Oh, don't get me wrong, my closet's wide, airy, and comfortable, but this Proposition One business is just too much. I'm sure your grandmother will drop it now, and without her grandstanding, it'll sink like a rock in this town."

"I think you overestimate the power of my grandmother," I said. And you underestimate her homophobia, I added silently.

"I don't think so," he said. "I've lived here all my life, and I remember when your grandfather brought Wilhelmina back here. It was just after World War Two. She hit this town like a tornado. Ruffled up the old girl," he jerked his thumb in the direction of Millicent, "but she's handled that smoothly enough. Idaho women are no match for these southern Jezebel types."

Somehow, I'd never pictured my grandmother as Jezebel. She was more like Aunt Pitty-Pat. I was about to tell him so when Agnes Merwin spoke up behind me.

"Hello, Bil," she said. Agnes made me nervous at the best of times, and I now found myself receiving the full smoky voice and sultry eyes treatment. I was sure it meant nothing. Agnes was the sort of woman who flirted with the world. "A double Scotch, Freddy, on the rocks."

"Coming right up."

The eyelids lowered a fraction of an inch further. "So, Bil, what have you been up to? Just moved back here, when was it?"

"End of May, and I've been up to nothing in particular, just going to school. How about you?"

"I'm bored," she said, taking a sip of her Scotch.

"I'm sure. I think maybe my grandmother should write a new play."

Agnes laughed, a low, fruity sound. "She should, but my boredom is a bit more global in scope." She leaned close and whispered into my ear, "You, on the other hand, seem to have lots of excitement on your hands."

I stepped back involuntarily. “I can handle it.”

She laid her hand on my arm. “There now, it’s all right. I’m sympathetic to your cause.”

Was I going to have to discuss my sexual orientation with the entire cast? “Thanks,” I said quickly. “I’ve got to go.”

She laughed. “Of course. Don’t keep Sylvie waiting.”

It was clear from her tone that while Kate might not know about Sylvie, Agnes certainly did. The resemblance between the sisters, between Sylvie and Helen, and all of them to one another was beginning to disturb me. There were distinct differences—Agnes was smooth and sleek, while Kate was more rough and ready—and yet having them all in the same room together was like watching a cloning experiment gone awry. I realized with a shock that I just wasn’t used to families that looked alike. In an adoptive family, the resemblances are all nurtured.

I made my way back to Tipper and Sylvie.

“I need to drop these off before I can get your food,” I said, handing them their drinks.

Sylvie grimaced. “I’m sorry, Bil. You don’t have to wait on me. I can get my own food.”

“Nonsense,” I replied. “It’s no trouble at all.”

Tipper smiled approvingly, and I felt the blush rising in my cheeks. “Here,” I thrust my orange juice at him, “hold this for me.”

I beat a hasty retreat and collected Sylvie’s food. When I got back, Kate and Fairfax had joined our party.

“Yes,” Fairfax said, “definitely a good crowd. I’m certainly pleased to see the mayor in attendance.”

“I’m sure you are,” Kate replied, nodding towards the mayor. “I’m surprised you’re not over there talking to her. You don’t usually pass up that kind of chance.”

“Here’s your food,” I whispered to Sylvie. “Have I missed anything?”

“Listen and learn,” she whispered back.

“She seems to be busy with Millicent,” Fairfax observed. “She certainly knows how to work a room. Good politician.”

“You used to be,” Kate replied. “I’m surprised you’re not mayor yourself. Politics used to interest you quite a bit, as I recall.”

“That was a long time ago. Longer than I care to remember.”

Kate laughed harshly. "Funny, I thought your memory stretched back to infinity."

I tugged at Sylvie's sleeve, and she whispered, "They hate each other. I don't know why."

"Your uncle's an ass?" I suggested.

"It's more than that. It's . . ."

"Really," Fairfax was saying, "I don't think this is the place."

Kate sighed and looked down at the cup in her hand, idly swirling the contents around. I took a deep sip of my orange juice. "So," she said, looking up at him suddenly, "have the police questioned you yet?"

I choked on my juice. Fairfax looked startled, though he didn't seem nearly as surprised as Sylvie looked and I felt. The orange juice made its way up my nose and into my sinuses. I sputtered, and Tipper began slapping me on the back. I recovered sufficiently to stand up. Sylvie was watching Fairfax intently.

"*Have* they questioned you?" Sylvie asked.

Fairfax looked at her. Kate was no longer paying attention. She was staring at something over his shoulder, as if she were uninterested in his answer. He stammered a bit before he said, "Why should they?"

Kate turned back to him. "Why not? You were saying just this afternoon how well you knew my late husband. I thought maybe he visited you before his arrest."

I glanced over at Tipper to see if he was following all of this. He had his back to us and was whispering excitedly to one of the Lesbian Avengers, whom I hadn't noticed before. Now, as I looked around the room, I saw Lesbian Avengers stationed against all four walls. A. J. was in the corner next to my mother, who was talking to Granny and gesturing wildly.

I tried to get Emma's attention. She was so intent on my grandmother that she didn't see me. A. J., however, winked and mouthed, "Meet me outside." I shook my head no.

I tugged at Sylvie's sleeve. "Something's up," I whispered. "I don't like this."

She nodded absentmindedly. Her attention was still fixed on Fairfax and her mother.

Fairfax put his fist to his lips and cleared his throat. "No," he said, "no, they haven't. That was all such a long time ago . . ."

"It seems like only yesterday," Kate said flatly. "I have a long memory."

Sylvie grasped my hand, lacing her fingers with mine. We all waited in silence for Fairfax to respond, the conversations around us fading to background noise as we concentrated our attention. As he opened his mouth to speak, a horribly familiar shriek came winging through the air.

"For God's sake, of course I know she's a lesbian. She's my daughter!"

As if on cue, the Lesbian Avengers pulled long torches from behind their backs and set them alight.

"The Lesbian Avengers eat fire!" they cried, shoving the torches down their throats.

Next to the drinks table, Granny, Helen, and my mother were posed like three monkeys. Granny was in the middle, leaning backwards with her hands over her eyes. Helen had clapped her hands over her ears, her mouth frozen open in mid-gasp, and my mother stood to one side, gazing in wonder at the Lesbian Avengers. She was shaking from head to toe with laughter.

Tipper was the first to break the silence.

"Now that's what I call theater," he cried, clapping enthusiastically.

Chapter 16

Granny mouthed something that looked suspiciously like "I could just die" and fled the room. Helen made eye contact with her father, and he took his cue to bounce over to her side. He was soon patting her on the back and plying her with drink.

Their torches extinguished, the Lesbian Avengers gathered in the far corner and marched out of the room. I ignored A. J.'s wave, and she left with the others. Kate and Sylvie looked down at their shoes. I prayed for a natural disaster.

Instead, I was swept up by Captain Schwartz.

"Come on, Bil," she said, firmly wrapping her arm around my shoulders. She nodded crisply to Kate and Sylvie. "Excuse us, ladies, we need some fresh air." Before I knew it, we were outside, and Captain Schwartz was lighting up a thin, brown cigar.

She leaned against the back wall of the stage, one booted foot resting against the top of a bicycle rail. When she finished her cigar, she ground it out beneath her heel. She seemed to be waiting for me to speak first, so I said, "Thanks, Captain."

She brushed this off. "It was nothing. Tipper should have helped you, but I'm afraid he was preoccupied by the floor show."

"You don't approve of the Lesbian Avengers?"

"I don't," she replied, shaking her head, "but what do I know? I'm an old Southern lady. Where I come from, you don't crash parties, not even to make political statements. By my reckoning, that will have lost us more friends than it gained."

"Conservative streak a mile wide," said a voice behind her. Tipper stepped out of the shadows, followed closely by Sylvie. "Pay no attention to Rush Limbaugh there, pretending to be a lesbian."

She laughed. "I'm not that bad."

"Near enough as makes no difference." He paused next to the Captain, sniffing the air suspiciously. "Though I hope you haven't been out here puffing on a cheap cheroot, I'll do myself a favor and not ask. You promised you'd give them up."

The Captain shrugged, and Tipper shook his head in disgust. Sylvie came and stood close to me, and I smiled to let her know that I was fine.

"Heard any good jokes lately?" I asked.

"I'm sorry," she said. "If it's any consolation, I don't think you're the Pee Wee Herman of Cowslip."

"I don't know about that," Tipper cut in, "but I do think that three outings in less than twenty-four hours is some sort of record. Do you want to come home with us? You could stay for a few days, give things time to settle down."

"You mean give myself time to settle down."

"That too," he agreed. "Matricide is a crime, whatever the circumstances. Isn't that right, Mama?"

The Captain said very seriously, "You're always welcome at our house, Bil. You're family."

Sylvie had moved close enough almost to touch. The cast party was beginning to break up, and a few people were staggering out of the back door. Helen was one of them. She gave us a brief glance and walked on.

"Thank you," I said, "but I believe I'll go home. I'm sure Emma is sorry." In fact, I was sure she wasn't. I planned to go to work with a sledgehammer until she was. "Besides, I actually have some studying to do. I have classes tomorrow, and considering my track record over the last couple of weeks, I think I should not only attend but try paying attention."

The Captain and Tipper excused themselves discreetly. When they were gone, Sylvie put her hands on my shoulders.

"You'll be all right, won't you?"

"It's not the end of the world. I'll be fine."

She gave me a long, measuring look. "Okay," she said. "I'll be up late tonight studying for a botany test tomorrow. You can call me if you want to."

"Botany," I said musingly.

"Yes, botany."

"And drama."

"Yes, botany and drama. They go together like fish and bicycles."

"I suppose you wanted to keep your options open?"

She laughed. "Why not? I always liked acting and set design, but I never kidded myself about making a living as an actor. I'm naturally pragmatic. I chose botany and graduate school in Cowslip over waiting tables in Los Angeles, waiting for my big break. What about you? What do you do with English and psychology?"

"Analyze your family," I replied, "and then write a book about them. Consider the case of B, small-town lesbian . . ."

"Make it a screenplay," she laughed, "and I'll play you."

"Typical Hollywood casting. Up on the big screen, I suddenly become a beautiful blond."

Her hands had been moving over my shoulders. Now they stopped and grasped my upper arms. I waited for a moment, daring to hope. Then I realized that she was gripping me like a coach grips a player.

"You're beautiful," she said simply.

I wanted to curl up and die. She was so earnest, as if I looked like someone who needed to be bucked up on this point. I remembered Tipper's plan to clean me up and take me out shopping, and I felt queasy. Then she smiled and took that one, critical step closer. People were continuing to come out of the theater. I didn't care. She wrapped her arms around my neck and closed her eyes. I leaned towards her.

"Bil!"

My mother's voice rang out like the shot heard round the world, and Sylvie and I sprang apart as if an electric fence had dropped down between us. "Bil! Can you give me a jump-start? I left my headlights on, and the car's deader than a doornail."

❖❖❖

I watched Sylvie walk off into the darkness and turned to face my mother. She was staring at me as if we were the last two passengers on the *Marie Celeste*.

"Well?" I said at last.

"Well what?"

"Even you cannot possibly be that dense."

"Bil," Emma purred, "I know you're mad, but I was provoked. You know how your grandmother is—she's more than flesh and blood can stand."

"Is that the best you can do?"

"I am sorry," she said, with almost convincing sincerity. Then, as I felt my resolve slipping, she made a fatal mistake. "I can't believe you're holding a grudge."

She could rage like a hurricane now, I'd gotten the furniture up off the floor and my windows were taped shut. "You're not sorry, Emma, you just want off the hook. Well, I'm not going to let you off. And you can wipe that ridiculous pout off your face because I'm not fooled."

This made her pout all the more.

"Where did you park your car?" I sighed.

"Out past Traveler's Rest, hell and gone from here."

The battery was a lost cause. I spent half an hour trying to jump-start it, but the car just made a sick, grinding sound and then conked out.

"She's given up the ghost," I said. "You'll have to ride home with me."

"But . . ."

"But nothing," I interrupted. "No one is going to steal that hunk of shit. You can come back tomorrow with Hugh. He may be able to figure something out."

She hemmed and hawed until I pointed out that I would be more than happy to abandon her at Traveler's Rest. We said very little on the drive home. I didn't particularly feel like talking, and Emma was maintaining an injured silence. One of my mother's worst characteristics is that she's incapable of keeping a feeling all to herself. Through some bizarre reverse empathy, she makes me feel it too. By the time I pulled into the driveway, I almost felt guilty for being annoyed with her.

"Just once," I said, switching off the ignition, "I'd like to have feelings of my own."

"What are you talking about?"

"I'd like to get good and pissed at you and not feel bad about it. You deserve my anger. You deserve to have me hold a grudge."

"And I deserve to be told the truth firsthand," she replied. "Not by your father and certainly not by your grandmother. You could have confided in me at any time, Bil. Have I ever given you any cause to think I wouldn't be happy that you're a lesbian?"

She was out the door before I could answer. I considered arguing with her, trying to explain how I felt. I also considered chasing her down and telling her that she wasn't the fucking pivot point of creation. She stopped about ten feet in front of me to shake a rock out of her shoe, and I had a vision, brief but satisfying, of running her down in the driveway. Too bad I'd switched off the engine.

My sisters' cars were all parked in the driveway. It was an old pattern—they had bagged out of going to the play, and they wanted to stay in Emma's good graces. They were here to bow and scrape until she forgave them. I felt sick.

They were all seated in their accustomed places. Ruth and Sarah were on the sofa, Hugh was in Archie, and Naomi was in Edith. The only surprise was Sam, who came walking in from the kitchen with a glass of milk in his hand.

"What are you doing here?"

"I live here," he replied, puzzled.

"Since when? You've spent the entire week with . . ."

"That slut," Emma interrupted.

Sam glared at her. My sisters were shifting about nervously, and I wondered if Hugh had told them. It didn't seem likely. They were probably just antsy waiting for the Sam and Emma fight to begin. If that happened, my moment would be lost. My mother folded her arms across her chest and opened her mouth.

"Hugh," I said quickly, "would you please turn off the TV? I've got something to say, and I'd like everyone to hear it all at once."

"But I'm watching that!" Sam objected.

"You can watch Bugs Bunny some other time, you selfish little fucker. For now, you can just sit down and shut up."

He sat down. As Emma stepped forward to sit down beside him, I grabbed her firmly by the elbow.

"No, ma'am," I said. "You sit between Ruth and Sarah. This is not going to be the Sam and Emma show, not tonight."

Emma cast a pitiful glance at Hugh, who ignored her, and did as she was told. Ruth and Sarah sat forward on the sofa with visible interest.

I cleared my throat and began speaking. I was surprised to hear my own voice. It was clear and confident, not unlike Captain Schwartz's.

"I want you to hear this from me, and I want you to know that it's something I'm happy to tell you. It's something I'm happy about. I'm a lesbian. I love women. A lot." I wasn't sure how to finish, so I just said, "Thank you," and leaned back against the front door.

I surveyed their faces. Ruth was blinking slowly and thoughtfully, as if she were having trouble processing the information. Sarah was smiling, and when I looked at her, she winked at me. Naomi's mouth was hanging open. I wish I'd had a camera to capture that expression for the family Christmas cards. Sam was clearly puzzled. Lesbian wasn't a part of his daily vocabulary.

My mother sat quietly, looking down at her lap. Hugh, however, was grinning broadly. He stood up, tapped out his ever-present pipe, and then crossed the room and shook my hand.

"Well done," he said warmly, and then in a deeper, quieter voice, "Good for you, Bil."

Then he turned to the rest of the room and said, "Who would like a cup of coffee? I feel like making a fresh pot. How about you, honey?"

I nodded, though the last thing I need was a jolt of caffeine.

"I'd like coffee," Ruth said.

"Me, too," Sarah chimed in.

I crossed the room and sat down in Hugh's chair.

"Jesus Christ, Naomi. Close your mouth, will you?" She closed her mouth.

"So," said Emma, looking up.

"You just watch yourself," I snapped, pointing at her. "I'm not through with you." Really, though, I was through. I wanted to bask in the aftermath of disclosure and savor my new freedom. It felt good.

"Go ahead," I said, gesturing to the room at large. "The rest of you have permission to talk."

Sarah spoke first. "Well, like Dad, I say good for you, Bil. I just have one question—why doesn't Emma get to talk?"

I pointed at Emma and shrugged. "Get her to tell you."

My mother put a hand on her chest and asked primly, "May I speak now?"

"Don't be facetious, Ma. Get over yourself."

"First, let me say that I'm as happy for you, Bil, as your father is—don't make that face at me, I am. Now, as for the rest, Bil is being unjust. We were at the cast party, which none of you bothered to attend, leaving me to cover for you . . ."

Ruth cut her off. "We never go to Granny's cast party, just like we never go to her plays. What does this have to do with Bil coming out?"

"Thank you," I replied. "Nothing. It has nothing to do with my coming out. What happened is that Emma here decided to out me to a room full of people. I think she was trying to kill Granny."

"Did she succeed?" Sarah asked hopefully.

"No."

"More's the pity." She looked at Emma. "You should have told her *you* were gay."

"I wasn't thinking on my toes," Emma replied. "But look, Bil is putting the worst possible spin on all of this. Your grandmother came to me and said she'd heard a dreadful rumor from a dreadful drag queen. I asked her what it was, and she whispered, shocked to the marrow, that she'd heard Bil was a lesbian. She'd asked Helen Merwin about it, and Helen had confirmed it."

"Helen!" Sarah and I shouted in unison.

"Yes, Helen. This is a small town, Bil. I've been hearing rumors for ages. I suspected long before your father told me this afternoon."

Naomi spoke for the first time. "Dad told you?"

"He did." Emma turned to me. "How could you tell your father before you told me? That was entirely unfair. When I got home, he broadsided me."

"I thought you were glad," I replied.

"And besides," Sarah added, "why should you get all the news first? Maybe Bil felt more comfortable telling Hugh."

My mother scowled, her lower lip jutting out.

"Stop it," Sarah said. "You look just like Mussolini when you do that. It's perfectly reasonable that Bil should tell Hugh first. I would."

"Explain that remark!"

We were interrupted by a loud whistle. Having gotten our attention, Ruth said quietly, "Excuse me, but we're getting off the topic. I want to know why Emma outed Bil to a roomful of people."

"Outing is a harsh word," Emma objected. "Your grandmother . . ."

"Granny was speaking quietly to you," I said.

"Your grandmother," Emma continued, undeterred, "did not ask me if it were true, she asked me if I knew. I just told her of course I did."

"You shouted," I corrected, "at the top of your lungs, 'Of course I know Bil's a lesbian, she's my daughter!'"

"That loud?" Ruth asked.

"Louder. She's got lungs like weather balloons."

"What an exaggeration. There are two sides to this story," Emma began.

Ruth held up her hand. "Thanks, but I think I've heard the truth. Bil," she smiled, "I'm glad for you, too. Also, I think you've got remarkable patience. If she'd done that to me, I'd have killed her."

"It did cross my mind."

"So," Sarah leaned forward conspiratorially, "do you have a girlfriend? Who is she? Is it anyone we know? Are you going to bring her home for the obligatory family supper?"

"Tomorrow is convenient," Emma piped in. "I'll cook something special."

"Would you knock it off? No, I don't have a girlfriend. Not at the moment, anyway."

"What are you talking about?" Emma interjected. "I thought you were seeing Sylvie Wood."

"Sylvie Wood?" Ruth echoed. "Burt Wood's daughter?"

"Emma," I said, "I don't believe you . . ."

"Well, that's tricky, isn't it?" Ruth went on. "I didn't know she was a lesbian."

"I knew that," Sarah interrupted. "Helen mentioned it one day when we were scheduled to work reference together. She likes this outing business almost as much as you do, Emma. It's bad form, you know. Maybe you should think about joining P-FLAG."

"What's P-FLAG?" Sam said.

"Parents and Families of Lesbians and Gays," Sarah said.

"Parents and Friends," I corrected. "But listen, Sylvie and I aren't . . ."

"It would be difficult if you were," Sarah interrupted. "Particularly considering Sam's connection to her late father. Still, stranger things have happened, I suppose."

"You're leaping to conclusions here," I said desperately. "If I were seeing her, I would hope that Sam's being in that jail cell . . ."

"I didn't kill anyone," Sam cut in. "You all talk about me like I'm not even here."

Emma said, "I'm sorry. We do, don't we? Bil, tell Sylvie to come at seven o'clock for dinner. What should I make?"

I took a deep breath. "Once and for all, Sylvie is not my girlfriend!"

Everyone stared at me.

"Well," Emma said in shocked tones, "I hope you're not leading her on. It doesn't pay to be promiscuous, you know. You'll get a reputation."

Hugh chose that moment to walk in with a tray full of mugs and a pot of coffee. He'd not only brought the sugar bowl but the creamer as well. I was touched. We all take our coffee black, but my father was clearly making an occasion of it. If I ever did bring Sylvie home for dinner, he'd probably propose a toast. Unfortunately, Hugh's idea of fine wine is Gallo in a box.

Naomi took the first cup of coffee. She stared at me severely.

"In the midst of all this thronging admiration," she said grimly, "there are a few harsh realities you need to consider."

We all tensed up, even Sam.

Naomi stiffened her upper lip and continued. "This family is not normal. Congratulations are not what you're going to hear when you get outside of this living room. And you can all stop looking at me like that. I've got nothing against gay people, but . . ."

"Some of my best friends are gay?" Emma suggested.

"And," Sarah added, "I've heard that if you've ever been gay on Saturday night, you'll never go straight again."

Naomi's cheeks puffed out, reddened, and then sank back in. She was breathing heavily, a sure sign that we were about to be treated to a magnificent display of righteous indignation. Our family had never cared enough for social conventions to suit Naomi. She wanted us to be regular, decent, and quiet, and it seemed as if we never did anything but deliberately and gleefully let her down. She stood up, looming over us like a thunderhead, and addressed the room at large.

"You always do this, all of you—you never think anything through. You don't think about the consequences, and anyone who raises an objection, who points out a problem, that person is automatically dismissed as a regressive bigot. When are you going to face the fact that you can't have everything? There's a price to be paid for the choices you make. Here you all are, patting Bil on the back for being true to herself, as if that's all there is to it. Well, that isn't all there is. What's she going to do now? What will other people think?"

"Who cares?" Hugh asked. "You can't live by anyone's lights but your own."

"That," she snapped, "has nothing to do with reality." She turned to me. "Have you thought about what this might mean for your future? The doors this might shut? Are you ready for some people to treat you like a pariah?"

"Naomi!" Sarah and Ruth exclaimed in unison. Now it was my turn to sit with my mouth hanging open.

Undaunted, she went on. "I'm not saying this to hurt your feelings, Bil. I'm telling you this for your own good. All this liberal goodness is fine in theory, but we don't live in a platonic Never-Never Land."

"Thanks for the update," Sarah said. "Why don't you go home and polish up your jackboots?" When the door had slammed behind Naomi, she added, "In Plato's *Republic*, they got rid of all the lawyers. Clever old Plato."

Ruth offered to have a word with her. I told her not to bother—I couldn't remember a time when I'd ever cared what Naomi thought. I did, however, encourage Sarah to make peace when she felt up to it. Naomi wasn't a jackbooted Nazi—she wasn't even wildly conservative. She was just white, straight, and conventional. Whatever hostility I might face in the world outside our living room, at least I wasn't odd-woman-out within the bosom of my family.

Ruth poured herself another cup of coffee. "I don't know if this is the time," she said, "but I've got some news for you. It's about Sam."

Sam had been sinking slowly into the cushions of the love seat. Now he perked up. “What about me?”

“I’ve seen Burt Wood’s autopsy results,” Ruth answered, pushing her glasses up on her nose. “The lab work is back from Spokane. Deb Trilby phoned me. She’s an ER physician, but she does some occasional work for the coroner’s office. She’s also an old pal. I called in a favor.”

“Well?” Emma and I said in unison.

“Do you know what Datura is?”

“Something chemical?” I suggested.

“More like something botanical. Burt Wood died because he ingested a quantity of jimsonweed or one of its cousins.”

Sam, in a puzzled tone, said, “So?”

Ruth smiled. “So, unless you got the munchies for some jimsonweed, it won’t turn up in your urinalysis. I’d say you were off the hook.”

Chapter 17

It's great to have a doctor in the family, and sometimes, it's even okay to have a lawyer, but no one is handier than a librarian. Within five minutes, Sarah had us logged on and surfing the Internet for information on the Datura genus.

We learned that there were a lot of varieties of Datura plants, some wild, some cultivated, and all of them toxic. Jimsonweed sometimes got harvested with hay, or the seeds got mixed up in grain, and livestock accidentally ate it, rendering themselves temporarily crazy. Sometimes, it even killed them. More frequent than livestock poisonings, however, were human poisonings. Children ate jimsonweed because they didn't know any better; teenagers and adults ate it because they wanted to get high. Datura plants contained tropane alkaloids, which were hallucinogenic. They could also be fatal if administered in sufficient quantities, particularly if the ingester wasn't in the best of health.

According to Ruth, our dead man had hepatitis B, and there were enough plant seeds in his stomach and intestines to kill a healthy man. Emma and I experienced one of those rare moments when we had the same thought at the same time.

"That couldn't have been an accident," we said simultaneously.

"It seems unlikely," Ruth agreed. "I suppose he might have committed suicide, but there are certainly easier ways to go. Atropine poisoning causes delirium, hallucinations, dry mouth, decreased bowel activity, increased heart rate—it's thoroughly unpleasant."

"I don't see how any of this gets me off the hook," Sam said. "He probably didn't kill himself, so that means someone else killed him. According to the county prosecutor, that means me."

"But if you haven't taken it yourself, I don't see how she could," Ruth explained. "As I understand it, the case against you is primarily based on the idea that you were both taking the same substance. When the urinalysis comes back, it will be clear of any tropane alkaloids," she lifted an eyebrow suggestively, "if not other illicit substances."

Sam stared off into the distance.

"Is this a common plant?" I asked.

"Looks to me like it grows all over the place," Sarah said, flipping through computer screens.

"Then why would Sam be off the hook? If people eat these plant seeds to get high, then how do we know that Sam hasn't eaten them?"

"Because," he snapped, "I don't know anything about this plant."

"That wouldn't stop you from eating it," Sarah replied. "Or selling it."

"Perhaps I was too hasty," Ruth admitted. "What I should have said is that if the police need a positive match on the urinalysis to charge Sam, then he's in the clear. I suppose he could have supplied the jimsonweed, but they'll have to find some other way to prove it. He couldn't have eaten it." Though her glasses had slipped down to the end of her nose again, she didn't bother to push them back up. "Because of the hepatitis, Wood was immune suppressed. A much smaller dose would have been sufficient to kill him. Chemotherapy also destroys the immune system."

Sam looked puzzled.

"In other words," Ruth explained, "if you'd eaten a load of jimsonweed, you'd have been dead before you pissed into that specimen jar."

I went in to school early the next morning, hoping to catch Sarah at the library before class. She always worked the morning shift on the reference desk, usually leaving her house around seven o'clock.

I got to the library around eight-thirty. Sarah was six feet tall, so

I didn't have any trouble spotting her among the shelves. She was without question the great beauty in our family. Her skin was dark brown, and her features strong and prominent, particularly her cheekbones. She wore her hair in a crew cut and, because she was near-sighted, she also wore small, round glasses. The overall effect was John Lennon meets Grace Jones. Ten people a day probably asked her why she was a librarian and not a model. The simple answer was that she never wanted to be anything but a librarian. She loved books, and she loved to read. She did her undergraduate degree in English at Cowslip, and then she went to the University of Washington for her master's in Library Science. Her first job was in Seattle Public Library, and I think in some ways she would have preferred to stay there, but my family—meaning, of course, my mother—exerted an irresistible pull. Sarah took the first job she could get that was close to home.

As she reached up to reshelve a book, I snuck up behind her.

"Why doesn't this library subscribe to the *National Enquirer*?"

"Shit is not included in our collection development policy," she replied, not bothering to look around. "You think you're being funny. You don't know how many questions I get every day that are worse than that."

"I'll bite. How many?"

She lowered her voice and pointed surreptitiously at a young man in a T-shirt that said Veni, Vidi, Vomiti. "Frank Lloyd Wright over there just asked me why we don't have any architecture books. Apparently, he went into the stacks and searched all of the shelves marked A. I've just spent half an hour trying to explain the Library of Congress classification system to him."

"So what's he doing now?"

"Pretending he knows how to search the online catalog. In a few minutes, he'll come and ask me for help."

"You don't volunteer it?"

"Not to the snotty," she replied. "They have to ask. Politely."

"I don't know how you stand it. I was wondering if you'd had a chance to do that research I asked you about."

"You mean trying to find you some contemporary accounts of Burt Wood's disappearance? I made some photocopies for you, though I don't know why you're still interested. You heard what Ruth said.

Sam's pretty much out of it now, unless they can prove he's been selling nickel-bags of jimsonweed."

"Anything's possible. In the meantime, I'm still curious. I'd like to know more about the whole Burt Wood, Frank Frost thing."

She pursed her lips and stared at me suspiciously. "This wouldn't have anything to do with Sylvie not-your-girlfriend Wood?"

"So what if it does? Are you the library police?"

"No," she replied smoothly, "I'm a highly trained information specialist. I see that you woke up on the wrong side of your bed of nails, but I'll help you anyway because that's just the kind of decent, hard-working person I am. Besides," she tossed over her shoulder as she walked back to the reference desk, "I remember what it was like to be young and in love."

"Knock it off."

She rifled through several folders in the files behind the desk, looking increasingly aggravated. "That's strange," she said. "I could have sworn I left it down here."

"Left what?"

"A file with your name on it," she replied. "I managed to gather a few things for you yesterday afternoon, and I put them all together in a manila folder."

"Could you have put it in your office?"

She ran a hand through her hair and gazed up thoughtfully. "I might have. Can you hold the fort for a minute? If anyone asks for help, tell them I'll be back."

She raced up the stairs, leaving me to surf the Internet on the reference computer. I was reading an online magazine when she came back ten minutes later.

"Sorry," she said, breathing heavily. "It wasn't upstairs either. I don't know what could have happened to it. I can ask Helen this afternoon."

"Why would you ask Mildew?"

"Shh," she said. "I try not to call her that here. We have to work together."

"You mean she was down here when you were looking all of that stuff up?"

"Part of the time. We try to have at least two librarians and one higher-ranking staff member on the desk during the peak hours. Sundays are fairly slow, but things tend to pick up around noon. That's when Mil . . . Helen comes in. She likes to work on weekends."

"Freak," I replied automatically. My mind was already elsewhere.

"I suppose I can look it all up again," Sarah said thoughtfully. "What a pain in the ass, though."

"I'd be very grateful."

"You'll be concretely grateful," she replied. "You'll be buying me dinner."

"It's a deal. The restaurant of your choice."

"I'll call you as soon as I've gotten it all together. Maybe Helen knows where it is. Her nickname around here is 'the Eye.' Not a lot gets past her."

Somehow, that didn't surprise me. I knew where that folder was, and now I also knew the identity of the shadowy figure who had perched up on the hillside at Kate's house, watching us from behind the bush. And she probably used my fucking binoculars, too.

I met Sylvie outside of my abnormal psych class. She seemed neither surprised to see me nor particularly happy. She gave me the same look she had given me on Saturday when we met at Traveler's Rest.

"Hi," I said doubtfully.

She looked down at her boots. "Hi."

"I went to see Sarah this morning. She says she'll call me when she's got something."

"Okay."

She stole quick, angry glances at me from beneath half-closed eyelids, and I thought about asking her why she was mad. My experience with the same question on Saturday told me not to bother. Instead, I said, "This will be the second time Sarah's looked up your father and Frank. She had a bunch of news clippings in a folder. Helen seems to have stolen it."

That got her attention. She looked up at me now, her eyes wide open.

"The folder had my name on it. Sarah left it down at the reference desk yesterday, while Helen was working. Now, the folder's missing."

"What makes you think she took it?"

I shrugged. "I don't know. She's nosy. Maybe she found it on the desk, saw my name, and thought it would be fun to fuck with me." I didn't really believe this, but it was as good a reason as any. "We had a run-in the weekend before last at my mother's house. Helen and Granny were pamphleteering for Proposition One. She called me a dyke."

"That sounds like her," Sylvie agreed. "If it's true, it explains a lot of things."

"Like what?"

She was beginning to thaw towards me. She looked up and gave me a genuine, friendly smile. "Like nothing," she said. "It doesn't matter. You're right, she doesn't like you, but she doesn't like me either. I don't know why she hasn't outed me to my mother. She's certainly threatened to often enough."

I thought it best not to mention that she'd outed her to Sarah. "There's a word for women like Helen, but it's rarely used outside of a kennel."

"Wait," she said, "I know that one. It's Joan Crawford, right?"

"Very good," I smiled. "It's from *The Women*. Have we seen all the same old movies?"

She laughed. "Either that or we've taken all the same film studies courses."

"Look," I stepped closer and put my hand on her arm. "Do you want to go somewhere?"

She shook her head. "I can't. I have that botany test."

Having managed to get this far, I decided to press my luck. "After botany?"

"Well," she hesitated, looking down at her boots again, "actually, I have a prior engagement. I would if I could, Bil, but I really can't cancel this."

"It's okay," I said quickly. I knew what prior engagement meant—it meant someone who was not me. "I understand. Another time."

"Definitely. I could even call you tonight, if you like."

My reply was terse, giving away more than I had intended. "I don't know if Sarah will be finished by then."

She smiled tentatively. "I could call you anyway."

"Okay."

As soon as she was around the corner, I walked across the lobby and picked up the pay phone. Tipper answered on the second ring.

"Stop the Prop!" he cried. "But in the meantime, let's chat."

"It's me, Tipper. Can I come over?"

"What's the matter?"

"I was thinking I'd throw myself under a train."

"Don't do that, you're the answer to my prayers. Mama's taken the car, the Faeries are taking a nap, and I want to go shoe shopping!"

Chapter 18

When I pulled up to the gate, Tipper was leaning against it, wearing a crisp, white, button-down shirt. The shirt was tucked neatly into his jeans, and he was wearing a broad, black leather belt with a big silver buckle. The finishing touch to this YMCA drag was a pair of construction boots.

"You look like Barbie's dream date."

He closed his eyes and fluttered a hand over his chest. "My heart belongs to Ken. Actually, I wore this for you. This is going to be your new look."

"My what? Look, I thought we were going shoe shopping, which means you try on a thousand pairs, and I just sit and watch."

"We'll do that, too. Nevertheless, it's about time someone took you in hand. You're a mess. I don't just mean your clothes, I mean you generally. You've looked like death eating a cracker for over a week."

I sighed. "Tipper, I'm exhausted. I'm behind in every class, and . . ."

"And you need my advice but don't know how to ask for it. Don't worry," he smiled, "I don't expect you to tell me right away. For now, just relax and drive."

"Fine." I pulled out into the highway and headed for town. "Where are we going?"

"Spokane," he replied. "Don't miss the exit."

"Spokane? But that's two hours away!"

"Then you'd better put your foot down because that's where we're going. Only farmer's wives shop in Cowslip, and besides, you and I are going to spend some quality time, just the two of us. Close your mouth, I will brook no argument. You can have one afternoon with no Emma, no Sam, and," he paused for effect, "none of your other little problems."

It was a long drive from Cowslip to Spokane, even at seventy miles an hour. The highway ran up the middle of nowhere, past a lot of grain elevators and a couple of one-horse towns. Otherwise, it was all wheat and barley fields, as far as the eye could see.

Once we were outside of Cowslip, Tipper rolled down the window and stuck his head out, letting the wind blow through his hair.

"Free at last, free at last! Thank God almighty!"

I grabbed his arm and gave it a yank. "Come back inside before you're decapitated."

"In that case, you'll have to put something good on the stereo," he said, settling back down in his seat. "I need music."

"I thought we were going to have quality time."

"We can't do that without an appropriate soundtrack. What have you got?"

"I don't know. There are some cassettes in that case on the floor, down by your feet."

He flipped through them for several minutes, pulling out those he liked and setting them on the seat between us. And then he pulled out a cassette he didn't like.

"What," he asked loudly, "is this?"

I squinted at the cover. "It looks suspiciously like *New Miserable Experience* by the Gin Blossoms."

"Well the title fits. How did one of A. J.'s cassettes get into your truck?"

"How do you know it's hers?"

"Elementary, my dear. One, I happen to know that you hate the Gin Blossoms. Two," he waved the case in front of me, "she's written her name on it."

"Get that out of my face," I said irritably. "I can't see to drive."

"You can't see period. Once and for all, are you done with that woman or not?"

"I am done with her." This statement earned me a slap on the arm. With some irritation, I said, "Look, do you need an anger management class? Talk, don't hit."

"I can hit you all I like, we're practically sisters. Now, what gives with A. J.? She'd better not be the reason you want to throw yourself under a train."

"She's not. That cassette's been in here since last spring."

"Hmmph."

"It has!"

"I know for a fact," he said sternly, "that she was in your company quite recently."

"She wasn't in my truck." He glared at me. I sighed. "It was just that once, Tipper—the night we all went to Fiesta Jack's. I was weakened by alcohol, as you well know."

"Oh no," he shook his head. "You can't blame this on me. I drank just as much as you did, and I successfully repelled the advances of a very determined Suzy."

"Oh, Suzy. He'd proposition a lamppost."

"That doesn't mean he's easy to fight off. And like you, I've had a long dry spell."

"If I acknowledge your moral superiority, will you leave me alone?"

"No, but thanks anyway." He peered at me closely. "Just once?"

"Yes, for Christ's sake! I'd know, wouldn't I? What is this anyway, the third degree? I thought this was going to be a day without, as you said, my little problems."

"It wasn't my intention to grill you," he relented. "It's just that . . . well, you might as well know now as later. After you left the party last night, the Lesbian Avengers met at the Cowslip Café to plan their next action. The Faeries and I decided to intercept them. Do you know what they're planning, by the way? A kiss-in on Union Square."

"I don't care if they're kissing asses on Union Square. What's this got to do with me?"

"Innuendo. They were all talking about your big outing, and A. J., always the center of attention, told them that you were her—now wait, let me get this right—I think she said that you were her primary partner."

"Her what?"

"Allow me to translate. She said you were her girlfriend *du jour*, her main squeeze, and her all-around chief fuck buddy."

"Enough, I get the picture." I tried to concentrate on the road ahead. I wasn't sure I wanted to know, but I asked, "Who else was there?"

"You don't want to know," he confirmed.

"Tell me anyway."

He rolled his eyes despairingly. "The entire Merwin clan was sitting at the table next to us. A. J. flapped her lips, and Helen took dictation. And believe me that was not the first time A. J. has told that story. She's blabbed about your recent escapade all over town. Last night, as soon as I got a chance, I dragged your ex aside and put the fear of God in her, but I'm afraid it was way too late."

For a moment, I gazed at him, horrified. I looked back at the road just in time to notice that I had drifted into the southbound lane. I jerked the steering wheel sharply to the right, throwing Tipper against the door.

"Don't kill us! You might wish you were dead, but I don't."

I gripped the steering wheel tightly. "Goddamn that Helen, she's everywhere."

"She's a regular machine," he agreed.

We said nothing more for several miles. Tipper chose a tape and popped it into the stereo. It was Aimee Mann's *Whatever*, one of his favorite albums.

"Honey," he said finally, "what were you thinking? I thought it was all over with her."

"I wasn't thinking, Tipper. She was beautiful, and I was stupid. That pretty much sums up every romance I've ever had."

"If it's any comfort," he said, "I've been equally stupid myself."

"Tom?" He nodded. "Is it serious?"

"I'm serious. I don't know if he is."

"I see."

He sighed heavily. "I've broken rule number one in the Gay Scout's handbook: make sure you both want the same thing."

"What do you want?"

"A husband and seven children. I don't know what he wants. Maybe I'm just another ride on the gay rodeo for him."

"I doubt that," I said, "but if you need a place to get away and think, my home is your home. You can even have my bed."

"Promise to change the sheets?"

"Anything for you, Tipper."

"You're a peach." Changing tone, he continued briskly, "Enough about me. Why were you going to throw yourself under a train? We've eliminated A. J., so it must be . . ."

"It is," I admitted. I paused for a moment. How could I explain without explaining everything? He was clearly waiting, so I had to try. I said, "Sometimes, it seems to be going well, and I think I'm on the right track. Then I arrange to meet her or I run into her somewhere, and she cuts me dead. I saw her today and invited her out for coffee. She said she had a prior engagement. She was just blowing me off."

"If you believe that, you're an idiot," he observed matter-of-factly. "There are two factors at work here. The first is Helen Merwin. I'll bet you dollars to doughnuts that she got straight on the phone last night and told her dear cousin that you are a cad. That's the bad news. The good news is that if she didn't care for you, she wouldn't cut you dead. What you've been experiencing, you naïve fool, are jealous fits."

"You're insane," I said.

"Nonetheless, you know that I am always right."

"And always modest."

"Who has time for modesty? I have to fix your life so I can get on with my own. Now be quiet while I continue my analysis. Do you want to know how you ended up in bed with A. J.?"

I didn't answer.

"Well?" he persisted.

"Sorry, I thought that was rhetorical."

"It was not. First, tell me exactly what happened. I want the complete chain of events—leading up to, not during," he clarified.

I shrugged. How did it happen? Did I run into her by chance or by design? I couldn't remember. "I left Fiesta Jack's and walked in the general direction of Ruth and Naomi's place. I paused outside of the Underground to get my bearings, and there she was." I added, "In the right light, Tipper, she really does look like Elizabeth Taylor."

"So do I," he snapped. "Bil, you don't understand women at all."

"And you do?"

"I understand her type well enough. That was a pre-emptive strike. She laid a trap, and you stuck your big feet right in it. Sleeping with you was purely an act of sabotage. She was marking out her territory, sending a signal to Sylvie and any other interested party—dibs on this one, she's mine."

"What, like a dog?"

"Not the exact word I was thinking of," he said, "but you get the picture. A. J. wants Sylvie to think you two are an ongoing item, very much involved in the present tense. She's done a good job of it, too."

Listening to Tipper was like driving past a car wreck. I didn't want to see the dead bodies, and yet I couldn't stop rubbernecking.

"Look," Tipper continued seriously, "you were entitled to a grudge fuck."

"That's not . . ."

"Will you stop interrupting me? That's clearly what it was. I'm on your side, remember?" I had to promise to let him have his say before he'd continue. "You should have made a clean break with A. J., but I realize that's not the lesbian way. Lesbians prefer to beat the dead horse already in their stable rather than look for a fresh pony. You need to wake up, Bil, because you've got a fresh pony who's saddled up, hitched, and ready to ride."

"What an attractive analogy."

"I am perfectly serious," he said. "A. J. is rotten to the core. She wants you for a trophy because you'd look nice hanging over her sofa. You broke up with her, and she hates that."

"She drove me to it!" I protested. "And you've just pointed out that she doesn't give a shit about me. I'm a convenience to her, like a public toilet."

"Now who's making attractive analogies? Look, don't argue with me. If she can't have you back, she at least wants you to suffer for having dumped her. The question is, what are you going to do about it?"

We had reached Colfax, Washington, a notorious speed trap. I slowed down to twenty-five and crept along Main Street.

"Tipper, do you really think Sylvie is interested?"

He raised an eyebrow, but didn't answer. We passed through Colfax without incident, so when we reached the top of the hill at the edge of town, I put my foot down.

"You're a seven," he said suddenly.

"I'm a what?"

"A seven on the butch-femme scale. It goes from one to ten, one being maximum femme and ten being maximum butch. My mother is an eleven. You are a seven, and Sylvie is a four."

"What about the motorcycle?"

"That's why she's a four and not a three. Now this is what we've got to work with—you're naturally attracted to one another. We need to play to your complementary strengths."

He stared at me for so long I asked if he was measuring me for drapes.

"Shut up," he said. "I was wrong about the suit and tie, but I'm right about cleaning you up. Crisp white shirts and lace-up oxfords; that's what you need."

There was no point in arguing. I knew as much about clothes as I knew about particle physics. Besides, he was probably right. Could it hurt to retire Mr. Bubble and a few of my other more wretched T-shirts?

"Okay," I said, "I'm a seven, and Sylvie's a four. What's A. J.?"

"Easy," he replied. "A perfect ten."

"She's not a butch!"

"No, she's a bitch. I've changed scales."

We started with Nordstrom's and finished up at The Bon Marché, stopping at a hundred and fifty stores in between and leaving a trail of bemused salesgirls in our wake. I bought two button-down shirts and, at Tipper's insistence, a pair of brown wing tips, which I wore out of the store.

Tipper bought a pair of high-heeled pumps, which he described as "billboard slippers." They were red and glittering with four-inch spike heels, so I didn't need to ask what they were advertising. I did suggest that he buy a silver-tipped cane to stop himself from falling over, and he informed me in a voice too shrill for comfort that they weren't walking-around shoes. They were staring-at-the-ceiling shoes.

He could have gone on shopping until the stores closed. I was a lesser mortal. At half past six I said, "Tipper, I'm beat. Can we take a break for dinner? Maybe even a beer?"

He put an arm around my shoulders and gave me a friendly squeeze. "Of course, honey. You've been a brave little butch, and you deserve a Budweiser. I know just the place."

Ten minutes later, we were sitting in Jackie J's, a les-bi-gay bar and grill downtown. I ordered a bacon cheeseburger, and Tipper had a Caesar salad with dressing on the side. The bar was crowded, and we had to wait well over half an hour for our food. In the meantime, people came and went. We had just started eating when I saw her. At a table in the far corner of the room, in light so dim I could barely make her out, Sylvie sat with a tall, dark-haired woman who looked familiar to me. The woman was handsome, broad-shouldered with small, well-rounded breasts. I could scarcely help noticing the latter as she was wearing a tight V-necked sweater. They were clearly together, and judging from the intensity of their conversation, she was no casual pick up. She was the prior engagement.

"What is the matter with you?" Tipper asked. "Stomach cramps?" He started to turn around in his chair, and I grabbed his arm.

"Don't look," I said, crouching down so as to be less visible.

"Why not?"

"Sylvie's here."

"So? Let's ask her to join us," he said, attempting to turn around again.

"We can't." I gripped his arm tightly and dropped my voice to a low whisper. "She's not alone."

"Oh. Would you like a menu to hide behind?"

"Don't be funny."

"Okay. Would you like to leave?"

"We'd have to walk right past them."

Tipper considered the possibilities and then shook his head. "It looks like we'll have to wait. Just eat your dinner, and I'll try to shield you from view as much as possible. If you'll stop staring at her, she'll be less likely to notice you."

I made a conscious effort to look away, but I couldn't resist sneaking glances. It took me several minutes to place the other woman. She was one of the fire-eating Lesbian Avengers who had made Sunday night so memorable. They downed at least two rounds of drinks, and then, apparently without Sylvie noticing me, they got up and disappeared among the pool tables in the back room. I let out the breath I hadn't realized I was holding.

"Is the coast clear?" Tipper asked.

"They've gone into the billiard room. Go ahead, eat your dinner."

"Look, maybe she's just a friend."

"No one has friends who look like that."

"Look like what? I wasn't allowed to turn around."

"Like k.d. lang."

He paused to consider this. "Like k.d. lang on Grammy night or when she's caught by the paparazzi on her way to put out the trash?"

"Grammy night. When she's won."

"I'll eat quickly," he said, forking a huge pile of lettuce into his mouth.

I wadded up my napkin and tossed it onto the middle of my plate. What right did I have to be miserable? I was no better than A. J. I'd behaved like a drunken slut, both in Fiesta Jack's and afterwards, and I didn't have any legitimate claim on Sylvie, anyway. Tipper was my friend. He thought I should have my pick of the dykes of the world. Sylvie might have other ideas.

We drove home to the accompaniment of Ella Fitzgerald. I had requested Janis Ian. Tipper dismissed this as music to commit suicide by and pointed out that he couldn't die until he'd slept with all of the Seattle Mariners. I reminded him that he already had a sweetheart, which he dismissed with a wave of his hand before popping the *Cole Porter Songbook* into the cassette deck.

It was close to eleven by the time we reached Fort Sister. I pulled into the gravel drive, my headlights pointing at the front gate. The silver padlock flashed in my high beams, and I found myself thinking about Sylvie and Kate and Sam's dead cell-mate. I turned the engine off.

"What's up?" Tipper asked. "Are you coming in?"

"No," I said. "I was just thinking of something. The man who died . . ."

"Sylvie's father?"

I nodded. "Yeah. You said he was out here, and that's why you got the padlock."

"I know it's useless. It's only for psychological reassurance."

I shook my head. "That's not what I mean. What did he want? What did he say to Cedar Tree that made your mother put a padlock on your gate? People don't even lock their cars in Cowslip, much less their front doors or their front gates."

Tipper thought for a moment. "I don't think he actually spoke to Cedar Tree, he just scared her. It's not all that surprising, is it?"

"What do you mean?"

"Well," he continued, "Cedar's out communing with nature, worshipping the moon or something, and she sees this figure creeping along the edge of the woods. When she screamed, he ran off. She probably thought she'd conjured him up with one of her smudge sticks."

"This was at night?"

"Just after nine," he said. "Still light enough to see, but dark enough to be creepy. But that was on Wednesday, I think. He came back the next day."

"He was here twice?"

"That's what Cedar Tree says. He was walking along the edge of the property early the next morning. Cedar Tree saw him, and my mother went out to have a word with him. He said he was just passing through, and then he tried to bum some money off of her."

"Did she give him any?"

"Probably."

"But she put the lock on the gate?"

He shrugged. "I guess she didn't want to have to shoot him. Some people see that you're a soft touch, and they decide to come back in the night for seconds."

I nodded. "What did your mother do after that? Can you think of anything else?"

He closed his eyes and leaned back against the seat. "She called the neighbors," he said.

"Including Kate Wood?"

"Of course. When Cedar Tree caught him on Thursday morning, he was on the old footpath that runs past the dugouts. As you know, that goes straight up over the ridge and drops down onto Kate's farm. She lives there all alone with only a couple of dogs for protection. I don't know if she has a gun or not. My mother offered to send over an armed squadron. I believe that Kate thanked her politely but turned the offer down."

"Did she say if he'd been to her place?"

"No," Tipper said, "she didn't. Of course, considering who he was, I guess it's not too surprising. It's got to be unnerving when your husband comes traipsing back after sixteen years. You can have someone declared dead after seven."

We sat quietly for a moment. I thought of telling him Sylvie's story and seeing what he made of it. I'd trust Tipper with my life, but in the dark, I couldn't seem to dismiss what Sylvie thought she had seen in her backyard as the wishful thinking of an abused child. Tipper seemed to guess some of what was on my mind.

"You're wondering if he made it all the way over to Kate's, aren't you?"

I shook my head. "No, I know that he did. Sylvie told me." I explained about her seeing him in her mother's kitchen on Thursday. "What I'm wondering is what he was doing over here on your mother's property."

"Maybe he didn't know about my mother," he said, "or how she feels about trespassers. We moved here after he did his vanishing act. If he was walking along the road, a detour across our place would cut nearly three miles off his trip."

"Unless your mother happened to shoot him."

"True." He looked at me closely. I avoided making eye contact. "Let me sum up, for you," he said at last. "You think Sam is in the clear. If Sylvie's father was murdered, that leaves one or two suspects very close to home."

I started the truck. "I've got to be going."

He shook his head, smiling. "Goodnight, honey. When you want to tell me about it, and I do mean all about it, give me a call."

He leaned over and gave me a peck on the cheek before he got out. I watched him climb over the fence, shining my headlights down the gravel driveway until he was well out of sight. Then I backed out. Instead of driving straight home, I drove up the road to Kate's. I missed the entrance the first time and had to back up. I pulled in and drove part of the way up to her house. Then I shifted the truck into neutral and turned the headlights off.

I didn't get out. The trees were thick on either side of the drive, and it was impossible to see the house—you couldn't see that until you were about fifty yards from it. The only light visible was a halogen bulb mounted on the front of the barn. I could see the glow from where I was parked, but it illuminated nothing.

I sat there for about a quarter of an hour, thinking. The woods seemed to close in on either side of the truck. I locked my door and then reached over to lock the passenger side. I don't know what I thought I was locking out, ghosts maybe.

Chapter 19

When I got home, I found a note from Emma pinned to my pillow. It said, "Emergency Room." I drove back into town.

I met Hugh down in the lobby. It was where I expected to find him; he avoided being up in the ER with Sam whenever possible. Unlike my mother, who loved talking hospital jargon with the doctors, Hugh was completely at a loss. If a physician told him decapitation was the cure for a headache, my father would say, "Do what you think is best."

"What's happening?" I asked, sitting down in the vinyl seat next to him.

"It's pretty bad," he said. "Sam's also making it a lot worse than it has to be."

"Of course."

He smiled. "He's been vomiting all day, couldn't seem to stop. He's not vomiting now, but he's so potassium-depleted that he can't walk. His muscles don't work properly. He's had a liter of potassium solution, and he's refusing to drink any more. They're up there trying to work out some kind of compromise."

"So you came down here?"

"I'm not going to sit up there and listen to him yelling at the nurses. Everyone's doing their best."

The nurses never minded the yelling as much as my father did. They considered it an occupational hazard and didn't seem to take it personally.

I said, "Is it life-threatening?"

Hugh seemed to shrink before my eyes. I noticed the gray in his hair and the ashy stubble on his chin. I always forgot my father's age; he was three years older than Emma. To me, he always seemed about forty. That was the last time I could remember him having a birthday with a specific age attached to it. He looked at me over the top of his half-glasses.

"I don't know. I asked your mother that."

"And what did she say?"

"She said the heart's a muscle, too, just like his legs. It could stop beating."

I let this sink in. "Can I go up?"

"Sure. They probably won't let you stay very long. Not unless you can convince him to drink another liter of potassium."

The nurse was pumping up a blood-pressure cuff when I went in.

"That fucking pinches," Sam snapped. He was wearing his usual hospital outfit, a pair of boxer shorts and a tank top. He refused to wear the gowns that tied up the back. "Take it off."

"She has to take your blood pressure," Emma explained calmly. She was wearing her hospital face—patient, unflappable, and as much a part of the routine as Sam's outfit. "Just relax."

"Fuck off."

I sat down on the windowsill, as far out of the way as possible. The nurse's face was a complete blank. She finished her count and stuck a Thermoscan thermometer in his ear.

"The doctor will be by in a couple of minutes to talk about your options."

"She can forget it, I'm not drinking any more of that shit."

The nurse smiled mechanically and left the room. Sam was watching TV. The six million dollar man ran across the screen in slow motion.

"That's what I need," Sam said. "New fucking legs."

Emma shook her head. She was fussing around the bed, tucking the blankets in beneath him. "What you need is to do what you're told. If you want to walk out of here, you've got to drink another liter."

"Then I won't be walking out."

Emma punched the mute button on the TV remote. "Hi, Bil," she said cheerfully. "I see you got my note."

I kept my features carefully neutral. My mother was hell in the sheriff's office, but she didn't allow emotion to intrude in the hospital room. Anyone caught crying got kicked out the door.

"Hi, Sam."

"Hi," he said, not looking at me.

Emma gave me her do-something look. I made no sign that I'd seen it.

"Could we turn the sound up a little?" I asked. "I think this is the episode with the Fembots."

Sam nodded. "It's two parts, and they're showing them back-to-back. It's some kind of *Six Million Dollar Man* and *Bionic Woman* marathon."

"Oh good."

Emma sat down in a chair next to the bed, looking more old and tired than Hugh. "I don't know how you can watch this trash."

"You know," I said, ignoring her, "I wonder if they'll ever make a feature film out of this. They're making one of *The Brady Bunch*."

"And they've done *The Beverly Hillbillies*," Sam added.

"Exactly. You'd think this would be an obvious choice. It's got everything—action, technology, the chance for some really spectacular special effects. Who would you get to play Steve Austin? Arnold Schwarzenegger?"

Sam shook his head dismissively. "No. Maybe Steven Seagal, or that guy who played Batman."

"Michael Keaton?"

"Yeah."

Emma gave me the look again, meaning press him now into doing what we want. I ignored her. I couldn't hammer him like that, even when he needed it.

"I used to want to be bionic," I said. "I wanted to fall out of an airplane just so I could get the arms and legs. I never really wanted the ear, though. I thought the bionic eye was much cooler."

"That's because you already had the ear," Emma observed. "Everything I said went down in your little notebook."

Sam smiled, and I hoped his humor was improving. "Remember when Sarah went as Wonder Woman for Halloween?"

"Who could forget that? We dipped the boobs on one of Emma's old bras in baby shoe bronzer. Then she painted Dad's climbing rope gold and hung it on her belt."

"And she stole Naomi's high-heeled boots out of her closet and spray-painted them red."

"Agony," I said. "All hell broke loose when she came out into the living room."

Emma, seeing our mission was nearly accomplished, smiled now. "Be sure to confine your reminiscing to this room and away from Naomi. She still hasn't forgiven Sarah."

"She never forgives anyone," I said. Sam nodded in agreement.

We settled down to watch the Fembots in companionable silence. Sam was approaching the point where he'd be pliable enough to discuss that second liter of potassium, but he hadn't reached it yet. My mother was champing at the bit, so much so that she nearly jumped out of her skin when the doctor, a short, round, competent-looking woman, came in.

Emma stood up. "I hope you can talk some sense into him," she said.

The doctor smiled and looked at my brother. She extended her hand. "Hi, Sam. Dr. Nordquist has gone off duty. I'm Deborah Trilby. I've heard about you from your sister, Ruth. We're friends."

He took her hand reluctantly but said nothing.

"We need to discuss your options here. As you know, potassium depletion is a very serious thing. The first step was to get your vomiting under control, which you've done. The second step is to get your potassium levels back up to normal. That'll restore your muscle function."

"I know all this," Sam said. "I've been here for hours."

"Listen," my mother interrupted, "you've got to be made to see sense. Either you drink that other liter . . ."

Sam had opened his mouth, no doubt to tell Emma to fuck off again, but Dr. Trilby intervened. "You must be Mrs. Hardy. I've heard a lot about you." Dr. Trilby smiled enigmatically. "And you must be Bil," she said, turning to me. "I've heard a lot about you, too."

Turning to my mother, she said, "Mrs. Hardy, it's my practice to consult with my adult patients in private. If you and Bil wouldn't mind leaving the room for a few minutes, I'll run over Sam's options with him, and then he can make a decision."

"What options?" Emma argued. "He can drink the rest of that potassium or he can die. I don't see why I should leave the room and let him kill himself."

"Nevertheless," I stood up and took her arm, "we're going."

"Bil," Emma objected, "I've never been asked to leave the room before."

"She means hospital room," I said to Dr. Trilby. "She's been asked to leave lots of other rooms."

"Sam is my son," Emma began.

"Sam is twenty-two," I finished firmly, "a grown man by any standards. He can make his own medical decisions. We'll see you later, Sam."

My brother, who had been slouching into a monumental sulk, sat up and turned the television off, something I'd never seen him do while in the hospital. Even when doctors asked him to turn it off, he either ignored them or turned up the sound. Dr. Trilby sat down on the edge of the bed, and I gave Emma a firm push, propelling her into the hallway and shutting the door behind us.

"Bil . . ."

"Come on," I said.

"I should be in there!"

"Bullshit. You should be letting him make his own decisions, not babying him."

She had been walking as if on autopilot toward the elevator. Now she stopped, folding her arms across her chest and glaring at me.

"What does Deborah Trilby know about it? She's not even his doctor."

"She's a friend of Ruth's," I replied. "She passed on the information about Burt Wood's autopsy results. Didn't the name ring a bell with you?"

This surprised her enough to allow me to get her moving again. "I forgot that." Then, recalling her anger, she said, "Whoever she is, her high-handed treatment . . ."

"Will get Sam to drink that second liter of potassium," I replied, guiding Emma onto the elevator and pushing the button for the basement. "I'm sure of it."

"She's an asshole," my mother observed bitterly. "I've never been shuffled off like that, and she couldn't have done it without your help."

"The point, Ma," I paused and looked her in the eye, "is that she's right. Sam needs to be making these decisions for himself."

She opened her mouth to object, but I cut her off. "When he got sick, he was still a teenager. You had to make his decisions for him back then. It's different now. I'm sure he still wants you there, but he needs—he deserves—the dignity of being treated like an adult."

"You know he's going to die, don't you?"

I shrugged, looking away.

"You need to prepare yourself." Her voice was quieter now, though her tone was still strident.

"No, I don't," I said at last, and I was surprised to hear that my voice was firm and steady. "Ever since Sam's relapse, you've been telling me that I need to get ready, that I need to make my mind up to the fact that he's going to die. Well, Emma, he's not dead yet. There are no guarantees—any one of us could get run down by a bus tomorrow. You've got to stop throwing dirt in his face."

I stepped out of the elevator and headed down the hallway to the cafeteria. I didn't look back to see if Emma was behind me or not. I bought a cup of coffee from one of the vending machines and sat down at a table near the back door. My mother sat down and lit a cigarette.

"No smoking," I said automatically.

"I don't give a rat's ass. Besides, we're the only ones down here."

We sat in silence until the ash on her cigarette was over an inch long.

"I'm not throwing dirt in his face," she said. "I'm just—it's hard to explain. I made my mind up five years ago that I'd fight like hell to keep him alive, but I need to make sure that I won't have any regrets. I've got to do everything I can for him, however crazy it seems to the rest of you."

I reached across and took her hand. After staring at our hands for a second or two, she patted mine. She stubbed her cigarette out in the nearly empty coffee cup and leaned back in her chair.

"He's a grown man, Ma. Just because he acts like a teenager doesn't mean we should treat him like one."

"Sometimes," she said, "you sound just like your father."

Back upstairs, Sam was sitting up in bed, drinking his second liter of potassium. He looked completely disgusted. *The Six Million Dollar Man* was back, and Steve Austin was ripping the plastic face off an OSI secretary to reveal an evil Fembot. I resumed my perch on the windowsill.

"Did I miss anything?"

"I don't know. I just turned it back on."

I pointed at his cup. "Does that taste bad or what?"

He nodded. "Like shit, but it beats having it pumped up your ass as an enema."

I made a mental note to congratulate Dr. Trilby.

"Let me get this straight," I said, for maybe the fifth time. "We know that Burt Wood was killed by tropanic poisoning."

My mother bent her head to light a cigarette. "Basically. The seeds he ate . . ."

"Or was fed," I interrupted, stabbing a fork into my pancakes. "Are you sure you don't want anything to eat?"

Emma shook her head. "Just nicotine for me."

It was five a.m., and we were sitting in the House of Pancakes. Hugh had gone home, and Dr. Trilby had thrown us out of the ER so that Sam could rest undisturbed. Emma and I were both wide-awake. It was clear that Sam's lymphoma had reached some sort of apex, and the next couple of weeks would be critical. For now, at least, Sam was out of immediate danger.

"So the seeds Burt ate," Emma continued, "or was fed, contained tropane alkaloids. Highly toxic. All the cops found in your brother's urine was evidence of THC, but that was enough for a warrant. They searched the house Monday afternoon."

"My bedroom too?"

She nodded. "I'm afraid so."

I thought about the more questionable reading material I kept in a box under my bed and inwardly winced.

"Your brother began vomiting sometime after you left yesterday morning and kept it up non-stop for most of the day. The sheriff's deputies showed up at three, and I had to juggle taking care of your brother with seeing to it that they didn't rip the place apart."

"Did they find anything?"

"Of course."

"Oh, Jesus. What are you going to do?" I had visions of the Drug Enforcement Agency bankrupting my parents and seizing the family homestead.

"Nothing," she said. I raised my eyebrows at this, and she smiled. "Your brother has a corrupt supplier. There were no psilocybin mushrooms in his stash. For future reference, by the way, psilocybin is the technical term. No one calls them magic mushrooms anymore. Anyhow, it turns out they were dried shiitakes, just like you said."

"You didn't destroy that bag?" I asked, aghast.

"Of course I did. Your brother had another bag. It was in the bottom of his closet, stuffed into the toe of an old sneaker. Originally there might have been one or two of the real thing mixed in, but I doubt it. I think it's a case of your brother having the intent, if not the connections. He's in trouble for the THC, but since he's a cancer patient, I don't think they'll pursue it. As for the rest, Campbell and Young were fishing. They've got an inconvenient death on their hands, and the law in this town has been looking for something good to pin on your brother. He is, as Campbell says, a corrupting influence on younger people."

"Meaning Francie? Don't make me laugh. When did you talk to Campbell?"

"In between vomiting bouts. I think it was about six-thirty. I called to read her the riot act. That's when I learned that the deputies had taken those mushrooms to a horticulturist who took one look and laughed in their faces. Campbell hasn't given up entirely; she's going to pressure your brother to name his source."

"For shiitakes? Try Safeway."

"You're forgetting about his urine test. She wants to know where Sam got the pot."

I poured more syrup on my pancakes. "Do you think he'll spill the beans?"

"Your brother turn nark? Not a chance."

"Your familiarity with the language of the street is terrifying. If I were you, I'd start encouraging Sam to cooperate. It might help get him out of this mess."

"You think so? I'll have you know that Campbell suggested that your brother is the tip of a massive drug underground."

"Oh, come on. Cowslip doesn't have an underground. There's always been a stoner population, just like there have always been farmers and Republicans. Everyone knows who they are. Sam's been a pothead since junior high."

My mother rolled her eyes and toked on her cigarette. "You exaggerate. Everyone tries pot a time or two; it's a rite of passage. Your brother wasn't a serious user until his diagnosis." She inhaled deeply and then blew the smoke out of the side of her mouth. My mother is under the impression that if she doesn't exhale directly in your face, then you're not breathing second-hand smoke.

I shook my head sadly and said, "You live in a dream world, Emma," though it was clear that she was no longer paying attention.

Disease doesn't exist in a vacuum; its effects radiate outwards. Cancer grows, changes, weakens or gets stronger while its host goes on about his business. Every time Sam was in the ER, I expected the world to grind to a halt, but it never did. The cancer pursued its course, the Lewis County sheriffs pursued theirs, and Sam endured. In some ways, he even prospered. In the ordinary course of events, he was a petty criminal, but sometimes it seemed as if non-Hodgkin's lymphoma had transformed him into someone else, someone brave and death-defying. I often felt a strange kind of admiration for him.

My pancakes had been rendered inedible, so I pushed the plate away. I also traded my ash-covered mug for a fresh cup from another table. "So the only thing they found in his bedroom were the dried mushrooms? No pot?"

She shook her head.

"It's a good thing you had Bucky's Salvage haul those wrecks out of our yard before they had a chance to search them."

"You don't think . . ."

"He spent a lot of time out there working on those cars, but they never seemed to look any better, did they?" She had nothing to say to this. Just for the record, I asked, "How bad was his score on the urine test?"

She stubbed out her cigarette. "Well, they measure THC in parts per million. Judging from your brother's parts, he was smoking a joint in the squad car."

"Smoking . . ."

"He says eating, actually. When he heard the sirens, he stuffed everything he had into his mouth, chewed it up and swallowed it. He says he ate at least a quarter bag of stems and pieces."

"Don't you mean leaves?"

"No, I mean the stems, the buds, and the dregs of a stash. He and Francie took care of the leaves some time ago. They were saving the buds for a special occasion."

Emma opened a new pack of menthols.

"It's a stretch," I said, "but maybe a good lawyer could get him off."

"With his record?"

"Okay, maybe they could send him to some sort of twelve-step program."

Emma laughed harshly. "It doesn't matter anyway because your brother is going to jail. To jail or to his grave or maybe both. It's like that game, the lady or the tiger, only he's got two tigers."

What could I say? It didn't seem to matter anymore that he'd made one of the tigers himself. He was out of choices, and I wanted to help him. "What can we do?"

"Do you suppose Bucky has crushed those cars?" my mother asked. "God knows they weren't worth saving for parts. The Buick didn't have any wheels, and the Impala didn't have an engine."

I thought for a moment and said, "If they're smart enough to think of the cars, I'll just say that anything they find is mine. I don't have a record, so the most that could happen is I'd get a weekend in jail or some community service."

Emma closed her eyes and rested her forehead on her fingertips. Smoke curled up from her cigarette and wound its way to the ceiling. When she finally looked up again, I was surprised to see that she was smiling. "I am obsessive, aren't I?" she said.

"What do you mean?"

"I mean that you clearly think I'd make soup out of you and feed it to Sam. I'm beginning to have a pretty clear picture of the past five years, and just this once, while I have this blinding flash of clarity and reason, I want you to know that I'm sorry. People will tell you that mothers don't have favorites, Bil, and that's true. I love all of my children equally, but Sam and I—we have a different kind of bond. He needs something from me that the rest of you don't. Because he's sick. But I can tell you right now that I would never allow you to go to jail to save your brother. He's made his bed, and now he can lie in it."

She looked bone-tired, and I wanted to do something for her. Unfortunately, I couldn't think of anything. Her choices were all tigers, too.

"Emma," I said, "that man who died in Sam's cell—what would you say if I told you that he wasn't Burt Wood? He was Frank Frost."

She answered without any hesitation at all. "I'd say that you haven't lost your talent for eavesdropping."

Chapter 20

Emma and I talked until six-thirty, when I dropped her off at the hospital. Like it or not, I had to see Sylvie. The weather had turned decidedly cold, and the forecasters predicted an early frost. Though the sun was up, the sky was low and dark, and the wind was blowing fiercely. I needed to sleep, but I couldn't and wouldn't until I'd talked to her.

Sylvie's apartment was on the third floor of an old building downtown, not far from the Cowslip Café. I rang the doorbell several times. There was no answer. I was contemplating my next move when someone tapped me on the shoulder.

It was Sylvie. She stood there in her bomber jacket, her head cocked to one side. The jacket was zipped all the way up, and her hair was pulled back into a short ponytail. Her cheeks were wind-burned, not surprising if she'd ridden a long way in a cold wind.

"You'd better come in," she said.

I followed her through the front door and into the large hallway.

"I'm going into the kitchen to make us some coffee."

I shook my head. "I don't want any."

"I do. You can wait in the living room."

She was brisk though not unfriendly. I went into the living room and sat down on the sofa. I hadn't paid much attention to my surroundings the night I slept over. I realized now that it didn't look like a student's apartment. The sofa was slip-covered in a soft, white cotton twill, and it looked new. There was a large abstract painting hanging on the wall above the fireplace. There were no posters anywhere, just photographs and watercolors, all framed and matted. I wondered what Sylvie would make of the poster of "Monarch of the Glen" that Emma had nailed up over our sofa. Not that I was likely to be taking her home anytime soon.

She came back with two mugs. Coffee for me, like it or not. I would have preferred a pillow.

"I forgot the sugar," she said. "I'll be back in a second."

No matter which way I tried to sit on the sofa, I felt awkward. The cushions were too soft, and they seemed determined to surround me and suck me into their depths. That explained the sore back I'd gotten the night I'd slept over. I finally opted for sitting sideways, my back against the arm and one leg drawn up, the ankle resting on the opposite knee. When Sylvie came back with the sugar, I realized that I probably looked like a *GQ* ad, but it was too late to try to reposition myself.

She sat down on the opposite end of the sofa and drew her legs up beneath her.

"Comfortable?"

"Ecstatic. Your couch is trying to eat me alive."

"It's probably hungry. I haven't fed it any guests lately."

"So, how have you been since yesterday morning?"

"Fine," she yawned. "And yourself?"

"Just peachy," I yawned in response. "Never better."

We sat in awkward silence for a minute. I didn't want it, but I took a big swig of my coffee, burning the tip of my tongue and spilling at least half a cup down the front of my shirt.

"Goddamn it to hell!"

Sylvie flinched. I felt horrible and tired. I put the cup down on the coffee table and stood up. "I'm sorry. I'm going to get an ice cube. I burned my tongue."

She stood up as well. "Do you want to change your shirt? I've probably got something you could borrow."

I looked down at my front, covered in hot brown liquid. "Yeah, if you don't mind."

"Sit down," she said. "I'll get you that ice cube as well."

She came back with a soft blue T-shirt and a glass of ice water. I fished out a cube and popped it into my mouth.

"The bathroom's at the end of the hall. You can change in there."

I nodded and left the room, my tongue now too frozen to speak. When I came back, she was standing by the window, looking out. I sat down and sank back into the sofa cushions. Still looking out the window, she said, "I guess you heard."

"Heard what?"

She turned around and regarded me closely, leaning back against the sill. "About my mother. Isn't that why you're here?" I nodded as if I knew what she meant. "They haven't charged her with anything yet."

"I saw you in Spokane yesterday," I said, no longer able to hold it in.

"Really?" She raised her eyebrows but otherwise made no other reaction. "That must have been in the afternoon."

"Early evening," I corrected.

She nodded. "I got home just after eleven. There was a message on my answering machine. I went down to the sheriff's office to see if there was anything I could do. They aren't holding her as a suspect, they just wanted to ask her some questions."

"Like what?"

"Had she seen him, had he called her, did he want money."

"Did they ask her about the identification?"

"No, or if they did, she didn't tell me about it. I left my bike at the station and drove her home in her truck."

"What did she say?"

Sylvie came back over and sat down, this time next to me rather than at the other end of the sofa. "They're now treating this as a murder investigation. According to the autopsy results, it wasn't an overdose. He was poisoned."

"I know."

She looked up sharply, her eyes an intense green. "Bil, why are you here? Has your mother been . . . ?"

"No, at least not yet. I'm here because the shit has hit the fan." The cushion against my back was cool and soft, and despite my agitation, I felt myself beginning to drift off. If I could just sleep for fifteen minutes, I was sure everything would make sense.

"What's happened? Bil," Sylvie grabbed my leg and shook me. "Bil!"

I struggled back to the surface. "My mother knows that man was Frank Frost, and if the coroner checks your father's medical records, he'll know, too."

"Why? Bil," she shook me again. "Why?"

"The dead man had three kidneys. My mother says Frank had three. He used to make some stupid joke about being able to drink fifty percent more than a normal man."

Sylvie repeated slowly, "He had three kidneys. So they might know he's not my father, but it doesn't follow that they'll necessarily know he's Frank. It's a genetic abnormality. Unless they pull Frank's records . . ."

I nodded in agreement; the action made me dizzy. I kicked my shoes off and drew my feet up, resting them against Sylvie's thigh.

"Bil?"

Her face was suddenly very close to mine. I didn't open my eyes.

"I saw you in Spokane," I said again.

"Be quiet," she whispered against my ear. "We'll talk about it later."

I woke up with a start. The sun was shining in my eyes through a chink in the blinds. I blinked once or twice and then sat bolt upright. Sylvie was sitting in a rocking chair, facing me though her eyes were closed. When I swung my feet down onto the floor, she opened them and yawned.

"Feel better?"

"Do you know what time it is?"

She looked at her watch. "Eleven-thirty."

"And it's Tuesday?" She nodded. "Then I don't feel any better. I should have been in French three hours ago. I need to call home. Can I use your phone?"

"There's one in the kitchen and one in my bedroom. You'll have more privacy in my bedroom."

"Thanks."

I sat down on the edge of Sylvie's bed, a futon on a low wooden frame. The walls were cream-colored and plastered with a lot of framed photos of vintage motorcycles. I recognized the old Harley-Davidsons, but the other bikes were obscure.

My father answered on the second ring. Emma and Sam were still at the hospital, and Sam was walking again. Hugh wasn't sure when he'd be released. Knowing my brother, he'd check himself out in the next hour or so.

I went back into the living room. Sylvie had moved from the rocking chair to the sofa. I sat down next to her.

"Is everything okay?"

"It's back to normal, anyway." I covered up a yawn with the back of my hand. "I'm sorry I fell asleep like that. I didn't mean to."

"Don't be sorry," she smiled. "But if you feel awake enough, I'd like you to finish what you were saying."

"About Frank and his three kidneys?"

"And everything that led up to it."

I began with coming home to find the note on my pillow and wound up with Emma and I sitting in the House of Pancakes.

"So, I just blurted it right out. I said, what would you say if I told you the dead man was Frank Frost? She didn't even bat an eyelash. She said that's exactly who she thought it was, and for proof, she brought up the three kidneys. My sister Ruth got a look at the autopsy report."

Sylvie was watching me intently. The gold rims around her pupils were shining brightly. "My father only had one kidney. He had a younger sister on dialysis. She died shortly after the transplant surgery. I think it was the only unselfish thing he ever did."

I said nothing, waiting for her to continue.

"So they must know. They know she lied, and they want to know why."

"Maybe," I agreed, "but it could be that she made a legitimate mistake. Maybe she really thought it was Burt."

Sylvie leaned back against the arm of the sofa and closed her eyes. "You still don't believe me."

"I'm just trying to cover all of the bases. You were six years old. Your father disappeared sixteen years ago. If you saw what you think you saw, if it wasn't a dream, then he's dead, and that means that your mother deliberately lied to the sheriff. If he's not dead, then he might have changed a lot. Your mother might have forgotten exactly what he looked like. Either way, there are a lot of possibilities that the sheriff will have to take into account. The best thing your mother can do right now is to keep telling the same story, even if they ask her a thousand times. That's what my mother's doing, even with me."

"Did you ask her about my father?"

"No, I didn't. I couldn't. She wanted to know how I knew that was Frank and not Burt. I told her the truth—that you'd seen him in your mother's kitchen the day before he died."

"What did she say?"

"She said he probably wanted money. Frank was always short on cash. She was just surprised that he waited this long to come back."

"Maybe he didn't. Maybe he's been getting his money long distance."

"Blackmail?"

She nodded. "What if he knew what happened to my father? He might even have guessed. My mother's not poor—my grandfather left her the bulk of his estate. He didn't approve of Aunt Agnes marrying Fairfax, so he wrote a lopsided will. My mother tried to make amends, but Agnes wouldn't touch it. She said she and Fairfax had plenty of money."

"Do they?"

"He's got family money, or so he says. Haven't you heard about his rich East Coast relatives?"

"Endlessly from my grandmother, who's impressed by that kind of thing. Before she claims you as her friend, she sets you up on a spreadsheet."

Sylvie laughed. She looked more relaxed now, but her fingers played nervously with a loose thread on the sofa.

"So," she said, "do you have any classes this afternoon?"

"Two. Do you need me to leave?"

"That's not what I meant. I was just thinking that if you were free . . ."

"I'm free," I replied too quickly. "I've missed one, why not miss them all?"

She smiled. "You might wish you hadn't said that. I've got a confession to make, Bil. Before you fell asleep, you said something about having seen me in Spokane. Do you mind if I ask you when exactly that was?"

I avoided her gaze, not wanting her to read anything in my response. It was bad enough that I'd quizzed her about it. She was free to do whatever she liked, and with whomever.

"In Jackie J's," I replied, keeping my voice as neutral as possible. "Tipper and I went shopping and then to Jackie's for dinner."

She seemed embarrassed, and I stared at her, puzzled.

"Oh, I thought you'd seen me earlier."

"Where were you earlier?" I asked, unable to keep myself from sounding suspicious.

"That's the confession part. I ignored your advice and went to see a private detective. I found his name in the Spokane phonebook."

I must have looked as dumbfounded as I felt.

"I just . . . I wanted to see if there was anything he could do that we couldn't. I know what you said about poking around quietly, but I got scared. I called this guy, and then I went up to see him. He said he'd be discreet."

"And?"

"I don't know. He was more expensive than you thought—he wanted five hundred dollars a day. That was all I had in my savings account."

I looked around me dubiously, and Sylvie blushed. "My mother's footing the bills while I'm in college. She set up a joint checking account for me, and she gets all the statements. I closed my savings account and paid the detective in cash."

"You don't have to explain."

"You think I'm a spoiled rich kid."

"No, I don't. Who am I to talk, anyway? My father just gave me four hundred dollars to pay for a truck repair. I haven't worked since I came back from Seattle. I live at home on student loans and mooch off my parents. If anyone's spoiled, it's me." And I certainly didn't know what it was like to be terrified of my own father, I thought silently.

She said, "I gave him an abbreviated version of what's been going on, leaving out what I saw that night in the backyard, and asked him to look into Frank's disappearance. I hired him for one day on the condition that he not come down to Cowslip to interview anyone."

"What can he possibly find out that way?"

"He says he does most of his work by fax, Internet, and telephone.

Except for the divorce cases, of course, which seem to constitute the bulk of his business."

"He follows cheating spouses around?"

She nodded. "Gruesome, isn't it? I think he's a photographer who got into investigative work."

I hoped she hadn't wasted her five hundred bucks. I also hoped that he'd be as discreet as he'd promised. "So, when do you get your report?"

"Tonight," she replied. "Five hundred dollars paid for twenty-four hours. That's why I wanted to know if you were busy. Are you up for another trip to Spokane?"

"Why doesn't he just phone you?"

"I'd rather he didn't. I'm probably just being paranoid, but I don't want his name cropping up on any record of calls either to or from this number. I called him from a pay phone to make the appointment. Besides, I'd rather meet with him face to face."

"I'd probably have done the same thing. When do you want to leave?"

"He told me to be there at eight, so we don't need to leave here until six. You can go back to sleep if you want, either here or in my room."

"Don't you have a roommate?"

She laughed. "Not so you can tell. She spends every waking moment these days with the Lesbian Avengers, planning actions."

"What about you? You went to the early meetings, didn't you?"

She shrugged. "I decided it wasn't for me. I'm not the Lesbian Avenger type."

"Obviously," I smiled ruefully, "neither am I. A. J. used to . . ." I stopped short. A. J. was the last person I wanted to bring up. My stomach did three jackknifes and a swan dive before Sylvie spoke.

"What about A. J.?"

I forced myself to meet her look squarely. I might be a fuck-up, but I wasn't a wimp. "A. J. used to call me a Saturday night dyke. I don't think she meant it as a compliment."

"Probably not."

I stared at the floor, the window, anywhere but directly at Sylvie. Finally, feeling a desperate need to say something, I said, "I'll take the sofa. I've gotten used to it, and you'll be more comfortable in your own bed."

"Fine," she agreed. "Should I set the alarm for five p.m.?"

"That's fine. It usually takes me about half an hour to wake up completely." She got up to leave. "One more thing," I said, stopping her. "You don't by any chance have a contact lens case and some saline, do you?"

"I don't," she said, "but I'm sure Nancy does. I didn't know you wore contacts."

"You don't remember my glasses? I got them in first grade. They were hideous."

"Guess I forgot. I'll go search Nancy's room."

She came back a few minutes later with a case and a bottle of disinfecting solution.

"It's a good thing Nancy wears contacts," I said, peeling a lens off my eye and depositing it into the case. "These were beginning to fuse to my corneas."

"She doesn't," Sylvie said. "My roommate is a bit of a Casanova. She keeps a spare toothbrush, contact lens stuff, and anything else an overnight guest might need in the bottom drawer of her dresser."

"She's a regular Girl Scout," I observed wryly.

"Good thing for you that she is. Can I get you anything before I hit the hay? A blanket, a glass of water?"

A goodnight kiss?

"Nothing," I answered. "Just give me a good shake at five, and if I don't wake up right away, be persistent. I'm a heavy sleeper."

"Right. Sweet dreams."

Chapter 21

A low, sexy voice was murmuring in my ear. "Do you want to take a shower?"

I smiled, my eyes still shut. "That sounds like fun."

"You've got time for a quick one," the voice went on, "but you'll have to get up now."

"What about you?"

"I've already showered," she said. "It's your turn. I picked out some jeans and a T-shirt I think will fit you. I stole the jeans from Nancy. You two are about the same size."

I opened my eyes, awake now.

"Could you hand me my lens case? I left it on the coffee table, and I can't see a thing."

"Here you go," she said.

Sylvie came into focus, and I smiled at her. She looked fresh, like she'd actually had a full eight hours of sleep. Her hair was tucked back behind her ears, and gold hoop earrings reflected onto the golden skin of her neck.

"I think I'll take that shower," I said, painfully aware of my own disheveled grubbiness.

"There's a clean towel on the rack, and the clothes are on the vanity. I hope you don't mind," she looked away, "but I got a pair of boxer shorts for Christmas. I've never worn them."

"It wouldn't matter if you had," I said without thinking. "I grew up with four siblings. Wearing other people's underwear is not a novelty."

To stop the perpetual motion of my mouth, I hurried off to the bathroom. Even though I desperately wanted to linger under the hot spray, I got in and out quickly. I dried off and examined the clothes on the vanity. Nicely faded button-fly jeans, a white T-shirt, and the boxer shorts, which were plaid. She'd even thought to supply a pair of socks.

"You ready to go?"

"All but the shoes," I replied. "You know, I've got a new shirt out in the truck. Tipper picked it out for me yesterday. He tried to make me buy a necktie as well."

"I love women who wear neckties," she said.

My heart stopped, and then resumed beating at a rapid rate.

Sylvie handed me her bomber jacket. "Here, you'll need this. It's pretty cold out there."

"What about you?"

"I've got a red anorak my mother bought me. She's always complaining that I never wear it. I don't really like it."

"Count yourself lucky. I expect your mother has better taste than mine."

I followed her down to the parking lot. The wind was biting, and I began to wish I had a hat. Sylvie seemed oblivious to it. I hoped she wasn't one of those die-hard prairie women. Emma always said I had thin blood, which was her way of saying that I was a wuss.

"It's really cold," Sylvie said.

Thank God. This being Idaho, the parking lot was filled with four-by-fours, and at least three of them were red Toyotas. It took me a moment to figure out which one was mine.

"She's over here," I said at last. "I really should get a bumper sticker or something to help me spot her."

"She? Have you named your truck?"

I began to feel foolish until I saw that she was smiling at me.

"Sue, Sue the Toyota. I'm an animist at heart. I don't name my shoes or anything, but I do name motor vehicles."

She laughed. "It's a nice truck," she observed, climbing in. "I love my bike, but it's not practical. Come November, I'll have to borrow the farm truck."

"It's fine to be practical," I said, "but I long to be exciting. I love motorcycles. Emma would have a cow if I ever got one, though."

"You can ride mine anytime you like."

"Really?"

"Have you ever ridden before?"

"Sure. Tipper had a dirt bike when we were in high school. Since I practically lived at Fort Sister, I learned to ride around the same time I learned to shoot. My mother was furious. She's violently opposed to motorcycles and firearms. Don't ask me to explain it. She used to be quite the tomboy herself. In fact, she had a motorcycle when she met my father. She was the scourge of my poor grandmother's life. Imagine grooming a debutante and ending up with Dennis Hopper."

Sylvie laughed. "You can ride my bike without fear of recrimination. Just make sure your mother doesn't see you."

"Is your detective downtown or on the outskirts of town?"

"Downtown, just head for Division Street. I'll give you directions once we get there."

I backed out of the parking lot and headed for the Washington border. We drove along in silence, Sylvie resting her head against the window. Once we were heading north through the rolling wheat fields of the Palouse, I looked over at her. Her eyes were tightly shut, though I didn't think she was asleep. Still, she didn't open her eyes and we didn't speak to one another until we were thirty miles outside of Spokane.

"Where to?" I asked quietly.

Sylvie yawned and stretched. "When we get to the Division Street exit, take any of the streets that head downtown. Park wherever you can in the shopping district. We can walk from there."

I nodded. "Do you mind if I turn on the radio or play a cassette or something?"

"No, I don't mind. I didn't think your radio worked."

"Oh, it works fine. I just didn't want to wake you."

"That was nice, but I wasn't really asleep."

I picked a cassette at random from the pile on the seat between us and hoped it wouldn't betray my bad taste. I listened to a lot of different kinds of music, but in the car, I liked to play stuff I could sing to. As it turned out, it was one of the tapes I'd compiled myself, various tracks from various albums that had taken my fancy.

Sylvie smiled happily as the first strains of Willie Nelson's *Stardust* began to play. "That's excellent, Bil. I was afraid it was going to be Melissa Etheridge."

Now I was truly worried. "Don't you like Melissa Etheridge?"

"Don't panic," she laughed. "Of course I do. They'd revoke my dyke membership if I didn't. Still, it's nice to hear something different. Every time I get into a lesbian's car these days, she's playing Melissa or k.d. lang or the Indigo Girls. This used to be the love that dare not speak its name."

"And now it won't shut up?" I shook my head and smiled. "Aren't you a little too young to be jaded?"

She laughed and stretched again, her breasts pressing against the front of her shirt. I gripped the steering wheel tightly and concentrated on the road, willing myself to be a paragon of self-control. Besides, she might not listen to k.d. lang, but that didn't stop her from dining with her twin.

"I suppose I am jaded," she said. "Just ignore me. I love all of them. Well, most of them."

"Care to be more specific?"

"Not until I know you better. I don't want to end up on your bad side."

"I don't have a bad side."

She closed her eyes again. The picture of her sitting in Jackie J's swam before my eyes and splashed cold water on my libido. I slackened my grip on the steering wheel. When I turned onto Division Street, she sat up and yawned. At Sylvie's direction, I parked the truck in front of Nordstrom's. It was quarter to eight.

After we'd walked about seven blocks, I said, "I could have parked closer. There are plenty of spaces around here."

"I think they're vacant for a reason. I didn't want anything to happen to your truck."

"How about my body?"

"I'll take care of that." She stopped and smiled reassuringly. "I've been taking karate for the past five years. It was my mother's idea. She takes it too."

Two blocks later, Sylvie stopped in front of an iron-barred display window for a place called Jackson's Pawn Shop. I stared at it dubiously.

"It's upstairs," she said. "You have to go through the back of the shop to get to the staircase."

Cowslip had two pawnshops, both of them seedy. Jackson's Pawn Shop made them look like Nordstrom's. As I followed Sylvie past toasters, electric guitars, baby strollers, and ice skates, I grew depressed. How much did a pawnshop pay for a blender, two or three dollars? Whatever it was, someone was desperate enough to take it.

A fat, greasy man sat behind a glass counter in the back of the shop and stared at us through long, sticky bangs. Lying on the floor at his feet was the inevitable pit bull. It looked up as we walked by, its big square face perfectly placid. Why couldn't people just get Labradors?

"Nice dog," I said.

The fat man laughed and the dog laid back down with the side of his face pressed flat against the dirty tile floor. We walked down a short hallway and through a freshly painted white door marked Reginald Brown Investigations. Brown's office was at the top of a narrow, carpeted staircase that stank of stale cigarettes and urine.

"I'm sorry," Sylvie said. "I found this guy in the phone book. I guess I was desperate."

"It's okay," I lied. "Sam's dragged me to worse places."

Reginald Brown was his own receptionist. We knocked on the door, and he yelled for us to come in. I whispered in Sylvie's ear, "If I made my living spying on cheating spouses, I'd be more careful."

"Shh," she said, "he'll hear you."

We went in, and Brown stood up to greet us. He was smiling. I'd been expecting a low-rent Philip Marlowe. The man who reached out gleefully to shake our hands was young, not much older than Sylvie and I, and instead of a trench coat and fedora, he was wearing nearly the same outfit I had on. His office was nice, too. Big and airy, with new carpet and good furniture.

"Hello, Miss Wood and friend," he said, nodding at me. "Please, sit down."

I looked around his office. It was fairly large, with two rooms leading off the west wall. The door nearest Sylvie and me had a red light next to it, probably a dark room. Decoration was minimal, a couple of Ansel Adams posters. It was clear how Reggie spent his money—his computer must have cost a mint. Fifteen-inch monitor, color scanner, and, sitting on the desk in front of him, a digital camera that cost God only knew what. The box the camera had come in was sitting on the floor next to his desk, and the manual lay open in front of him, so I suspected this was a recent innovation. He saw me looking at the camera and ran his hand over it protectively.

"Nice system," I said.

Brown smiled again, and I noticed for the first time that he was wearing braces.

"Thanks. It's all tax deductible, too."

Sylvie cleared her throat, and Brown quit grinning.

"Well," he said, "let me tell you what I've learned. If you'd give me a couple more days . . ."

"I can't afford a couple more days," she replied firmly.

"Right," he said sadly. "Anyhow, I followed your instructions to the letter. I called all of the people on your list and told them I was with the Associated Press. I said we were interested in the Burt Wood story, missing for nearly twenty years and then he turns up dead. I contacted the Lewis County Historical Society—a lot of good stuff there—and told the woman in charge, what's her name?" He glanced down at his notes. "Millicent Rutherford."

I elbowed Sylvie and mouthed the word, "Christ."

"Shh," she said.

Reggie Brown read on. "I told Mrs. Rutherford that we were thinking of focusing on the tie-in with the Frost robbery, although that isn't really the right word, as it was actually an embezzlement. Anyhow," he turned his back to us and opened a file on the computer. "Sorry. I haven't printed it all out. Some is still on the computer. I'll have to mail it to you."

"That's fine," Sylvie said.

"Right. Fred Maguire. Not much there. He was thrilled to be talking to the Associated Press, and it was hard to keep him focused. Free with the gossip. Said everyone suspected Frost was gay, but people were surprised by Wood. Frost and Wood went to high school together and were roommates for a while at Cowslip College. After that, Frost dropped out and went to work for Lewis County. He was an assessor."

He clicked the mouse and a small window opened in the lower right-hand corner of the screen. "I also did a little research into the Lewis County records. Public information, you know," he grinned back over his shoulder. "Just started putting it all on computer a few years ago. They're starting with the older stuff and working forward, rather than the later stuff and working back. Good thing, eh? Anyhow, Frost began working for the county in June of 1975. Nothing untoward until January 1976, when the county clerk wrote a memo to the Lewis County Commissioners detailing some problem with accounts in the assessor's office. There's a second memo in February saying that it was human error and everything was now hunky-dory."

He closed the window and read on. "Millicent Rutherford refused to discuss the Frost case in any detail, but she suggested I call Wilhelmina Aldershot. Lots of information there. Mrs. Aldershot claims that Frost was essentially a bisexual rent boy. On the condition that she not be quoted by name, she told me he'd had arrangements with Maguire, Burt Wood, and both Agnes and Fairfax Merwin. Maguire seems like a possibility. He has arrest records in New York and Chicago for solicitation. That could mean anything, of course."

Granny. I wondered just how much of her information was accurate and how much was idle speculation. About fifty-fifty, I decided, with a frosting of embellishment.

"The next people I talked to were Agnes and Fairfax Merwin. As you suggested," Reggie continued, with another over-the-shoulder smile, "I called her at home and him at the office. He flatly refused to talk to me and hung up. She was a little more forthcoming. She absolutely denied that Frost and Wood were having an affair—in fact, she was adamant about it. One thing I found interesting was that unlike the other folks I interviewed, she knew the exact dates on which the men disappeared. She last saw Frost on July first, and Wood on the third. She gave times and locations. On the night of July third, she saw Frost at a bar, the Wheatland, drinking a beer. She said she was there two-stepping with her husband. On July fourth, she claims to have seen Burt Wood's motorcycle at a rest stop on Highway 95. It was after two o'clock in the morning, and she was coming back from Spokane. Mrs.

Merwin said she waited around for several minutes to say hello, but he didn't come back to the bike. Eventually she left, as it was late and she needed to get home."

Heavy trucks rumbled by on the street outside, and I found myself listening hard to catch every word. Brown turned off his screen and turned back to the desk. "I checked on the bank transactions you asked about, and, for at least the past two years, money has gone out of Katherine Wood's account at regular intervals, five thousand dollars at a time. It may have been going on longer, but that's as far back as I could get. The transfers have been made quarterly, and they were in house, from one account at Pioneers Bank to another. The receiving account is held jointly by Kate Wood and Agnes Merwin. One other transaction might interest you—two transfers have been made from that jointly held account to a bank in New York. Here," he handed her a piece of paper. "The money went through an intermediary account on the way to its final destination. This is the name of the bank and the account number where it ended up."

Sylvie looked down at the paper he'd handed her before passing it on to me without comment. It was a list of names, banks, and transactions. Most of it seemed to be in Greek, but it was clear that the name on the destination account was Charles Gibb. So much for my theory of the spontaneous alias. I looked at the other names listed.

"So this intermediary account you mentioned—it's called the Fitzhugh Corporation? What's that?"

Brown wiggled his eyebrows up and down like Groucho Marx. "A blind, I think. I haven't been able to find out anything about Fitzhugh except that it isn't publicly traded. The Gibb account was dormant for a long time. Money began moving into it again a couple of months ago, all from Fitzhugh. As I said yesterday, if I had more time . . ."

Sylvie shook her head impatiently. Brown shrugged and continued, "I tracked them down as best I could, but I'm not a financial wizard."

"You're a hacker," I said.

Brown looked wounded. As if to sooth himself, he ran his hand absently over the digital camera. "I'm a private investigator."

"Is that everything?" Sylvie asked.

"Without another day or two to work on this . . ." Receiving no encouragement, he went on, "I'll tell you what I'd do if I were you. The classic detective's advice is *cherchez la femme*. In this case, I'd *cherchez la moolah*. Access your mother's accounts. All you need is the last four digits of her social security number and her mother's maiden name. Then, follow the connection between Wood and Frost. They'd known one another for a long time, and they both worked for the county as assessors."

"Assessors," I mused.

Brown stared at me blankly for a moment and then laughed. "An assessor determines how much property tax you have to pay," he explained, as if he were talking to a particularly dim-witted farm animal.

"I know that. I was just thinking."

"Really?" he smirked.

Sylvie stood up and offered him her hand. "Thank you for your time, Mr. Brown. This has been very interesting."

"If there's anything else I can do," he began.

Cut your fee in half so we can pay you for an extra day, I thought.

Half an hour later, we were on the other side of town at a combination bookstore and coffeehouse called Ellie's. Our waitress had just served us two coffees. What we'd actually ordered were two hot teas. I sighed and dumped three packets of white sugar into mine. Sylvie shook her head in disbelief.

"You'll rot your teeth."

"Not a chance, see?" I gave her a wide smile. "Strong and white, if a little gapped up front."

"Nice choppers," she agreed. "I thought you took your coffee black."

"I do," I said. "Usually. But tonight, I need the jolt. Caffeine plus sugar, the poor woman's crack cocaine. So what's this about a jointly held account?" I cocked my head and looked at her closely. "How did Brown get into your mother's bank accounts anyway? Isn't that illegal?"

She shrugged. "Through me. I gave him her maiden name and the last four digits of my own social security number. That was enough to run a full credit report on me."

"On you?"

"Yes, on me. My mother and I have a couple of joint accounts. I knew once he got into those, he'd be able to get into hers."

"But not without her permission."

"No," she agreed. "Not legally."

"Shit, Sylvie. He could rob you—he could rob your mother blind!"

"I don't think so. I'm not crazy. He's licensed with the state of Washington. He has to follow certain rules."

"But still, your mother's bank accounts . . ."

"A couple of those accounts are held jointly," she repeated. "I never look at the money. I just withdraw what I need, I let my mother know how much, and we call it good. I could have looked most of that stuff up myself."

"Then why didn't you?"

"Because our joint accounts are held in two small-town banks in the small town of Cowslip, Idaho. You don't think Betty Jane Oliver down at the Wheatland Bank might mention to my mother that I'd been making inquiries? She and my mom went to high school together. Or, how about this: picture me asking my Uncle Fairfax at Pioneers Bank for a record of all balances and withdrawals? No. It was better to have Reggie Brown asking the questions."

"Under what guise? He couldn't tell the bank he was with the Associated Press."

"No." She looked thoughtful. "He could have told them he was with a credit card agency or a brokerage or something. My mother has investments everywhere. No one would think anything of it."

Meaning Reggie Brown probably broke the law, I thought, but I didn't argue. Kate wasn't my mother, and the Woods' money wasn't anything to do with me, either. I said, "Listen, I've got a savings account with exactly a hundred bucks in it. I can't touch that, not if I want to keep my checking account open. Now, my checking account has about three dollars and fifty cents in it. I don't understand banks. I don't understand money. What I know about investments would fit in this coffee cup, with plenty of room left over for the coffee. I was completely lost in Brown's office. I only understood about twenty percent of what he was saying. Why does your mother have an account with Agnes?"

"I don't know—they barely speak. When my mother offered to

share the inheritance from my grandfather, Agnes turned her down flat, so that can't be it. Did you get a look at the balance? It's just over ten thousand dollars."

"That's a lot of dough."

She nodded. "I asked Brown to look into my mother's finances because I wanted to know if she was being blackmailed. The fact that he was able to trace a connection to Charles Gibb tells me she was."

"Maybe. Brown traced a connection from your mother *and* Agnes to Gibb, and it went through this Fitzhugh thing first. If that's a blind, then what does Agnes have to do with it?"

"I don't know."

I tasted my coffee and stirred another teaspoon of sugar into it. "What are you going to do?"

"Exactly what Brown said, look for the money. The problem is that I'm no more a financial wizard than he is. Before I do anything, I want more information on Frost."

"That's where I come in," I said. "Sarah should have finished that research by now. We'll see what she's got and take it from there."

Sylvie gazed up at me. "I'm glad you came today, Bil. I feel better when you're with me."

I wondered if I could be reading her wrong or just losing my mind. Everything she did and said was driving me crazy. During the three-block walk from the truck to the coffeehouse, she'd kept bumping into me and then excusing herself. There was a positive charge in the air between us, and my skin was buzzing.

She looked away first. After a few moments, she said, "This place is lesbian-owned."

The walls were plastered with big posters of Eleanor Roosevelt, Audre Lorde, and Angela Davis.

"I'd never have guessed."

"Smart ass."

"That's me," I laughed. "Actually, it does kind of surprise me. This is the first lesbian coffeehouse I've been to that has real sugar. Usually, you have to make do with molasses or something like that. Tipper and I went to one place in Seattle where we had our choice of either honey or maple syrup. It was disgusting."

"No need to worry about that here. Ellie's as big a sugar fiend as you are."

"Is she the owner?"

"She is." The green eyes met mine for a moment and then looked down again. "I used to go out with her."

I could hardly have expected Sylvie not to have had girlfriends. Probably lots of them. I wondered if Ellie was the k.d. lang I'd seen her with at Jackie J's.

"Isn't she a little young to own a coffee shop?"

Sylvie frowned. "Young? Ellie's thirty-five."

Not the same woman. "You must have been in diapers. Who is this cradle snatcher?"

"Shh," she said, laughing. "I don't think she's here, but who knows? She might be in the back checking her stock. She's paranoid about people ripping her off."

Sylvie looked into her coffee, gently swirling it with a spoon. The coffeehouse wasn't particularly crowded, and aside from the fact that one of Sylvie's ex-girlfriends owned it, I liked the atmosphere. Me'shell NdegeOcello was playing over the sound system, and the posters of famous feminists reminded me of my parents' den in the seventies. Someone had even slapped a "Feminism Spoken Here" sticker on the cash register.

The coffee was also good, if wrong. There were empty tables on either side of us, and the people sitting in the corners were absorbed in their newspapers and conversations. Sylvie was giving me a bemused look, and I felt the flush rising in my cheeks.

She said, "You wouldn't pass me a packet or two of that sugar, would you? The cream as well. I think I'll splurge today." She stirred two packets into her own cup.

"Don't believe the hype. Sugar is good for you."

She laughed, and took a sip. "Delicious. Deadly, but delicious."

If I'd been offered my pick of DNA, I'd have made Sylvie Wood. Exactly. Everything about her was perfect, from the faint freckles that ran across the bridge of her nose to the way she licked a drop of cream from her top lip. I wanted to ask her about the woman at Jackie J's, but how could I? With A. J.'s help, I'd pulled the rug out from under my own big feet.

"Would you pass me another sugar packet?"

"What?" I said, shocked out of my reverie.

"Sugar?"

I moved the whole container of packets over to her. She stirred in two more.

"Can we talk?" I asked.

"I thought that's what we were doing."

"We are," I said slowly, "and we aren't. What are we doing here? I mean you and me, not this stuff with our mothers."

Sylvie leaned back in her chair, balancing it on two legs. Before I could stop myself, I yelled, "Four on the floor!" She laughed and brought all four of the chair's legs back down with a loud thump.

My cheeks were on fire. "I'm sorry. That's what my mother always says."

"Bil." She leaned across the table and gazed at me, her fingers touching my face. "Your eyes are very blue, dark blue with snowy caps around the pupils. They're beautiful."

I took her hand. "What do you want to do?"

"I want to go home, and I want you to come with me."

"I can't take your sofa anymore. I feel like I spent the night in traction."

"I think you know," she said slowly, "that you won't have to."

"Then let's go," I replied, pushing my chair back. "It's a long drive."

"Wait." She laid her hand on my arm. Reluctantly, I sat back down. "There's something else I want to talk to you about, something I want to explain. It's about my father."

"Are you going to tell me the whole story?"

"What do you mean?" She pulled her hand back and put it in her lap.

I thought for a moment, trying to put feelings and impressions into words. "If what you saw was real," I said at last, "if you didn't imagine it, or dream it, or just wish that it were so, then I think your mother had more than one reason to kill him. He did more than just pinch the back of your neck and shove you around, didn't he? Your mother wasn't just afraid for herself, she was afraid for you. You were in some danger."

"Go on," she said quietly.

I shrugged—I didn't know any more. She sat very still. I reached across the table and held my hand out to her. She looked at it for a moment before she took it. Suddenly she seemed far away, and I wanted to bring her back to me. I touched her chin, lifting her face up so I could look at her.

"It's all right, Sylvie. He's gone. He can't hurt you anymore."

"How did you know?"

I laced my fingers with hers. "Intuition. I was afraid of your father. I've also been wondering what it would take for me to kill a man, the father of my child, and never look back. I'd probably want to murder someone who beat me up or killed my dog, but would I do it? It had to be something more."

She said, "On the day he died, I accidentally knocked my father's motorcycle over in the driveway. I broke something on it, and he choked me until I passed out. I don't remember anything after that, except what I saw that night. My mother knew we had to get away from him."

I nodded slowly. "But a divorce couldn't guarantee that. He might fight it or try to get joint custody."

"Or kill us. I think that's why your mother helped that night. She'd been trying to get my mother to leave for a long time. She knew we couldn't just walk out; we had to go somewhere that he couldn't find us."

She looked away. I held her hand tightly, squeezing it until she returned the pressure of my fingers. When she looked at me again, her eyes were clear. That made me sadder than if she'd been weeping uncontrollably. It also made me angry. Sylvie had learned to hide her feelings, to push them down out of sight where no one could find them and use them against her.

I looked down at our hands resting entwined on the table.

"Come on," I said. "I'll take you home."

Chapter 22

As much as I wanted to be with her, I wasn't looking forward to the drive back. I suddenly felt very tired. Outside of Spokane, the highway was dark and windy. Occasional gusts shook the truck, and by the time we were halfway home, fat drops of rain were pelting against the windshield.

"Only forty-five more miles," I said with mock cheerfulness.

"I'm sorry."

I looked at her. It was dark, but the dashboard lights caught the glow of tears on her cheeks.

"No, I'm sorry. I didn't mean anything. I'm always a jerk when I'm driving."

She wiped her eyes and then laughed. "It's not you. I just haven't had to talk about this for a very long time. It's hard."

I cast her another quick glance. The rain was coming down harder, and if it continued, we'd have to pull over. "When you want to talk about it again, I'll listen."

She sat up and blew her nose into a handkerchief. "Thanks for the offer, but I'll be all right. Once a month, I tell it all to a well-paid therapist."

"Is that enough?"

"That's enough. I'm okay, really."

Her hand rested momentarily on my shoulder, and then she leaned back against the door. The rain slackened, so I let the speedometer creep back up to fifty-five. I switched my brights off and made do with the low beams, as they didn't reflect as badly in the fog that was drifting over the fields.

"Do you want to listen to some music or something? It's still a ways back to Cowslip."

"Sure. Something quiet, maybe?"

I located a soft jazz compilation and slipped it into the cassette deck. Sylvie closed her eyes and stretched out her legs. In five minutes, she was asleep. The rain slowed us down quite a lot, and it was after midnight when we got back to her apartment. I pulled into the parking lot and switched off the engine.

"Sylvie, we're here."

She stirred and opened her eyes slowly. "I'm sorry," she said. "I meant to keep you company. That's a long drive all by yourself."

"It's okay. I need to get you upstairs, though, before you fall asleep again."

"I'm awake," she yawned, "but would you mind carrying me up?"

I smiled. "No problem. I'll just sling you over my shoulder."

We dragged ourselves up the steps and paused at the front door while Sylvie dug around in her pocket for the key. The apartment was dark and quiet.

"Looks like Nancy's out again. I expect she's gone for the night."

"I don't believe you have a roommate. Nancy's imaginary, like Harvey the rabbit."

"As long as she pays her bills."

I followed Sylvie down the hallway and into her bedroom. She opened a dresser drawer, and I flung myself down on the bed, flat on my back.

"Bil . . ."

"I know. Do you want me to go?"

"No."

I propped myself up on one elbow. "It's okay, you know. We're both tired and upset. I can keep my hands to myself, but I'd like to stay. I don't want to drive home, and . . . and I want to be with you." There, I'd said it, and there was nothing I could do about it now.

She nodded quickly and turned away. "Pajamas? I think I have a pair of flannels in here."

"T-shirt and boxer shorts, if that's all right."

"That's fine." She turned around and leaned against the dresser, smiling. "It's what I wear, with the exception of the boxer shorts, anyway. I prefer jockeys, myself. Do you want the first shower?"

"I'd like a shower, but . . ." I looked down at my trousers.

"Don't worry. My mother gave me a three-pack of boxer shorts. The other two are still lying folded and new in the top drawer. In the meantime, you can use my robe. I'll fetch that contact lens case from Nancy's secret stash."

I showered quickly, giving my hair only a cursory scrub. When I got out, not only was the lens case lying on the vanity, so was the toothbrush from my night on the sofa. I hadn't even heard her come in. I brushed my teeth, combed my hair, and wrapped myself in the thick, white bathrobe.

When I came out, Sylvie was leaning against the wall outside the bathroom.

"All yours."

"Thanks. If you hear water running an hour from now and I still haven't come out, it means I've fallen asleep and drowned."

"If you're not out in five minutes, I'll beat the door down."

"My hero."

T-shirt, boxers, and, in case I wanted them, a pair of socks were waiting for me on the bed. I put on the shirt and shorts. Assuming Sylvie preferred the side of the bed nearest the alarm clock, I climbed in on the other side and fell quickly and completely asleep. I was vaguely aware of someone coming in and lying down next to me. She might even have kissed me. I couldn't be sure.

I woke up at a ridiculously early hour. Sylvie was still sound asleep, so I wrote her a note explaining that I'd be back in time to take us both to class. Then I got dressed in my borrowed jeans and her leather jacket, and drove to campus. The closest space I could get to the library was still half a mile away, so I fished around behind the seat and dug out a wool ski hat. It was hideous. I only kept it for emergencies.

I figured it was because I had the hat on that I ran into Naomi.

"Are you Doug or Bob Mackenzie?"

"Neither, hosehead. What the hell are you doing on campus?"

She sniffed and rubbed her nose. I was pleased to see that it was red and puffy. "Library research. Hats are for wimps, you know. You need to toughen up."

"That's right, only the weak get frostbite." The wind was chafing my hands and cheeks, but I was trapped in a prairie-woman standoff. I'd be damned if I'd admit I was cold before Naomi did. "You seem to have a cold."

"That's got nothing to do with the weather."

"Of course not. What kind of research are you doing?"

She shrugged. "I've been asked to do some *pro bono* work."

"Who for?"

"Your crowd, Stop the Prop."

I stared at her in amazement. "Well, fan my brow."

"Oh, shut up," she snapped. "I've agreed to do it because it's good for my career. In a couple of years, I'm blowing Cowslip and heading straight for D.C. Sarah and Ruth might be happy whiling away the hours in this Podunk, but I'm on to bigger and better things."

"Like what, Lambda Legal Defense?"

"Who knows? If you're smart, you'll quit standing there with your mouth hanging open. Between the hat and the mouth, you look like you're in training to be the village idiot."

I closed my mouth. "Is there any particular reason why you're so cross? Batteries give out on your vibrator?"

"If they did, I'd just raid your room for spares." She sighed heavily. "Actually, it's nothing to do with you or Stop the Prop. I'm changing jobs at the end of this month."

Naomi worked at the law firm of Fitzroy, Fitzroy, and McAnulty. They were the largest firm in Cowslip, and, by those standards, prestigious. Naomi had crowed for weeks when they'd hired her. I couldn't picture her leaving voluntarily.

I said, "Why? Is something the matter at Fuck, Fuck, and McNutt?"

"Everything is the matter," she replied, flinging her arms out for emphasis. "As you know, Fitzroy the Second kicked the bucket last spring. George McAnulty should have become the senior partner, but there was an office coup, and Fitzroy the Third got the jump on him."

"How'd he manage that?"

She gave a short laugh. "Third is a sneaky weasel bastard, that's how. It's impossible to work for him—he's such a liar." She shoved her hands deeply into her jacket pockets. I was pleased to see that the wind was beginning to get to her, too.

"A lying lawyer, imagine that. What's your new job?"

"You're now looking at a Lewis County Public Defender."

I allowed my mouth to hang open again. "You? Law and Order, Hang 'em High Hardy? What happened to your life's ambition to be richer than Croesus?"

"Politics, sweetie. Didn't I just explain that to you? I need a broader range of experience than I'm getting at Fitzroy. I'd rather work for the county prosecutor's office, but this will do for now. It'll give me some criminal experience."

"No shit," I laughed. "It'll give you chance to defend the Sams and Francies of the world. They'll take away your Republican Party membership, you know."

"I voted for Ross Perot in the last election."

"Then you really are crazy. Does Emma know about this yet? She must be wetting her pants."

Naomi smiled, which made her look like the Grinch. "I haven't told her yet. Are you going to be home tonight? You can have a front row seat."

"Sorry, I've got other plans. You'll have to videotape it for me—she'll be delighted. She'll paint her ass blue and dance the fandango."

"No doubt. Now, if you'll excuse me."

"Are you off?" I asked innocently, suppressing a shiver.

"Of course," Naomi replied. "It's freezing out here."

Winner takes all. I decided not to gloat. "I'm actually on my way to the library as well. I'll walk you over."

"If you must."

Naomi made for the staircase as soon as we were in the door, which saved me the trouble of dumping her so I could talk to Sarah alone. Just as I'd expected, my sister was working the reference desk.

"Hi, Toots. Any messages for me?"

She reached under the desk and pulled out a fat manila folder. "You're in luck, pal. That's two hours of my precious time. I hope you appreciate it."

"Believe me, I do."

"Good. I'll be waiting for my Chinese dinner."

"Name the time, and I'll be there."

She laughed. "Don't worry, I will. So, infant, what's up? Your absence at the dinner table last night was noticed. No need to fret, though—your favorite sister covered for you."

"Even if you hadn't been my favorite before, you would be now. What were you doing at home on a Tuesday? Didn't you have a date?"

"I did," she said, "but that was later. I wanted to check up on Sam, so I ate dinner with Emma and Hugh and then met my date at the Art House. They were having a Marlon Brando festival."

"Does this date have a name?"

"Gary Smart."

I nearly swallowed my own tongue. "My abnormal psychology professor?" She nodded, and I said, "Does he know I'm your sister?"

"He does," she replied, "and now I know that you've missed more classes than you've attended. I covered for you there as well. I told him all about our family and our recent difficulties with Sam, and he said you could make up any work that you'd missed."

I gave her my sincere thanks. "Would you mind going out with a few of my other professors? I skipped three classes yesterday."

She shrugged. "Depends on who they are. I've been on mercy dates before, but never for the sake of a sibling. Now," she glared at me intently, "fair is fair. Where were you last night?"

"Behaving myself," I answered carefully. "I'm not ready to talk about it just yet."

"Fine with me," she said, raising an eyebrow. "Whenever."

"So, what's in the folder?"

"You'll have to see for yourself. Contemporary articles from the *Herald-Examiner* and a couple from the Spokane papers."

"You're amazing."

She nodded. "Aren't I just? Now, you have to pay my price. You have to tell me if you want all this information because Emma still has you working on Sam detail."

"I thought your price was a Chinese dinner."

She shook her head. "This is different." When I didn't answer, she said, "Look Bil, I know you get really involved in all of Sam's dramas, but I wouldn't worry too much about this. Naomi says they don't have a case. If possession of some shiitake mushrooms means you might have poisoned Burt Wood, then everyone who makes stir-fry is a suspect."

"That reminds me," I said. "Do you have any pictures of Datura plants? While I'm here, I might as well . . ."

"Fine," she laughed. "Do you have a few minutes?"

"I've got time. Thanks."

"You're welcome. Librarianship—it's not just a job, it's an adventure."

I got back to Sylvie's apartment at eight-thirty. She answered the door dressed and ready for class.

"Have you missed many classes this semester?" I asked.

She frowned. "A couple. How about you?"

"I've missed more than I've attended, but I have a secret weapon. Let's go sit down."

I led the way to the living room, and we sat down on the engulfing sofa.

"What's up?"

I showed her the manila envelope. "I think we should bag class and start putting two and two together. We can read through all of this stuff I just got from Sarah and maybe match it up with what we learned from Mr. Brown."

"I'm with you," she said, "even if it means blowing off classes tomorrow as well."

There were only ten articles. Sylvie and I took five each and then traded. They all said pretty much the same thing. The police believed Burt Wood and Frank Frost had left Cowslip in one another's company. Only two of the articles stated directly that Frost and Wood might be homosexuals. The *Cowslip Herald-Examiner* didn't mention it.

I found the details of Wood's disappearance interesting. According to several sources, he and Frost had a standing date every Fourth of July. No matter what day of the week the Fourth fell on, Wood and Frost made a weekend of it. It was a tradition they'd started in high school. They met in Spokane on the Fourth, rented a room in some dumpy hotel, and then spent several days touring the sleazy strip bars. On July third, 1978, Wood was supposed to drive his motorcycle up to a bar in Spokane called Clyde's Corner, where he'd arranged to meet Frost. Wood had booked a room at a motor inn called the Fifth Wheel—a room with two double beds, the *Herald-Examiner* carefully pointed out. The reservations were for the third through the sixth. The Fifth Wheel usually did a booming hourly business, especially on holidays, so, when neither man showed up, the manager let the room to someone else.

Some of the articles gave details about each man's height, weight, and distinguishing features. Similar builds, similar features; they even had matching mustaches. They could have been brothers. Or Castro clones. They also described what each was last seen wearing. Details about both cases were sparse, and the missing money was only mentioned in connection with Frank. There was a brief flurry of articles over the course of two weeks, and then it all stopped. The power of gossip and Mayor Frost, I suspected. People thought they had an answer to what had happened to the two men, and Frank's father's money effectively closed the official investigation. Vernon Young, now Lieutenant Young, was in charge of both cases.

"Did you get to the part about Vernon Young?"

Sylvie nodded. "He's the one who called my mother to make the identification. Hoping to clear up an old case, I suppose."

"Or hoping for some free publicity during his run for sheriff."

The articles about Wood were vague. Though they mentioned his wife and daughter, Sylvie was never mentioned by name. Wood's mother, Miriam, had given a couple of brief interviews. Otherwise, the articles focused on the circumstances of his disappearance rather than on his personality or character.

Frank, on the other hand, was discussed with thinly disguised salaciousness. He seemed to have lived his last year in Cowslip in constant peril of being run out of town on a rail. He'd been gone for nearly a week before anyone noticed that the county was missing a large sum of money. All of the articles had a field day with his juvenile record. I knew from my brother's experience that while juvey records are technically sealed, Cowslip was too small for that to mean anything in practice. People talked, people speculated, and the newspaper wrote what they had to say, carefully phrasing accusations as questions. Before he turned eighteen, Frank had been arrested several times for everything from possession with intent to sell to indecent exposure. After his eighteenth birthday, he either got smarter or just more careful. The *Herald-Examiner* mentioned two speeding tickets but nothing else.

In the back of the folder were two photos. Sylvie pulled them out first.

"My father," she said. A man with a bushy black mustache stared out at me, younger than when I'd known him. His eyebrows were heavy, almost meeting at the bridge of his nose, and his hair was short and straight, parted high on the left-hand side. According to the caption, he was a college sophomore.

I flipped it over and laid it face down on the coffee table. "Can I see the other one?"

The second photo was blurry, and it looked as if it had been cropped from a larger picture. Frost's head was too large for the frame, and there was no background either above or on either side. I couldn't tell if the blurring was the fault of the original or the photocopy. He had a broad, toothy grin and thick, dark hair cut in a shoulder-length shag. Like Wood, he also had a thick, dark mustache. He might not have made the grade as a Castro clone, but he wasn't bad looking.

"Do you think he was gay?"

Sylvie considered the picture, her head tilted to one side. "I don't know. Maybe he was just a tourist."

"Are you bi-phobic?"

I was suddenly swept up in a green gaze, sharp and intense. "No. Are you bisexual?"

I shook my head. "Just plain old lesbian. How about you?"

"Never slept with a man and don't want to."

I put the folder down on top of the pictures and sat back, pressing the palms of my hands against my eyes. The photocopies had been fuzzy and difficult to read. Sylvie tucked her feet up beneath her and sat cross-legged, facing me.

"Do you know any bisexuals?"

I nodded.

"A. J.?"

"Yes. That's how she identified at the time, anyway. I don't know what she is now that she's running around with the Lesbian Avengers. If you showed her a penis these days, she'd probably say, 'Who, me?'"

"When did you break up?"

"Officially? Five months ago. It had been coming for a long time, though. The crunch came when she called me one night and said she'd decided to embark on a life of non-monogamy. I moved onto the sofa, and a month later, I moved back to Cowslip."

"Oh."

"Oh?"

She shrugged and sat upright, hugging her knees to her chest. "I thought maybe it was more recent than that."

Lying didn't seem like a particularly good idea, though I admit I considered it. "Two weeks ago, I made a big mistake. The grapevine in this town being what it is, I'm sure you already know about it. I spent one night with her. It was stupid, and I was sick and sorry."

"If she's been sleeping with men . . ."

"We were safe," I said quickly.

She shook her head. "Do you still . . . ?"

"No, I don't. I thought I did, and when we broke up, I was devastated. Now, I think I was just naïve. I need to quit expecting every woman I date to want to marry me."

She laughed. "Does that mean I should cancel the cake?"

"Does that mean that we're . . . ?"

"I think we should, don't you?" Before I could answer, she let go of her knees and laid a finger against my lips. "On second thought, don't answer that. If I let you talk, you'll talk your way right out of this."

I opened my mouth to speak, but she put her hands on my shoulders and pushed me back against the sofa. She looked at me for one long moment, and then she kissed me. A surge of electricity ran from the top of my head down to my stomach and then back up again. I wrapped my arms around her waist and pulled her close, kissing her back with a vengeance. I was rewarded by her sharp intake of breath.

Her hands slid under my T-shirt, and I sank deeper into the sofa cushions.

She stopped just long enough to say, "My room?"

"Who needs a room?" I asked, pulling her to me again.

We were breathing quickly now, and the blood was pounding in my ears, deafening me. I traced three fingers up the inside of her thigh and over the zipper of her jeans. I opened the top button and unzipped, slipping my hand down into her underwear. I pressed in, and she thrust her hips against me. I kissed the hollow place just above her collar bone, and she groaned.

Sylvie was pulling the T-shirt off and over my head when I heard a key being turned in the front door lock.

"Shit," she said, sitting bolt upright. I yanked my shirt back down and ran a hand through my hair, trying desperately to snap to attention. Sylvie had her back to me now, and she was zipping up her jeans.

"Hi Sylvie," said a voice in the doorway. "What's going on?"

Then, I saw her. What's more, she saw me.

"Oh, hi." Her voice was chilly. "Haven't we met?"

"I've got to go," I said, pushing past her in a mad dash to get to the front door.

"Bil," I heard Sylvie call, "wait!"

I paused in the doorway. Sylvie put a tentative hand on my arm.

"Where are you going?"

"I don't know. Look, I'll call you, okay?"

"You don't have to go."

"Tonight," I said. "I promise."

I cast a quick look at the woman standing behind her, and then I left. It was the woman I'd seen Sylvie with at Jackie J's.

Chapter 23

I took the steps as quickly as I could, tripping over the last two in my hurry to get out to the parking lot. I reached my truck and managed to get in and shut the door before I burst into tears.

The woman had keys to Sylvie's apartment. I wanted to hate her, but I couldn't get past hating myself for being so stupid. What was it with me and non-monogamous women? For a long time, I rested my forehead against the steering wheel. Then I sat up and looked at my face in the rearview mirror. My eyes were red and swollen. I wiped them off as best I could on the sleeve of my borrowed T-shirt. It smelled like Sylvie.

As I shifted the truck into reverse, someone tapped on the passenger-side window. I shifted back into neutral, and she got in.

I said, "If you and I were the last people on earth, A. J., I'd still shove you out the door at fifty-five miles per hour."

She laughed and shrugged her shoulders. "You don't mean that, and you look to me like you could use a friend."

"I could. You, however, have never answered that description."

She shook her head sadly, and I switched off the engine. "Come on, Bil. You don't hate me nearly as much as you pretend to, and I don't hate you at all. Let's bury the hatchet and be friends. You want to tell me why you're sitting in a parking lot, sobbing your eyes out?"

"I'm not sobbing."

"Fine. Why are you crying then?"

"You can't imagine," I said, turning the full force of my anger and frustration on her, "that I would tell you?"

She backed away but made no move to get out of the truck.

"I didn't realize it was that serious."

I looked at her. I couldn't remember the last time I'd seen her wearing anything other than a femme fatale combat kit, but now she had on a soft, ivory-colored fisherman's sweater and a pair of loose khaki pants. Her hair was combed back behind her ears, and the only makeup she was wearing was a little mascara.

"What are you talking about?"

"You and Sylvie Wood," she said. "I didn't realize you were serious about her."

"What do you know about it?"

"Not as much as I thought. It was pretty clear that afternoon at the coffee house that she was flirting with you. It was also clear that you were responding. I just didn't think you were serious."

"What did you think?" I leaned back in my seat and waited for her to continue.

"I thought you'd seen me," she said finally. "I was sitting inside by the front window when you came in. I thought maybe you were putting on a show for my benefit."

I was puzzled. "Why would you think that?"

She looked at me for a moment. "Because I'm stupid," she replied, and then she blinked and looked away. "I thought maybe we could . . . I don't know. Pick up where we'd left off."

"We didn't leave off very pleasantly."

"I know that. I guess I just hoped. Then that night I met you outside of the Underground . . . Bil, I never wanted to break up with you, I just wanted to . . ."

"Branch out?" I suggested.

"You make it sound cheap."

I laughed. I might as well tell the truth. Any dignity I might have had was now lying in a heap on Sylvie's sofa. "You hurt me, A. J. I thought I was in love with you, but we don't have anything in common. We don't look at things the same way. It's true that I didn't just stop caring about you when we broke up."

"And now?"

"Look at me." She looked up, and I pushed a wayward strand of hair back behind her ear. "I think I'm in love with Sylvie. I don't know how she feels about me, not yet."

She said nothing for a minute or two. "So you've opted for monogamous bliss."

Monogamous? Maybe. I'd push like hell for it, though in that moment, I knew I'd take Sylvie on whatever terms she offered. I nodded.

A. J. said, "Can we do the lesbian thing and still be friends?"

"Maybe." I laughed. "You know, I used to lie awake at night thinking about how much I hated you. If that wasn't love, I don't know what is."

She smiled. "Thanks, I think."

I held my hand out to her. She took it, holding it for a moment in both of hers.

"So," she said, "why did you come tearing out of Sylvie's apartment like that? I was sitting in the car, waiting for Nancy, and you ran past me like the building was on fire."

"I left because . . ." I stopped, finally putting it all together.

"Because?"

I felt the urge to burst into tears again. "I left because I'm a fucking idiot. Nancy's her roommate, the Lesbian Avenger."

She nodded. "She's the one who invited the rest of us here to help organize. I can't believe you haven't met her yet."

"I thought she was imaginary."

"You what?"

"I've just humiliated myself, as usual."

She laughed. "Actually, I think this is good. Not the humiliation," she explained, "but the fact that you're in love with Sylvie. She's in love with you, too, you know. I wasn't planning to tell you that, but I guess I owe it to you. She's a lucky girl."

"What are you talking about? She lives with this Nancy woman."

"Who do you think told me? In fact, I spent most of last night holding Nancy's hand and listening to a catalog of the wonders of Sylvie Wood. She's so gorgeous, she's so smart, and she's so blind to the charms of the woman who shares her apartment. Nancy would like nothing better than to settle down to a life of dull monotony . . ."

"That's monogamy," I corrected, "and how would you know it's dull?"

"Touché. Anyhow, she apparently confessed her devotion the other night and got turned down flat. Sylvie was kind and apologetic, but she's all wrapped up in someone else."

"How do you know it's me?"

"Don't be a dork. I'm already getting fed up with being the sympathetic and platonic friend, so don't drag this out. You're in love with Sylvie, and she's clearly in love with you. So there." She leaned forward and grasped my chin in her hand. "Perk up."

"What the hell was she doing with Nancy in Spokane then?"

"Nancy's from Spokane. If you're talking about Monday afternoon, Sylvie offered to give her a ride home. Nancy wanted to beg her mother for some extra cash. We've got a big event coming up. In fact, I've been trying to call you about it. Are you free on Friday night? There's going to be a town meeting and . . ." A. J. laughed. "Are you listening?"

"I'm sorry."

"Don't be. It does seem a little unfair that Sylvie has two tall, dark, and handsome women weeping over her, and all I get to do is sit and console them. Suddenly I've turned into Miss Lonely Hearts."

I smiled at her. "A. J., I could just kiss you."

"I think you're going to have to," she replied. "It's my standard fee for services rendered."

I leaned across the seat, intending to give her a chaste little peck, but she pulled me to her and kissed me hard. Very gently, I pushed her away.

"Just checking," she said.

"You always were one hell of a kisser."

I could see Sylvie's living room window from the parking lot.

She said, "Go back upstairs, Bil, and give it the old college try, but I warn you—lesbians should be careful who they sleep with because one way or another, they're stuck with them forever. I don't think I have any friends I haven't slept with."

"Tell me about it."

"All right," she said, smiling. "Actually, I haven't slept with Nancy."

"I expect you'll soon remedy that. Besides, you know for a fact that she's available."

"And what about you?" she asked, gesturing in the direction of Sylvie's living-room window.

I shook my head. "I don't think I can go back just yet. This time, I've truly surpassed my humiliation threshold. I need to drive around for a while and get myself together."

"I don't know what you did up there, but don't leave it too long. You're very good at backing yourself into impossible corners." She opened the door and climbed out. "You might try calling me sometime. I've left my number with your mother about ten thousand times, and you know where I'm staying. I'm here until the election. After that, you can call me in Seattle."

"Okay."

"Do you mean it?"

"I said okay, didn't I?"

"Don't get huffy. If you do call me, though, don't tell Tipper. I don't think he likes me very much. I don't know what you told him."

"The god's own truth," I replied sternly. "No embellishments necessary."

She actually looked moderately embarrassed. "Well, try to put in a good word for me now. The Avengers and I have to work with him and his mother for at least another month, and she looks to me like she's packing a concealed weapon."

"Get out of here," I said. "What's her face is over there waiting for you." Nancy had emerged at the bottom of the staircase and was hesitating on the edge of the parking lot.

A. J. blew me a kiss and closed the door. The clock on the dashboard said it was eleven o'clock. I cast one last glance up at Sylvie's window. I couldn't face her, not yet. I'd been too stupid for words.

I started the truck and headed for Fort Sister.

The padlock was off and the gate was open, so I drove all the way to the front door. Captain Schwartz was out on the softball field, shooting skeet with a 12-gauge over-and-under. Jane was pulling clay pigeons for her two at a time. I stopped for a moment to watch her. Captain Schwartz never missed. She blew two pigeons to glory before she lowered the shotgun and waved to me.

"He's in the kitchen making omelets," she called, removing her hearing protection.

"Everyone else?" I called back.

"Ha! If you mean that load of lazy queens, they're still lolling about in their bunks."

I walked around the back of the house to the kitchen. Tipper was standing by the stove, flipping an omelet into the air with a quick flick of his wrist.

"How do you do that? You're as amazing with a skillet as your mother is with a shotgun."

"I'm showing off," Tipper replied. "Just like her."

"Why is she showing off?"

"Why do you think? It's been Annie-Oakley-gets-laid all week. She'll be shooting through quarters with a target pistol next. Here," he said, sliding the omelet onto a plate and handing it to me. "Sit down and eat this. The Faeries are all upstairs sleeping it off."

"Wild night?"

"All the way around," he said, joining me at the table. "We sat up late with the Folksong Army playing truth or dare. We always picked truth, and they always picked dare. You can see which is more exhausting. Toast?"

"Please. And butter."

When we'd finished eating, he said, "So, are you ready to tell me everything? You should be warned that I know some of it."

"Like what?"

"Well, we could start with where you've been for the past two days." He held up his hand to forestall any comment. "Don't interrupt. I won't ask what you've been up to, not yet anyway, because I know you haven't been up to it with A. J. She and the Avengers had their kiss-in at Union Square yesterday afternoon, and you and someone else were conspicuous by your absence. Now, as for the rest, you might have told me about Sam's near-death experience, about Burt Wood's autopsy, and about the fact that they've taken Kate Wood in for questioning."

I stared at him blankly, and he laughed. "As you might recall, one of our county cops has a thing going on with Miss Suzy."

"So, Suzy and the sheriff's deputy. Is it true love?"

"Who knows? It's lasted longer than most of his relationships. I can't tell if it's the great sex or the great information. Suzy loves having that inside edge. He's like the living embodiment of *Hard Copy*."

"And what about you?"

"I'm hard, but I'm no copy."

"Shut up," I said. "I mean what about you and Tom? How's that working out?"

He shrugged. "It's fun, but I don't think it's the real thing."

I opened my mouth to say I was sorry. Instead I said, "Hold out for the real thing."

He smiled and took a sip of his coffee. "You want to tell me about it?"

"I love her, Tipper."

"And you've spent the past two days proving it."

"Don't be crass," I said. "I'm serious. Besides, we haven't actually . . ."

Tipper interrupted me by spraying a mouthful of orange juice across the table. "What were you doing that night in the dugouts? What have you been up to for the last forty-eight hours? Don't tell me you've just been sitting around talking!"

"That night in the dugouts, she was upset," I said. "We both were. She told me . . ."

"She told you she was really a man? I can't think of any other reason you wouldn't go for it. This isn't the Bil I know. This one's all talk and no action. In fact, I've now changed my mind about Tom. There's a lot to be said for mindless fucking."

"Will you shut up?" Tipper rolled his eyes and sighed. "Listen," I continued, "this is serious in more ways than one. The man who died—who was murdered in the Lewis County Jail." I dropped my voice. "He wasn't Sylvie's father, he was Frank Frost."

I gave him an expurgated version of the story, much like the one Sylvie had told Reginald Brown. I said that she'd recognized Frank in Kate's kitchen on the Thursday before he died, and I also mentioned the fact that the dead man had three kidneys.

He stared thoughtfully at his now-empty coffee mug. He said, "I knew about the kidneys."

"Suzy's flatfoot?"

"Yeah. They must know by now that he isn't Burt Wood."

"Yes, I expect they do. Could I have some more toast?"

He nodded slowly. "Yes. I mean, no." More than half an hour had passed since my arrival, and the sounds of Radical Faeries stirring in their beds began to drift down the stairs. "Look, I'm going to make a phone call, and then you and I are going for a walk. Wait here—I'll be right back."

As I waited, I thought about Sylvie and what she must be thinking. She might be hurt or furious or both. In any case, I didn't see how I was going to make it up to her, and the longer I waited, the worse it would be.

"Come on," Tipper said.

"I'm sorry. I think I need to go. I've done something really stupid, and now . . ."

"And now," he said firmly, "you're going for a walk. We're going to get some fresh air into you and clear your head, and as soon as you're back in fighting form, you can leave here and resume battle. Come on, no arguments."

As Tipper had predicted, the Captain had abandoned the shotgun in favor of a target pistol, which she was teaching Jane how to shoot. They were both seated on the ground, aiming at a paper bull's-eye about forty yards away. Jane sat in front of the Captain, who reached around from behind to steady her arms.

"Love is in the air," I sang softly, "everywhere I look around."

"And if you lived out here," he replied, "you'd get every sight and every sound. I wish my mother would Sheetrock the whole house or at least buy a good stereo."

I laughed. "Where are we going?"

"We're retracing the mystery man's steps. When Cedar Tree saw him, he was heading up toward the top of the ridge. Keep your eyes open for clues, Nancy Drew. We're sleuthing."

"Lead on, chum."

We walked along uneventfully. I looked idly on either side of the footpath for jimsonweed, briefly entertaining a fantasy that our dead man might have stopped for a snack. I saw nothing that looked like the plant in the picture Sarah had given me. The path up to the top of the ridge seemed steeper than before, and tall as I was, I still struggled to keep up with Tipper's long strides. The trees were thick on either side, though the underbrush was dry and easily trod under foot. Just before the ruined house were the remnants of a barbed-wire fence. There was once a gate across the top of the path, but it had long since rotted and fallen to one side. Tipper stopped now and examined it.

"You're not going to believe this," he said. He held a strand of barbed wire between his thumb and forefinger. A two-inch swatch of dirty fabric clung to one of the barbs. "You want to take this back to your lab and give it a DNA test?"

I took the swatch from the fence. It was a belt loop from a pair of blue jeans. A breeze was beginning to pick up. It rustled through the cottonwoods, and their silvery green leaves hummed to us. I wished I'd thought to take Sylvie's jacket when I'd stormed out of the apartment.

I said, "This could be anyone's."

"It could," he agreed.

Still, it might have been Frank's. After all, we knew he'd been on the property. "Suzy's mole might be able to tell us if our victim's jeans were missing a loop. Do you think he can be trusted to ask a subtle question?"

"Ha!" Tipper said. "Wish in one hand, shit in the other, and see which fills up first. I'll try wording the question for him and see if I can get him to memorize it."

"Good plan. Would you mind walking all the way up to the ruined house? I'd like to take another look around."

"Sure thing," he agreed.

We walked in silence to the top of the ridge. Tipper was moving more slowly now, so I got to the foundation walls before he did. I saw them immediately. In fact, they were perched on a corner so I couldn't miss them.

I picked up the binoculars.

"Lucky find," Tipper said, coming up behind me. "I wonder who those belong to."

"My father."

He raised his eyebrows, and I told him about my time behind the bush, spying.

"Helen Merwin left them up here. While we've been poking around about Burt and Frank, she's been spying on us. I think Kate was being blackmailed."

The brown eyes met mine and held my gaze for a long moment. "Why?"

"I can't answer that."

There was a long pause. "Okay," he said slowly. "Why Helen? Is there any particular reason she might want to spy on you? Is she . . ." His eyes narrowed. "Please tell me you didn't sleep with her."

"For God's sake," I snapped, "are you barking mad? I have never in my life been that desperate. I'd sooner sleep with Cedar Tree. Or a bucket of razor blades. Or you."

"Fine," he said, "there's no need to get nasty." He gave me a pinch on the arm. "If I were unkind, I'd point out that you haven't always been . . . um . . ."

"Lucky?" I suggested.

"Choosy," he replied, and it was my turn to pinch him. "The question," he continued, "is if Helen has been spying on you, what are you going to do about it?"

"That depends on what . . ." I began before I could catch myself.

Tipper smiled. "Call it situational ethics. I'd do exactly the same thing. I didn't expect you to go running off to the sheriff's department; Sylvie's got to be your top priority."

"I don't suppose I should be counting my chickens, should I?"

"That's right. You can't cluck until you fuck."

"Excuse me?" I said sharply.

He laughed. "Lighten up, Bil, everything will work out. Now that we're up here, though, don't you want to look around? If you want to play detective, you'll have to detect. Police work is about more than being a uniform queen. Of course, being a uniform queen helps."

"Just look around, would you?"

We kicked through the pine needles, and once again, Tipper scored.

"What is it?"

"It," he said, "is a folded piece of paper. Would you care to open it? It might be a wadded-up bit of chewing gum, but I don't think so."

The paper he handed me had been folded over and over again,

until it looked like one of the paper footballs we used to flick at each other in ninth grade algebra class. I unfolded it carefully. It had been rained on and the corners were still soggy. Despite my care, it ripped.

"It's a page out of the Cowslip telephone book," Tipper said. "I can't read it, the ink's all runny."

"It's more than one page. I don't think I can get them apart."

"Can you see what's on the front and back, then?"

I held it up to the bright light coming through a gap in the trees. "It's Magnusson through Metcalf on this side, and Rowe through Spencer on the other. I think there's a page in the middle here, but I don't have a prayer of figuring out what that one says."

"Do you think it means anything?"

"Maybe." I thought it might mean a lot. Maguire and Merwin were on the first page, and Rutherford was on the back. The page in the middle might have listed the numbers for Wilhelmina Aldershot, Kate Wood, or Emma Hardy. There was no way of telling.

Tipper regarded me with undisguised suspicion. "I find it hard to believe that you're keeping secrets from me of all people. I'm your best friend in the entire world."

It was true, and I would have trusted him with my life.

"I'm sorry," I said. "You know all of my secrets, Tipper. These are someone else's."

He nodded, and I hoped he understood.

"Can I look at those pages?"

He stared at them for a minute or two, looking thoughtful. Then he handed them back to me.

"What do you think?"

"I don't really know what I'm looking at," he said. "I think it might be a list of suspects. Is that close?"

"That's close," I conceded.

"If you and Sylvie ever feel like you want to talk about it, call me. I'm no detective, but I'm a good brainstormer. I'm also discreet."

"Really?" I laughed.

"When I have to be," he replied seriously.

A lot of questions were hanging in the air between us, and I wanted to fill the space with some sign that I trusted him. I wanted him to know that if it were just up to me, I'd confide in him completely. I asked, "Tipper, who would want to kill Frank Frost?"

"Someone with something to hide. Find the motive, find your murderer. Your brother makes for an unsatisfying suspect, and according to Suzy's source, the prosecutor isn't really interested in him. She's just trying to make it look like this investigation is going somewhere."

"She'd also like to put him in prison for something. He's a pain in the ass."

Tipper was silent.

I said, "You know in high school, when you lost that fountain pen you loved? You didn't lose it. I stepped on it with my great big clod-hopping boot. I broke the hell out of it. I tried to find a replacement but . . ."

"Shh." Tipper smiled and wrapped his arm around my shoulder. "It's okay. You don't need to prove yourself to me. Don't tell me any more secrets. I was just having a jealous fit. I never considered A. J. much of a threat, but I'm beginning to suspect that you love Sylvie better than you do me. That's going to take some getting used to." He smiled again. "And I knew about the fountain pen. There were bits of it embedded in the sole of your great big clod-hopping boot. I also knew how bad you felt about it. You're more important to me than a fountain pen, Bil—even an irreplaceable antique like that one."

"Oh shit, Tipper, I . . ."

"Go on, you fool," he laughed. "Antique, my ass. I bought it at a pawnshop in Seattle. I think it cost all of three dollars. Listen, according to Suzy's mole, they're questioning everyone who was even remotely associated with either Frost or Wood. Fairfax and Agnes Merwin, Fred Maguire, Millicent Rutherford. They even called your grandmother."

"Really?"

"Really. That didn't make sense to me yesterday, but it does now. If the deceased is Frost and not Wood, then your grandmother knew him quite well. He was part of that whole community theater crowd. Didn't you know that?"

I shook my head.

"You're no Nancy Drew," he observed. "If I were you, I'd pay a visit to my prospective bride and discuss your latest clues. Besides, it's not nice to keep a lady waiting."

"What are you talking about?"

He grinned. "She called out here looking for you about fifteen minutes before you arrived. She told me you'd gone storming out of her apartment. She didn't say why, but I can guess. The course of true love never did run smooth. She knows you're here because I called before we left for our little walk. I told her I'd give you a good talking to and send you straight back downtown. There now, I've discharged my duty."

I stood aside so Tipper could blaze a trail back down the hill. Just as he brushed past me, I reached out and held his arm. "Why would Frost come up here?"

"Shortcut," he said. "And besides, there used to be a fairly decent house up here until my mother knocked it down. It was dirty and full of spiders, but the walls were solid and the roof didn't leak. He might have been thinking it would be a good place to squat while he sorted himself out. Back in his day, this was a favorite pothead hang out."

"You're pretty clever."

"Nonsense," he said. "Process of elimination. I have quizzed my mother thoroughly about this and learned that on Thursday, she caught him coming out of one of the guest cabins. He'd clearly snuck back after his encounter with Cedar Tree and slept in one of them."

"Did you . . . ?"

"Of course I searched it. There was nothing there."

"Wait," I said. "One more question. Since you seem to know everything else, who is Suzy's deputy boyfriend?"

"This is just a guess," he said thoughtfully, "but I think it's Donny Smith."

I was dumbfounded. "You're shitting me! A nice Mormon boy with a man like Suzy?"

"They make a lovely couple," he sighed. "Do you think they'll have a temple wedding?"

Chapter 24

I pulled into Sylvie's parking lot just after two o'clock. I thought about running up the stairs, but it wouldn't do to arrive out of breath. Plus my feet were blistered from my morning's trek. I vowed never to hike in wing tips again. In fact, as soon as I found my lost hiking boots, I was never taking them off my feet.

On the way up the stairs, I began to worry. What if she wasn't home? What if she looked through the peephole and decided not to answer?

"I should have called from Tipper's place," I mumbled to myself.

Still, I only hesitated a moment before knocking. What was the worst that could happen? Several creative possibilities suggested themselves. I was mulling over appropriate responses to each miserable scenario when the door opened.

She stood there, barefoot and smiling. Music was playing in the background and, after a moment or two, I recognized it as Sarah McLachlan's *Solace*. One of my favorites.

"I was just in the neighborhood," I said.

"Were you? Well, maybe you'd like to come in."

She opened the door wide, and I stepped inside.

"Have a seat in the living room. I'll only be a moment."

She came back with two mugs and set them down on the coffee table.

"Haven't we done this before?"

She smiled and sat down beside me. "It's déjà vu. If you wait a minute, it will pass. Besides, that's hot chocolate. I thought it might satisfy your sweet tooth."

"Sweet teeth, you mean."

Sylvie watched me with a bemused expression I found both uncomfortable and exhilarating.

"I took a hike out at Fort Sister." I told her what I knew about Frost's movements, and I showed her the belt loop and the pages from the telephone book.

"He's been blackmailing your mother. Nothing else makes sense."

"Someone has," she agreed. "That would explain the transactions from her account."

"You don't think it was Frank?"

"I don't know." She shrugged, cupping her mug in both hands. "I don't know much about the ins and outs of her finances. She gives me a monthly allowance. It's disgusting, isn't it?"

"Will you quit apologizing? A lot of parents put their kids through college."

"I don't know anyone else who has an expense account."

I laughed. She smiled ruefully and continued. "My mother owns a lot of stocks. She inherited some from my grandfather, but she's bought and sold those several times over. I know she felt guilty about the disposition of my grandfather's estate—he only left Agnes a thousand dollars. Spite money, she called it. Maybe Agnes changed her mind, and my mother's now supplementing her income. I do know that my mom's very good with stocks."

"Hugh plays the market," I said. "He's got about fifty thousand in various stocks."

She smiled. "When my grandfather died, he left my mother the farm and three hundred thousand dollars. She's turned that into three million."

My jaw dropped.

"Now do you see why I'm embarrassed?"

"No, but . . ."

"It's a lot of money, and the land has appreciated as well. We haven't had to run a working farm since my grandfather died. That was the year before my father disappeared."

I was amazed. There were a lot of wealthy landowners living around Cowslip, but I didn't know any of them personally. Kate Wood had taken ordinary, farm-family wealth and turned it into a fortune.

"Why doesn't she just pack up and move away from here?"

"Why do you think? My father is bound to have moldered away by now. If she thought to dump quick lime on him, the evidence might have been destroyed in a matter of weeks, but how could she be sure? She stays because she can't leave."

"That statement . . . you said there was ten thousand in that account?"

She shook her head. "Yes and no. It was only in there for a day before it was transferred out. I don't know how my mother's accounts work, or why she has so many. She seems to know what she's doing."

I could see that she was tired, and I felt stupid for not having come back sooner. I didn't know where to begin. Sylvie had pulled her knees up and was regarding me cautiously, waiting. It was now or never. I took a deep breath and waded in.

"I'm sorry. I shouldn't have run out of here like that. It was stupid. Even worse, it was unchivalrous and cowardly. I was . . . overwhelmed. Upset. Mostly, I was jealous."

"I appreciate the apology," she said, "but I'm a bit confused by it. First, why do you think you were unchivalrous?"

"You were tucking your clothes back in. I should have stayed, not left you on your own to smooth things over. That was pretty pathetic."

She shook her head and smiled slowly. In the dim light of the living room, her eyes were a rich, dark green. "Nancy sees me tucking my clothes in all the time. She lives here. Besides, it was her turn to catch me in an awkward moment for a change."

"Do you catch her a lot?"

"Fairly often."

"I understand she wants to mend her ways and become monogamous. With you."

"Who told you that?"

"I ran into A. J. in the parking lot. She's the one who clued me in to Nancy's true identity. I should have guessed that she was your roommate, but I wasn't thinking clearly. I saw you with her at Jackie J's and recognized her from the Lesbian Avengers' fire-eating performance, so I just assumed . . ."

"Assumed what?"

"That you weren't just together, you were together."

Though her arms were still folded across her knees, her face was beginning to lose its guarded look. "Why would you think that?"

"Because Nancy's so goddamned ugly," I snapped. "Come on, Sylvie. You live with a big lesbian wet dream."

She tried to frown, but she was stifling a laugh. "You're not doing a very good job with this apology," she said, "but go on. I want to hear all about how attractive you find my roommate."

"That's not what I meant. It's just that she's . . . oh, never mind. I saw you together, and I thought you were lovers, and I flipped out. There, happy now?"

She certainly looked happy. She had let go of her knees and stretched out on the sofa, laughing, her feet just inches from my lap.

"Don't look at me like it's a physical impossibility," I said. "Why wouldn't you be with her?"

"I've never been interested in Nancy."

"She's interested in you."

"It's just a passing fancy. She's got a big group of Lesbian Avengers to choose from. I'm sure she won't go begging."

"Not if A. J. has anything to say about it."

"Does that bother you?" She wasn't looking at me now, as if the answer didn't matter one way or the other, though her feet had edged closer to my thigh.

"No, it doesn't matter."

"Nancy really isn't my type at all, you know."

"And A. J. and I have finally sorted ourselves out. I don't like her, but I no longer feel morally obliged to hate her."

"Well, that's progress, I suppose. Do you feel obliged to do anything else with her?"

She looked at me now, and I met her gaze without flinching. "No."

We sat in silence for a moment, she in her corner and me in mine, with her legs stretched out between us. The auto-reverse on her tape deck clicked and began playing another Sarah McLachlan album, *Fumbling Toward Ecstasy*. I stood up.

"Bil," she said, tentatively, "I'm sorry to grill you like that. Please don't leave."

"Maybe this is too soon," I said. I was immediately sorry, and I wasn't exactly sure why I'd said it. Perhaps I was trying to force an admission out of her, something other than the fact that she wanted to sleep with me. I didn't expect to hear that she was madly in love with me. I just wanted some indication that she might someday get to that point.

She looked away again. "Maybe you're not as over A. J. as you think."

I laughed, and she looked up quickly.

"You don't know just how over her I am." I sat back down on the sofa, lifted her feet, and put them on my lap. "I don't care what she does. What I meant to say was maybe this is too soon for us. Maybe I'm pushing you."

She flexed her toes and shifted her weight against the cushions. I lifted her left foot and stroked it gently.

"Harder," she said, smiling. "Do you mind?"

"Not at all. I have a foot fetish."

"Hmm, lucky me," she yawned. "You're not pushing me, Bil. I broke up with Ellie a long time ago. That was my first real relationship, and I had a lot of things to work out about who I was and what I wanted to be. The age difference didn't help. She always felt awkward about me. She didn't like to introduce this kid barely out of high school to her friends and then have to explain that I was her girlfriend. She was afraid they'd say she was a . . ."

"Cradle snatcher," I finished for her. "I'm really sorry, Sylvie. I'm always putting my foot in my mouth."

"Is that what you mean by a foot fetish?"

I laughed, and she shifted against the cushions, lifting her hips in order to stretch out more completely.

"It's okay," she said. "I wasn't offended. The age difference wasn't a big deal to me—in fact, I was glad of it. I wanted her to be in control of the whole thing, to be responsible for it. It gave me the space I needed to really come out to myself. I'd dated women my own age, and it always felt awkward and experimental. We were only together for a year, but Ellie gave me confidence. I'm grateful to her for that."

I shifted her feet and stood up again. She looked up tentatively, and I smiled.

"I'm not leaving," I said, reaching a hand down to help her up. "But if one of us doesn't get up, we'll probably spend the rest of the day sitting here talking about our ex-girlfriends."

She stood up, her face only a few inches from mine. "What do you have in mind?"

"I was thinking that if we went into your bedroom and locked the door, I might be able to kiss you without disaster raining down upon us."

"I hope you plan to do more than just kiss me," she replied. Her head was tilted slightly to one side, her breasts brushing against mine.

"Are you sure?"

She shook her head and laughed. "Bil, you're an idiot. I've been sure for ages. Do I need to drag you into the bedroom before you change your mind?"

"I won't change my mind."

"How can I be sure of that? Only a few hours ago . . ."

I kissed her. She fell back onto the sofa, pulling me on top of her. I gave a second's thought to the possibility that Nancy might walk in again, but when Sylvie's hands found their way under my shirt, I didn't care anymore. I pulled it up over my head and tossed it into the corner. Sylvie sat up briefly and did the same with hers.

She moved down beneath me, trailing kisses from my neck to my navel. When she reached the top of my jeans, she unbuttoned them, and I sat up so she could pull them off.

"What is it about a woman in boxer shorts?" she asked, tugging at them.

I said, "If you keep that up, I'm going to faint. Come on, your jeans, too."

"Whose idea was this anyway?"

She pushed me over onto my back, and I wrapped my arms around her waist, wanting to feel her weight pushing me into the thick cushions. She pulled off my shorts and threw them in the general direction of my T-shirt and jeans. Then she hesitated above me for a moment, her breath warm and fast.

"Don't wait," I said. I was already embarrassingly ready, and her hands were all over me, the fingers skating around the edges. "Please."

She leaned down to kiss me. Her teeth tugged at my bottom lip, and I kissed her hard, winding my fingers into her hair.

"Anything you want to tell me?" she whispered.

"I'm safe," I said. "Don't worry."

"I'm not worried. I'm safe, too. Any other instructions?"

I thought for a moment. "I want to do this until we can't walk anymore."

She laughed. "It's a shame you're so shy."

"Shut up and kiss me."

For the next hour and a half, I forgot about everything and everyone else. I didn't care who came in the front door—Nancy, the Pope, or a marching band, it was all the same to me.

Afterwards, we were lying quietly, trying to catch our breath. Sylvie moved to get up. I pulled her back down on top of me. "Don't," I said. "I'm naked under here, you know."

She laughed. "And I'm getting pretty cold up here. I thought maybe we could move to my bedroom. There are blankets in there, and my bed isn't nearly as devouring as this sofa."

I made love to Sylvie again almost as soon as we touched the sheets, moving quickly and confidently where I had expected to be slow and tentative. She said nothing, and I stopped at one point to make sure I was doing what she wanted.

"What you're doing," she said, pushing me back down and gripping my shoulders so tightly it hurt, "is perfect."

She came in a great, silent wave, overwhelming in its intensity. Her back arched and stiffened, and her thighs closed on either side of my head, pushing me in and holding me there. Then, she released me and was still. I moved up to lie beside her, and she smiled and stroked the back of my neck. She was beautiful, more so now than I ever could have imagined. I wanted to open her up like a birthday present.

"I'm going to kiss every inch of you."

"Be my guest," she laughed.

When I reached the slight curve of her stomach, just below her navel, I paused.

"What's the matter?"

"Nothing's the matter." I moved up to lie beside her, propping myself up on one elbow so I could look at her. She rolled over onto her side, facing me, and I rested my hand on the curve of her hip. "This morning, I told Tipper that I was in love with you. I should have told you first."

I waited, letting my admission hang in the air between us.

She smiled. "You can tell me now."

"I love you, Sylvie."

"I love you, too. I'm glad you said it first. I was afraid to."

I rested my head on her shoulder, and she combed her fingers through my hair.

"Bil?"

"Mmm?"

"What kind of relationship do you want?"

"We've only been together for a few hours. Are you sure you want me to answer that?" The fingers in my hair stopped moving. I opened my eyes and put my hand on her cheek, forcing her to look at me. "I didn't mean that like it sounded. What I meant was that my answer might scare you. Sylvie, I want to stay here like this forever. I'm thinking long-term and . . . exclusive."

She was silent for a long moment.

"If that's not what you want," I said quickly, "it's okay. I won't show up at your front door tomorrow with all my worldly possessions, I promise, and—" I took a deep breath "—and if you want to see other people, I'll understand. Well, I'll try to understand."

Sylvie laughed, and then she grew serious again. "I want to be long-term and exclusive with you, Bil. More than anything. I'm just afraid."

"Why?"

"Because we've got so much strange history hanging over us. There are so many things that could go wrong, so much beyond our control."

I climbed into bed, tucked the blankets around us, and held her tightly. "Nothing will change the way I feel about you. I don't care what happened in the past, and what happens in the future doesn't matter to me, either. I don't want to think about my mother or yours, not now."

"How did you know?"

I smiled and kissed her lightly. "Why wouldn't you be thinking about your mother? I was thinking about mine. It's a supreme act of will to forget about my mother."

"I wonder what Freud would make of that."

"Believe me," I laughed, "I wasn't thinking about her the entire time. My mother is the original anti-aphrodisiac."

At that, her hands began moving beneath the blankets again, and soon, I couldn't even remember my own name, much less my mother's.

I woke up at four o'clock, just as the first light of morning began to show through the blinds. I lay back against the pillows, savoring the moment and the woman next to me, who was still sound asleep. I eased my arm out from under her back and got up. She stirred, rolled over, and went back to sleep.

I opened the bedroom door and stuck my head out cautiously. The coast was clear—there was no sign of Nancy. I closed the door behind me and crept quietly down the hall. I found my boxer shorts and T-shirt and put them on. The manila folder was still on the coffee table where we'd left it. I read each of the articles again and then looked at the photos. Something about Frank's picture still bothered me. I stared at for several minutes before I figured out what it was.

The blurring wasn't a result of the photocopying. Burt's picture was perfectly clear. If Sarah had copied them on the same machine, they both should have been clear. I suspected that Frank's face had not only been cropped from a larger photo but blown up as well. That's why the background was obliterated. I checked the clock. Sarah wouldn't be in her office for another three hours. I put everything back into the manila folder and climbed back into bed.

Sylvie rolled over and wrapped an arm around my waist. I kissed her, and she murmured something against my lips that sounded suspiciously like my name. I thought about waking her up right there and then but decided that would be pushing my luck.

Chapter 25

Sylvie came into the kitchen just as I was dialing Sarah's number. She kissed me and stumbled over to the refrigerator, staring into it as if it might hand her something to eat.

Sarah picked up on the third ring.

"Hi Sis, what are you up to?"

"Tearing my hair out," she replied. "What do you want?"

"Information."

"I'm going to start charging."

I briefly explained what I wanted.

"Let me get into *LexisNexis*, and I'll get back to you," she said.

"Considering the sorts of things he got up to before he left Cowslip, he might have been embraced by the long arms of the law at some point. Is there any way you can check prison records or something?"

"Nationwide?" She considered for a moment. "I'll talk to Susan Ferguson, the government documents librarian. I'll call you back when I'm finished. Are you at home?"

"No," I said quickly. "I'm not."

"I thought it was too quiet. You know Emma bailed Sam out this morning. Another crisis has been averted."

"What do you mean she bailed him out?"

"You mean you haven't seen it?"

"I don't even know what you're talking about."

"Where have you been, Bil, under a rock?" She paused significantly and then laughed. "On second thought, don't answer that. Just do yourself a big favor and take a good look at the billboard next to Safeway when you drive home. If you drive home."

"Very funny."

"It is, really. Don't worry about Sam. He's regained the use of his legs and is up to his old tricks again. I never thought I'd be relieved to have him arrested."

"It's mighty peculiar."

"Everything is fine at home. Just drop by the Safeway sometime today."

"I will. Why don't we meet for dinner? You can give me the information then. The Golden Dragon at five?"

"I don't know," she hesitated.

"There's someone I want you to meet. You don't have another date with Gary Smart, do you?"

She laughed. "For you, Bil, I'll break it."

"You can do better than him, Sarah."

"Have you looked around lately? This is Cowslip, honey, not the Riviera. Good-looking men don't just fall out of trees."

"Gary Smart looks like he did."

"Fine," she said, laughing. "I just want you to know that I'm not giving up a free dinner. Bring plenty of money. I want the soup and the egg roll."

"And lychee fruit for dessert. Gotcha. One more thing—what do you know about Agnes and Fairfax Merwin, Fred Maguire, and Millicent Rutherford?"

"The exact same things you do. Millicent is one of Granny's oldest friends, if you use that term loosely. She and the rest of them are all community theater cronies. If you think I'm going to dig out twenty years' worth of newspaper clippings about local productions, you're crazy. Especially not for a cheap Chinese dinner. If you want information about Millicent and company, go straight to the source. Call your grandmother."

"You're a hard woman, Sarah. I'll see you at five."

I put the receiver back on its hook and turned to Sylvie, who was leaning against the kitchen counter. She yawned.

"You should have woken me up. I was afraid you'd absconded in the night."

"Not a chance," I replied. "Can I get you a cup of coffee?"

"You're an angel." She'd put on a white T-shirt and a pair of underwear. I stopped on the way to give her a kiss.

"Hey, wait a second," she said, pulling me back to her. "That was woefully inadequate."

Several minutes later I said, "Satisfied?"

"Not yet," she smiled, "but I think I need that coffee first."

"Your wish is my command."

"Do you mind if I go sit in the living room? The tile on this floor is freezing."

"You should steal a pair of socks from your dresser. That's what I did."

"I'll try to remember that."

A few minutes later, I joined her in the living room. She was reading the newspaper clippings.

"Do me a favor," I said, "and take a closer look at that picture of Frank. Do you notice anything strange about it?"

She contemplated it for a minute or two and then shook her head. "What am I looking for?"

"It's the same size as your father's yearbook photo, but it's cropped from another picture. When I was on the high school yearbook staff, we cropped pictures for people who didn't show up for their annual photo. I think that's what they've done with Frank."

"Okay." She sipped her coffee.

"I'm wondering where that photo came from. I don't think it's a sports shot—his hair isn't messed up, and he's not wearing a uniform. I'm guessing it's taken from some dramatic production or another. As you well know, the Cowslip College drama department and the Cowslip Community Theatre are separated in name only. I want to find the original of that photo. I've asked Sarah to get me copies of the *Cowslipper* for the years Frank was in college."

"What will that tell us?"

"I don't know. It might give us an idea of how long he'd been using his alias. If he was Charlie Gibb before he left Cowslip, then perhaps he had some help with his embezzling. That would mean your mother wasn't the only blackmail possibility."

"Clever," she observed. "You should be a detective when you grow up."

She leaned against me, and we sat together in companionable silence. Then she sat up.

"Well, what are we going to do until we get Sarah's report on the activities of the late Frank Frost? If I was eavesdropping correctly, you've asked her to run a more complete search for any reference to either him or my father."

"Right. She's checking *LexisNexis* and the *New York Times Index* for any reference to either of them. Charlie Gibb might not have been Frank's only alias. Maybe he used one closer to home, like his best friend's name. You'd need to pick aliases that were easy to remember. I suppose we need to think of a way to flush out Frank's killer. If we can do that, then maybe the sheriff's department won't care that your mother misidentified the body. We might even be able to convince them that it was an honest mistake."

Sylvie stared at me. "Then you don't think my mother killed Frank?"

"No, I don't. It doesn't make sense. When did that money start moving into Gibb's account?"

She thought for a moment. "Four or five months ago."

"Right. If Kate was being blackmailed, then why? As far as we know, she only has one secret to hide. How would Frank have known? Even if the rumor that he was believed to have run off with your father reached him, why would he assume that meant that your father was dead?"

"Much less that my mother had killed him," she agreed.

"And another thing—those transfers to Gibb came out of your mother's joint account with Agnes. Frank might have been blackmailing her or Fairfax. I think either of them is a more likely prospect than your mother."

"I've been so fixated on my mother and her part in this that I haven't seen any of the other possibilities. What could Frank have had on Agnes?"

"Who knows? Maybe it's a sex thing. Our poisoner could even have been dear cousin Helen." I described my afternoon on the hillside next to her mother's kitchen and told her about the shadowy figure on the hillside.

"Yesterday, I found my dad's binoculars on the wall of the ruined house. Helen's too young to have been mixed up with Frank, but she might know if one of her parents were in trouble. And there was that strange conversation at the cast party when your mother asked Fairfax if the police had questioned him."

"You know," she said thoughtfully, "Helen's been pretty weird lately." Seeing the look on my face, she laughed and amended that to "weirder than usual." "That night I met you at Traveler's Rest, for example. Do you remember?"

I thought back. "You were really angry, I remember that."

She blushed and nodded. "That's because Helen took me aside to warn me about you. She said you were a notorious slut and that you'd lead me to rack and ruin. She's known I'm a lesbian for years, though I've always refused to discuss it with her. I wasn't surprised that she brought you up—she'd seen us together—but, well, she named names."

"A. J.?"

"And others."

"There weren't that many, for God's sake. Two . . ."

"Three, total. Not including me. I don't care," she added, "just so long as it stops with three."

"You mean four. You've now joined my harem."

She laughed. "I don't know how she finds these things out, but she always knows. It's like she's doing research or something."

"She's an amateur Reginald Brown." We looked at one another. "I don't know about you, Sylvie, but that gives me the creeps."

"Helen has that effect on people."

"She's been snooping around. I wonder what she knows."

Sylvie shivered, and I pulled her closer. I tried to picture Helen Merwin as a blackmailer, gathering rumors and gossip from all of her old lady friends. She seemed more like the poison-pen type, but perhaps she had a mercenary streak.

"About my mother, Bil—do you think she's better off just confessing and taking the consequences? I can testify that it was justifiable homicide."

I shook my head. "Maybe as a last resort. I don't see how it would help her with the Frost case, though. I think it would just add fuel to the fire."

I didn't add that after hiding the body for sixteen years, Kate might have a hard time proving justifiable homicide, even with Sylvie's testimony. I also didn't know how to keep my mother's part in the whole affair from coming out during a trial, and it seemed better to me to let sleeping dogs lie if it were at all possible.

"I think we should go talk to your aunt," I said.

"Agnes? What for?"

"You heard what Brown said—rumor has it that she and Frank were having an affair. Let's go over this afternoon. We could go now, but sooner or later, I've got to go back to class."

She laughed. "I don't think I've ever been this close to flunking out, but I don't care. Do you think they'd give me a medical drop?"

"You're not sick."

"I'm exhausted."

"That's your own fault," I smiled.

"No," she objected, "it's yours, not that I'm complaining. What time is your first class?"

"Ten. How about you?"

"Ten as well." She glanced at the clock. "It's only eight-thirty now."

I considered this a proposition. "Shall I exhaust you again?"

"Not if I exhaust you first."

It was three o'clock when we knocked on the Merwins' front door. There was only one car in the driveway, a silver Volvo, which Sylvie identified as belonging to Agnes. I hoped she was home alone. Helen was supposed to be at the library with Sarah, and Fairfax should have been at the bank. I didn't fancy trying to quiz Agnes in front of either of them. We knocked a couple of times and were nearly ready to give up when Agnes suddenly appeared in the doorway. She looked a little the worse for wear, like she had slept neither well nor long enough. She was mightily hung over, and her eyes were bloodshot.

"Sylvie?" She sounded more surprised than annoyed. Then she saw me. "And Bil Hardy. My goodness. Is anything the matter? Is Kate all right?"

"Nothing's wrong," Sylvie assured her. "We just wanted to ask you about some things. Could we come in? Just for a minute," she added, when Agnes seemed to hesitate.

"Sure, that's fine." She led us into the living room. "Can I get you anything to drink?"

I shook my head, and Sylvie said no.

"Well, I'm going to get one, and a couple of aspirin as well. I've had a long night. Please make yourselves comfortable."

Sylvie and I sat down on the love seat, a mission oak style affair with brown leather cushions. The whole room was tastefully and expensively decorated. The floor was hardwood, with a large oriental rug covering the area in front of the sofa. It looked like an antique. No tacky chartreuse recliners graced the Merwin parlor, and the central feature of the Hardy living room, the television set, was nowhere in sight. Two wing chairs covered in tapestry fabric with matching ottomans sat on either side of a large stone fireplace. The mantel was wooden and beautifully carved. It was also well polished, but I guessed Agnes was not responsible for that. She didn't look like the dusting type.

Agnes came back with a huge glass of soda that gave off strong whiffs of gin. She sat down carefully on the sofa across from us and sipped her drink.

"You know the police have taken my mother in for questioning about Burt's death," Sylvie said suddenly.

Agnes paused before speaking. "I didn't know that, but it doesn't surprise me. They've been questioning everyone."

"You as well?"

"Me as well. And Fairfax, Millicent, Fred, and," gesturing at me, "Bil's poor grandmother."

"So who do you think poisoned him?"

She looked at me and smiled. "Someone who wanted him dead, of course. That could be almost anyone. Sylvie, here, for example. I don't think she liked him very much."

Sylvie's body went tense beside me. I resisted the urge to get up and slap the drink out of Agnes' hand. "This isn't public knowledge yet," I said, "but it wasn't Burt Wood who was killed. It was your old friend, Frank Frost."

For a brief moment, the mask dropped and I saw that she was startled, maybe even frightened. It didn't last long. She schooled her features into a perfect picture of calm indifference.

"I don't know what makes you say that. My sister identified the body."

"The dead man had three kidneys. Burt Wood only had one."

"How unpleasant," she replied, gazing at me with hooded green eyes. "I suppose you've seen the autopsy report. How did you manage that?"

"A little bird told me. This does seem to change the playing field, doesn't it?"

"After all this time," Agnes said, almost to herself. "Imagine." She took another sip of her drink.

"Who would want to kill Frank?" Sylvie asked.

"I don't know. Just about anyone, I suppose. He wore out his welcome here long before he disappeared. People like that usually do."

"Like what?"

She laughed. "Good-looking but worthless. Frank was small-minded; he might even have been stupid. I don't mean that he was mentally deficient, but he was one of those people with perfectly average intellects who are convinced they're geniuses."

"You seem to know a lot about it."

Agnes smiled at me. "Sweetheart, I live with two others just like him." She held up her glass in mock salute. "Here's to Einstein and Madame Curie. Are you sure you won't change your mind and have a drink?"

"No thanks."

"Suit yourself."

"Aunt Agnes," Sylvie said, leaning forward on the love seat, "what do you remember about my father? Do you think he and Frank ever . . . do you think they were having an affair?"

Agnes seemed to think carefully before she answered.

"Is that what this visit's really about?"

Sylvie shrugged. "I'm trying to make sense of it, I guess. I really can't ask my mother."

"I can see why." The look Agnes gave her was almost kind. "I hated your father, Sylvie. I thought Kate was crazy to marry him, and once she had, I don't know why she didn't divorce him. But then, divorces in our family are rather rare. There would have been hell to pay, especially as far as our mother was concerned. Catholics, you know," she said, nodding to me. "It nearly killed Mother when Kate and I married Episcopalians. When I was five, I overheard my parents arguing one night about whether or not my father was going to wear a condom. He didn't want to risk having another baby, but my mother insisted on the rhythm method."

"Who won?"

She looked at me as if I were an idiot. "She did, obviously. Nine months later, I had a sister named Kate."

I noticed a movement then, just a shadow, out of the corner of my eye. A large, black cat walked through the doorway and jumped up on Agnes' lap. The shadow had seemed too big for a cat, but there was no further movement.

"As to Frank and your father," Agnes said, "I don't think so. I think your father was doggedly heterosexual. And his motto was the more, the merrier. He liked power and control. The first time your mother ever brought him home to meet our parents, he made a pass at me out in the barn. He did that a lot. He was always switched on, and he didn't know how to take no for an answer."

I'll bet you didn't say no, I thought, but I said nothing. Sylvie gave an involuntary shudder, and I put my arm around her. She leaned against me. Agnes watched us carefully. I didn't care what she thought.

"Frank was another thing entirely," she continued smoothly. "You've probably heard that he was bisexual. I don't have any evidence to back it up, but I think that's true. He and Fred Maguire got into an argument one night when we were rehearsing *Cat on a Hot Tin Roof.* Fred hurled some ugly accusations at Frank, and Frank punched him in the face. Fairfax had to pull Frank off of him. Later that night, someone trashed our new car."

"Frank?"

"No, it was Fred. He thought Fairfax was having an affair with Frank."

"Was he?"

She laughed. "I have no idea. I never bothered to ask. And now, ladies, if you don't mind, I'm going upstairs to lie down. My head is throbbing."

❖❖❖

I shifted into reverse and backed slowly out of the driveway. The Merwins lived in a gentrified bungalow on Exmoor Street, not far from the house where A. J. and the Lesbian Avengers were staying. They had a "Vernon Young for Sheriff" sign in the middle of their front lawn. I gave myself a dog-like shake.

"What are you doing?"

"Getting rid of Merwin cooties. That was so weird."

"I know. Agnes has always been strange."

"Must be where Helen gets it. It's unnerving to experience your aunt in her natural habitat."

"You've never been to her house?"

"No, that was my maiden voyage. By the way, did you get the feeling that we might have had an eavesdropper? Something moved past the living-room doorway. I don't know if it was the cat or a trick of the light."

"I must not have been paying attention. When did you notice it?"

"Agnes was talking about her parents playing Vatican roulette, and the cat came in and hopped on her lap. He's a big bastard, isn't he? He must weigh about twenty pounds."

"The cat actually belongs to Fairfax. His name is Ford Madox Ford, if you can imagine that. I was more focused on that huge glass of gin and tonic." She frowned. "Do you think she's an alcoholic?"

"She sure as hell isn't a teetotaler. That wasn't a glass, it was an aquarium."

At the corner of Exmoor and Broad, I turned the wrong way onto A. J.'s street without realizing it. There was nowhere else to turn around, so I drove all the way to the end, stopping at the fence separating the houses from Lilac Trailer Court. The yards up and down the street were badly overgrown, and the strip of ground next to the fence was especially wild. Clumps of crabgrass fought a losing battle with Scotch thistle and other noxious weeds. I had put the truck into reverse for a three-point turn before I realized what I was looking at.

"Wait here," I said, hopping out of the truck.

It only took a moment. I picked a weed next to the fence and handed it to her.

"You're the botanist," I said. "You tell me what that is."

"Jimsonweed," she replied. "I recognize it from the picture your sister gave us."

"Frank was seen around here, and my brother practically lives just over there in trailer number eight. It's also convenient to a few other people."

"Yes," she agreed. "Fred doesn't live too far from here. Within walking distance, anyway."

It began to rain as soon as we turned onto Main Street. Safeway, the scene of Sam's failed shoplifting spree, stood on the corner. It wasn't until I actually saw the billboard that I remembered what Sarah had said about his recent arrest. There, painted in runny red letters over an advertisement encouraging literacy, were the words "Francie Stokes is a b-i-c-h."

Chapter 26

Reluctantly, Sylvie and I agreed to part company for the time being. I needed to let Emma know that I was alive and well, and Sylvie needed to check in with her mother. I dropped her off at Kate's farm, promising to pick her up again in time for dinner with Sarah. Then, I girded my loins and drove home to face the wrath.

Emma was sitting in her accustomed place on the sofa, reading the *Herald-Examiner.* She looked over the top of it as I came in.

"Could it be . . . yes, it's Amelia Earhardt. How was the Pacific? Run out of gas?"

"Very funny."

"It's not funny at all," she replied. "I suppose I can call the sheriff now and tell him to stop dragging the Elk River. I don't know what gets into you kids. First, you disappear. Then, your brother checks himself out of the hospital and takes off God knows where. He reappeared last night via a collect call from the jail. Now, you come strolling in looking like the dog's dinner."

I sat down in Archie Bunker and folded my arms across my chest. "I'm a grown woman, Emma."

"You're an inconsiderate snot. You might have called to let me know that you were all right. 'Officer, I last saw my youngest daughter at the House of Pancakes.' That would have made a nice epitaph, don't you think?"

I pointed at the cordless phone sitting on the coffee table next to her. "I've spoken to both Sarah and Naomi. They knew where I was. I thought one of them would have called you."

"It wasn't their responsibility."

There was no answer to this. She was right.

"I'm going to ask one more time. Where have you been?"

"I refuse to answer that, but I am sorry that I didn't call you."

"Sylvie Wood." It was a statement, not a question. The angry tone was now at war with the I-knew-it voice. "You should have called me."

"I'm sorry," I said again, "and yes, I know that all the prisoners in jail are sorry. I won't make the same mistake again. I'll get an apartment in town—then you won't have to worry about me."

Her ears pricked up like a cocker spaniel's. "You'll what?"

"Don't try and talk me out of it, Emma. I need a place of my own."

She scowled and put the newspaper down, spreading it out flat on her lap.

"You can't afford it."

"I'll get a roommate."

"Bil, you've only just come back."

"That's come out, not come back."

"Don't split hairs. You can't just move in with Sylvie like that, all harum-scarum. Have you talked to her about this? Is it her idea?"

I sighed. "Sylvie already has a roommate, Ma. What I'm talking about is a place of my own, and I don't want to discuss it with you. Can we please move on?" Not giving her time to object, I said quickly, "Sarah told me you bailed Sam out this morning. Where is he now?"

"Who knows? Did you see the re-spray he gave the billboard at Safeway?"

I blew a stray lock of hair out of my eyes. "That's your son, always ready with the illiterate *mot juste*. Any idea what inspired him?"

"What do you think? Francie Stokes and her itchy, twitchy twat."

"That's catchy, Ma. You should put it to music."

She was slapping the newspaper so that it made a rhythmic popping noise.

"After breakfast, when you dropped me off at the hospital, he was up and making phone calls. Brian Sorenson—you remember him, big skinny blond kid—answered Francie's phone. He told your brother that Francie was still in bed asleep. You can imagine the rest."

"It might have been perfectly innocent."

The hand rested temporarily. "Innocent?"

"Come on, Emma. Francie's place is a flophouse. So what if Brian was there? There were probably twenty-five other people as well, all watching cartoons."

My mother shook her head. "You are naïve. Sam wasn't around to give her what she wanted, so she hooked up with someone else. I wish this were a permanent arrangement, but sooner or later, she'll crook her little finger, and your idiot brother will be right back there, plowing up that garden of earthly delights."

"You know," I slipped Archie back into his fully reclined position, "your interest in your son's sex life is unnatural. You should think about getting a therapist."

"Don't push me, Bil," my mother snapped. "I'm on the thin edge."

"If Francie is putting out as much as you say she is, I don't see how the cops can pin this billboard thing on Sam. Anybody could have painted that sign."

"When they stopped him for questioning, they found a can of red spray paint in the back seat of the car, and he still had some of it running down his arm." A pained expression had planted itself on my mother's face. She looked like she had indigestion.

"Tell me the truth, Ma. What did you do when you saw that billboard?"

"What do you mean what did I do?"

"You laughed, didn't you? You thought it was funny."

"I didn't think it was funny when they arrested him."

"But you thought the billboard was funny. You probably wet your pants laughing." She looked away, and I knew I'd hit the nail on the head. "Sam has the will to live, Ma."

"Sam has the will to live dangerously."

"What the hell's the difference?"

Sylvie and I got to the Golden Dragon right on time, and we only had to wait forty-five minutes for Sarah, a family record. She came in carrying an overstuffed purple backpack and a fat briefcase, which appeared to be made out of brightly colored swamp grass. She spent several minutes trying to disentangle herself from her wet overcoat, and several more trying to find a place to hang it where it wouldn't drip on all the jackets around it. In some ways, Sarah takes after my mother—she's a hurricane with an orderly Rolodex at its eye.

"Sorry," she said, sitting down damply in the booth next to Sylvie. "I've just been trying to track down a facsimile edition of *Beowulf.* We had one on the shelves, but it's gone missing. No one's checked it out, so it's misshelved or lost or stolen, and . . ."

"Oh dear," I interrupted. "So, what did you find out?"

She shook her head, laughing. "Have you ordered family style or do I at least get to look at the menu?" She turned and smiled at Sylvie. "It's true that Bil was raised by wolves, but I'm sure that any moment now, she'll think to reintroduce us as it's been years since we last met."

"Sylvie Wood, Sarah 'Miss Manners' Hardy."

"Pleased to meet you again," Sylvie said, shaking Sarah's hand.

"Likewise, I'm sure," Sarah said. "You were my first babysitting job, did you know that? Your mother dropped you off at our house one night, and I got to officially watch you and be paid for it. I wasn't old enough to babysit on my own, so Emma was the real babysitter. I took it all very seriously anyway."

"I hope I behaved myself."

"Perfectly. I wouldn't mind having a child just like you. Of course, thanks to Bil here, I'll never have any children of my own. I was supposed to have a dinner date with a rich professor who might have taken me away from all this."

"There are plenty of fish in the sea," I interrupted. "I'd go for the Hunan prawns. Whatever you do, give the Mongolian beef a miss. It always tastes like combat boot marinated in cornstarch and soy sauce."

"Prawns it is. I hope there are lots of onions in it. I'm covering reference again from nine to midnight, so I'll be breathing on the patrons."

"Are you working double shifts or something?"

"I'm covering for the department head. She had a tooth out this morning."

"You do get the plum jobs."

"Do you like being a librarian?" Sylvie asked.

"Sometimes. I love books, and I like my co-workers. I even like one or two of the patrons."

A gangly girl wearing an Alpha Phi sweatshirt took our order, and our dinner soon arrived. Mine was soon eaten. Sylvie pushed her chicken around with a chopstick, while Sarah chewed each bite thirty-two times. My sister is beautiful but sloppy. No matter how slowly she eats, she always drips. At home, she ties a napkin around her neck like the last of the hillbilly gourmands. Thankfully, she doesn't resort to this trick in public. I tried to be patient as she chewed, but curiosity got the better of my manners.

"Well?"

I had to wait for her to finish chewing. "Well what?"

"What did you find out?"

Sarah picked up a prawn with her chopsticks and dangled it precariously over her stained bosom. "Would you like to see the paperwork, or should I just summarize?"

"Is the paperwork particularly interesting?"

Sarah considered the question, and then she considered me. "I'll summarize," she decided. "I don't know where Frost spent the last sixteen years, but I do know where he spent the last twelve. He was in prison in upstate New York. They paroled him five months ago."

"Any idea what he was in for?"

"Of course I know," she laughed. "There were three charges, grand theft, burglary, and malicious destruction of property. None of these would have sent him up for all that long, but he already had a police record as long as your arm. He was what they call an habitual offender."

"What are you talking about? Wasn't theft, burglary, and that other thing enough?"

"Malicious destruction of property," Sarah said. "Either you haven't paid much attention to the many dramas involving our baby brother, or you never listen to what Naomi has to say. Why should taxpayers in a state the size of New York care about an insect like Frost? He was a non-violent offender. You don't get the chair for this sort of thing, not even in Idaho. And that reminds me, I've been reading about Frank's sins here in Cowslip. I went back a little further in my research than you asked me to, and I found an interesting snippet from the weekly police report about him stealing money from Emmet Rutherford."

"Millicent's husband?"

She nodded.

"How much?"

"Quite a lot for a sixteen-year-old. Frost tried to make off with about two thousand dollars from the till at Rutherford's Farm Supply. He was working there at the time."

Sylvie was surprised. "Really?"

Sarah nodded, chewing a prawn. Then, with an inclusive gesture in my direction, she added, "So was our mother, and so was your father, but they're not mentioned in the newspaper."

"I knew Emma worked there," I said, "but not Frost and Wood. How did you find this out?"

She gave me a smug smile. "Special collections, sweetheart. When John Fredericks died—he was the sheriff from 1950 until 1982—his widow donated all of his papers to the library. A lot of shit is donated to libraries. If it's really junk, like someone's old *National Geographic* collection, we toss it out, or sell it, or recycle it. Fredericks was a fairly important figure, so we kept his stuff. Notes, diaries, conspiracy theories—the widow Fredericks even gave us all of his dirty magazines."

"So what do you know?"

"Judging from his taste in porn, he had a thing for lactating women."

"Please, Sylvie's still trying to eat."

"No," Sylvie pushed her plate away, "I'm done. Did my father have anything to do with Frank stealing from Emmet Rutherford?"

Sarah stabbed the air with her chopsticks. "Remember, this is just Fredericks speculating; he couldn't prove anything. Your father was working the till on the day the money went missing. Fredericks thought he either gave Frank access to the till, or he wasn't minding the store. At first, Emmet suspected Wood, but then the money turned up in Frank's bedroom. Now," she speared up another prawn, "here's the interesting part. This all comes up in Fredericks' diary as background for his theory about the missing money from the county clerk's office. He reckoned that Burt and Frank were in it together, with Frank, as history suggests, taking the heat. Officer Young . . ."

"Now Lieutenant," I said.

"Now-Lieutenant Young didn't agree with this theory. Fredericks dismisses him as an idiot."

"What did Young think?"

She shook her head. "Fredericks doesn't say. He makes a few tart observations about Young's intellect, or the lack thereof, but that's it."

"So," Sylvie asked, "what exactly did they do? How do you steal a quarter of a million dollars from a county assessor's office?"

"Well, you'd have to get someone like my father to explain the accounting parts to you, but essentially, there was some trick to the way Frank assessed properties, particularly large farms. He figured their values correctly, but then he under-reported to the county. When the taxes rolled in, they pocketed the excess. Fredericks had been watching them for at least six months before they vanished, but he couldn't figure out where exactly the money was going. He thought someone was laundering it for them."

"Did he say who?"

She shook her head. "He didn't have a clue. Burt and Frank were always together, but your father doesn't seem to have had any other friends. Frank was involved with the community theater crowd and some assorted Cowslip low-lifes, known drug dealers, that sort of thing."

I chewed on a forkful of rice. If Burt and Frank had been in on the embezzlement together, maybe they really had been planning to abscond together. It surprised me to think that part of the rumor might be true after all.

"Wait," I said. "Frank did community theater. That's where he met his money launderer."

"Yes," Sarah agreed affably, "it's bound to be our grandmother. No doubt she's secretly rich, and we should start being nice to her, or she'll leave it all to Helen Merwin."

"Very funny," I replied. "I was thinking of Fairfax Merwin, actually—he's the banker."

My sister winked at Sylvie. "She's smarter than she looks. So, would you like to take a look at the other possible suspects? I have here our college yearbook, the *Cowslipper*, for the year 1966. That's the last year Frank was in school. Take a look at page sixty-seven."

It was a photo of the college drama department, and they were all there. There were two productions during the school year and one in the summer. In the fall, Frank had played Brick to Agnes' Maggie in *Cat on a Hot Tin Roof.* Fred Maguire was resplendent as Big Daddy in his ice cream suit and Panama hat. There was a large picture of my grandmother and Millicent playing opposite Fairfax's Mortimer in the spring production of *Arsenic and Old Lace*. Fred was in that photo as well, dressed up like Teddy Roosevelt. The summer production was *Our Town*. I looked again at the photo of Frank.

"What do you think?" I asked, passing the book to Sylvie.

"Same picture," she agreed. "Someone's cropped it, like you said."

Sarah shook her head. "You've lost me. Who's cropped what?"

"The pictures in the folder of Burt and Frank. I noticed this morning that Frank's looked like it had been cut from a larger photo. I'm pretty sure this is the original."

Sarah shrugged. "I still don't know what you're talking about. I didn't give you any photos. That's why I thought you wanted a copy of the *Cowslipper*."

"Well if you didn't put the photos in there, then who . . ."

I suddenly had a vision of my binoculars sitting at the top of the ridge, waiting for me.

"Goddamn her, what's she up to?"

"Who?"

"Helen, of course. She's stole the first file you made, and she's tampered with this one."

Sarah considered this. "But why?"

"Because she's fucking with us, that's why."

My sister slammed her hand down on the table with so much force that people stopped eating throughout the restaurant. "Nosy bitch! I once caught her looking up a patron's circulation record. She doesn't work in circulation, so she had no legitimate reason for wanting to know what he read. I reprimanded her, of course. That's a direct violation of ALA policy."

"American Library Association," I translated for Sylvie's benefit. "It's the librarian version of the FBI."

"It is not," Sarah snapped. "ALA sets the standards for my profession, and we take two things very seriously—freedom of speech and patron privacy. You can tell a lot from someone's reading list, and people have a right to read what they want without comment or censorship. If I find out she took that folder, I'm going to knock her fool head off."

"What do you know about jimsonweed?"

Sylvie's head had been resting on my stomach, but now she moved up to lie down beside me.

"You do have a one-track mind, don't you?"

"I have two tracks, actually. Now I've switched to the other one. Have you ever done anything with Datura?"

"I know the genus, but that's about it. I suppose I could talk to my botany professor."

I rolled over. Her arm was resting on top of the sheet, her skin tan against the white cotton. I traced a line from her wrist to the top of her shoulder. "The whole plant is toxic, but apparently, the seeds are the worst part. The stuff I read said they don't taste unpleasant, so I suppose it would be easy enough to slip them into someone's food. Among our suspects, who do you think would know enough about plants to poison someone?"

Sylvie shrugged. "You and I know enough. It's a matter of reading the right books, knowing where to find your plant, and then harvesting the seeds. It's down to motive and opportunity, which puts my mother pretty high on the list, though it could have been anyone. I think we need to trace the money."

"Reginald Brown again?"

"I don't see what choice we have. If it takes him more than a day or two, though, there's no way I can pay him, not without my mother knowing about it."

I moved closer, so that our bodies were touching. "It's cold in here," I explained. "I've got a credit card, we could max that out."

She shook her head. "Don't do that. I'll figure something out."

"We could try scaring someone. We could call everyone up and say, 'I know who you are, and I saw what you did,' and then see what happens."

She laughed. "Now you're being ridiculous."

"Probably." I traced my fingers back up her arm and rested them on the back of her neck. She closed her eyes. "Sylvie?"

"There's an extra blanket in the bottom drawer of my dresser."

"That's not it."

She smiled, her eyes still closed. "Don't tell me. Your train has switched tracks?"

"I think my train has derailed."

Chapter 27

I had two hours to kill before I was due to meet Sylvie at her place. We planned to attend the Proposition One debate scheduled for seven o'clock at the Cowslip Community Center.

I had just enough time to go to the gym. I hadn't been for over a week, and it felt so good to lift weights again that I did a full body workout, knowing I'd be sorry later. On my way out, I ran into Tipper and Suzy.

"Well?" Tipper said, lifting a perfectly arched eyebrow.

I looked away. "Well what?"

"That answers my question." He held me at arm's length and surveyed me from head to toe. "And it certainly suits you, I must say. You look fabulous. Doesn't she, Suzy?"

"She does indeed. One might say glowing."

"If I'm glowing, then you are radioactive. Any idea what the forum will be like tonight?"

Tipper nodded. "The editor of the *Herald-Examiner* will act as moderator. On our side, we have the pastor of the Unitarian Church, a lawyer for the ACLU, and a spokeswoman from the Idaho Library Association. The forces of evil have our Republican representative to the state legislature and the charming and effervescent Reverend Jones."

"How come we have three and they only have two?"

Suzy laughed. "They were counting on the minister from the

American Baptist Church, but unfortunately, they didn't check with him first. He opposes Proposition One."

"I just hope it doesn't look too lopsided," Tipper sighed. "If we want to win over the muddled middle, then this needs to be a real debate. We need to win on points, not numbers."

Suzy disagreed. "Who cares if it's lopsided, just so long as we win? Besides, Jones by himself is a match for any two reasonable people. He'll be whipping out the hellfire, brimstone, and Leviticus, and the rhetoric will get so hot that any reasonable argument will just burst into flames."

"That bad?"

"Take my word for it, sweetie," he replied. "It won't be pretty."

It was just after four when I got to Sylvie's apartment. I took the stairs quickly, still pumped up from my workout. Nancy answered the door on the second knock. She looked less than pleased to see me again.

"She's not here," she said shortly and moved to close the door.

"Wait . . . where is she?" She shrugged. "Well, could I leave a message? A note?"

She stared at me for a long moment before saying, "Wait here," and disappearing into the living room. She came back with an envelope and handed it to me. "She left this for you."

It was addressed in Sylvie's firm, dark script. I walked back down the stairs slowly, waiting until I got into my truck to open it. It said:

> **Bil—I've gone out to my mother's to talk some things over before the meeting tonight. I'll walk over the ridge and meet you at Tipper's. I love you, Sylvie.**

That was it. I sat for a minute trying to figure out what it meant and came up with several possibilities. The one that worried me the most was that she might confront her mother with what we knew, or at least what we suspected. I didn't want her to do that without me. I'd come to accept the idea that Kate had killed her husband and that my mother had helped her hide the evidence, and whether I liked it or not, it was now my secret, too.

I went home to shower and change before heading out to Tipper's.

Emma and Sam were sitting on the sofa, watching cartoons. My mother was laughing heartily, and Sam looked happy and relaxed. I briefly considered asking them to come to the meeting and then decided against it. If it was going to be as awful as Suzy seemed to think, then I didn't want them there.

I reached Tipper's house at five-thirty. He and his mother were sitting side by side on the softball field, shooting at targets. Everyone else was sitting behind them with their hands over their ears. I got out of the truck, waiting until Tipper had fired before shutting my door. He waved at me.

"Bil, come over here. I've got a bet with Mommie dearest. If she wins, she gets to smoke in the kitchen." He sniffed in disgust.

"I see. And if you win?"

"Then I get a prescription for the nicotine patch," the Captain replied.

"So how does this work," I asked, "and what you using?" I squinted down the firing range at the targets, which were about two hundred yards away.

".308's," the Captain said. "Tipper's using his old Winchester 70, but mine's an 800 action Remington. Look at that," she held the rifle out for me to admire.

"It's beautiful," I said, shuddering to think how much money the Captain must have dropped at gun shows over the years. "But is it entirely fair?"

"Shut up," Tipper said. "My old Winchester is perfectly good. We're shooting five groups of three at two hundred yards. That should separate the fags from the dykes."

"Sitting, not prone?" I asked.

"Sitting. Although I did offer to let her lie down, seeing as she's an old lady."

"And I offered to shoot an apple off his head," the Captain grinned.

"You'll never get a decisive outcome at two hundred," I objected. "You're both too good. Why not make it one group of three at three hundred yards?"

Tipper and his mother looked at one another.

"Three hundred, prone," Tipper said.

"Sitting," the Captain answered, unable to resist the challenge.

She was wearing her amber shooting glasses and clearly feeling cocky.

Tipper looked at me doubtfully, but he agreed.

"Hold this," the Captain said, handing me her rifle. I held it as I'd been taught, the breech resting on the crook of my arm, the barrel pointing down at the ground. The Captain and Jane walked out onto the field to move the targets back.

"Thanks a hell of a lot," Tipper whispered. "Now you've guaranteed that my mother will get emphysema, and I'll have to live with a smoke-filled kitchen."

The Captain came back and sat down. There was some rustling behind us until I gave Suzy the eye. He settled down quietly to watch. The Captain and Tipper each fired three shots.

"Shall I do the honors?" I asked. I retrieved the targets from the bullet traps and brought them back for inspection. Both groupings were good, but one was slightly better than the other.

"Sorry," I said, handing the Captain the targets.

Tipper handed his rifle to me, hiked up his skirt, and danced around the field. The Captain took it well, though I caught her closely inspecting the sight on her rifle.

In the kitchen, the Captain made a show of breaking her cigars in two and throwing them into the trash. Then we gathered around the table, the Radical Faeries perched up on the counters, and we discussed strategy.

We decided that the thing to do was ask intelligent questions and to remain calm at all costs, no matter what was said. We needed to look like reasonable people. Jane suggested at one point that perhaps Tipper and Suzy should consider wearing suits, but the Captain said, "Nonsense, Jane. This is about who we are, not who they think we are."

In the end, Suzy opted for a plaid kilt with a neat white blouse, and Tipper just wore jeans.

"I'm having a butch spell," he explained. "I expect it will pass."

We waited until a quarter to seven for Sylvie. Then the others got ready to leave, and I promised to follow as soon as Sylvie arrived. As they were climbing into their cars, a full-size pickup truck came up the driveway. It stopped in front of the house, and Kate and Sylvie stepped out.

"Sorry we're late," Sylvie said, kissing me. "My mother's decided to come to the meeting."

I was too surprised to know what to say. Thankfully, the Captain came to my rescue, stepping forward and holding out her hand. "Hi Kate," she said. "I'm glad you're with us."

Kate smiled and shook her hand. "Every little bit counts. These are scary times for all of us."

"They are indeed. So, who's riding with whom? Tipper's driving my car, and Jane's driving the van. I assume Sylvie's riding with Bil."

"I can take someone," Kate offered, "possibly even two, if you don't mind being cramped."

"You can take me," the Captain replied. "The van always makes me a little seasick."

Jane looked as if she were about to object. Then she thought better of it and took her place behind the wheel. The Faeries piled into the station wagon, the Folksong Army into the van, and we rode in a convoy to the Community Center.

As we drove downtown, I took Sylvie's hand.

"So, I guess you're now out to your mother?"

"I'm out," she said, smiling. "I told her about us, so I guess you could say we're out."

When we arrived at the Community Center, there was a large crowd already assembled. The Lesbian Avengers were sitting on the front row, all wearing T-shirts that featured a ticking bomb and the logo, "Lesbian Avengers—We Recruit." They looked like a cross between Dykes on Bikes and the Guardian Angels, and I envied them. A. J. smiled, and I nodded and waved. Sylvie gave me a sharp pinch on the backside, which made me laugh.

Sarah and Ruth were in the audience, as was my grandmother. They sat on opposite sides of the room, my sisters just three rows in front of me. Sarah turned around and winked, and Ruth looked over her shoulder and raised her eyebrows. I tried to ignore them, though I made sure that Granny saw me by waving every time she turned her head. Reluctantly, she waved back. Helen was with her, scowling, as usual.

"I think Reverend Jones has brought an amen corner," I whispered to Tipper.

"Don't worry," he said. "We've got our own."

The moderator, a tall man with an ill-fitting toupee, introduced the combatants and then began the debate by reading the text of Proposition One. The legalese seemed a little fudged to me, but the gist of it was that no law protecting the civil rights of gays or lesbians could be passed in any county or town in the state of Idaho. There was also a lot of language about prohibiting state funds from being used to promote homosexuality.

The woman from the Idaho Library Association spoke first. She spoke eloquently and at length about those parts of the proposition that would affect the purchase and distribution of library materials. If Proposition One were enacted, she said, collection development at both public and academic libraries would be seriously compromised. She also estimated that it would cost an astronomical amount of money if libraries were forced to restrict access to any materials regarding homosexuality to those over eighteen.

"We'd have to set up something akin to the beaded curtain at your local video store," she said. "This proposition is so broadly worded that we might have to restrict access to the Bible, which, as you are aware, makes some mention of homosexuality."

The Republican representative, Phil McCauley, was given two minutes to respond. His answer was that the Idaho Library Association exaggerated both the scope of the law and its potential costs. Then he gave a speech about tradition and family values. The idea of two gay people raising a child seemed to make him particularly unhappy.

"The gay agenda," he said, "has to do with social engineering. The American family is currently under attack, and homosexuality contributes to our moral decline."

"I wish I could make myself temporarily deaf," I whispered to Sylvie. She wrapped her arm around my waist but said nothing.

The Reverend Jones agreed to let the UCC minister and the ACLU attorney speak one after the other, and he allowed McCauley to deliver the rebuttal for both of them. This gave him the chance to make a big closing speech and then walk off in godly triumph.

He rose to speak, smiling, his helmet of brown hair perfectly sprayed into place. He looked handsome and distinguished in a plastic way. Worse yet, he looked plausible. Suzy stirred in his seat. The Captain laid a hand on his knee and squeezed it reassuringly.

Jones began by reading from Genesis: "For this reason, a man will leave his father and mother, and be united to his wife, and they will become one flesh." He looked out at us and nodded slowly, as if the meaning of what he'd said was only just beginning to dawn on him.

"Friends, we are all born of one man and one woman. This is the human condition as God has created it, as he has intended it to be, and as it has indeed remained for time immemorial. The fact that we are made by the union of male and female is what unites us and defines us. In supporting Proposition One, what you are being asked to do is simply to reaffirm the laws of nature, created by God, and recognized and revered by our Judeo-Christian forefathers."

Several heads on the right-hand side of the room had already begun to nod in affirmation, including my grandmother's. I resisted the urge to go over and shake her until her false teeth rattled. Jones spoke on, smiling often and spreading his arms open wide. He didn't avoid looking at our side of the room, instead casting benevolent and even beseeching looks our way whenever possible. The Lesbian Avengers remained motionless, their arms folded across their chests.

I glanced over at Suzy, who was sitting very still in his seat, crying. I thought about the time he'd spent in Exodus International, and I felt sorry for all the times I'd found him really irritating. The Captain put her arm around his waist, pulling him close, and Jeff, who was sitting behind him, leaned forward and whispered something in his ear. Suzy nodded and sat up, wiping his eyes.

Jones went on with his sermon, in full swing now and feeling his power. When he finished, several of his supporters applauded.

Then, it was time for the questions. One of the Lesbian Avengers asked Jones and McCauley if they followed all of the restrictions laid down in Leviticus.

"Do you eat shellfish," she asked, "or wear blended fabrics?"

Jones smiled and gave a brief lecture on St. Paul's thinking about Jewish dietary laws.

There were a few questions for the ACLU attorney and a couple for the UCC minister about open and affirming congregations. She was a good speaker, as effective in her way as Jones, if not as showy. Then, just as things were beginning to wind down, I stood up to ask a question. Summoning the whole of my biblical knowledge, which, thanks to my mother's strident atheism, was sadly limited, I said to Jones, "You spoke earlier of Paul's vision. Just which parts of the Bible do you want to see written into Idaho code?"

He smiled. "Paul is very clear on those parts of the law which are important in a Christian civilization." Then, looking back at his amen corner, he said, "We should never apologize for our beliefs, and we should never back down."

There was scattered applause, but Tipper interrupted, saying, "Excuse me, but I believe that the Bible calls for the stoning of law-breakers. Do you think we should be stoned?"

Jones paused, and in that moment of hesitation, Suzy stood up. His eyes were red but dry. He said, "Who knowing the judgment of God, that they which commit such things are worthy of death, not only do the same, but have pleasure in them that do them."

For the first time, Jones dropped the smile. His jaws clenched, and in his booming pulpit voice he said, "Thou shalt not lie with mankind, as with womankind. It is an abomination."

"Judge not, lest ye yourselves be judged and found wanting," Suzy replied. "I sleep with men, sir. Do you think that I should be killed?"

"I make no apologies for the word of God," Jones said firmly. "His will be done."

The debate, for all intents and purposes, was over. There were a few shocked gasps, but a scary number of people clapped. In the confusion that followed, several people left the room. One of them was my grandmother. I didn't dare to hope that she'd seen the light. It was more likely that she wanted to be first in line to the bathroom.

As Suzy brushed past on his way out the back door, I touched his arm.

"You were great," I said. "You certainly know your Bible."

He smiled grimly. "I also know Jones' son. Biblically."

Chapter 28

Sylvie and I went for drinks and doughnuts with the Radical Faeries. Kate, Captain Schwartz, and the Folksong Army all declined, pleading old age and fear of insomnia. We took two outdoor tables at the Cowslip Café and pushed them together.

Suzy lit a cigarette. "I feel it's incumbent upon me to get in the good reverend's face whenever I can. I owe that much to the memory of Trevor Jones."

"Did he . . . is he dead?" I asked.

Suzy laughed. "No. He's living in queer bliss in Portland, Oregon with a lovely Jewish man named Jacob. I meant the memory of our relationship. Between his father and mine, plus all the time we spent together in Exodus, we just couldn't make it work. Two fundamentalist preachers' kids—it was a nightmare. Besides, it would take more than proselytizing to kill Trevor. Or me, for that matter."

"It would take stoning," Tipper observed. "Can you believe that bastard?"

We sat in silence for a while. Then, gradually, small conversations began to build up again. Jeff and Brian argued about the Seattle Mariners, Alan and Suzy told each other off-color butt jokes, and Tom did his best to flirt with Tipper, who pretended to be indifferent.

"Well," I said to Sylvie, "here we are, odd dykes out."

"Do you really mind?" She was leaning back in her chair, holding my hand. People walked by, and one or two cast us a backward glance.

“I don’t mind at all. Sometimes, it’s nice to be alone in a big crowd.”

“There is safety in numbers,” she agreed. She looked tired but happy.

“What did you say to your mother?”

“I told her about us. I said that I loved you, and that I wanted to be out to her.”

“And what did she say?”

“First,” she squeezed my hand, “she said how much she liked you. She said she was happy for us. Most of all, she was happy that I told her. Then we talked about my father.”

“Your father?” I sat up in my chair.

“Not about that,” she said in a low voice. “We talked about the rumors. I told her how I felt about them, how they’d kept me from telling her long after I knew I was gay. She said she was sorry she hadn’t contradicted the story before, but she didn’t know how to broach the subject. She’s thought for a long time that I might be a lesbian. She didn’t want to ask, and she didn’t know why I hadn’t told her. Bil, I believe her. That’s why she didn’t say anything. I think . . .”

We were interrupted by a tap on my shoulder. A. J. and Nancy stood behind us. A. J. was smiling her broad, sharky grin.

“I thought you might be here,” she said.

“What do you want?” Tipper piped up. “Planning to set fire to downtown Cowslip to promote lesbian visibility?”

“I don’t know why you hate me,” A. J. replied. “I’ve never done anything to you, and the Lesbian Avengers have already done a lot of good.” She turned back to Sylvie and me. “I wanted to see if you two could come to our meeting on Sunday night. We’re planning an action.”

“Maybe,” I said. “What do you have in mind?”

“Sword-swallowing,” Suzy suggested.

“Walking on hot coals,” added Brian.

“Parachuting.”

“Pie-eating contest.”

“Hair pie.”

“That’s enough out of you, Suzy,” I snapped. “You’re starting to sound exactly like my mother.” Suzy laughed. “Give me a call tomorrow night or," I nodded at Nancy, "you can tell Sylvie. We'll see—it depends on the action."

"Actually," A. J. said, "what we have in mind is phone-banking, calling up registered voters and asking how they plan to vote on this issue. If they say yes, we ask them to reconsider. If they don't know, we offer to give them more information. It's easy, really. Then we're going to do some canvassing door to door."

None of the Faeries had anything to say to this. I looked at Sylvie, and she nodded.

"If that's what you're doing," I said, "you can count us in."

A. J. smiled. As she and Nancy turned to go, she said, "You really need to get some new friends, Bil. You can't be a fag hag all your life."

Sylvie and I both opened our mouths to speak, but Suzy beat us to it.

"I prefer the term queer peer, myself."

"How about fruit bat," Jeff suggested.

"Or fruit fly?"

"Or fruit loop?"

A. J. and Nancy stalked off. We waited until they were a reasonable distance away before we laughed. Tipper just shook his head.

"I really should have had you committed when you took up with her. I think you were having a psychotic episode."

"You should be nicer to me," I replied, "considering the fact that I saved you from a smoke-filled kitchen this afternoon."

"What are you talking about?"

"I switched the targets. Your mother actually won. The closest groupings were hers."

He paused for a moment and then grinned. "I owe you," he said.

"Yes, you do. You and the Faeries can get your asses in gear and help the Lesbian Avengers canvass door to door and run that phone bank."

Sylvie and I stayed at the café for some time after the Faeries had left. I longed to go back to her apartment, but she'd promised to spend the night with her mother. She felt that coming to the meeting was her mother's first tentative step out of the closet, and she wanted to talk to her. When I could no longer resist the evil glares of the café's wait staff, who wanted to close up shop, I pushed my chair back and bowed to the inevitable.

I started the truck and turned on the headlights. It was another dark, cloudy night. I kept telling myself that I needed to be more sensitive to other people's needs, but I didn't want to go home and sleep in my own bed. Sylvie reached over and tickled the back of my neck.

"You might not believe this," she said, "but this isn't the way I wanted to spend tonight."

"I know. Your mother needs you, and besides, you promised."

"That doesn't make it easy."

"But tomorrow is Saturday. We've got the whole weekend ahead of us."

"And Nancy's going to be up in Spokane until Sunday night. It'll be just the two of us."

"Thanks," I said. "Now tonight is bound to be a living hell. I'll be forced to sit around with my mother and brother watching championship wrestling, praying for the hours to pass."

We were on the highway three or four miles from Kate's farm, just past Fort Sister's driveway, when a car pulled out to pass us. I couldn't see into the interior, and it didn't have its headlights on. It pulled up parallel to me, but it didn't pull ahead.

"Idiot," I said, slowing down. "What he's doing, playing chicken?"

Suddenly, the car swerved into my lane, narrowly missing the side of my truck.

I slammed on the brakes and went into a skid. We'd been doing about fifty-five, and we were still going at least thirty when the truck jumped the shoulder and went into the ditch. I just had time to yell "Shit!" before we plowed into a tree with cacophony of scraping metal and an ominous hissing sound.

When I opened my eyes, the hood was buckled up towards the windshield like an old bed sheet. The truck tried to run for a few seconds after impact, and then it knocked twice and died. I closed my eyes again and listened, afraid to look at Sylvie. The hissing sound was definitely mechanical, not human. I guessed it was the radiator. I opened my eyes.

Sylvie's hands gripped the dashboard tightly, and she was breathing like a locomotive.

"Oh God, honey, are you okay?"

She nodded. "Just bruised, I think. The seatbelt—thank God for this seatbelt—knocked the wind out of me. Are you all right?"

"I'm fine, but I thought you were . . ." I burst into tears. "My poor truck."

Sylvie unbuckled herself and slid across the seat as best she could. She put her arms around me and held me tightly.

"It's okay. Neither of us is hurt, and that's the important thing, right?"

"That bastard ran us off deliberately," I said. "He didn't have his fucking lights on. He . . ."

A terrifying thought occurred to me.

"We've got to get out of here," I said, opening my door and pulling her behind me. "Come on, let's go."

I stepped out of the truck and directly into a two-foot deep hole. I lost my footing and Sylvie, already off balance, nearly fell out of the truck on top of me. She righted herself in time and got out carefully.

"Help me up," I said. "We've got to get out of here quickly."

"Why? Bil, what's . . ."

I motioned for her to be quiet. I heard a sound up the road from us. A car was turning around on the highway ahead, just around the curve.

"I've twisted my ankle," I said, grabbing the door handle and pulling myself up. "I can walk on it if you'll help me, but it's important that we get away from here as quickly as possible. We're not far from Tipper's. We need to make for those trees. Are you ready?"

She didn't answer. She must have been afraid because I certainly was.

"It's okay," I said. "I know these woods."

I hoped I knew them better than the driver of the car coming back down the road. Whoever it was, they were driving slowly. I could hear the tires crunching on the asphalt.

"Let's go."

We had just reached the tree line when the car drove past. It was too dark to make out the model, and its headlights were still turned off. We moved into the trees, and I turned to look back at the truck. The impact had knocked out my headlights. The taillights, however, glowed red in the dark. I wished I'd had the presence of mind to turn them off.

The car stopped on the shoulder just above us, and someone stepped out. I caught a glimpse of a crowbar in their hand, which made me think it would be best if we didn't stick around.

Sylvie had seen it, too. "Come on," she whispered. "Quickly and quietly."

We made an ungodly amount of noise; it sounded as if we were stepping on every dry twig in the forest. I stopped for a moment and listened for the sound of an engine starting and a car driving away. I didn't hear it. My ankle was really starting to ache. I motioned for Sylvie to move faster. I thought we were within a quarter of a mile of Tipper's house.

After another fifty yards or so, we stopped again. That's when I heard a twig snap behind us. We'd been followed into the woods.

"Run," I whispered to Sylvie.

"No." She reached around my waist to get a firmer grip. "Let's go!"

No longer even trying to be quiet, we ran for all we were worth. I cast one quick glance over my shoulder and thought I saw the shadow only about twenty yards behind us. I ignored the pain in my ankle and put as much weight as I could on it, praying that the adrenaline rush would produce enough endorphins to get me through. When I finally caught sight of the lights on the softball diamond, I yelled with all my might.

"Help!"

We stumbled into the back fence just behind Jeff, who was backing up for a fly ball.

"Nice catch," I said. Then I let go of Sylvie and pitched forward in a dead faint.

Chapter 29

I woke up in Tipper's bed. Sylvie was sitting next to me, crying, and Tipper was standing behind her, patting her on the back. The Captain was pacing furiously up and down the room. When she saw that my eyes were open, she stopped.

"How do you feel?"

I was having difficulty focusing. I said, "Like the biggest wimp on earth."

"You hit your head," she said. "You've got a big gash on your forehead. Sylvie thinks you hit the windshield, and Suzy thinks you might need stitches."

"What would Suzy know about it?" I tried to sit up and instantly regretted it.

"Lie back down," Tipper said firmly.

Sylvie wrapped her arm around my shoulders and eased me onto the pillow.

"In a former life," Tipper continued, "Suzy was an emergency room nurse. He's older than he looks. He says you're to lie down and wait for an ambulance."

"No ambulance."

"Bil . . ." Sylvie began.

"Call Ruth," I said, closing my eyes because the room had begun to spin. "She can come look at me. I don't want to go to the hospital. I don't want to leave here."

I was suddenly filled with terror at the thought of leaving Fort Sister. I wanted to stay with Captain Schwartz and her armory of guns.

"And I don't want you to go anywhere, either," I added to Sylvie.

She squeezed my hand and kissed me on the top of my head. "I'm here, Bil. I won't go anywhere."

Tipper left the room, and I heard him consulting with Suzy out in the hallway. I strained to hear what they were saying. Tipper came back into the room and walked to the edge of the bed.

"Suzy says that you're a jackass, but he thinks you'll be okay. You've had a whack on the head, but he doesn't think you're concussed. He's butterflied your cut, which should hold you for now. Do you two want to tell us what happened?"

I looked at Sylvie. She said, "Some nut ran us off the road. He didn't have his lights on, and he swerved into our lane. We crashed into a tree on the edge of your property."

Captain Schwartz turned to Tipper and said in an accusing tone, "I told you I heard tires screeching on the highway."

"Mama," Tipper said, "I will never doubt your bionic hearing again." Then he turned to me. "I'm sorry, Bil. We got up a game to decompress after the town meeting. It got pretty noisy, and then Suzy insisted on having a disco soundtrack blaring out across the field. Mama heard you yell for help, but I didn't know you were there until you stumbled out of the woods."

His eyes filled with tears.

"It's okay. We're both okay."

He grabbed a tissue and blew his nose loudly. "Why were you yelling for help?"

Sylvie answered him. "Because the person who ran us off the road decided to finish the job with a crowbar. He chased us through the woods."

"Someone from that debate tonight? Someone followed you?"

I didn't think it was anyone from the meeting. The Reverend Jones might want to stone me, but if he were going to kill anyone, he'd probably start with Suzy. I looked at Sylvie, whose expression was inscrutable.

"I don't know who it was," I said.

The look I'd given Sylvie was not lost on Tipper. "Damn it, Bil—you're running around playing private detective, not watching whose toes you might be stepping on, and now you've got someone mad enough to want to kill you. I might just kill you myself if you keep it up. If you know something, take it to the sheriff. Those pages from the telephone book . . ."

The Captain was still in the room, so I cut in quickly, "Ixnay, you idiot."

He glared at me.

Captain Schwartz leaned over the other side of the bed and laid a large, cool hand on my cheek. "I hope Suzy's right that you're not concussed. Your sister needs to check you out. Why would someone want to kill you?"

"I . . ."

"She's been sticking her nose where it doesn't belong. No pun intended," he added, lifting an eyebrow. "She's been asking questions about our recent murder, and I expect she might have asked one question too many."

"Why are you . . ." the Captain began. Then she looked at Sylvie and smiled. "I sent Cedar Tree and Jane to fetch your mother, Sylvie. She should be here any minute now. I've also called your mother, Bil."

"Great," I muttered.

The sounds of a great consternation rose up the staircase, and my mother swept into the room, followed closely by Kate.

"Bil!" she wailed, sailing over to my bedside.

"Come on, Tipper," said the Captain. "Let's go downstairs and call Ruth."

They closed the door, and my mother felt me up and down for contusions and bruises, creating many new ones in the process.

"Knock it off, Emma. Ruth will be here soon."

"What happened?"

"Some bastard tried to kill us," I said. "Ran us off the road and then chased us down with a crowbar. We made it here just in time to keep from getting our heads bashed in."

"But why would anyone want to . . . that goddamn meeting! I got a phone call from your grandmother, and I told her I hoped she was happy. She was shocked to death, but I said you lie down with dogs, you get up with fleas. Did you get a look at him? Have you called the sheriff?"

"If you will shut up," I said slowly and carefully, "I'll answer all of your questions. First, we don't know that it was someone from the meeting. It might have been someone closer to home."

"Why . . ." she began, and then stopped.

Kate cast a quick glance from Sylvie to me. She said, "Two sheriff's deputies were waiting for me when I got home tonight. They had some more questions about the man who died. I misidentified his body, but I think you already know that."

I looked at Emma, who was staring resolutely at her toes. Kate continued.

"The autopsy made it clear that he wasn't your father. I haven't been charged with anything, though I think that might just be a matter of time. I told them it was a mistake, but why should they believe me? I have every reason to lie."

She walked over and stood beside her daughter, her hands hanging loosely at her sides. Sylvie looked up at her and waited. The blood had drained from Kate's face, and she swayed a little, as if she were going to be sick. Sylvie reached out and took her mother's hand, though she made no other move to comfort her. No one said anything for at least a minute.

Then, Kate spoke to Sylvie. "How much do you remember?"

Sylvie didn't answer. She looked past her mother at me.

I said, "She woke up and saw you through the kitchen door. Both of you. She watched you bury his body in the backyard."

Kate said, "Oh."

My mother said nothing. She had a curious expression on her face. Sylvie waited.

"I planned to leave him," Kate said. "I planned to leave on the fifth. I knew he'd be gone for at least five days, and that would give me time to get you out of the state. I had enough money, and I had a college friend who lived in California. Actually, Emma knew her better than I did—she was an attorney in family law. She worked with battered women, and she'd arranged Emma's adoption of Sam. We were going to leave on Wednesday morning, the day after your father left for

Spokane. But there was a problem, something went wrong with his motorcycle."

"I knocked it over," Sylvie said. "It bent something on the engine."

"The clamp holding the throttle cable," my mother said. I looked at her, bemused. She shrugged. "It was nothing, easily fixed."

Kate wiped her eyes with her fingertips. "He was enraged. I thought you were in bed asleep, but I heard him yelling at you, and I knew. When I came out the back door, he was holding you in the air by your neck, choking you. I tried to pull his hands off. He wouldn't let go. Then, he dropped you. I thought you were dead, but when I got to you, you were still breathing. I carried you into the house and laid you on the kitchen table. He followed me in. I'd put the dog down that morning, and the gun was still out. I wanted to kill him."

"It wasn't premeditated," I said. "You could have pleaded self-defense. You had the evidence."

"It wouldn't have mattered," she said. "Men who beat their wives and children still get custody, even now. I didn't have a chance in a court of law and he knew it—he knew. We'd been married for just over a year when I met someone, a woman. I would have left with her, but I couldn't."

"You were pregnant," Sylvie said, her voice expressionless. "Did he rape you?"

Kate closed her eyes. "No, not then. I married Burt to please my parents. I know my mother suspected I was a lesbian; she hinted at it once or twice. My marriage shut her up. After that, what could she say?"

"Why didn't you have an abortion?"

"Because I didn't want one. Sylvie," Kate took her daughter by the arms and turned to face her, "I wanted you. I don't regret the choices I made because I have you."

She didn't go on. Sylvie was crying silently now, still holding her mother's hand. They didn't look quite real to me.

"Emma," I began, "maybe we should . . ."

Emma blinked once and then spoke. "Kate called me when she was sure he was dead. We talked about what to do. Although he'd beaten her severely, the loaded rifle made it look like premeditated murder.

She might have taken her chances in court, but Sylvie needed her mother. And so I told your father the only lie I've ever told him. I said that Sylvie was sick, and that I was going over to keep Kate company. When I got there, we stripped him naked and buried him. I burned his clothes in the barbecue pit out back, all except for his shoes. Kate put those in the trunk of her car, and we dropped them in the river in Spokane. We had four days before he was due back to clean up the mess and work out a story."

"What was the story?" I asked.

"We kept it simple," Emma said. "He left for Spokane. He never got there. Kate waited until the day after he was due back, and she reported him missing." She looked at me, her gaze firm and unwavering. "If I had to do it over again, I'd do the same thing."

"How did you know Frank wouldn't report him missing? He was expecting him in Spokane."

My mother shrugged. "We didn't think that far ahead. Sometimes, you just get lucky. Frank was long gone. Someone in the assessor's office noticed the money was missing about the same time they noticed Frank was. That was on Monday, July . . . what? The tenth, I think. Anyhow, within a week, the rumors were flying all over town. We couldn't have guessed that people would link the disappearances, but we knew Frank wasn't going to be calling the police to report anything. He'd stolen two hundred and fifty thousand of Lewis County's dollars."

"If Burt wasn't going to Spokane to meet Frank . . ."

"He was going to meet someone else," my mother said. "Someone who wasn't all that eager to step forward and report that Burt was a no-show."

"I think I know," Sylvie said. "He was meeting Agnes. She said she saw his motorcycle that night at a rest stop on Highway 95."

Neither my mother nor Kate seemed surprised by this.

"What about his motorcycle?" I asked.

Emma smiled ruefully. "You do think of everything, don't you? How long have you known about this, or guessed about it, anyway?"

"About three weeks. What did you do with the motorcycle?"

"She rode it up to Spokane," Kate said. "We waited until Sylvie was asleep. I put her in the back seat and followed in my car. When we came to a quiet, out-of-the-way bridge, we pushed it into the Spokane River." She looked at my mother. "You were right about seeing Agnes."

Emma nodded. "I thought so. I saw someone standing next to the bike when I looked out the men's room door. It looked like her, and I wondered what she was doing there at four o'clock in the morning."

"You were in the men's room?" I said.

"Of course I was in the men's room. I was supposed to be Burt. What would I have been doing in the ladies' room? Agnes was on her way back from Spokane, thinking no doubt that Burt had stood her up. It's a wonder she didn't hang around—she was brazen enough. We were lucky she didn't notice the car."

"She did," Kate said. Emma, Sylvie, and I all stared at her. "She told me about a week after I'd reported him missing. I made up a lie about having a fight and following him to Spokane. I said I thought he was having an affair, and that meeting Frank was just a sham."

"What did she say?" Emma asked.

"She laughed. In her own way, I think she really did hate him."

"Hmmph," said my mother. "Funny way of showing it."

"No," Kate said slowly. "She doesn't like me, but she's my sister. I'm sure he picked her just to punish me. He probably thought it was funny. He can't have been kind to her."

"Did she say what she was doing at that rest stop in the middle of the night?" Sylvie asked.

"She said she was on her way home from Spokane. I didn't ask questions. It was clear to her that I knew she and Burt were having an affair."

I was no longer interested in the travails of Agnes. She made me sick. Against Sylvie's objections, I pulled myself to a sitting position, resting my back against the pillows.

"So you shot him," I said.

No one answered. Kate seemed stricken by a sudden pain, and my mother looked at the ceiling. Sylvie, who had been holding her mother's hand, let it go now and came over to sit by me on the bed. I put my arm around her.

"No," Kate said at last. "I didn't. I meant to, but I didn't. When he saw the gun, he charged at me. I panicked. He hit me, and I knocked the back of my head against the kitchen floor. I remember him grabbing my throat, just like he had Sylvie. Then I passed out. When I woke up, he was lying on his back in the kitchen doorway. Sylvie was sitting next to me, crying, and he was dead."

"Then who . . ."

Kate and my mother both looked at Sylvie.

Ruth came and pronounced me bruised but not concussed. My ankle was also badly bruised, but likewise neither sprained nor broken. I couldn't stop the Captain from calling the sheriff's department, and that meant I had to answer a lot of questions about what had happened. They inspected the truck and then came back and tried to get me to blow into a Breathalyzer bag. This infuriated everyone, especially my mother.

Emma went home just after midnight. I convinced Kate and Sylvie to spend the night at Fort Sister. The Captain gave up her bed for them, but sometime in the night, Sylvie crept out and joined me upstairs. Though Tipper was asleep on the floor beside me and I had a hell of a headache, I was glad to have her close to me.

"I planned all of this just so you'd have to stay with me tonight," I said.

She said, "Shut up, you fool," and she kissed me.

I woke with a start just after seven in the morning.

"Oh fuck!"

Sylvie and Tipper both sat bolt upright.

"What?"

"The pages from the telephone book. I left them and the folder of newspaper clippings in the truck. And," I turned to Sylvie, "all of that stuff from Reginald Brown. It's on the front seat. What if the cops found it last night?"

"So?" Tipper said. "It's just research. Your brother was a suspect. You've got a right to be curious."

Sylvie and I exchanged significant looks.

"They'll get the wrong idea," I explained quickly. "And they'll start looking somewhere they shouldn't. I've got to know if they found it."

"Well," Tipper said, lying back down on the floor, "you don't have to know right this minute. There's nothing you can do about it, so why don't you go back to sleep."

"I'm getting up," I said.

"Bil," Sylvie laid a hand on my arm. "That's not a good idea. I'll walk out and check." She stood up.

"Not by yourself, you won't. I'm going with you."

"I don't want to fight with you, Bil."

Tipper sat up and sighed heavily. "Who the hell can sleep with you two in the room? I'll go."

He shoved me back down roughly.

"Ouch."

"Don't be such a baby," he said.

As soon as he'd gone down the stairs, I said, "Do you remember now?"

Sylvie shook her head. "I don't remember anything, not yet, but I must have pulled the trigger, Bil. That's what my mother and Emma think happened."

"You were only six," I began, but she shook her head.

"It's okay, I don't blame myself, maybe because I don't remember it. I'm relieved to know that my mother didn't kill him. My mother's not a murderer."

"And neither are you," I said, forcing her to look at me. "I hope you know that."

"I wanted him dead," she said quietly. "I used to lie in my bed sometimes, listening to him fighting with my mother, and my whole body would shake. I thought if I could just concentrate hard enough, I could kill him by wishing."

I didn't know what to say. I'd never felt rage like that; I'd never had to. I pulled her close to me and stroked her hair. She said nothing for a few moments and then, "I wish I could remember."

"No you don't," I murmured against her ear. "Please don't think about it."

"I don't even remember waking up and going to sit by my mother."

"You were terrified; you've blocked it all out." I rested my hand on the thin, soft curve of her stomach. "It'll come back to you soon enough, and when it does, I'll be there."

She laid her hand on top of mine. "If they'd reported it for what it was, even if there'd been a trial, it would all be over and done with now. It would all be in the past, and I could forget about it. I know they thought they were doing the right thing, but I wish . . ."

I said, "I think they thought that you'd been through enough, and that it would be better if he just disappeared. You do things when you're upset and confused that you wouldn't ordinarily do. Maybe if she'd been thinking clearly, your mother would have called the police, though they might not have believed that a six-year-old could have pulled the trigger. An overzealous prosecutor, a difficult sheriff, there were any number of things for your mother to be afraid of, and she'd been afraid for a very long time. And," I added, "this is a small town."

She looked at me, puzzled.

"People know everyone's business here," I said, "and they never forget anything. Your mother had to send you to a private school in Washington because people were whispering that your father ran off with another man."

She said, "Imagine if they'd known that his own daughter killed him."

It took Tipper half an hour to walk to the truck and back. Sylvie and I watched him cross the softball diamond from the bedroom window. I climbed back into bed and pulled the covers up to my neck.

"That's a very nice impersonation of a person doing what she knows is good for her," he said, flinging the door open, "but I saw you in the window. You're impossible."

"Did you find the folder?" I said, sitting up.

"It wasn't there."

"Then the cops have it." Sylvie looked resigned.

Tipper shook his head, reached into his shirt, and pulled out his cell phone. He waved it at us for emphasis. "No, they don't. I called them."

"You what? What did you say?"

"What do you think I said? I asked them if they'd taken a folder out of your truck."

"You . . ."

"Don't be stupid, Bil—what could it hurt? If they had found the folder, the damage was already done. If they didn't have it, why would it be suspicious to ask? I didn't tell them what was in it. It might have been your homework, for all they knew."

"Jesus Christ," I said.

"So what we have now," Tipper observed, "is a murderer with a folder full of photocopies."

"And a 1966 copy of the *Cowslipper*. I'm going to be really popular with Sarah if I've lost a book that she's checked out to herself."

Chapter 30

I called Emma and told her that Tipper would be driving me home. I said good-bye to Kate, who was sitting on the living-room sofa, and to Captain Schwartz, who was sitting next to her. Howitzer Jane sat across the room in a rocking chair, pretending to read the newspaper while casting worried glances at the Captain and Kate. I said good-bye to her as well.

The Captain told me she'd keep an eye on Sylvie and Kate, and that she'd tow my truck back to her place. Cedar Tree knew something about bodywork, and the Captain was sure she wouldn't mind taking a look at it.

The Radical Faeries were, of course, not yet awake. Sylvie walked me out to the car, where Tipper was already waiting behind the wheel with the engine running.

"Do you want me to come with you?" she asked.

"Of course I do, but I expect the whole family is there. I'd like to have them all sorted out before I bring you home for the first official visit." Lowering my voice so Tipper wouldn't hear, I said, "We'll talk about everything this afternoon. Go take care of your mother."

"And you take care of yours. Will you call when you're done? I can come pick you up."

"If my head feels better, I'll just borrow Emma's car. She owes me."

I got into the car and rolled the window down. Sylvie leaned in and kissed me.

"Drive slowly," she said. Tipper saluted, and she laughed. "I'll see you in a couple of hours?"

I nodded. "I'm just putting in an appearance to show them all that I'm still alive. I'll get out as soon as I've showered and changed."

When we pulled in at home, all the cars were in the driveway.

Tipper said, "Shall I wait out here in case you need to make a fast getaway?"

"No, you go on home. I can handle them."

He kissed me on the top of my head and waved good-bye.

Ruth, Sarah, and Emma were on the sofa, Hugh was in Archie Bunker, and Naomi sat in Edith. Sam was parked on the floor in front of my mother, and she was scratching his back.

"Here, Bil," Hugh said, standing up. "Sit here."

"Thanks."

"You look okay," Ruth said. "How do you feel?"

"I need a shower and some clean clothes, then I'll be right as rain."

"You should take it easy. Spend the day in bed, sleeping."

"I can't—I've got things to do." I turned to look at Emma. "Can I borrow the car?"

"Of course," she said, "but I think Ruth is right. You need to lie down today, not run all over the place like nothing's the matter."

"Can I have the keys?"

"Sure, but . . ."

"I need them now," I insisted.

She shook her head, but she fished them out of her pocket and tossed them to me.

"Hugh," I said, avoiding Emma's eye. "If you were going to embezzle some money from a county office, how would you do it? I mean, where would you put it if you didn't want to get caught? You couldn't just deposit it into your own bank account."

"I'm assuming this is hypothetical?"

I nodded.

"Well," he took his pipe out of his front pocket and tapped the bowl against his palm, "It would depend on how much money was involved, where it had come from, and who might notice it was missing. You'd need to be someone or know someone with a lot of financial experience and resources, someone who knew how to hide money. That's not all that rare; people hide money from the tax man every day."

"Where would you hide it?"

"I'd hide it in my mattress," he said, "but I'm not much of an embezzler. In a stock account, different bank accounts, dummy corporations, that sort of thing."

I could feel Emma watching me.

"Thanks. Time for that shower," I said, getting up.

Naomi cleared her throat. "One more thing. Granny called me. She wants everyone to know that she'll no longer be working for Proposition One."

"What prompted this change of heart?" Hugh asked. "Was she struck by lightning?"

"No such luck," Emma complained.

"What she said was that she would never understand the gay lifestyle, but she didn't believe in stoning people to death, particularly not members of her family."

"Christ," Emma said. "To her, gay-bashing is just bad manners."

"I'll settle for that," I replied.

I drove carefully, though with little regard for the speed limit. I had planned to drive straight to Kate's; instead, I took the turn off into town. Sylvie needed some time alone with her mother, and I thought I had a good idea of what had become of that folder. I pulled into Granny's driveway just before eleven o'clock.

Granny's car was there, an old, orange Volkswagen Beetle. She'd had it as long as I could remember. My grandmother was one of those drivers who caused accidents but never had one herself. She might drive out into a busy intersection without looking, create a five-car pile-up behind her, and cruise on as if nothing had happened.

I knocked on her door before walking in. This was standard practice in my family, and I was unlikely to disturb Granny in anything illicit, not at eleven o'clock on a Saturday morning. After last night's debate, she might decide to skip church, but she wouldn't miss having morning tea with her weirdo friend.

My grandmother's house smelled strongly of old widow lady, a pungent combination of ancient carpet, slow-running drains, and boiled cabbage. I reeled a little in the doorway. However, I had a job to do, even if it required breathing through my mouth. Sure enough, there were Granny and Helen sitting at the dining room table with a deck of playing cards laid out before them. Helen and her old lady friends—she might have been sitting in a field of lavender for all the notice she paid. I got myself a glass of iced tea and sat down at the table.

"We're playing gin rummy," Granny said. "Can I deal you a hand?"

"I prefer poker."

Helen pointed at the bandage on my forehead. "What's the matter with you?"

"Someone tried to kill me last night," I answered nonchalantly. Her eyes narrowed for a fraction of a second. I turned back to my grandmother, who was shuffling the cards in her hand.

"You and your stories," Granny said. "You were always making things up as a child. I told your mother it was just plain lying, but she said you were being creative. You know I never read fiction, only biography. Why would I want to read something someone else has made up? Millicent is always reading those trashy romance novels. I picked one up—it was pornographic, full of Venus mounds and men's members and . . ."

"I get the picture," I said. "I'm glad to see you're your old self again, Granny. Naomi says you're no longer working for Proposition One."

The look Granny gave me was almost coherent. "I was very shocked last night. Imagine declaring that the Bible told you to kill people. It's blasphemy."

I shrugged. "It's true."

"Don't argue with me, Wilhelmina. That's your mother's bad influence."

"Sorry. Maybe I've got the wrong Bible."

"It could be," she said. "The Catholics have their own Bible, and then there's that red-letter version. Your grandfather bought me one of those, but I refused to use it. That red lettering looked, well . . ."

"Satanic?" I suggested.

"I didn't like to say it."

"So," I said, sipping my tea, "did you know that the man who died in Sam's jail cell wasn't Burt Wood after all? It was actually Frank Frost."

"I heard a rumor," Granny said, putting down her cards and gazing at me eagerly. "It hasn't been in the newspaper yet."

I tapped the side of my nose. "I saw an advance copy of the autopsy report."

"Ruth?"

"Shhh," I said, with a pointed look at Helen. "The walls have ears. Between you and me, I don't think Frank had anything to do with Burt Wood. I think he left town because he'd embezzled all of that money, and he came back because he thought he could cash in on someone who'd helped him."

"An accomplice?" Granny whispered.

"I think so." I got up and drained the last of my tea. "Anyhow, I've got to be going. Things to do. I just wanted to check on you, see how you were after last night."

Granny nodded, as if I checked on her all the time. "Thank you, I'm fine." Then she added, "You know, Wilhelmina really doesn't suit you. It's good that they call you Bil."

This was as close as I was going to get to an apology. "I think so."

"You were named after me. The Wilhelmina, not the Eleanor. I don't know where they got your middle name."

"Eleanor Roosevelt."

"No, I remember. Eleanor of Aquitaine. Your mother loved *The Lion in Winter.* Katharine Hepburn was one of her favorite actresses. You were nearly Wilhelmina Katharine, with a 'K.' It might have been Catherine with a 'C' but then your initials would have been WC, and that's what the English call their toilet . . ."

"I think," I said, "that I'd better be going."

My grandmother looked at me. "I like people, all people. I'm not really a misogynist."

"Perhaps," Helen suggested, "you mean misanthrope."

"No," Granny continued, "I mean curmudgeon."

And they let you drive, and they let you vote, I thought to myself. Terrifying. I put my empty glass in the dish drainer. Granny would never mention my sexual orientation to me directly. She'd talk about me behind my back, but she wouldn't take a chance on me telling her to go to hell.

"Was there anything else?" Helen asked.

"Just visiting my grandmother. No crime in that."

"Curiosity killed the cat," Helen said, staring pointedly at the bandage on my forehead. She rocked back and forth in her chair, smiling. I stared back at her until she started to hum. Though my knowledge of eighties music was far from comprehensive, I recognized the first bars of "Tainted Love."

I leaned close to her, resting the palms of my hands on the table. "And what would you know about that, Mildew?"

Helen stopped humming and looked down at my hands, still pressed against the table in front of her. "You said someone tried to kill you. They must have had a reason."

Before I could ask her if she knew exactly what that reason was, she looked back up at me and said abruptly, "You're my cousin's lover, aren't you?"

"Yes, I am."

"My mother thinks it's genetic," she said, "like eye color or hemophilia. I don't. I think it's a sin and that you're both going to hell. Book of Leviticus."

My grandmother watched this exchange in silence but her ears were flapping. As soon as I was gone, she'd be on the phone to my mother like a shot. I smiled at Helen. Righteous anger wasn't genetic, it was nurtured, and I'd learned how to use it at the knee of a master.

"Hmm," I said, "do you eat shellfish, Helen?"

"Yes."

"Leviticus forbids that."

Her eyes narrowed. "Don't lecture me," she said. "It's better than what you eat."

"My goodness, Helen, could you possibly be referring to . . . oral sex? Ah well, I like shrimp, too. I suppose that doubles my chances of a hot hereafter." I turned to smile at my grandmother. "Thanks for the tea, Granny, but I have to be on my way. Mustn't keep a lady waiting."

And with that, I spun on my heel and headed out the door, not wanting them to see that my cheeks were burning. I didn't know where my grenades would land, but I felt I'd lobbed them in the right direction. Helen would tell her parents, and Granny could be counted on to cite chapter and verse to anyone who would hold still long enough to listen. Now, I just had to find Sylvie and wait for all hell to break loose.

Chapter 31

The drive to Kate's house gave me time to think. My money was on Fairfax as Frank's accomplice. Sylvie had asked her mother point blank about blackmail, and Kate admitted that Frank had come by twice in the days before he died to ask her for money. He hinted that he could make life uncomfortable for her. She called his bluff. Frank knew Burt hadn't left town with him; he didn't know anything else.

It also seemed to me that there might be two blackmailers at work. Kate and Agnes had a joint account at Pioneers Bank, and Kate transferred money into it regularly. But would twenty thousand a year be enough for Agnes if she really knew something about Burt's disappearance? I didn't think so. Agnes had been written out of her father's will, and Kate had gotten everything, or close to it. Agnes was bound to be bitter. Why not take it all?

Fairfax was another possibility, a blackmailer who was also being blackmailed. He certainly had access to Kate's accounts at Pioneers Bank. The question in my mind was whether or not the embezzlement conspiracy had spread out beyond him, Burt, and Frank. For all I knew, maybe half the town knew about it. Maybe my father was right, and the money was stuffed in someone's mattress.

When I reached the top of Kate's driveway, the dogs raced over to sniff me. Priscilla wagged her tail. Elvis stood back warily. I swallowed my fear and held my hand out to him. He edged closer until his nose was touching my fingers. Then he wagged his tail as well.

I reached down and scratched behind his ears, and he licked my hand. "You big fraud," I said. We walked in a heaving, tail-wagging mass to the front door, and I knocked. Sylvie appeared around the corner of the house, wearing a baseball shirt and a pair of cut-offs. She was barefoot.

"Why didn't you go to the kitchen door?" she said. "No one ever uses this one."

"As this is my first formal call as your official girlfriend, I thought the front door was more suitable."

"Idiot," she replied, putting her arms around me. I kissed her.

"You've got to quit going around barefoot," I said, breaking away to catch my breath. "You know I've got a thing for naked feet."

She laughed. "Remind me to throw away all of my shoes. Do you want to go inside?"

"Sure. Where's your mom?"

"Running around town. At two, she has a coffee and a cigarette date back here with your mother." I lifted an eyebrow at this information. Sylvie just shrugged. "Why not? Now that we know, maybe that old barrier is gone for good."

"And now that we're together, they've got to start behaving like in-laws instead of outlaws."

"Something like that."

I followed her around the side of the house and into the kitchen. An open book lay on the table in front of her chair. I picked it up and read the title: *No Fond Return of Love.*

"Have you read it?"

I nodded. "I love Barbara Pym. Generally, though, I have pretty debased tastes. When I'm not reading something highbrow for class, I prefer paperback mysteries and lesbian trash. You got any issues of *On Our Backs*?"

"You'll have to check under my bed. Why don't we go through to the living room? We can neck on the sofa."

"You really are my kind of woman."

I propped my feet up on the coffee table, resting them on a magazine so my heels wouldn't make black marks. I put my arm around Sylvie and she leaned against me, her head resting on my shoulder. Then I told her about my visit with Granny.

"Did Helen really say that?"

"Yeah."

"She's dreadful. I'm glad you called her on it. So you lobbed your grenades. Now what?"

"Now we wait to see what happens."

She sighed and shook her head. "That sounds dangerous, especially considering what happened last night."

"Maybe. I didn't know what else to do. We'll just have to be extra careful."

"Right," she said, "that's certainly a word I associate with you."

"That's me, careful and shy."

We sat there happily quiet for a long time. Eventually I said, "So, what did your mother have to do in town?"

"She went to see Lieutenant Young." I sat up at this news. She pulled me back down. "Don't get upset. We decided that the best thing for her to do was to go in of her own free will and say that she'd made a mistake. Burt and Frank were the same age, they were the same height and weight and hair color, and she hadn't seen either of them for nearly two decades. She could have made a legitimate mistake, and it was clear that Young was pressuring her. He didn't wait for the autopsy report. He didn't check dental records . . ."

"I've been wondering about that. Why not?"

"The autopsy took longer than expected, and once the results arrived, Young didn't have anything to compare them to. There was no real investigation into either my father's disappearance or Frank's, so he'd never asked for medical records. Besides, he thought he knew whose body it was. Remember that anonymous tip? Someone called Young and said they'd seen my father wandering around town."

"Yes," I said, "and I wonder just who that was. The nosy Helen?"

Sylvie shrugged. "Who knows? It wasn't until Young learned that the dead man had three kidneys that he asked for my father's records. Having three kidneys is weird, and Frank had mentioned it to people. Anyhow, it took quite a while to locate them. My father's doctor was ancient—he was the same doctor who'd delivered him. When he died, his practice was sold to another doctor, and that doctor in turn sold it to someone else. The files were a mess, all stacked up in boxes in a back room, waiting to be transferred to computer."

"So he thought he had a well-known corpse on his hands, and he pushed your mother to identify him. It was probably the most excitement he's had in years."

"He's running for sheriff. A splashy case would get his name in the newspaper. Alice Campbell is running for re-election, and I'm sure that's the reason she was so determined to nail your brother. She wanted to be seen cleaning up the streets of Lewis County."

"Do you think they'll believe your mother?"

"I hope so. She really didn't have anything to do with Frank's death, I'm sure of that."

"You're not worried then?"

"No," she said, shaking her head. "No one was blackmailing my mother. She told me last night that she's been giving Agnes twenty thousand a year since my grandfather died. My mother didn't approve of the will, and she wanted to make amends. At first, Agnes refused. Then she changed her mind. For some reason, she didn't want a lump sum, and she didn't want anyone to know about the payments. There might be a connection between Agnes and Frank, but there's nothing between him and my mother. Bil—are you listening to me?"

I kissed the spot just behind her ear where her pulse throbbed. Then I worked my way down her long, smooth neck, around the line of her jaw, and, finally, back to her mouth.

"It's getting late," she said eventually. "They'll be here soon."

"Who cares?"

She laughed. "You're supposed to be resting. Remember your head?"

"I'm young and resilient. I'll let you know if I feel like my head is going to explode or something."

"Gee, thanks. That might be messy." She leaned back against the sofa cushions and stayed there for several seconds with her eyes closed. Then suddenly she stood up. "Come on," she said, reaching a hand down to help me up.

"Where are we going?"

"To my apartment. Just because our mothers are going to be here at two doesn't mean we need to. I'll leave a note, and they can call us. Right now, I need music, television, and something to read besides *Mother Jones.* Not to mention the fact that there's nothing to eat in this house, and none of the pizza places deliver outside city limits."

"Pizza sounds like a very good idea, pepperoni and lots of mushrooms." She was pulling me forward, but now I stopped.

"What is it?"

"Mushrooms," I said. "Did you ever ask your botany professor about jimsonweed?"

She shook her head. "He was useless, so I talked to the agricultural extension agent on campus. Jimsonweed grows all over town. That thing you picked by Lilac Trailer Court is actually a variety called Angel's Trumpet."

I sighed. "Well, that doesn't reduce our number of suspects then, does it? I suppose Frank was an only child?"

"He was. Why?"

"Just wondering if I missed a suspect."

"I'm afraid you'll have to make do with your grenades," she said, pulling on my arm again. "Let's go."

"Wait a second." I fished the keys out of my pocket and handed them to her. "Would you mind sailing my mother's boat? I feel a little dizzy."

"Do you have a headache?"

I pulled her to me. "Do you have a cure?"

"Wake up. Bil, wake up."

"Why?"

"It's after six. My mother just called. Your mother's there and they want to talk to us."

My eyelids felt glued to my corneas. "Shit, I've slept in my contact lenses again."

"I'll get the saline from Nancy's room. Your clothes are around here somewhere. Sit up, Bil." I felt an arm behind my back, lifting me up. "Try to get dressed. It sounded important."

"Okay, I'm awake."

When Sylvie and I pulled into the driveway, Hugh's car was parked next to Kate's.

"They're probably in the kitchen," Sylvie said, using her foot to push a dancing dog out of her path. "Elvis, behave yourself. Get down."

We made our way past the dogs and entered the kitchen. Kate and Emma were sitting at the table, cups of coffee in their hands and guilty looks on their faces.

I sniffed the air, which was filled with sickly sweet smoke. "What is that smell? Oh my god!"

"Relax," Emma said, waving her hand to dissipate the smoke. "I found it in the pocket of your brother's jacket this morning. It's no big deal."

"In his jacket . . . so you thought you'd just toke up? What the hell has gotten into you?"

Sylvie was staring at her mother in disbelief. Kate at least had the good grace to look embarrassed. My mother was shrugging it off.

"Sorry," Kate said. "I haven't done it since college." She cast a puzzled look at my mother. "Funny, it doesn't seem to have the same kick, does it? I don't feel a thing."

"You're telling me," my mother agreed.

I drew myself up. "If I'd known the two of you were going to be hopped up on Mary Jane, I'd have stayed in town. Come on, Sylvie."

Emma gave me a sour look. "Don't be such a prude. We only had one puff each, and then I stubbed it out. It was just a whim."

All things considered, I would have preferred a mother who was a little less human. In the last few weeks, I'd learned more about her than I'd ever wanted to know. Still, Sylvie wasn't nearly as bent out of shape as I was, so when she sat down, I relented.

"One puff and then you stubbed it out? I just hope that thing smoking under the toe of your shoe isn't burning a hole in the tile, Emma."

"Christ on a cracker," she said, knocking her forehead on the table as she bent down to retrieve the burning roach.

"Don't worry about it now, Em," Kate said, leaning back in her chair. "We need new tile in here anyway. My father put this linoleum down when he built the place. It's probably asbestos."

"Lucky old you," I said to Emma. She ignored me. I took a seat at the table, and Sylvie and I waited. After a minute or so, Kate spoke.

"Complications," she said, holding her hand out to Sylvie. "Fortuitous complications. I think that's why we were feeling a little frivolous. I learned something down at the sheriff's office that I hadn't expected. A bridge maintenance crew has found your father's motorcycle."

"They found it four months ago," Emma interrupted. "They were doing a routine inspection on some pylons, and a couple of bridge divers for the highway department came across it. The bike was wedged under some rocks. Urban sprawl hasn't reached that far yet, so it was just sitting there."

I looked first at Emma, then at Kate, and then back at Emma again.

"What are you talking about?"

My mother reached into her purse and pulled out two cigarettes, lighting both and handing one to Kate. "He was always a lunatic on that bike, even his mother said so. He'd had several accidents. We thought they'd find it sixteen years ago. They wouldn't find a body, of course, but that could have been swept down river, eaten by coyotes . . ."

"Please," I said. "Spare us the details. Why would you want them to find his bike?"

"An accident," Emma said. "We didn't plan to make him disappear without a trace—we expected someone to look for him. When the bridge crew found it, they dragged it out of the river and read the number on the license plate. Then, they reported it to the highway patrol. The bike was clearly old, and it seemed to have been junked, so the highway patrol reported it to the Department of Motor Vehicles. They, in turn, sent the paperwork to Boise because it was an Idaho tag. That paperwork wasn't processed until the first of last week; it was treated as a low-priority title search."

"Bureaucrats," Sylvie snapped. "That's been sitting on someone's desk all summer long. They could have saved us all a lot of trouble."

"I'm still not getting this," I said. "Why are you feeling frivolous? Aren't the police going to look for a body to go with the motorcycle?"

Kate smiled, and it lit up her entire face. She looked ten years younger.

"They don't expect to find one, not after all this time. They assume that Burt ran off the highway sixteen years ago and drowned. When I went in today and told them that I knew I'd made a mistake, they believed me. I said it looked enough like him to actually be him, and I just wanted some closure. I said after all this time, I thought we deserved it."

"And that," my mother said, "was exactly what they wanted to hear. For all intents and purposes, the case is now closed."

We all sat there, letting this sink in.

"Wait," Sylvie said quietly, "what about Frank? I want to know why you didn't tell them it was him. After all this time, Mom, why did you tell such a dangerous lie?"

Kate stubbed her cigarette out in the ashtray and regarded her daughter seriously. "At first, it was because I panicked. Young asked me if I could identify the man, and without thinking I said, 'Yes.' Then I realized that he meant Burt, and I was confused and scared. That's when I thought, why shouldn't he be Burt? Frank didn't have any living relatives. I didn't know then that he'd been poisoned, or that he'd died in a jail cell with Sam. I didn't know about any of that until afterwards, when it was too late."

"Sylvie," she took her daughter's hand and leaned forward until they were face to face, "I was selfish. I thought it would make things easier for us. If we finally had a corpse to bury in Cowslip Cemetery, then we'd be free. Your father was a bad man. I was sorry for the way things happened, but I wasn't sorry that he was dead. I was relieved—God help me, I was glad. As it turned out, he still managed to blight our lives. We've spent nearly twenty years in a kind of limbo. I thought if I could just lay claim to being a widow, an obvious widow, then we could shut the door on Burt Wood and start talking freely to one another. I'm a lesbian who's spent most of her life hiding behind rumors and lies, and I wanted to stop. One last big lie, and then it could all be over."

Sylvie had been staring down at her hands, wrapped tightly around her mother's. Now she looked up. "It wasn't the lies, I understood those. It was the fact that you never told me that the rumors about my father and Frank weren't true. Being a widow isn't the solution, Mom. You've got to be who you are, someone completely apart from my father. I've known for a long time that I was a lesbian, and I've known about you, but I could never talk about it. That made me feel more lonely than you can possibly imagine."

Kate stood up and reached out to her daughter, who embraced her without hesitation. "I'm so sorry," she said.

"I hope you're taking notes," I said to Emma.

She looked shocked. "I'm not hugging you."

"I meant that you could learn to say you're sorry once in a while. It wouldn't kill you."

"I'll consult my physician and get back to you."

Chapter 32

The next day was beautiful, and the evening looked set to be fair as well. Tipper had invited us over to Fort Sister for a game of softball, and we'd managed to convince Kate to come along.

Sylvie was in her bedroom changing clothes while her mother and I waited in the kitchen. Kate sat at the table, and I leaned against the counter next to the back door. My head was much better than it had been the day before, though for some reason, I felt dizzier when I sat down than when I stood up.

"Was Frank gay?" I asked.

Kate shook her head. "I don't know; we never discussed it. I suspect he was more of an opportunist. Whatever his sexual orientation was, I just thought of him as greedy."

"*Radix malorum cupiditas est.*"

Kate smiled. "The love of money is the root of all evil—high school Latin?" I nodded. She tapped herself on the chest with an index finger. "Catholic school. The one thing I can say with certainty is that Frank was a pathological liar. I remember him lying for no reason at all about things that didn't really matter. He made up stories, and then he seemed to believe them. After Emmet Rutherford died, Frank told people that Millicent was paying him to have sex with her." She laughed at the look on my face. "Millicent was more attractive thirty years ago."

"If you say so. Did anyone believe him?"

"It didn't matter if they believed him or not, they passed the stories on."

"No smoke without fire?"

"Exactly."

The clock struck five.

She said, "I wonder what's keeping Sylvie."

"I'll go check." Before I could move, there was a knock on the back door.

It was Fairfax. Kate frowned and got up to let him in. He looked a little the worse for wear. His hair was uncombed, and his clothes didn't have their usual freshly pressed look. He walked in the door and right past me without seeming to notice that I was there.

"Do you mind if I sit down?"

"Be my guest," Kate said. "We're leaving in a few minutes, though."

He sat down heavily and licked his lips.

"I think I'll go upstairs now," I said, excusing myself. He waved a hand at me.

"Don't bother. I'm sure none of this will come as a surprise to you."

I looked at Kate, who just shook her head. I had a feeling that my grenade had exploded, but I hadn't expected this man, who seemed resigned and defeated before he'd even begun.

He said, "I know that I'm not your favorite person, Kate, but neither of us wants to see Agnes hurt. I didn't kill Frank, and I don't know who did. I understand that you've been cleared. All of that was such a long time ago. Please, let it go."

"Fairfax," Kate said seriously, "I don't know what you're talking about."

He looked at me. I just shrugged. Some of the life seemed to come back into him now, and his voice became animated. "But the other night at the cast party, you asked me about Frank. I thought you knew."

"So you did see him," Kate said, her voice low and even. "I knew you had to be lying. You two were always hand in glove. I suppose he wanted money."

Fairfax looked nervous, but he said nothing.

Kate went on, "So, why should I believe that you didn't kill him?"

"Because I didn't."

I sat down at the table, not wanting to leave Kate alone with him. The long hairs he usually combed over his bald spot were hanging down loosely to one side, and his face was a nasty gray color. He was equal parts pitiful and disgusting. For a long moment, he stared at a spot on the wall behind Kate's head, and then he turned to me. I noticed for the first time that his eyes were the same washed-out gray as his skin.

"Then you must have done it," he said. "You're clever. You called the bank, gave the teller the right information, dug around in a few records that were none of your business. What do you care, Bil? Your brother is out of harm's way, and I'm just a little man in a little bank in a little backwater town. I'm not innocent, but I think I've paid enough."

"I didn't call the bank," I began. Then I stopped. Reggie Brown called the bank; Reggie Brown dug around. And what if Fairfax had the folder from my truck?

He waited for me to continue. I shook my head. In desperation, he turned back to Kate. "You should understand. We've both made mistakes. Tell her," he said, pointing at me. "This is my life—it's not a game."

"Boom," I said suddenly. They both stared at me, and I continued, "You're talking about embezzling, Fairfax. Sixteen years ago, you helped Frank park some stolen money from the county in some dummy bank accounts, possibly a dummy corporation. You aided and abetted. He paid you some percentage, but after four years of wild living and twelve years in a New York prison, he didn't have anything left. So, he decided to hit you up for some hush money. Is that right?"

He didn't look away. "Someone has been poking around in my wife's bank records, and," he pointed at Kate, "in hers. It was someone who claimed to be with a brokerage firm. Lying about that sort of thing is a federal offense, Bil."

"Really?"

His eyes narrowed slightly. "Really."

"Well," I shrugged, "it wasn't me. It takes a professional sleaze-bag to get that kind of information."

"Who was it, Bil?" he asked quietly, the menace now gone from his voice. "It wasn't anyone from the sheriff's department. They'd just get a subpoena. Why would anyone else care?"

I thought about trying to string him along, maybe extracting a complete confession, but I was no Reginald Brown. It was true that Fairfax Merwin was a crook. At that moment, however, he just looked like a sad old fuck-up.

"Don't worry," I said. "I was just trying to clear my brother. I don't care what you did or didn't do. If you say you didn't kill Frank, then I believe you. The question now is who did? Someone ran Sylvie and me off the road two nights ago, and then they chased us through the woods with a crowbar. Whoever it was also stole a folder full of information off the front seat of my truck, information about Frank and Burt and you."

He scratched the palm of his left hand and stared at me. Kate, who had been watching in silence, lit a cigarette. Almost as an afterthought, she offered him one. He took it, sucking about half of it up in one long drag, and stubbing out the rest in the ashtray.

"I wasn't born rich," he said. "I worked my way through college, and I worked my way up in the bank. Then, I married a rich girl. Her father hated me on sight, wouldn't even give me a chance. When he died, he cut her out of his will with a thousand spite dollars. He left all the rest to her younger sister, Kate."

"I've made that up to her," Kate said, her face tense. "I've given her twenty thousand a year for the past twenty years."

"In quarterly transfers," I said.

Kate looked at me. "How did you know that?"

I shrugged. "I heard it from a hacker. I'll explain later."

Fairfax went on as if neither of us had spoken. "You could have given us half then, not kept us on like a charity case. If I'd had two hundred thousand, I'd have a fortune now." He paused and glared at her bitterly. "I'd be as rich as you are."

"I did what I thought was best," she said.

He laughed. "You didn't like me any more than your father did. My wife's family, the McAfees, are one of the first families of Cowslip," he said to me, waving his hand in the air. "They're the descendants of homesteaders. That's all that counts for anything around here. The Merwins have a very distinguished pedigree, as a matter of fact. I've got ancestors who came over on the *Mayflower*."

"And gambled or drank away what little they brought with them," Kate cut in. "No one cared about your family, Fairfax. It was you—you were the problem. You married my sister because you wanted money. When you didn't get it, you became a crook. I'm tired of lying to save your feelings. If you want to know why I didn't give my sister a lump sum, you'll have to ask her."

"I know why you didn't give it to her," he said, angrily. "Because you're greedy."

"I didn't give it to her," Kate said, her voice cold with fury, "because she asked me not to."

He slammed both hands down on the table, knocking the ashtray to the floor.

"That's a lie! If your father had known what you are . . ."

"Don't hesitate," Kate said. "You can say lesbian. I am out now, and things are going to change around here. No more secrets. Agnes didn't get the money because our father knew that was why you married her. Your failures are your own, Fairfax. You can't blame them on me."

Beads of sweat had broken out on his forehead, and he was breathing heavily. His cheeks, which had been so gray, were now flushed an angry purple. I waited for the explosion, but none came. Instead, he put his head in his hands and sobbed.

Kate said, "How much did you get for hiding Frank's money? Half? A quarter? Did you even get as much as you had to pay him later?"

Fairfax didn't answer. I felt someone move behind me. I'd been sitting with my back to the living room, and I turned around now, expecting to see Sylvie. She was there, but directly behind her stood Helen Merwin. I knew something was wrong. Sylvie caught my eye, and I followed her gaze down and back. It was then that I saw the gun in Helen's hand.

Kate caught sight of the pistol at the same time I did. "My god."

Helen ignored her. "Sit down," she said, shoving Sylvie into the remaining kitchen chair.

Fairfax shook his head slowly. "Helen, where did you get that?"

"From your dresser, of course."

"But why?"

"Why?" Helen said, as if the reason she was waving a gun around was self-evident. "I've done my best to keep you out of jail, and there you sit, telling them everything."

"Helen," Fairfax said again. "What are you doing?"

"You killed Frank. I'm keeping you from going to prison."

"But I didn't kill him."

Helen just shook her head, as if she were talking to a deluded child. "Of course you did; there's no one else. Frank was a blackmailer. You helped him with the embezzling, and he knew about Mother and Uncle Burt. I've figured it out, Dad. Mother doesn't have the presence of mind to kill anyone, and besides, she's too selfish to think of saving you."

Fairfax put his hands up in defeat, as if this wasn't the first time she'd pointed a gun at him. I stared at Helen in amazement. It's one thing to joke about someone being a lunatic; it's another to know for certain.

"What are you going to do?" I asked. "You can't just shoot us."

She laughed. "Why not? Let's see—that's one, two, three lesbians. No great loss."

This would have been my moment to charge her, but I was no Captain Schwartz. I didn't want to be shot. All I wanted was for Sylvie, Kate, and me to leave that kitchen alive. I thought about Sylvie and her karate lessons and hoped she wouldn't do something stupid. I looked at her, trying silently to convey this. She inclined her head slightly but made no other sign.

"Honey," Fairfax said, "you have to listen to me. I did not kill Frank."

Helen smiled sadly. "You killed him just like you killed Uncle Burt. I saw him on Thursday, coming out of the bank, and when I heard he was dead, I knew what had happened. You don't need to lie to me. Let me help you."

I was having a hard time looking anywhere but at the gun. When I did, I realized that everyone was staring at Fairfax. He licked his lips again.

"You?" Kate said. "You killed Burt?"

Fairfax didn't answer. Helen was giving us a look of pure hatred, and the gun was shaking in her hand.

"You were wrong," she said to Kate. "He married my mother because he loved her. The poor fool still loves her, despite the fact that she never thinks of anyone but herself. You know she was meeting your husband for that July the Fourth weekend? At the time, I thought you must be an idiot. I was fourteen, and I could see what was going on. They were doing it right under your nose, in cars, in cheap hotels, in our living room. My mother is a drunken whore."

"Shut up," Fairfax said.

"What?"

"Please," he said, "don't talk about your mother like that."

Helen closed her eyes, and still, none of us moved.

"He came out here to confront your husband," she held up the pistol, "and he brought this to help persuade him. When he got here, you were out cold on the kitchen floor, and you," she pointed at Sylvie, "were lying on the kitchen table. My father thought you were both dead. When Uncle Burt walked through that kitchen door, he shot him. Imagine what he must have felt, thinking that my mother was planning to spend the weekend fucking a man who'd killed her own sister."

"Helen," Kate said. "How do you know this?"

"Because I was here. I hid on the floor behind the front seat of our car, and when he drove out here, I came with him. The same way I came out today."

No one said anything. The dogs were now barking, but no one paid them any mind. Fairfax was staring at the table, and Kate and Sylvie were looking at one another. I'd been praying for Captain Schwartz to come storming through the back door, guns blazing, but that was beginning to seem increasingly unlikely. In the end, she was just like every other survivalist—her guns were only good for winning potatoes and turkeys.

It was now or never. I stood up slowly. "Put the gun down, Helen. You've got the folder, go ahead and destroy it. It's in our best interests to forget about this."

She laughed. "A budding psychologist—I'm so lucky that you're here to talk me out of shooting you. You might even save me from the firing squad. You can get me some help, a good therapist, and everything will be fine. Sit down and shut up, Wilhelmina."

I sat down. As slowly and carefully as I could, I said, "You can't shoot all of us, Helen. As soon as you've fired one bullet, the rest will be on you."

She gave me the same look now that she'd given me at my grandmother's dining-room table.

"Fine," she said. "Why don't I just shoot *you*?"

It was then that my miracle arrived. The screen door flew open with a bang, and there she stood, five feet tall, a half-eaten hamburger in her hand and ketchup dripping down the front of her purple sweatshirt. Her voice exploded across the kitchen like a cannonball.

"Put that gun down, Helen Merwin—you are not in a fucking movie!"

In another second, my mother was across the room. She took the gun out of Helen's hand, emptied the bullets into the trashcan, and handed the empty weapon to me.

"Now," she said, "who wants to tell me what the hell is going on here?"

After Fairfax took Helen away, I described the chain of events to my mother as best I could. She was still having trouble grasping the details.

"Okay, I see how, but why?"

"Agnes," I said.

"He was jealous?" My mother shook her head as if this were some alien emotion. "He just shot him dead and left him there on the kitchen floor? What did he think was going to happen?"

"He didn't know. You heard him—he went home, and he sat and waited. Agnes came back from Spokane and told some lie about where she'd been. He pretended to believe her. I'm sure he had a nasty couple of days, but the next thing he knew, Burt had been reported missing. Then, he started to wonder. Maybe Burt wasn't really dead. Maybe someone else finished him off. I think he guessed what happened, and he just kept his mouth shut. When the rumors started flying about Frank and Burt, he did his best to fan them along. Once something becomes common knowledge, it's nearly impossible to convince people that it isn't true."

Sylvie sat next to me on the sofa with her eyes closed. I could see that she was clenching her jaw. Otherwise, she gave nothing away. Kate sat next to my mother. She'd taken her shoes off and propped her feet up on an ottoman.

"That son of a bitch," my mother spat out. "And he says it's all Kate's fault for not handing over half the inheritance?"

Kate sighed and shook her head. "Agnes didn't want him getting his hands on a lump sum. He's wanted to be rich all his life, but he's a speculator. He takes wild risks, and it all blows up in his face."

"Everything he touches turns from sugar to shit," Emma agreed. "Jesus, what a nerve."

"Nerve," Kate said, "and desperation. I wish I'd been thinking more clearly. Burt was shot right in the heart. No child could have done that, not unless she was damn lucky."

Sylvie flinched, and I tightened my arm around her. Once and for all, she needed to hear the absolute truth, knowing that neither she nor her mother was to blame.

"Is there any possibility he set you up deliberately?" I asked.

Kate shook her head. "I don't think so. That's not to say that he wouldn't have been happy for me to take the blame. I guessed a long time ago that he helped Frank embezzle that money from the assessor's office. He's greedy, and he's selfish."

"What did you do with the rifle?"

"Threw it in the Elk River," my mother said. "I never thought to open the breech and look for a bullet. No doubt it's still in there. Unless, of course, Fairfax had the presence of mind to fire it off into the night."

"It was a .22?"

Kate nodded. "Just like the pistol. Even if the wound had been bigger, I might not have noticed."

For the first time since we'd come into the living room, Sylvie spoke. "All this time," she said. "Hiding and lying and being afraid. All those secrets we didn't need to keep. No childhood for me, and no life for you. What a waste."

Kate got up and came over to sit down beside her. She put her head close to her daughter's, and I could see very clearly what Sylvie might look like in thirty years. She'd still be blond, but gray streaks would appear at her temples, and the golden color of her skin would darken and subdue.

She said, "I'm far more sorry about the years you lost than I am for anything I might have missed. I was lucky enough to have a good childhood, and that's what I wanted for you. I'd give anything to have been able to give you that."

When Sylvie spoke again she said, "We still don't know who poisoned Frank. Fairfax said he had nothing to do with that. We're back at square one."

Emma stirred in her seat. "No, we're not. None of you thought to ask me why I stopped by here in the first place. And, by the way, it's lucky I did. Bil didn't seem to be getting through to Helen."

"I don't have your way with freaks," I agreed. "So, why did you stop by?"

My mother was smiling. "Because I wanted to tell you that the county prosecutor has persuaded Sam to name his drug supplier."

"What's that got to do with anything?"

Emma lit a cigarette now and prepared to pontificate. "What it's got to do with is fraud. Users often support their habit by becoming dealers, but Sam's supplier came up with an even better plan. In addition to dried shiitake mushrooms, Sam's friend has also been selling pre-rolled joints filled with dried-up weeds. Not weed, but weeds. A tiny bit of pot for verisimilitude and the rest all garbage. As you may recall, the Lilac Trailer Court has been Cowslip's French Connection since Kate and I were in college."

"Then Sam really did . . ." I began.

"No," my mother said firmly, "he didn't. Frank made the mistake of stopping by Lilac, looking for a quick fix. On Thursday, he had a few drinks in that bar downtown, the one that plays all the loud music."

"The Underground?"

"That's the one. He had a few, and then he bought a few, and once he'd made friends with a couple of likely looking ne'er-do-wells, they gave him directions to the right trailer, and he bought some joints. Unfortunately for him, he never got a chance to smoke them. When the sheriff's deputies picked him up, he swallowed them."

"The first time they arrested him or the second?" They all looked at me. "He was picked up twice," I explained. "Tipper told me—he got it from an inside source at the sheriff's department. He was arrested once at noon, and then again later in the afternoon. The first time, they just drove him out into the county and dropped him off with instructions to beat it to Spokane. It's what they always do with vagrants."

"It must have been the noon arrest," my mother said thoughtfully. "That would have given the jimsonweed time to work in his gut over the next couple of hours."

"So why has Sam suddenly decided to name names?"

Emma smiled grimly. "Because his supplier was stupid enough to try the dried-weed trick on *him* yesterday. He fired up a joint, took one whiff, and went ballistic. Your brother might not know his mushrooms, but he is a connoisseur of pot."

Kate laughed out loud, and I could see that Sylvie was suppressing a smile. My mother looked at me.

"Aren't you going to ask me the name of this entrepreneur?"

"I don't need to," I said. "Her name is Francie Stokes."

Epilogue

We won the Proposition One fight by about three thousand votes. Its supporters promised to get it onto the ballot again for the 1996 election. Our joy was also tempered by the full slate of homophobes who were elected to the Idaho legislature and to represent us in the federal government. Still, a small victory was a victory nevertheless.

Nancy moved out of Sylvie's apartment at the end of November, and I moved in. In fact, I was already living there—I just wasn't paying rent. When it became official, I told Hugh first, and then I told Emma.

Sam was sitting on the front porch the day Sylvie and I came to collect the last of my boxes. He looked good. His skin was a rich brown, and he smiled easily. On the days after chemo, he often looked dull and ashy, and, on the really bad days, he had the look of someone who was living in two worlds. His eyes seemed to look through you and on to some other place. I tried to be present on those days, and afterwards, I always went home and rested with my head on Sylvie's chest, listening to her heartbeat.

Francie Stokes was sent to reform school, and potheads all over Cowslip took joints, both good and bad, and flushed them down the toilet. Initially, she was charged with manslaughter, but her public defender, Naomi, pled her down. My mother, the old hypocrite, was furious.

Helen continued to work in the library. Her eyes took on a tranquilized look, and we all hoped she was getting some therapy. Sylvie and I knew that she was the one who'd chased us through the woods that night with a crowbar—she told us. She wasn't trying to kill us, she said. She just wanted to scare us. She succeeded. Sylvie seemed to think we'd been in no real danger, but if she'd caught up with us, I didn't doubt that she'd have taken a whack with that crowbar. Why not? She hated us both. And if we'd seen her, well, who knew?

Helen was also the one who phoned in the anonymous tip to Young. I wondered about this for a long time. She wanted Burt Wood officially dead and buried just as much as Kate did, but why would she care if the body was correctly identified as Frank? Though Sarah knew next to nothing of the whole Helen, Fairfax, Burt Wood saga, she was the one who gave me the best insight into how Helen could stir around in the past and present and fuck things up so badly.

I stopped by the library one day and Sarah, frazzled as usual, waved a stack of Post-It notes in my face.

"She doesn't think," Sarah said. "She doesn't plan. Would you look at this?"

"It's a bunch of Post-It notes."

"Oh no it isn't," she said. "It's that moron's idea of serial title change."

"You're losing me," I said.

"We have a computer check-in system," Sarah wailed. "We make serial title changes on that. We do not put Post-It notes over the new titles telling patrons it's really the old title. Don't you get it?"

I shook my head. "I'm not a librarian."

"Neither is she," Sarah snapped. "And she never will be. Everything Helen Merwin touches turns from sugar to shit."

I agreed. Wholeheartedly.

Late at night, Sylvie and I talked about our families and their collective secrets. At first, we were both afraid that the whole story would have to come out. After all, Fairfax Merwin had killed a man. Gradually, however, we began to realize that this was a fact Sylvie and her mother had already lived with for sixteen years, and I wasn't willing to destroy her family and my own to avenge someone like Burt Wood. If Fairfax had a conscience, we had to assume that was punishment enough.

My mother wasn't worried at all. "Every small town is a collection of conspiracies," she said. "You can't imagine we've got dibs on the only horrible secret in Cowslip."

Eventually we agreed—by silent mutual consent—never to mention it again.

Sylvie and I passed through the fall semester with appalling grades. By spring, however, we had settled into a satisfying domesticity and our grades improved. The Lesbian Avengers dispersed to fight new battles, and the Faeries, with the exception of Suzy, went back to Seattle. Suzy stayed and moved in with Donny Smith, who, wonder of wonders, came out. At first, things were tense in the sheriff's department, but Donny said his co-workers were generally supportive. Sheriff Young set the positive tone—like my father, it seemed he'd had a lesbian aunt.

Tipper returned to Seattle and the University of Washington, still ambivalent about his relationship with Tom. He often called and left messages on our answering machine for Ward and June Cleaver.

One Saturday night in January, Sylvie and I sat on the devouring sofa and listened to *Fumbling Toward Ecstasy*. We had just begun to reminisce when someone pounded on the front door. Though I could guess who it was, I put my shirt back on and went to answer it anyway.

My mother pushed past me and marched straight into the living room.

"Sorry to interrupt," she said, "but we need you at the hospital."

Sylvie slipped up behind me and put an arm around my waist. We'd been waiting for the results of Sam's latest tests. I took a deep breath and let it out slowly.

"I'm ready. Just let me get my coat on."

"I'm coming too," Sylvie said. "If that's all right."

Emma laughed. "Of course it's all right, the more, the merrier. You might want to bring your camera, too—God knows he won't be able to stop you from taking pictures."

"You mean this isn't . . . he's not . . ."

"Your brother," she said, "fell off the back of some bimbo's moped and the tailpipe burned a hole in his ass. He's hanging up in a traction harness and screaming at all the nurses. Are you coming?"

"With pleasure," I said.

Joan Opyr

Joan Opyr's real parents were the Queen and King of the Circus. Though born and bred in Raleigh, NC, she now considers herself a Wild Westerner through and through, from the top of her Resistol hat to the soles of her Justin ropers. A gifted novelist, Joan also believes that she was the inspiration for the Black-Eyed Peas song, "My Humps."

Professionally, Joan is the Northern Idaho Editor for New West Magazine (www.newwest.net), a regular humor columnist for a number of newspapers, and, each and every Sunday, she co-hosts The Auntie Establishment and Brother Carl Show on Radio Free Moscow (www.krfp.org). Joan graduated from North Carolina State University twice, though you'd never know it to talk to her. In 1993, she finished the coursework for a PhD in Old English from The Ohio State University. She will never finish her dissertation.

Joan has been happily married to the same woman since the Crimean War. They live in Moscow, Idaho, with their two lovely children, three dogs, three cats, a dozen chickens, and a complete set of resident in-laws. Joan is a die-hard, yellow dog Democrat, who takes an active interest in local affairs—so active, in fact, that she's thinking of training one of her dogs (or perhaps a chicken) in the fine art of bomb-sniffing.

As for her hobbies, well, she hardly likes to say.

Please visit Joan's website at www.joanopyr.com or feel free to email her at joanopyr@moscow.com. She can't promise that she'll answer promptly, but she's notorious for answering thoroughly.

Bywater Books

HOSTAGE TO MURDER
A Lindsay Gordon Mystery

by V.L. McDermid

"One of my favorite authors, Val McDermid is an important writer—witty, never sentimental, taking us through mean streets with the dexterity of a Chandler." Sara Paretsky

Lindsay Gordon—investigative journalist, tenacious sleuth and unashamed lesbian—is facing a midlife crisis. Back in her native Scotland after a long absence, she has no job, no friends, and no desire to even think about her girlfriend's worrying preoccupations. A chance encounter with freelance reporter Rory McLaren offers her an irresistible invitation to open a new chapter in her life. From there it is just a short step to political corruption and other juicy stories—all welcome distractions from Lindsay's problems at home. But when a local car dealer's stepson is kidnapped, Lindsay and Rory trade journalism for detection. The trail leads them to St. Petersburg and a dangerous snatch-back operation that will test Lindsay to her absolute limits in every area of her life.

ISBN 1-932859-02-0 $12.95